CHEYLA

Highway of Infinity

JENNY MAC

JENNY MAC

CHEYLA

The Author JENNY MAC was born in the Country of
Central Australia, but now lives near the ocean on the
Central Coast of NSW in Australia, where she completed
the sequel 'CHEYLA' to her first Novel 'April Rain.'
From The Australian Outback Series.

For the latest information on Jenny Mac
Visit her Website at: www.jennymac.com.au

JENNY MAC

Titles by Jenny Mac

'The Australian Outback Series'

Acknowledgements

A big thank you to my family for their continued
support, and moments that I will always treasure.

CHEYLA is a Fiction Novel.

Some towns, places, or areas in this Novel, are fictional.
All products devised within the Author's imagination.
Characters are fictional, and bear no reference to anyone.

JENNY MAC

Chapter 1

Tenderly she rested her head on the massive breadth of his shoulder where she could feel the rise, and fall of his relaxed breathing. She inhaled deeply to succumb to his manly aroma, an essence of the land, and of leather.

His warm breath softly fanned her face as she watched him sleeping soundly. 'He is so beautiful, but also so very masculine.' she thought. 'But how do I reach his heart?' Sadly though, somehow she felt he would never be hers.

Their lovemaking had been so fierce, almost reckless even, but fired with wild abandonment. 'He was leaving! She sensed it! Felt it in her heart!' In distraction, she began leisurely, to trace a pathway down his superb physique, and her fingers, almost featherlike in touch, caressed each taut muscle from his shoulder to his belly button.

Bronze suntanned skin glistened to the first rays of the early morning light that crept in the window, and a lock from his deep golden hair fell across his forehead, and she just ached with the want of him. Already she felt her own arousal stirring her body urgently. She needed him inside her again believing it was the only hold she had over him, so she glided her fingers down to take him in her hand.

His eyes opened slowly as he grabbed her, and lifted her up so effortlessly. She sat across to straddle his body but held him as she stared into his captivating eyes. His erection became so hard that it was difficult to encompass as it throbbed in her hands, and desperately she tried to guide it into her aching body. His penetration was thrust so deep inside that she felt he was cleaving her apart, and she screamed out with pleasure. She could not get enough of him. Then as they reached a climax together it simply left her breathless, and yearning for more as she collapsed on top of him, and began to shower kisses over his body, and she lifted her head to seek the tenderness of his lips.

"She's dying!" he muttered suddenly, as he rolled her aside, then he lithely jumped from the bed to grab for his clothes on the floor to don his trousers.

"Who's dying?" asked Leila as he headed for the door with his shirt tossed over his shoulder, his shoes in his hand, but his mind elsewhere. He turned towards her.

"I'm sorry but Ol Mother is dying, so I must go to her!" he replied absently, then he quickly disappeared through the door, and closed it behind him.

She took refuge in her pillow, and sobbed. 'Why did I let myself fall in love with him? He loves with such a passion, but then pulls back into that dark place of non-commitment almost like a man possessed struggling with something constantly eating away at him.' she thought.

She realized now for the first time that this was a huge problem he had. 'He will always be a lost soul just seeking to be free from whatever haunts him, until he finds what it is that he is searching for. Or when his questions are finally answered!' she thought to herself.

Sadly though she still wanted him, it was impossible to say no to him. He had woven his web around her so tightly that she was suffocating with her love for him. She rose quickly from the bed, and rushed over to the window to watch as he climbed up into his 4WD. Her thoughts wildly consumed her, as she watched him drive away. 'What are his plans? Where is he going? Will he be back?' 'Maybe she would never see him again!' she realized.

* * *

Seeing her lying there, her tiny shrunken frame was so pitiful to look upon as she sank deeply into the bed.

Her ashen face seemed almost consumed with deep pain, but was ageless still, though the deep furrows in her face proved the lie. 'How she had lived for so long, he did not know! She has to be ancient!' he thought to himself.

In his youth she had seemed old even then, but he had given her a new lease on life. 'The only Grandmother he ever had, but the only Mother he knew.' and he loved her.

Fear gripped him as he approached the hospital bed. His first thought was that she was already gone, until he touched her hand, and her wise old eyes fluttered, then opened wide to stare at him with recognition, but bared a calmness within her knowing sight that had witnessed thousands of sunsets upon the distant horizon.

"Cheyla, ya bin com ta see me!' she mumbled shakily in a voice that rasped so softly, he leant closer to hear her.

"I'm here Ol Mother!" he whispered, his voice was so

soft, and gentle, but was breaking up with emotion.

"Did ya read tha letters thet I give ta ya Cheyla?" she asked, then she gasped. "Tis all I hav ta help ya. They be importin Cheyla!" she rasped, as a worried look creased her brow. "Tis ya roots Cheyla! Ya go find!" she said.

He looked at her sadly. 'Who was he really?' he asked himself. 'Where was his roots, his beginning?' So many times throughout his life he had asked her. 'Where do I come from Ol Mother? Who was my real Mother?' But she had brushed his questions aside in haste, not wanting to talk about it. 'She had named him Cheyla from birth. His name had some very special meaning, and her translation meant the shallows where he was born.' he was told.

'It was the only name he ever had.' They all lived in the bush, but were constantly on the move to different places. His only family, his only friends, were within her clan, an Aboriginal Tribe. He knew at an early age that he was very different from other aboriginal children in the tribe when they had started questioning, and teasing him.

'But that was way back.'

* * *

They had sat arguing as they both watched the water swirling, and surging as it passed the bank.

"Why ya got ta be damn stubborn Cheyla? Tis danger there an Ol Mother will be so mad at ya if she finds out!" muttered his friend in anquish.

"Then don't tell her then!" Cheyla replied.

Water gushed about him as he waded into its depths. Thrilled by the danger of the running water, and the feel of its strength, he whooped with glee, and gladly he let it push him along with the wild current that emanated from the waterfall cascading into the creek from the hillside.

Even at this tender age of seven he was fearless, and so confident in his own ability. His young body, sturdy, and so strong for his age as he rode the current effortlessly downstream, then swam strongly across to a sandy bank.

Laughing, he pulled himself from the water's depths to climb the bank, and the sun glistened on his wet body, and brought out the highlights in his hair.

"Don't ya do thet agin Cheyla, ya bin frightnin me!" spluttered Jono. "Why ya havta be recklus all tha time.... he paused, then stared. "Your hair Cheyla, it be go golden like the sunshine!" he uttered. "An ya skin, it be all shiny like, lot lighter than mine. My skin be black like Mamma! Why thet be Cheyla?" Jono asked inquisitively.

"Jus stop askin me silly questions I can't answer Jono!" Cheyla replied curtly, annoyed with him.

* * *

Now in the final hours of her life she had decided to tell him all she knew. "Tis all in tha letters Cheyla, all I no! I no read, but they be sent ta tha posti man in tha town, an he give ta Jono. He be read ta me." she rasped.

"I read all the letters Ol Mother, thank you, but I don't have a lot to go on. I will leave soon, I think it could be a long journey, but I will think fondly of you!" he said.

"Tis in ya name Cheyla me thinks ya...her voice trailed off as she fought to continue her tale. Then she gasped to struggle for another breath, but it was to be her last, as her head lolled, and she finally slumped, then lay very still.

Cheyla bent over her quickly as he tried desperately to hear her last words, and his brow creased in puzzlement. He felt for her pulse, but it was gone. She had uttered her last words. Sadly he kissed her lips, and turned to go.

Cheyla's thoughts spiraled as he was walking outside. Deep grief overcome him for the loss of the only Mother he had ever known. But now he had some small clues to quench the constant burning inside him, though it was all just a huge puzzle for him to unravel as Ol Mother's last strained words remained a complete mystery to him.

'Tis in ya name!' she had said.

'What is in my name?' he wondered.

Childhood memories flashed before him of times that his friends teased him in jest, and he clung desperately to his upbringing in the bush, not knowing what lay ahead.

* * *

What ya got there Cheyla?" Juba had asked.

"I think they call it a hook!" he replied.

"Where ya git thet there hook?" asked his friend.

"I found it Juba. It was in the long grass by the creek, on some sorta line!" Cheyla answered.

"Ya no Cheyla, somtimes ya do strange things all tha time. How com ya know how ta fish thet way, with thet there line, an ya worm on ya hook? What be wrong with ya spear? Aint thet good nough no more?" asked Juba.

"I don't know Juba! Jus somethin tells me things!"

"Ya be makin me so scared now Cheyla. So ya hav som voices talkin ta ya?" asked Juba, and Cheyla chuckled.

"No Juba, jus som sort of feelins I get sometimes, like I jus know what ta do, that's all, an besides I always catch more fish than you!" he replied laughing.

"Ya eva think ya be diffrent ta us Cheyla? Ya not be a full aboriginal, are ya?" Juba asked.

"Stop with all tha questions now Juba!" Cheyla said.

"Its jus ya be lookin lot diffrent ta me an all tha others, thet's all. Not only is ya skin, an hair lighter, but yor eyes be green Cheyla. Why is thet? No one hav tha green eyes in the tribe!" stated his friend.

Cheyla shook his head, trying to make it all go away. "I jus don't know Juba!" he said. He had tried desperately to ignore his body, but he had noticed his reflection in the creek, and he too wanted answers to all his questions.

* * *

In the beginning it was easier. He was so young, and so oblivious to his surroundings. Just another aboriginal boy within the clan of the tribe who loved him deeply. He loved them too, but also he loved the land, the bush, and their complete freedom. It was what he was used to.

As he grew older though he became aware of his own body changes, also changes around him. The Aboriginals were moved from the bush on to reserves, then later they were given housing to live in by the Government in town, and this was quite strange to them all to adjust to.

However they all went to school there, and where his Aboriginal friends in the clan floundered Cheyla excelled, almost as if he had done it all before. His speech was even becoming different now as if he was born to it, but he still spoke the language of the tribe. He loved the learning, but something else he learned, was the value of money, so he started a part time job delivering papers every morning before school just to earn some money, and very soon he had become quite well known around town.

He sensed such uneasiness in the family now though. They all wanted to go home to Tenna. They all pined for the bush, the only real home they knew, the freedom they loved, on the land they loved. So sometimes they would all go walk-a-bout, just to go back for a while, and it was one of these times that changed Cheyla's life.

* * *

They had started out at first light. All trailing along with a purpose, each carrying something according to their size, even the children. Walking was no effort to them, it used to be their lifestyle, but it was the smiles that lit up their faces much later when they reached Tenna, the creek by the waterfall that pulled Cheyla's mouth into a smile as well, as he looked tenderly at them all.

Decidedly, as if they had never left, they then assumed their roles. Cheyla watched them closely. The older men grabbed up their spears, then went fishing, as the women prepared the makings for a fire, and the young girls took their sticks, then went fossicking in the bush for berries, and the edible plants, but it was Ol Mother that captured his attention as his eyes settled on her face which was all lit up just with pure pleasure. 'It was her homecoming.' he thought, and he sensed her release, but felt her pain.

'That is how he would always like to remember her.'

"You look so happy Ol Mother!" he said, as he walked up beside her, and smiled down at her.

"Cheyla, I be so happy cause it be a happy place!" she said, her ancient face smiling, as she looked up at him.

"What should I do Ol Mother?" he asked.

"Jus hav tha fun Cheyla for tha time we be here! Go!"

Cheyla looked hard at the ominous cliff face. "In that case then, there is something that I always wanted to do here, but I was far too little before." he replied.

She squinted as she looked up at him. "Ya no Cheyla, ya be so big now ma neck hurts ta look up at ya, but ya be tha good boy Cheyla, ya heart be big too, an ya body so big, an strong. Ya will be big man, an a great man one day Cheyla. Ya make Ol Mother proud ya hear!" she said.

"I will Ol Mother! I promise!" he answered.

"So where ya bin wantin ta go here then Cheyla?"

"There is some sort of hole up behind the waterfall, it might be a cave. I always wanted to look there, but when I climbed up to see, I was way too short to reach the ledge which overhung it, and not strong enough, so that is what I want to do now! Do we have any rope?" he asked.

"Yea Cheyla, there be rope there, but Cheyla!"

"I know what you are going to say Ol Mother. But I will be careful. You just said I was big, and strong! Didn't you?" he asked, as he smiled.

"Yea me did, me thinks Cheyla!" she replied.

"I'll be fine!" he said, and laughed but as he proceeded he noted. 'It was pure strength he needed too, if he was to swim against the current to the rocks under the waterfall.'

9

'How did I ever do this before when I was smaller, and so much younger too?' he thought to himself, as he clung desperately to the rocks, getting ready for the climb up.

He carried only the bare necessities. His knife, a metal spike, and he coiled a length of rope across himself which was tied tightly to the end of a solid stick, he had matches, though he guessed they would be wet if he needed them.

Water swirled strongly around him as he tied one end of the rope tightly around his waist, then he tightened his hold on the rocks as he swung the remaining rope high.

It clattered up onto the top of the ledge when the stick landed, but it found no purchase, then it came tumbling back down again. He grabbed at the stick, and tried again.

This time he aimed his throw much higher, and as he dragged the rope back the stick lodged in the crevice of the ledge above. He pulled down on it so tightly, then realizing it was stuck solid, he started pulling himself up until he finally reached the top, then hurled himself over the top of the ledge to sit upon it, then he looked out.

He knew Ol Mother would be watching him, so he sort her out, and waved. She looked so tiny as he looked down from the heights, but he could see her waving back.

Eager to explore Cheyla stood, and walked attentively along the ledge, only to disappear behind the waterfall.

There he was faced by a huge opening in the cliff face, but the entrance was totally covered by thick vines which crept into the crevices of the rocks, totally concealing it.

Quickly he grabbed for his knife from its sheath, then began the slow process of hacking them all away.

CHEYLA

* * *

Cheyla remembered the time very well, it was etched into his memory. He shook his head as he climbed into his 4WD, and started the engine, engaged the gears, to pull out from the hospital carpark. His memories were quite vivid of the turning point in his life that changed everything, as he headed towards home with a purpose.

* * *

It was a tunnel of some sort, he noticed, and as he pulled all the vines away the sunlight streamed in through the entrance so he cautiously walked inside. As he moved on deeper into the cave, both sides of the walls seemed to open up, becoming wider now, and water trickled down them from high above as he passed, but further ahead he could see light. As he emerged into a natural clearing, he realized that it was a cavern of some sort. Light streamed in from above as he looked up high at the opening in the cliff, and at all the water cascading down the walls into a huge rock pool. He just stared in total amazement.

'For all the years they had lived around here, no-one even knew this cavern was here.' he thought to himself.

Immediately he just wanted to explore this new-found place, so quickly he moved to where the light from above was shining through. Something bright had attracted his attention, and he was in haste to see what it was when his foot rolled on a rock, and he slipped, and fell heavily. As he rose he grabbed the rock, it was heavy so he gripped it with two hands ready to toss it into the pool, but a glow stilled his hand as the sun's rays hit, and it shone brightly.

Drawing his knife quickly from his scabbard, he then crouched down on his haunches, and tried to scrape the outer covering away. Soon several pieces fell away, then immediately it gleamed to reveal some sort of gold metal.

Cheyla thought he knew what the metal was. Though he had never seen it before, he had heard about it often, and he wanted to convince himself of it as he tried to roll it around but he needed two hands as it was quite heavy, but quite unmistakable, like no other. 'Gold!' he thought.

'I have found gold!' He knew that many years ago this area had become very famous for its gold discoveries, and that the town originated from the gold rush days. There were still many abandoned mines around, he had learned about that history in his school lessons, and he had been very interested at the time, so he had read about it.

Quickly, he searched around to see if there were more, and he rolled over several big pieces of rock. He was not sure if they were all gold, they looked exactly like the first rock he had found, all covered in some covering. He knew they would weigh him down but he tried desperately to stuff them into his pockets, and down his shirtfront to no avail. Then as an afterthought, he looked up to see what had attracted his attention initially, and could see plainly the veins of yellow gold running through the rock face.

Shivers went up his spine like an electric impulse as the realization then hit him that his discovery was much more than he could comprehend. 'He had found gold, but what to do about it?' he had no idea. But that wasn't his only problem he soon realized when he reached the ledge, then he looked down through the waterfall at the swirling water below, and he knew then that he would definitely be pulled under from all the weight. 'This could take me quite a few trips.' he thought to himself. 'But getting all his samples back to town was going to be hard work also.'

He was exhausted when he finally sat crouched on the creek bed with his rocks attempting to make a sling for his back out of some old rags, and Ol Mother came near.

"What ya be doin there Cheyla?" she asked.

"I am making a sling to carry these rocks home. If they are what I think then we won't want for anything again!"

"What ya mean by thet Cheyla?" she asked.

"Look at this first one I found!" he said, holding it up.

"It be shiny, like somethin I be seen afore!" she replied.

"Yes shiny, like gold! I think its gold!" Cheyla replied.

"Yea thet be tha yella gold they be find round here fer sure. I be seein thet yella gold Cheyla, long time ago when they be findin it first in this here place!" said Ol Mother.

"Yes Ol Mother I think so, but don't tell the others just yet. First I want to make sure it is gold, and I don't know what to do about it yet either!" he said.

During the long walk back into town Cheyla pondered his predicament, but finally worked out some sort of plan.

Taking the steps two at a time Cheyla raced quickly up the stairwell. Mister Crawley always liked his paper delivered to his office inside the Bank, and Cheyla usually took it up to him, but today he had another reason to see him. He was exhausted, a little scared, but really excited as well, so with determination he knocked on his door.

"Enter!" the voice boomed out from within, so Cheyla turned the knob, pushed the door open, then purposely made his way inside with the newspaper casually tucked under his arm. He closed the door, and looked up.

"Good morning Mister Crawley!" he said cheerfully as he strode across the carpeted floor towards a huge timber desk where the Bank Manager sat staring out at him over the rim of his spectacles.

"Ah Cheyla! You have my paper! Well done young man, and thank you!" he said, as he set his glasses aside.

The room was expensively furnished. The long drapes encasing the windows were tied back to let the light stream in, and fell to the floor. Bookshelves, all laden with leather bound covered books lined the walls, and a hint of cigar smoke still lingered in the air as Cheyla moved forward to lean across the desk with the paper.

"It's good to see you Cheyla." said The Manager, as he set the paper aside. "So tell me what you are doing now you've finished school?" he asked.

Cheyla beamed. "Well Mister Crawley I have just been offered extra work at the printers, so I will be working full time from now on!" he replied.

"Well that is really good to hear Cheyla! So tell me, do you have a banking account set up so you can start saving your money?" he asked. Cheyla looked at him, puzzled.

"Eh! No Sir, not yet! Haven't thought of it." he said.

"We better organize that for you Cheyla! You have to save your money in case you need something. Or even a loan someday, who knows? We can organize an account for you now if you like?" he muttered, as he retrieved his glasses and pulled out some forms from his filing cabinet.

"Yes I guess so!" said Cheyla as he looked at the forms.

Cheyla's heart was racing fast. It wasn't only the space on the form he was looking at, where the first question asked for his last name that baffled him. It was what The Manager had said about getting a loan one day. 'He just had to have that land out at Tenna, and didn't know how.'

"Just fill out the form Cheyla, then take it downstairs to the teller. You will need just a small deposit to open the account, then whenever you want to, you can withdraw money, or make a deposit." he was saying. "Oh! You need to put your last name in there Cheyla!" he continued, as he pointed out the place on the form.

Cheyla's stomach began to churn, and little beads of perspiration suddenly appeared upon his forehead. He really felt quite sick. 'He didn't have a last name!' 'What should he do?' he wondered, as he looked at The Bank Manager. Winston Crawley laughed at his antics.

"You do possess a last name, don't you Cheyla?" he asked in jest. Cheyla moved to grab the pen, and as he leaned forward he felt the weight of the rock dragging in his pocket, then he laughed. "Of course I do Sir!" he said, as he wrote. "It is Cheyla Stone, Mister Crawley!"

So that was it! Just like that! He had a new name, and Cheyla wondered again what his real name should have been? 'He had never known, because he had never been given one!' he was thinking to himself.

The Manager interrupted his thoughts when he spoke.

"That's it Cheyla, just complete the form, and sign it, then take it downstairs when you leave."

Several thoughts raced through his mind as he bent to complete the form, and sign his new name. 'What to say? How to ask him?' Then a worried look crossed his brow.

"Is there something else Cheyla?" The Manager asked.

"Yes Sir, Mister Crawley! I was wanting to know more about the loan?" he asked. Mister Crawley laughed at him out loud. "You will need to save a lot of your money first Cheyla!" he replied. Sadness overcome him so badly, but he straightened to look into The Manager's eyes. "I see!" Cheyla said softly. "Thank you anyway Mister Crawley, for your help today. I'll go back to work now!" he said, as he backed away. Dismissing the rock that was dragging his pocket down, he turned to walk stiffly to the door.

Winston Crawley peered over his spectacles as he watched Cheyla walk away. 'There is something about this young boy that I like.' he mused. 'I'm sure he has something else on his mind. He was devastated just now I'm sure, something to do with a loan.' he thought.

Cheyla's hand gripped the doorknob in desperation to escape. He was wanting to get outside now, he couldn't breathe, so he turned the doorknob quickly just as The Manager's voice boomed out behind him. "Wait Cheyla! Come back a minute!" he called. Cheyla turned back to face him in surprise then walked slowly over to his desk.

"Sit down please Cheyla! I need to explain a bit more to you!" he said. Cheyla eased himself into the chair, and waited. "You know Cheyla you seem awfully young to be

16

wanting a loan, and it could take many years of saving before that can happen, but I haven't explained it fully!"

"Would you mind me asking what you need a loan for Cheyla?" he questioned, as he looked earnestly at him.

"No Sir! I need to buy some land! It is the land that I was born on, and lived on, long before we were all moved into town!" he replied.

"I see!" replied The Bank Manager, searching his face. "You do have a job now Cheyla, I guess that is a start, but unfortunately, unless you have some collateral as security for a loan, you will not be able to get one at this stage!" he said, not unkindly. "Then what is this collateral Mister Crawley?" Cheyla asked. "Well that would be something of great value that you usually put up as assurance that the loan would be repaid!" The Manager stated.

"I think I have that Sir!" Cheyla replied in earnest.

Winston Crawley just stared, trying to determine the truth of what Cheyla was saying. "What type of collateral are we talking about Cheyla?" he asked with interest.

Slowly he delved into his trousers to retrieve the rock, and pulled it out to firmly grasp it in two hands, and as Cheyla lifted it up in front of The Bank Managers eyes, it just gleamed in the early light.

Well I'll be… The Manager started to say as he just gaped at Cheyla, then rummaging around in his desk, produced a red cloth which he set out before him upon the desk. "May I?" he asked, pointing to the rock.

"Yes! Of course Sir!" replied Cheyla. Carefully, The Bank Manager took the rock from Cheyla, and set it upon the red cloth. He chuckled. "Well it has been quite a while since I have seen a nugget like this Cheyla! You do know what it is?" he queried.

"Yes Sir! I scraped away some of the outer covering to see it, but I think it must be gold! I have several more that are all the same!" Cheyla said.

"The outer covering will be a type of quartz, so to get to the gold, it has to be smelted. 'More you say?' Did you find these on the land you want to buy?" he asked.

Cheyla looked deep into his kind, honest face. "Yes Sir I did!" he then decided to say.

"Then here is what you should do quickly Cheyla. Go down to the Lands Department to stake your claim for the land you want, and go out with them and help peg it out. I will call to notify them that I have approved a loan for you. The Bank will arrange smelting of the nuggets, and pay you by the ounce of all gold yielded, and by the looks of it, you will have plenty left after repaying your loan! So then, what do you say about all that?" he asked.

Cheyla was dumfounded, and he replied shakily. "Yes Sir, and thank you so very much Sir!"

"Then what are you waiting for? Go!" came the reply.

"Yes Sir Mister Crawley!" Cheyla replied, as he turned around in bewilderment, then raced towards the door. He was ecstatic, beside himself, and he grabbed madly at the doorknob in haste trying to yank the door wide open to get outside. 'A loan? Yes! Yes! He laughed. 'I do actually have a loan!' 'So that was it! Just like that!' he pondered in disbelief. 'He was now to own the land that he loved.'

Chapter 2

Tenungeri the sign read as Cheyla braked at the gates. Over five hundred acres of rich undulating land was spread out before him, but then gradually receded as the formation of distant hills took over another aspect of the countryside to become steeped in thick bushland where a thing of beauty was displayed in the thrust of a waterfall as it gushed out over the rocks to tumble into the creek.

'Tenna Creek!' he thought to himself. 'My birthplace, and my property's name-sake. How lucky I have been!'

For some unknown reason Cheyla had wanted to raise cattle on his land, so at the very first opportunity he had bought more land to cater for his passion as a Landowner, and finally a cattle man. He scanned the countryside now, watching, as the cattle all roamed the paddocks that were prone to the rich, black soil, and were grazing contentedly on Mitchell grasses which swayed gently in the breeze.

His Property had almost doubled in size since his first purchase seventeen years ago, and today it was quite a large, prosperous Cattle Station, one of the very best, and biggest in The Territory of Australia. 'It was his pride, and joy.' he thought, as he gazed longingly over the pastures, and he felt the power of ownership surging through him, but inside a sense of gratefulness stayed within him.

He shook his head in disbelief as he done every day of his blessed life since he stumbled on his own gold mine, but eventually these feelings finally subsided, and he got out of his vehicle to walk slowly over to the double gates.

Only one thing still clouded his mind, forbidding him the luxury of complete contentedness, and he then pondered on what was before him, and what he now had to do. He swung the gates wide, then climbed up into his 4WD, and drove on through.

As he jumped down to close the gates, for the first time in his life he had a sense of direction, just a small inkling of hope to sate the obsession that burned inside him. He had Ol Mother to thank for that, but he hoped this new-found information from her was enough to solve all the mystery surrounding it, and that he wouldn't be too late.

He thought deeply of her now as he continued to drive along the winding gravel road that led on towards The Homestead, then became anxious, wanting to get all the organization in place. He had never even thought about a burial site on his Property before as no-one had died, so he had asked questions, and got approval. So now he had a plan, something fit for a grand old lady.

Suddenly his thoughts were momentarily interrupted as he swerved around the final bend, then he slowed to cross over the bridge where the creek flowed on swiftly beneath its timbers. He could make out the huts spread out on the rise above the creek which was home to his property workers, and families who mainly consisted of the aboriginals from Ol Mother's tribe, and some white people also, who were his hired hands.

Gravel flew up all around him as he accelerated on the final stretch towards the grid of the house paddock where he braked to slow down, and drove on to The Homestead, but purposely came to a standstill on the driveway as his home came into view, and he just sat looking at it.

'She always looks like a bride on her wedding day!' he thought. 'All white, and beautiful.' The grand sandstone, split-level brick Homestead sat gleaming in the sunlight amidst the colourful gardens, and lawns that surrounded it. Wide verandahs graced all the sides of the Homestead to take in magnificent views of the landscape portraying massive trees, rolling paddocks engulfed by the distant hills, as well as receiving the ultimate advantage of any breezes that were on offer. "Yes, beautiful!' he thought.

It was the end of a successful dry season, and all the mustering had been completed, but this year they were blessed with a few storms, and some rainfall, enough to keep the paddocks in a good state for the heat that was yet to come. Mostly the days were sunny in the dry, but it tended to get cool inside the sandstone house during the nights, and early mornings, so Cheyla was not surprised to notice that the fires had been lit inside the Homestead as he noted smoke billowing from chimneys on the roof.

Cheyla looked around his house paddock with pride. Nothing had been omitted when he had planned it all initially. Tenna Creek had always provided them with pure water throughout the house, though he had installed rain water tanks as well. There were meat houses, storage sheds for equipment, a separate hay storage shed, as well as a huge shed for the vehicles, and a separate workshop.

His inner stables stood proudly to cater specifically for his personal horses. He loved his horses, but he also had other work horses, and the stables for those, and the steel constructed cattle yards were in the adjoining paddock, much further down from where bungalows were situated for his permanent on-site workers, set amongst the gum trees, with a separate galley for their food to be prepared.

'Yes! This is my Home! I have built an empire here!' he thought to himself. 'Only now! Sadly I am leaving it.'

Looking up he noticed that Jono was walking towards him, so he waved. Jono had been his life-long friend. He had become big, and strong in the shoulders now he noticed, although his legs had still remained slender like sticks. His wiry black hair curled down to his shoulders, and his big brown eyes widened with delight as a smile spread across his face. Jono had been Property Manager at Tenungeri since day one, and Cheyla's right-hand man.

"So good ta see ya Cheyla!" Jono said, and he smiled, as their hands met in a solid handshake.

"Hi there Jono! My eyes hurt just looking at you!" he replied, lightly punching his shoulder, and they laughed together. "But it's good to see you too Jono!" he replied. "I would like a report on everything here while I've been in town however right now some more important things are to be discussed. I have a lot to talk to you about Jono, so let's go inside." he said, as he beckoned to him.

"Yea sure Cheyla, what's up!" asked Jono as he trailed along beside him, his grin disappearing as he sensed the big man's tone, and felt his stress. He knew him so well, but now he looked up at him, as if for the very first time.

'He would be about thirty-four now.' he guessed. But had grown to be the biggest man Jono had ever seen. His massive physique, tanned from the brutal sun, was lean but rippled with muscle providing him with unbelievable great strength, well contained within his excessive height.

His skin was almost bronze-like, dark golden hair fell long but loosely over a forehead framing deep green eyes where a real seriousness lay but yet a tenderness lingered, which Jono had always loved since they were kids.

'He's just a gentle giant.' he thought to himself.

'Cheyla Stone he had named himself initially, so long ago.' thought Jono, then he recalled how that had come about, and smiled knowingly to himself.

As Cheyla led the way into the house he could feel the warmth from the log fires immediately moderating the temperature throughout the rooms, and wood-smoke filled his nostrils as he walked through the house with a fragrance that he had always loved.

Omitting the entrance to the living room, he walked on down the hall, down the two steps, then along the wide hallway, down to the very end where the double doors to his study stood proud. Jono done his best to keep up with him as he strode out in front of him.

Cheyla leant hard against the huge brass handles on the doors to push them open, then walked immediately to the window, then towards the triple doors that led out to a balcony, where he drew all the heavy curtains aside, and light instantly flooded the room.

His study was a work of art. Bronze light fittings, and lamps were strategically placed to emphasize all the focal points of the room. One being a huge bookcase that filled an entire wall where leather bound books were artfully placed. Directly opposite where the embers of the newly lit fires smoldered in the recess, was the fireplace which took pride of place amidst a wall that was adorned with oil paintings of Bush Art depicting various scenes to capture the beauty of the Territory's Outback Country.

Ceramic pots overfilled with bush flowers spilled over, and could be detected in each nook, splashing their colour around the room. Upon an oversized mat centered on the slate floor to face the outside patio, stood a massive heavy timber desk which was graced by five black leather chairs placed to take in the scenery of the outdoors.

"Take a seat Jono." offered Cheyla, as he rounded the desk to take his place. "I have two very important things to discuss with you today." he added seriously.

Jono eased himself into the leather chair, and searched Cheyla's eyes. 'There be som worry there!' he thought, as he detected the creases appearing on his friends brow.

"Firstly I have very sad tidings Jono! Ol Mother passed away about an hour ago!" said Cheyla softly. "But I guess she has had a long life that you or I would not frown upon if we lived that long. But I guess that her pain has finally ended now, that is the only consolation we have I guess, but none of us will ever forget her, and that is why I have organized something very special for her." he added.

"I be sorry ta hear thet Cheyla, it be tha sad day for us all, but we all expectin it ta happen sometime. She be livin fer very long time, an yeah! She meant a lot ta us all! So what hav ya got planned Cheyla?" Jono asked.

There is a partially wooded area just before the base of the hills but closer to the falls at Tenna Creek! Do you know the specific paddock I mean Jono?" he asked.

"Yea me know tha place Cheyla." replied Jono.

"This is what I want you to do Jono! Get Henry to take a team of men up there, clear the undergrowth, and mark out a section large enough for a Cemetery. It will be our Cemetery for Tenungeri, so show him where to go!"

"Ol Mother will be the very first to be buried there. Her grave needs to be dug, and a cross made with words to say 'Rest in Peace Ol Mother.' If someone could do that then I'll be pleased, but everything must be ready today because tomorrow at 11 a.m. the undertaker from in town will be bringing her body out for burial." Cheyla said.

"Tis a great idea Cheyla. Ol Mother would like thet, she loved Tenna, so it be done. We will get onto it right away!" he said, as he got up to leave.

"Wait just a minute Jono. I have more to discuss with you. It's the second thing I need to talk about. It will also involve Henry. So after I talk to you first you can go and find him. We will all need to talk about things in depth."

Jono looked surprised as he sat back down in the chair. "What's up Cheyla, so what be on ya mind? I can tell somethin is disturbin ya but what else is there?" he asked.

"I have to go away Jono!" replied Cheyla.

"Goin away! Why Cheyla? But where ya bin goin to, an for how long ya be away?" asked his concerned friend.

"I don't know how long I will be away Jono, only that it could be quite a while. Do you remember all the letters that you read for Ol Mother some time back?" he asked.

"Yea I be rememba thet Cheyla, they be from som lady down in South Australia som place" Jono replied.

"Well Jono, Ol Mother has only just given those letters to me so I can read them also, and because they are the only source of information I have to find my real Mother, then I have to go, and search for her. I can't rest until I do this." Cheyla said sadly, as he looked into Jono's eyes.

"There was nothin in tha letters bout ya Mother, only som other lady's name who wrote em Cheyla" Jono said.

"Her name, but also her address!" said Cheyla. "That is my only key. Which is where I have to start looking, and I don't know where it will lead me to, but I have to follow it through. I just have to!" answered Cheyla.

"Did ya know also Cheyla, thet the lady who be from South Australia thet wrote tha letters, she be Ol Mother's Granddaughter, so she be aboriginal too" he added.

"No I didn't know that Jono. That is a surprise, thank you! That is vital information for me!" replied Cheyla.

"You do know Jono that I will be leaving you in charge while I am away! I know you are up to it, but tell me now if you think you can't handle anything." asked Cheyla.

"I be know everythin bout this property Cheyla. Ya know thet, jus wish ya weren't goin thet's all." Jono said.

"In that case we will go over all the finals details with Henry. I know you don't want me to go Jono, but please try to understand I may not have another chance. Go, and find Henry now, bring him here so we discuss everything, then he can get his men together, you can lead them up to the hillside so they can prepare the graveyard." he said.

Jono searched Cheyla's eyes earnestly, and he wanted more information, but suddenly he decided against it as their eyes connected, so he rose from his seat to leave.

"I won't be gone long then!" he said, then he walked across the room, and disappeared through the door.

Cheyla watched him leave. 'Such a good friend Jono had been to him.' he thought. "He would like very much for Jono to come with him, but he was relying on him to care for his Property. He busied himself while he waited by retrieving some paperwork from inside the big desk drawer, and grabbing a notebook, started to itemize a 'To do list' for Jono. Things he wanted done on a regular basis. He pulled out a sheet of paper from the pile, then compiled a list of jobs for Henry to keep on top of.

Henry Callen his overseer was a big man with a hearty laugh, and in the prime of his life. He was a white man who had earned his status as a Cattleman in The Outback Country, and had come into Cheyla's employ way back at the beginning when Cheyla intended running cattle on his Property. No other man apart from Jono, did Cheyla trust more with the running of his Property than Henry.

He was as straight, and as honest as they come. Tough, but very fair, and so dependable, and he got things done.

Cheyla looked up from his task as Henry's laugh rang out from the hallway beyond.

Henry Callen breezed through the doors, laughing loudly, as he shared a joke with Jono. His face was deeply tanned, and bared an almost leathered look as the tell-tale lines etched deeply into his face, and brow. His sun-bleached hair hung loosely about his face, and into his deep blue eyes. "Morning boss!" he called as he lithely crossed the room towards Cheyla seated at his desk.

'So strong, so agile he is. Just a few years older than me, though a force to be reckoned with I should think!' thought Cheyla, as he watched him walk towards him.

'Yes I have two good men to protect my Property.'

"Good morning Henry, Jono, come and take a load off, grab a chair." he said, as he gestured to the vacant seats.

Jono took the seat opposite Cheyla, and Henry pulled out the seat at the end of the desk, and eased his big frame into the softness of the leather chair.

"Henry I am not sure if Jono has filled you in with any information as yet, but due to the passing of Ol Mother, we have our work cut out for us today. I have instructed Jono as to what I want, and he will take you up to the site when you both leave here. Everything must be completed today. It will involve preparing a site for a Cemetery, Jono will tell you what I want! Any questions?" he asked.

'No questions boss, Jono can fill me in. I am very sorry to hear about Ol Mother, we will all miss her." he said.

CHEYLA

Cheyla looked at Henry sincerely. "Thank you Henry that is greatly appreciated, but just make sure your men do a good job." he said, as he looked at them both.

"Will do, that's for sure." replied Henry.

"Now we will discuss some things as I am going away. I will leave after the burial of Ol Mother tomorrow. I am leaving Jono in charge Henry, so you will report to him as if it was me. Are you ok with that?" asked Cheyla.

"Yes! Fine by me Boss." said Henry. "Good man!" said Cheyla, as he produced the sheet of paper, and handed it across the desk to Henry. "Just a list of things I want done, but just do what you always do best Henry that is looking after my cattle, the stock horses, paddocks, and fencing. If you need anything, just discuss it with Jono." he stated.

Henry looked over the sheet of paper. "All good here Boss. So you want the Cemetery area fenced?" he asked.

"Yes Henry, if you could organize your men to do that sometime after I am gone, then that would be good." he replied, as he turned his attention to Jono.

"Jono, you have total control of the Property! That is a big responsibility, are you ok with that?" he asked.

"Yea Cheyla, jus go an do what ya hav ta, an we all will be ok here." said Jono.

"Thanks Jono! But remember that you can contact me anytime on my phone, and I will ring you too. Your job is very important. Just keep all the staff happy, pay their wages, maintain The Homestead, and stables. This here notebook has all the information you need, keep it locked in the desk drawer with this bank card, and the details for you to pay all the bills. That's it!" said Cheyla.

"Yea ta be sure Cheyla." replied Jono as he clasped the proffered key then put it safely in his pocket. "Is that all I need ta know?' he asked.

"For now Jono!" replied Cheyla, then he rose from his seat as if to declare the meeting over.

"Then we had better move Henry, we have a lot to do today." stated Jono, as he pushed the chair back to stand.

"Yeah sure Jono, I am right behind you." said Henry. "Hope you have a good trip Cheyla." Henry said, as he climbed from the seat, then reached for the big man's hand. "Don't you worry about your Property Cheyla! Jono, and I will take care of things here!" he said, as their hands met in a firm handshake.

"Thank you Henry." replied Cheyla. "I don't need to tell you both how important this place is to me, however I will leave knowing it is in good hands. Now I have lots to do in preparation for my trip, but report back to me at the close of the day. Join me for dinner!" he said.

"Will do!" answered Jono, and Henry in unison.

Cheyla watched them closely as they crossed the floor, then disappeared through the doorway. He could hear Henry's laugh ringing out. 'Yeah a good team those two will be.' He pulled out the desk drawer to start clearing out his personal items in readiness for Jono. Preparing was endless so when he was done, he went to the kitchen.

Milly stood busying herself with something cooking on the stove top as he walked through the door.

"Morning Boss!" she uttered, as he entered the room.

"Morning Milly." he said as he approached her.

"Prepare dinner for two extras tonight. I have guests, and I guess you should know now that I am going away for a while. In my absence Jono will be in charge." he said.

"Yea sure Boss, but we will miss ya. How long ya bin goin for?" Milly asked.

"I am not sure Milly, but it could be a while." he said.

"What time ya want dinner tonight Boss?" she asked.

"Oh better make it for 7.30pm Milly, the guys might be late getting back today. Now I have to go across to the stables, then pack my things, so I'd better move." he said.

"What bout ya lunch Boss?" asked Milly.

"Lunch? Yes lunch would be good Milly." he laughed.

"But give me a couple of hours to get things done!"

"Sure Boss." she said.

Cheyla looked into her dark brown eyes, and smiled. 'Such good staff I have.' he thought. Milly had come to him on recommendation from a friend in town. She was a local aboriginal woman, not from the tribe that he grew up with. She was slim, and quite attractive though still single, and had been in his employ for many years.

"Thanks Milly I'm going to miss you, and of course, your cooking too." he laughed, as he headed for the door.

Much later he was residing on the verandah, a glass of whiskey sat at his right hand, and he relished the serenity of the day as it slipped away and dusk threatened to cheat him of his very last view of his Property when he noticed the workers returning. "Just in time men!" he called, as the rover stopped out front. "Dinner is at 7.30pm, drinks at 6.30pm. We will talk then." he said. "Ok!" Jono called.

Though the air next morning was cool, the sun was soon making its presence felt as they all followed.

Up ahead the hearse was slowly making its way along the winding dirt track, and just beyond the clouds of dust which swirled about behind it, the workers of Tenungeri trailed in a procession. The mixture of white, and of black people shared a purpose, and were all in mourning.

Some rode horseback, others sat together in the back of a dray, but the remainder preferred to walk, and the aboriginal women sang the mournful songs of a past life.

Cheyla sat his Rhone Stallion in silence, his face set in a mask of grief as he thought of his life, and Ol Mother. It was a long trek towards the hills, but as they neared the newly laid out Cemetery site, a sense of pride overcame him of his decision, and was impressed with what he saw. It was as the men had told him last night, all was in order.

It was a simple service, but everyone there knew the significance of it, and they lingered in respect, and Cheyla Mingled amongst them saying his goodbyes, then pulled Henry, and Jono aside. "I can't thank you both enough. I noticed the pegs for the fencing Henry, that is good. Give the people refreshments now Jono, but I must leave." he said, as he shook their hands, then mounted the Stallion. "Ya take care Cheyla." said Jono. "Safe travels Boss." said Henry. He waved as he cantered away. At the Homestead stables, he climbed into his 4WD, but paused at the front gates on impulse to look back longingly, just for one last time, then closed them attentively as if closing a chapter in his life. "When would he return?' he thought. 'Just how long does it take to find your true identity?' he wondered.

Chapter 3

A lice spread out before him. The MacDonnell Ranges seemed dark, and ominous against the failing light, but was no doubt a huge monument depicting the town as he approached it, and dominated its skyline.

Cheyla was enjoying himself, the hours had slipped by as the landscape captivated his interest, and only briefly, occasional thoughts of his Property, and the friends that he left behind, entered his mind to interrupt his journey.

He thought of his relationship with Leila, and realized that his feelings for Leila was purely platonic. He was not in love with her. She had not reached his heart in the way he expected. No-one had filled that gap for him yet, and he had experienced a few relationships over the years, so his vague thoughts slowly receded as the trip continued.

Suddenly he had acquired a sense of enthusiasm about travel, something he had never contemplated before, and he was liking it well enough. Visions of what may lay up ahead of him loomed up to capture his thoughts, but the despair that he had previously felt seemed to shrink into the back of his mind, as the pure excitement of seeing this beautiful Outback Country of Australia thrilled him.

A flashing neon sign attracted his attention. 'Hotel-Motel' it read, so he continued on towards it. As he crossed the bridge he noticed there was no water in the river, though the eroded high banks gave some evidence of previous water flow, it was just a dry river-bed now.

He chuckled to himself as he recalled reading newspapers that splashed photos across its pages of a famous Regatta that was held annually in this dry river-bed.

'I can just imagine it now.' he mused. 'People running a bizarre race in their make-shift boats, and flotillas, their legs poking through bottoms of their lovingly decorated inventions, feet digging into the sand for purchase as they scrambled to gain the lead, and striving to win the race.

He laughed to himself as he pulled into the reception area of the Motel, and got out of 4WD then walked inside where he rang the bell at the desk, and waited. 'Yes a nice shower, a good meal, a couple of drinks, and a good bed.' he thought. He was ready for a break for the night.

Later after he checked into a room, and was refreshed, he wandered across to The Hotel. He was forced to duck his head at the entrance as he pushed through the double doors to get inside, then headed for the bar.

He slipped onto a stool in the corner where he could look around, and study the mix of people in all the rooms.

The lighting was dimmed, creating a cozy atmosphere for the customers clad in their Sunday best as they chatted together in the dining area adjacent to where 'The Bistro' sign blinked, but in the bar area, he noticed workers were still in their work clothes, and enjoying an after work ale. It looked to be a popular place, people were still arriving, and as he looked into the lounge area he noticed a band was setting up their equipment in a corner of the room.

Suddenly he was aware of someone standing in front of him, and brought his attention back just as she spoke. "What will it be handsome?" she asked, as he looked up.

She was pretty. Long blond hair flowed to her waist, her mouth was large as she offered him a smile, and her blue eyes twinkled with mischief as she looked at him.

"I'll have a Johnny Red on Ice, with water." he replied, as he took in the shape of her body, and her firm breasts threatening to bust that button he was looking at.

"Sure!" she said, as she turned, her hair flipping across her shoulders, and she presented him with a back view.

Cheyla chuckled to himself as he watched her walking away. "Women!" he thought. 'Can't live with them, can't live without them.' He loved women, and secretly wished that one day he could settle down with a woman that he really loved, but he hadn't found the right one yet. 'Not for the want of trying though.' he thought.

Then she was back. Two coasters were placed in front of him. His chilled glass that contained the scotch was set upon one, and on the other, to his right hand side, a small jug with frosted sides containing the iced water.

He looked up in surprise. "Just how I like it! I find most people just add the water, so thank you." he said.

"My pleasure!" she said, and grinned. "I do get certain vibes from some customers, so I was just assuming you would like it that way mister eh…."What is your name?"

"My name is Cheyla Stone." he replied, then held out

his hand. She took it in hers. "Strange name." she said, as they shook hands. "It's a long story." he replied.

Immediately she laughed. "Sounds intriguing, it just so happens I like a good story, and I have heaps of time. I finish work in half an hour if you would like me to join you. My name is Anita, and I don't bite." she offered.

Cheyla laughed at her. "Pleased to meet you Anita, and I don't bite either, so I'd like it well enough if you would join me later." he replied.

"Good! That's settled then. Don't run away now." she said, laughing as she turned to carry on with her work.

Cheyla looked around the room. Everyone was eating, and chatting away in the dining room, and in the lounge, the band had struck a few chords, and then proceeded to play soft dinner music, adding to the mood for the select couples who approached the timber flooring sectioned off area which was the dancefloor. He drained his glass as he contemplated his next move but was startled by the voice.

"Like another?" she asked, as she stood before him.

"Yes I would Anita." he replied. "But before you go, I would like to ask you? That is if you want to, I mean! Seeing you are joining me later I would like it well enough if you would join me for dinner?" he asked.

She looked at him with a mischievous smile that lit her face. "Thought you would never ask!" she retorted. "I will finish in ten, so we will have plenty of time to eat dinner then." she offered, as she left in a swirl of hair.

Cheyla smiled. He was used to women being friendly with him, but this one was unlike the others he knew.

Suddenly she loomed beside him holding two drinks in her hand. "My shout." she said, as she handed him his scotch, then looked up, seeking his eyes. "Come with me!" she stated as she beckoned to him, and walked off.

He saw her hips sway as she crossed the floor, and he got up to follow her into a private alcove off the dining room which was screened by a wall divider with intricate patterns, and where lush bush plants grew in huge urns. Candles lit the semi-darkness of the room, and paintings of the Outback Country brought life to the walls.

Cheyla felt quite at home in this room, and as he eased himself into the softness of the bucket chair which graced the table, he commented so. "I like this room well enough, reminds me of home a bit, and I like the artwork, so much red, and orange in the paintings."

"That's because it is the heart of the red center here." she replied. "So you feel it is similar to your home here Cheyla? Isn't that the topic we agreed we would discuss tonight? The intriguing story of Cheyla Stone! His name, his life, his home?" she asked.

He looked at her, and thought. 'Well why not?' He had never really told anyone about his life, his beginning, only Jono, and the aborigines knew, but they were like family.

"Well I guess it wouldn't hurt seeing I promised you, but what say we order first. I'm starving, I could eat the leg off this table." he said in jest. "It's been a long day."

"Good, that is settled then!" said Anita, and then she laughed. "Yes I guess we should order first." she replied. She watched him as they made their selections, then the waiter came to take their order. Cheyla was a mysterious type, but very likeable, she was busting to hear his story.

"Where should I begin?" he asked, as he looked at her.

"It's your story! So it is entirely up to you what you say. Maybe the beginning would be a good place to start." she replied, as she gave him a cheeky grin.

"Well only if you have a story to share also!" he said.

"Of course I will." she said, as her grin widened.

The night slipped away as his story unfolded, deserted plates were whisked away un-noticed as the conversation became more intense. They both became oblivious to their surroundings as the drinks kept coming, and she was so engrossed by what he obviously had to get off his chest, she just listened. 'He seems to be a lost soul.' she thought to herself as he poured his heart out. She sat there gaping, wanting to interrupt to ask questions but choosing not too in case he stopped, as he seemed in a world of his own.

Slowly though, as he continued, Anita felt a tenderness towards this gentle giant of a man, and as she watched his face earnestly she detected a shadow seeming to cloud his beautiful green eyes as he spoke. His hidden pain now becoming evident on his face, and a deep sadness quickly overwhelmed her of his own private dilemma that tainted his life, leaving her own personal life input which she had elaborated on, was to pale in comparison, so her very next words seemed to choke in her throat as she tried to speak.

"Chey..la, I ca..n't begin to tell you how sorry I am, but you do have a lot to be thankful for, just be positive, and things will work out. However something is bugging me so there is something I must say to you Cheyla." she said.

"Thanks for listening Anita, I did ramble on a bit, but what is it you have to say?" he asked.

"Well I just can't help feeling there has to be a massive reason why any Mother would abandon her baby for the first instance! But then to leave him in the wilderness to be raised by Aborigines? Not the usual done thing I don't think. Have you thought at all about that?" she asked.

"Yes the thought has crossed my mind many times!" he stated, as his brow creased into a deep furrow.

"Well I don't want you to be disappointed that's all, so you had better steel yourself for rejection. That is all I will say on the matter, I hope it helps." Anita added.

"Yeah I know Anita, I realize that, but thanks." he said.

She looked at him earnestly. "Let's get out of here." she said. "Are you staying in The Motel here?" she asked.

"Ok then! Yes the Motel just out back." he replied. She dug into her purse, and retrieved some money. "That is for my meal, would you settle the bill Cheyla." she asked.

"No Anita! I will pay for our meals. My shout!"

"Cheyla! I do realize that you have more than enough to pay for my meal, but please don't! I pay my own way!"

He looked at her, but then realized that she wouldn't budge on the issue. Something that he was not used to, so he sub-mitted to her request. "Ok if that is what you want. Meet me out back." he replied, as he got up to pay the bill.

They swayed together as they walked. "You do know that I am leaving in the morning?" he asked, when they reached his room, and Cheyla fumbled his key in the lock.

"Yes I know Cheyla." she said, as she pushed through the door into the room, then flicked on the switch beside the door, and dimmed the lights.

"Cozy!" she said, as she closed the door, locked it, and moved towards him. Her hands reached up to caress his neck, and ear lobes, then slowly down inside his shirt, her fingers easing out the buttons of his shirt, one agonizing button at a time, as she gazed deeply into his eyes.

"Like a drink?" he stammered, as he held up the wine.

"Shush!" she said, as she took the wine, set it on the table, and then slowly reached out for him again.

Cheyla looked down at her. She was quite short, her head only coming up to his shoulder, so he reached for her, and lifted her high. She wrapped her legs around him, pressing her body close to his. Her mouth was wet as she sort his lips, her tongue seeking as it slipped deep inside his mouth, and he responded to her embrace.

Their kiss was a yearning, a wanting, and he moved to the bed, and set her down gently. Quickly he rid himself of his shoes, and clothes, and covered her body with his.

She watched as he mounted her, his magnificent body then touching hers radiated such a heat she could hardly bear it. Then his mouth was upon hers. Hot, and wet, and searching. His hands glided over her body as he fumbled with her fasteners. She rose to help him, and miraculously her clothes were whisked away, as his searching hands found, and caressed her secret parts. She gasped with the thrill of it. She clawed at his back trying to get closer.

His erection was hard against her tummy, his hands teasing her senses, her body to the point of oblivion, while at the same time his mouth was suckling her breasts ever so tenderly, barely nipping, and pulling at them until they stood proud, and tingled to send shivers through her body until she thought soon she would burst with elation.

In desperation she grabbed for him, and felt at once his manhood leap in her hand. Her fingers were unable to encompass its width, as she tried to guide him inside her.

"Help me!" she cried. As he thrust upwards, his penis glided into her, filling her being, and a scream of passion which could only be hers, escaped from her throat as she rode the waves of ecstasy to that place of completeness.

He felt her urgency as she grabbed him tightly to move with a motion that fired him, and he finally succumbed to his own desperate needs when he felt his release coming, and he thrust into her deeply, both of them unable to sate the raging fire within, sharing an escape from reality.

He rolled off her, then lay on his back just staring at the ceiling, unable to comprehend how he had become so reliant on expressing his true feelings to another person, but she had brought that out in him, not only during their conversation earlier, but now in this bed, and he turned to look at her now. She was a nice enough girl, she could certainly talk, and their love making had been good, but somehow he didn't feel that they could be a match. 'There was something missing, something so very important.' he told himself. 'What am I looking for?' he asked himself. 'I have had plenty of women throw themselves at me, but so far I haven't felt love. Surely that has to be.' he thought.

She sensed his thoughts, turning to look at him. "What is it Cheyla?" she asked. "What are you thinking?"

"Maybe nothing, but was thinking of our conversation earlier. I can't believe that for the first time in my life I have been able to talk to someone about my problems. I don't usually ramble on like that, so I guess I have you to thank for that Anita, but sorry to burden you." he replied.

"It was my pleasure Cheyla, and being here with you like this just seems to be right somehow. I know you have a lot to sort out Cheyla, and maybe you have a lot of pain ahead. Who knows? I hope not! So I hope it works out for you, but wherever you go just you remember that you are a special person Cheyla Stone, and I would love to be part of your life, but I know deep down that can never be, but if our paths cross again someday, I will welcome you with open arms, but now is definitely not the right time for you to get involved with anyone. However just remember you deserve to be accepted Cheyla, don't you settle for less!" she offered, as she got off the bed to grab at her clothes.

"Thank you Anita! What are you doing?" he asked.

"Getting dressed! I am going home now, I think that you need time to work out your plans." she replied.

He jumped quickly off the bed. "Then I will take you home! Where do you live?" he asked.

"Not far! In a unit, the street just behind the Hotel." "Then we walk together." he said, donning his trousers.

They walked in silence but at her front door she turned and kissed him full on the lips. "I will always remember you Cheyla Stone, good luck in your travels!" Then just as she had appeared, she was gone. Cheyla walked away.

Chapter 4

It was still dark out as he crossed the car park to reach his 4WD. He unlocked it to climb in, and started it up.

Lights at the all-night servo twinkled as he reached the highway, so he pulled into the driveway. He had drank a hasty cup of coffee before leaving the room, planning on stopping for breakfast at the first stop available, but now he needed petrol, and some supplies for this long trek that he knew was before him. He had gasped when he looked at the map earlier this morning, and realized just what he had taken on, and he wanted to get away very early as to alleviate the onslaught of the sun as it reached its zenith.

He filled up, checked the car, and grabbed some ice for his esky. Once inside he picked up some stores from the shelves he may need on the trip, and proceeded to pay.

"Morning!" said the guy behind the counter. "An early start to your trip? Where ya heading?" he asked.

"Well I plan on getting to South Australia, and visit The Flinders Ranges at some point. I guess it might be more appropriate to say that I will be just taking one stop at a time by the look of it." replied Cheyla with a laugh.

"Yeah! Think I know what ya mean." he said laughing.

"That is one long trip, but beautiful Country. Just take your time, and enjoy it, but just take care there is bound to be 'roos on the road." he said as he looked up at Cheyla.

"Thank you Mister, will do!" replied Cheyla as he left.

Back in the 4WD, he gunned the engine, and drove out to join the Highway which led south out of town. No-one was around, not even traffic on the road, and the morning silence unerringly comforting as he settled in for his trek.

Two hours later he noted the sky changing, there was a brightness slowly emerging that preceded the sun as it began its ascent above the ranges, then eventually loomed up displaying its brilliance, shunning darkness to provide light, and with it came the 'roos. Frightened by the vehicle they darted from the table drains where they were eating the sweet shoots of grass that had sprung up from a recent shower of rain, to cross in front of the vehicle, and Cheyla braked to avoid them. He had a bull bar across the front of the 4WD but he didn't want to hit a Kangaroo, he rather liked seeing them wild, and beautiful, hopping in flight.

As light spread over the land, he became more aware of other animals, and the beauty of the Countryside, so he slowed to take it all in. He drove on a bitumen road, but just alongside it wildflowers bloomed, and graced the paddocks where the earth had suddenly turned red, and the shrubbery, and bushes seemed to be tinged with gold as the golden orb highlighted them, bringing them to life.

'No wonder they call this The Red Center.' Cheyla was thinking to himself as he drove through the red earth, and the distant ranges now glowing in the morning light.

Unbelievable Country.' he thought. Even though his journey was for a specific purpose he was beginning to feel thankful for this new opportunity that had arisen.

He looked ahead, and suddenly the reality of it sank in. The Highway was so relentless. Unforgivably straight, and so endlessly long, as it stretched out before him as far as the eye could see, towards the distant horizon.

'A Highway of Infinity!' he assumed. 'The only way he could define it.' He knew Australia was large, but out here in the Red Center of it, alone on the highway, the vastness of it consumed you, and silence was oppressive.

Cheyla thought of his home where there were always people around him, something always happening most of the time, except his only quiet time was at the close of day when the sun was sinking low, and he sat watching it on the verandah, and looked out over his Property. So he had an affinity with this stillness, he liked it well enough.

As he travelled on he could feel the heat mounting in the cabin so he switched the air-con on. Up ahead though, the bitumen road seemed to look like a river as waves of heat hit it, playing tricks on his eyes as it swam before him to dance across the road forming some type of mirage.

In the haze as he topped a rise, he almost missed a sign at the side of the road, thinking it was not really there. He slowed down to read it. 'Revive, and Survive.' The sign read. 'Fuel, Food, and Drink.' One kilometer on left.

'Breakfast.' he thought, as he realized how hungry he was, and put his foot down until he came upon the turn-off where the sign read 'Roadhouse.' So he drove on in, and pulled into the car park, then parked his 4WD.

The Roadhouse was in the middle of no-where, and by the looks of it there wasn't much there he noticed. Just two small dwellings, a couple of fuel bowsers standing out front, a few signs that displayed food available at the café within, but there was a small building or shack really, built off the back of the café which looked to be some type of accommodation. 'The owners, or managers must live there.' he thought. 'What a lonely life they would lead.'

Cheyla walked towards the front door just as a lady appeared with a mop, and bucket in her hands.

"Can I help you lady?" he asked, while he watched her struggle to get through the door, so he held the door wide.

"Thank you young man!" she said, and set the bucket down to look up. "You have nice manners! I'll be back in one sec, just have to put these in the storeroom." she said.

"Are you open for breakfast yet?" he asked.

"Oh yes! Go in, the floors are dry. I'll be back to help you in a moment!" she said, picking up the bucket again.

It was a small establishment, he noticed as he walked inside. One long counter sat adjacent to the back wall, and was supposedly utilized as a servery for take-away food, but also catered for the sit-down tables scattered around close that Cheyla spied as he maneuvered a way through them, however a small alcove lured him inside which had a breakfast bar with high back stools that overlooked the Highway. So he went inside, and pulled out a stool, then grabbed a menu off the table, and checked it out.

Then he sat looking out at the wild Outback Country through the big windows of the Café, and shook his head.

CHEYLA

So much space, so wild, and untamed. 'How do people live out here?' he wondered. 'Just to rely on a friendly face from the tourists who passed by seemed a lonely way to live out your life.' he guessed. Deep in thought, Cheyla didn't hear, or notice the lady walking up to him, and was surprised when she spoke out next to him.

"Sorry about the wait mister. Usually open earlier, but only me here early, so I've had a lot to do." she said.

"That is quite ok. My name is Cheyla." he said in reply.

"Pleased to meet you Cheyla, Judith is my name." she offered her hand, and he took it in a handshake.

"I was just looking at the Countryside, so beautiful but raw too, if I may say that Judith. I was wondering what it was like living out here in the middle of no-where. Seems you don't have a lot of entertainment." he said.

"Yeah it's rough Country Cheyla, but not as bad as it seems. We do have people just like yourself that make our day, and believe it or not, there are Properties within the vicinity so we do tend to get together a fair bit. We have people on different rosters working here, so we also get a chance to go back to Alice, to kick up our heels." she said.

"I see!" said Cheyla, as he chuckled. "That makes it a little different, I thought you were isolated here." he said.

"No not at all, we probably get to see more people than town folk." she said, as she smiled at him. "So have you decided on breakfast yet Cheyla?" she asked.

"Sure have Judith!" he replied. "The big breakfast with the lot sounds good to me, and a coffee please." he said.

"Sounds like you have worked up a huge appetite, big fella, how far are you going?" she asked.

"Well I have to get to South Australia, and then to 'The Flinders Ranges,' eventually." he said.

"Long way to travel Cheyla, you better fill up your car too before you leave. There is other stops on the Highway, but if you fuel up at each stop you should be ok then." she replied. "I will go and get your breakfast now." she said.

"Ok thanks for the tip Judith, I might go out and fill up then while I am waiting for breakfast." he answered.

"Yeah, good idea Cheyla. I won't be long." she replied.

Heat seemed to sap his energy as he walked outside, and a hot breath of air fanned his face. 'It's going to be a hot one today.' Cheyla thought, as he looked across the road that was shimmering to the haze in the paddocks beyond. He checked his 4WD, washed the windows, then he filled up in haste to get back inside.

Breakfast was served as he sat up on the stool. With the pangs of hunger churning his insides Cheyla fell on it with a passion, devouring it in no time. Contentedly he leaned back in the high back stool sipping his coffee, and his eyes scanned the countryside. It was getting hotter out there now he could tell, as mirages seemed to dance along the highway, and steam seemed to rise from the red earth to form waves across the paddock, clouding his vision.

Suddenly something out there attracted his attention, and he focused hard. He thought he saw a man running in the haze, and as he concentrated he was convinced of it as he saw him fall, then get up again, and stagger on.

He was reeling on his feet, barely able to put one foot in front of the other as he headed towards the Roadhouse.

"Judith come quickly!" he called, not taking his eyes off the fellow in stress out there.

"What is it Cheyla?" Judith asked as she rushed over.

Cheyla pointed his chin in the direction as he spoke.

"Someone is in trouble out there. He can barely walk!"

"My goodness that looks like Charlie Rogers, but what the hell is he doing out there, and where is his car, he lives about six miles in but there is a road." she replied.

"Don't know but we better help him, he is not going to make it here." offered Cheyla, as he pushed back his stool, and rushed outside with Judith close on his heels.

Cheyla reached the man's side as he collapsed again for the last time, unable to get up, so he rolled him over. His mouth was so dry, his lips cracked, and caked with a white dry-looking spittle, and his eyes seemed to roll back in head, as he started mumbling something.

"He is dehydrated Judith, and it looks like he has been running for quite a while. Can you get some water, and something for him to lie on inside? I will bring him over to the Roadhouse." he stated, as he lifted him with ease, up over his shoulder, and strode out across the paddock.

"Yes sure Cheyla." Judith replied, as she gaped at him. 'Charlie Rogers was not a small man by any means. He was big, and tough, but in this big man's arms he looked like a small child.' she thought, then she raced away.

Judith set up a mattress for Charlie in a back room, and then at once Cheyla began to work on him. Sponging him down, lifting his head, and giving him small sips of water. Judith brought in a fan, plugged it in, and switched it on.

It was some time later, as he started to groan, and thrash his body about when the first signs of life appeared on his face as his colour returned, and the deep lines of stress slowly relaxed. His voice, which previously had been just a mumble, became coherent, and his eyes flew wide as he called out desperately, and grabbed at Cheyla's hand.

He looked up at the face that swam before his eyes, and detected someone there, and he stammered. "He..lp! Pl..ease, I..ne..ed ya he..lp Mister, can ya he..lp me?" he asked, as he lifted his head, and tried to get up of the floor.

Cheyla steadied him. "It's ok now mate, we're helping you, just take it easy, and lie back for a while!" he said.

"No! Can't!" he replied, more definitely now, pushing Cheyla's hand away to sit up. "Have to get help! Ya don't understand Mister. It's me wife that needs some help!"

He was raving now, and Cheyla listened intently.

"Was takin her to the hospital in Alice to be admitted this arvo!" he continued. "But had ta leave her in the car!" he sobbed, as tears filled his eyes to run down his cheeks.

"So your wife is sick is she?" asked Cheyla.

"More than sick!" said Charlie, as he looked up. "She's in labor now! An it's all my fault. It all started when I hit the hole, gave her one hell of a jolt that did!" he said.

"What hole?" asked Cheyla, trying to understand it.

"Was goin too fast, didn't see the hole until it was too late, an I hit a washout in the road, the front end got over, but the back of the car is lodged in a great hole. Tried, but couldn't budge it. Car's stuck solid about three miles back an my wife's in it, an in labor. Nothin I could do but run a shorter way cross country to try ta get help." he stressed.

Judith seemed to take things into consideration quickly, and now dominated the conversation.

"First things first!" she said. "I will go, and ring Marla. She is the mid-wife round here, and it looks like we need her services badly from what I hear. She lives about three miles back off the Highway towards Alice, so if she can leave immediately we can drive out to where Charlie's car is to get his wife, and bring her back here!" she said.

"Cheyla I hate to impose on you, and your trip, but are you able to help Charlie with his vehicle?" she asked, as she looked up at him in earnest. "Yeah sure Judith, my trip can wait, and I've got tow ropes, and anything I need in my 4WD, so it shouldn't be a problem." he replied.

"Yeah, but what about the hole?" Charlie asked, as he looked up at Cheyla. "That car's not movin." he said.

"Come on Charlie, let's get you up, and agile so I can get back there, and you just let me worry about the hole!" said Cheyla, as he pulled him onto wobbly legs. You ok?"

"Yeah I'll be ok, let's just get back there to my wife. Thanks a lot Mister!" he said.

"Cheyla is my name Charlie." he replied, and as they shook hands Charlie noted the iron-like grip in this big man's hand, and couldn't help but take in his physique as he looked up at him. "Thanks Cheyla!" offered Charlie.

"So Charlie, we will find you about three miles out on your property road, right?" asked Judith. "Yeah you can't miss it." said Charlie. "Right, see you there!" she said.

"Ok then, let's move now!" said Cheyla, and Charlie done his best to trail after him as he left the Roadhouse, and headed across the car park to his 4WD vehicle.

"Just point me in the direction Charlie, and we will get moving!" Cheyla said, as they climbed into his vehicle.

"Turn left when ya get out on the Highway, then about a mile further down take a right turn. It's a dirt road, an a bit muddy from the bit o rain we had but some gravel, but the corrugation is the worst. Guess my car is about two ta three miles in." Charlie replied.

"Sounds like a fun trip." said Cheyla, with a chuckle as he looked across at him. "You ok Charlie?" he asked.

"Yeah, I'm fine now, just worried about my wife that's all. It's all my fault! She is not due for another two weeks, an cause we live way out here the doctor in Alice wanted her admitted early, so that's where we was goin." he said.

"Don't blame yourself Charlie, these things happen all the time, but it will work out ok, you'll see." said Cheyla.

They could hear the screams as they approached the Ford Ute, its front end tilted in the air, but the back barely visible. Cheyla braked just short of the vehicle, and quickly they jumped out.

Cheyla assessed the situation at hand as he climbed into the hole where the back end of the truck was stuck. "You stay up there Charlie, and I will lift your wife up to you. So prepare the back seat of the 4WD to lie her down, there's pillows in the back, what's her name?" he called.

"Right." said Charlie in distress. "Her name is Lee!" he called, as he raced to the back of the 4WD, and was back peering over the edge in no time.

"Lee! My name is Cheyla, I am here with Charlie to help you. I am going to lift you up to him ok?" he stated.

Lee looked up at the friendly face, and though the pain was fierce she managed a smile.

"Thank you Cheyla, I am so pleased Charlie managed to get some help for us, I am as ready as I will ever be!"

"Good! On a count of three I will lift you, be brave." he said, then called to Charlie. "You ready Charlie?"

"Yeah, all is ready, just waitin here." called Charlie.

Cheyla scooped Lee up tenderly, and cradled her as he got her out of the car, then lifted her high, and passed her up to Charlie, who just looked at him in awe at the effort it would have taken, but he gripped her firmly, then he turned towards the 4WD. "You ok Lee? Marla is on her way." he said, and laid her on the back seat. "I'm ok now thank god you got help the pains are close now." she said.

Outside Cheyla was in action setting up the steel tow rope from his 4WD to the Ute. All was ready when Judith, and Marla drove up, so they transferred Lee into their car.

Charlie only had time to say 'Good Luck,' before she was whisked away as Marla put her foot down, and the car leapt forward on towards The Roadhouse. "So what happens now Cheyla?" he asked, his eyes following them.

"We have work to do Charlie! So this is the plan. Jump in the 4WD, but have it started, and ready to reverse tow when you see the Ute come up to the road level." he said.

"How's it gunna do that, what do ya mean Cheyla?" he asked. "I will lift it to the road level." said Cheyla as he jumped into the hole. Charlie gaped at him, and he was about to question him, but decided against it, so he ran to the 4WD, jumped in, and started the engine, and waited.

Cheyla shuffled his feet deep into the dirt to get a firm

stance, and flexed his huge muscles until they were loose.

He heard the engine running in his 4WD, his huge leg muscles flexed as he crouched down on his haunches, his both hands were searching for a secure grip under the body of the Ute until he was satisfied with his hold, then he summoned up all the power he had, his mighty legs pushing upwards, his biceps bulging with the effort as his arms, and legs straightened, and the Ute was lifted high.

Charlie sat listening to the throb of the engine. 'How on earth is he going to do this?' he thought, as he sat waiting. His eyes were almost mesmerized from staring at the front of the Ute, so when it actually started to move he thought he was imagining it. Then it moved again, and sat up more alert, and revved the engine in readiness.

He stared ahead unbelievably, as if he was watching a slow action replay of a movie. The front wheels of the Ute were firmly on the ground now, and slowly, inch by inch, the back end began rising from the hole. He was in total shock, but in awe of the man helping him, as he could not believe what he was witnessing right before his very eyes.

'I am a strong man myself.' he thought. 'But there was no way I could emulate this feat of strength! Just how strong is this man Cheyla Stone?' he asked himself, as he had never seen anything like it before, and probably in his lifetime, would never see the likes of it again.

Now he noticed the Ute was at road level, and Charlie sprang into action. He shoved the gear stick into reverse, and revved the engine, then slowly took the strain on the steel rope until it was taut, and using total pulling power, reversed the 4WD, and the Ute followed like a little lamb, and rolled along the road. Charlie braked to halt, and put the handbrake on, and shut the 4WD down, opened the door, and jumped down, and rushed to his Ute to check it out. He couldn't believe it, apart from a few dents, there was no damage underneath, and the tyres were intact.

Cheyla immediately emerged from the hole, then he climbed out. Seemingly he was none the worse for wear after his massive effort. He exercised his neck, and flexed, and shook his muscles just like a spaniel shedding water from its coat. "Well it's out Charlie!" he called out.

"Only cause of you!" called Charlie in response. "I am gob-smacked, you are just a legend Cheyla Stone! What massive strength you have." he said, as he punched his arm lightly. I can't begin to thank you enough. My Ute looks ok too, providing it starts, better try it!" he said, and he walked over, opened the door to climb in. As he hit the ignition the engine fired. "Ok we're out of here!" he said.

At the Roadhouse celebrations were in order, and as Judith led them to the back room where Lee had given birth, Charlie was presented with a bundle of joy. His face beamed as he cuddled his Son, then bent to kiss his wife.

"Well done Lee, I am so proud of you! Are you ok?"

"I am now, thanks to Cheyla!" laughed Lee.

"Congratulations you two, nice looking boy!" Cheyla said. "But I have to hit the road, this Highway is endless!" Charlie gripped his hand. "Thanks Cheyla! You will not believe what this guy done Lee! Wished I had my camera! He just lifted the car right out of the bloody hole, he did!"

Chapter 5

Far from the heart of the red center, in another part of the Country, the little town of Shallow Siding nestled in a beautiful valley, was blessed with a perfect day.

It was spring. Still coolness in the air, and evidence of blossoms on the trees, and gardens was obvious, though the sun now radiated some warmth in the early morning.

There was activity at the little Chapel on the outskirts of town as several people were taking things inside, and gardeners making final preparations to dress the gardens. A land-rover pulled into the curb, and parked out front.

Jacqueline Coby-Stringer opened the driver side door grabbed some things from the front seat, then locked the door, and made her way across the lawn to the path. She acknowledged the priest waiting for her on the front step.

"Good morning Father Simmons!" she said.

"Morning Jackie, we are blessed with a good day!"

"Yes it sure is Father Simmons. Is everything in order for this afternoon?" she asked. "Yes Jackie, all is prepared. I have already spoken with the photographer, and I have shown him the best places to be to take his shots. There are some ladies inside setting up the flowers." he replied.

"Excellent, I thank you Father!" She handed over a leather- bound book as she continued. "Would you mind placing this conspicuously at the entrance with this sign visible? It is a special request from Mary, as she would like all the guests to sign the book!"

"Yes Jackie, I shall!" he said, as he took the parcels.

"Thank you Father! Now I must check inside to see if that is in order? Oh also! This is for you!" she added, as she handed him an envelope.

He looked at the envelope, then slipped it into his vest.

"Thank you Jackie, by all means go inside." he said.

"Oh by the way! The organist will arrive at 4 pm." he said.

"Oh good, everyone is organized! What a treat." she said.

Anne Hardy was the first to attract her attention as Jacqueline walked inside the serene Chapel. "Over here Jackie!" she called from amidst all the floral blooms.

"Hi Anne! You girls are doing an excellent job, it looks so beautiful." offered Jacqueline, as she walked up to her.

"Hi Jackie! Oh, thank you! But the flowers are just so beautiful, it is not too difficult to arrange them, and the girls down the front there are such good helpers. I am so excited for Mary. It is going to be just a special day." she bubbled. "Are you all organized at home Jackie? Do you need help? That is going to be the best part. I can't wait!"

Jacqueline laughed. "You ought to know me Anne. Of course everything is organized! No help is needed, so just come, and enjoy. Are you, and Jake still staying over?"

"Of course!" said Anne. "Good! Seeing all is in order, I may leave for home, Melissa wants to ride early today."

"All is ok here Jackie! We are almost finished really, so off you go then. There are bound to be many things you must do there in preparation! I am guessing we will meet at the Chapel later this afternoon, shall we?" she queried.

"Yes after the service as arranged Anne. Thank you all so much for helping, remember to thank the girls for me!" Jacqueline said, giving a brief wave as she walked off.

"Bye Jackie see you later." said Anne.

Jacqueline's eyes squinted badly as she went outside the Chapel into brilliant sunshine. So she grabbed for her sunglasses out of her bag as she headed towards the Land Rover to unlock the door, then she slipped inside to start the engine. It was a four mile trip, so she was anxious now to leave, as she had promised Melissa she would be back.

On the trip home, the beautiful landscape escaped her attention as her thoughts turned to Mary Higgs.

'Yes today will be so special, she would make sure of that!' Mary had been everything to her in her lifetime. A nanny, a servant, a companion who had never deserted her, who always stuck by her, and was beside her through the worst years of her life. But most of all she had become her very dear friend. As she reached the Outback Gardens she drove straight down to the yards, shut the engine off, then slipped out of the rover, and walked over quietly.

She climbed the rails, then sat watching the two people she loved most in the world. As Mitch Stringer guided the Stallion around the holding yard, and urged him into a slow canter, Jacqueline Coby-Stringer's heart seemed to simply melt with pure pleasure from the sight of them.

Continuous whoops of sheer delight began to escape her Daughter's gaping mouth as she sat holding the reins tightly, while seated securely on the saddle in front of her Father, and Jacqueline laughed at her antics.

Melissa Anne Stringer was just over three years of age, but already she was showing signs of becoming a horse-woman. She just loved horses, and was forever wanting to ride, especially 'April Rain' whom she called 'Rain,' an easier name for her to say. She loved him, and he loved her too, and knew her well. He was so gentle with her on his back, taking tentative steps to protect her always.

Now as they slowly cantered to circle the yard the rays of sunshine seemed to highlight her already golden locks of ringlets, as she bobbed up, and down with the action. Quickly she looked over as if looking for her Mother, then called out loud when she noticed her. "Mother you came? Look at me Mother! I'm riding!" she laughed excitedly.

"Father is teaching me, but we are going faster today!"

Jacqueline's heart almost burst with pride as she called to her. "Good girl Melissa. You are riding! Well done!"

'How lucky she was.' she thought to herself. 'It didn't seem all that long ago when she thought her life was over, and that she would never have a Family of her own, but now she had a beautiful Daughter, a loving Husband, and many, many friends. Every day with them was a blessing.

There had always been a dark side to Jacqueline Coby-Stringer. Old memories that would never leave her kept resurfacing to haunt her for years to cloud her happiness, but she had overcome most of it, and now lived a full life.

Her mind wandered as those old thoughts crept in.

She looked up at Mitchell Stringer now. 'So impossibly handsome!' she thought. He still had that same effect on her as he did all those years ago, and her heart leapt inside her chest as she looked upon his face.' She loved him so.

She knew her state of mind had been restored only due to his patience, tenderness, his undying love for her, and a special bond which united them both to last throughout their lifetime. He was the perfect Husband, perfect Father to their Daughter, a great provider, and he was skilled at so many different things that had always astounded her, but his specialty was definitely horses, and other animals.

'He is a real-life Cowboy! Always was!' she mused.

Life at The Outback Gardens had become her passion, her life's blood put into it, as Jacqueline was involved in the running of it as much as Mitch, and his Son Pete.

However Jacqueline Coby-Stringer was a Coby born, and bred, and still was the sole Owner of 'Shallow Downs.' Their Property that was left to her by her Father, Clayton Coby, in his passing. It was a thriving property, and a large property of Cattle, and Wattle Plantations, but a Manager still operated it. To this day, Jacqueline had not stepped inside the newly appointed Homestead.

Her memories were just too raw.

Her only visit to the property 'Shallow Downs,' which was her childhood home, was a ritual every Sunday. But only to the Family Cemetery situated opposite the creek, where it was secluded below the base of the hills amongst huge gum trees, where her Mother, and Father lay to rest beside all the Families of Coby's that went before them.

All thoughts were washed away amidst the laughter from Mitch, and Melissa as he lifted her down from the saddle, and Jacqueline's Daughter ran towards her.

Jacqueline climbed down from the railings just in time to receive her Daughter who rushed towards her, and she folded her into her arms to hug her precious little body.

"You are such a clever girl Melissa! Father is teaching you well. You are actually riding." she said, as she gently eased her back so she could look into her beautiful green eyes, an imitation of her own, and the Coby's before her.

"Yes, I know Mother, isn't it excitin? But Father is just the best-est teacher!" she stated boldly. "I will be riding by myself soon!" she said in her childish chatter.

Jacqueline laughed particularly about the way Melissa persisted on trying to speak larger words way beyond her years, but at the same time a sense of pride overwhelmed Jacqueline. 'This Daughter they had produced was a little like her when she was young, and growing up. But very much like her Father also.' she thought. 'So confident, and capable at such a tender age. Just like we both were.'

But she knew deep down that stubbornness and pride ran true in her veins, cemented in her genes. Something that had passed down, not only from herself, but from her own Grandfather, Clayton Coby, who believed he could move mountains, so nothing was impossible. 'He usually succeeded too, he never ever gave in!' she recalled fondly.

Mitch sidled up beside her then he pulled her towards him into his arms. His mouth closed hers in a longing kiss of a new lover seeking attention, and Jacqueline matched his passion equally, until she felt her jacket being tugged.

She looked down at her Daughter's impatient face as she spoke. "We have a party to go to Mother, and Father, are we going right now, or not?" Jacqueline looked up at Mitch, who had a comical look on his face, and they both laughed, as he replied. "We were waiting for you Madam Butterfly! You have to get all prettied up first! So back to the Homestead pronto." he said, and that produced fits of giggles from Melissa who loved her Father's pet names.

Melissa skipped along in front, so they trailed behind her with their hands entwined. "She is so like your Father, Jackie," he said softly. "Yes I know!" she replied.

"Is everything ready in at The Chapel?" he asked her.

"Yes! Anne was there organizing it all, so we only have the reception to cater for Mitch." she replied. "I want it to be as wonderful as it can possibly be!" she added.

"It will be Jackie just trust me. We have many workers, and they have instructions, so it will be good!" he replied.

Back at The Homestead, when Jacqueline scrutinized the surroundings, she witnessed first-hand, the truth in what Mitch had said, and was more than pleased with what she saw. Somehow it rekindled times of long ago.

Ground lights adorned gardens magnificent in their blooms that graced the perimeter of the massive Marquee which was centered on the lawns to take up most of the grassed area. Coloured lights hung low in arrangements inside the Marquee so in darkness it would be a colourful display. Decorative candles stood proudly centering the tables dressed in decorations upon white tablecloths, and chairs backed in a cladding of white, and purple ribbons.

'Yes!' she thought. 'This is how I wanted it!' A perfect setting for a perfect lady, and her man. She felt privileged to be able to give her friend what she so richly deserved.

"Thank you Mitch, it is truly magical." she said, as she looked up at him, her own eyes misting over.

"Thought you might say that!" he drawled. "But come on Jackie, don't get all emotional, we have things to do!"

"But firstly. Let's all have lunch! I am famished. How about you Jackie?" he asked.

"Yes lunch would be nice. It's been a long morning!"

"Good that's settled then! Are you ready to have lunch miss youngest horse-rider of the year?" he asked Melissa in jest. Melissa giggled. "Oh Father you're so funny, and yes sir, I'm ready for lunch!" she replied, as a cheeky grin spread across her face that made them laugh.

"Right, then let's get cleaned up first!" he stated, as he grabbed both their hands, then steered them towards the stairs. "What say we three have lunch up on the balcony Jackie?" he asked. "Yes! Sounds good to me." she replied.

She chose their favourite table which took in the view of not only the gardens which were flourishing at the moment, but the water view of The Siding River winding its way through the property, and a back drop of distant hills brought in another element to admire. As Mitch re-joined them, they all enjoyed it, as far as the eye could see.

"It is so beautiful up here." remarked Jacqueline as she scanned the Countryside. "I do hope Mary likes our gift we chose for her." she said, as she looked at Mitch.

"Are you serious Jackie?" he asked in astonishment.

"Who wouldn't? It's the most perfect gift anyone can receive, and she's lucky to have such a generous friend!"

"Yes, but she won't be here anymore. She loves it here. Maybe she won't like that, and I will miss her also." said Jacqueline, as she looked up at Mitch with misty eyes.

"Jackie, you are getting sentimental again! Remember, everyone deserves a chance in life. That is something you are giving as a gift. What Mary decides about it will be up to her, and Drew I guess. Besides she will still be working here, and at Shallow Downs, so I don't see a problem. You will see her most days." he offered decidedly.

"You do have a way of simplifying everything Mitch!" said Jacqueline, as she squeezed his hand. "Thank you!"

"Good, that's settled! Now, I went down to speak with May, and to order lunch, she knows we are up here. Mary is joining us also. I ran into her in the kitchen." said Mitch.

May Jeffries was house cook at 'The Outback Gardens Homestead,' she had been for many years. "Really Mitch? That is just perfect." said Jacqueline, with a smile.

Mary sat on the tapestry chair in front of her mirror, and stared blankly at the face reflecting her image. 'What is wrong with you?' she asked of herself. 'Her eyes looked sad, her hands trembled, and she was fighting her body to gain control. 'You do love Drew, don't you?' she asked the face staring back at her. 'You know you do, and he loves you too! 'So what is the problem?' she queried.

'Maybe I need to get out of this room. Go downstairs to have lunch, that would be relaxing.' she thought, as she pushed the chair back in determination to cross the room.

She opened the door, closing it softly behind her, then approached the staircase which led down to the kitchen.

To her surprise Mitch was there talking to May, and he looked up as she walked in. "Mary! Good to see you up, and about. Pleased you came down, how would you like to join us upstairs for lunch? We've just finished the all- important riding lesson, so we're all hungry!" he said, and laughed, as looked at her. "You ok Mary?" he asked.

"Me be ok me thinks Mister Stringer. Jus be a bit shaky taday. But hungry too, so I love ta join ya all!" she replied. "Good! Jackie will soon sort you out, and Mary please call me Mitch." he said. "I be try Mister Stringer." she said.

Mary Higgs had been a servant most of her life. Her heritage being from an aboriginal clan. She found it disrespectful to call her bosses by their first names. It took her a very long time, many years really, to address Jacqueline Coby by her first name. She recalled how that had come about, and she shook her head at the memory.

'So much they had shared together!' she thought of this person who had become her very dearest friend.

She reached the top of the stairs, and stepped shakily out to the balcony, and into the sunshine. Her steps were very tentative as she approached the table with her nerves quite obviously reflected upon her fearful face as she tried her best to smile at the Coby-Stringer family sitting there.

They all looked up but it was Jacqueline Coby-Stringer who spoke out, then took control as she stared at Mary's face. "Come! Sit by me Mary!" "Mitch would you mind taking Melissa for a walk to get us some drinks please?"

"Maybe a little brandy, lime, and lemonade would be nice for us ladies. Is that suitable Mary?" she asked.

"Ya think I should hav a drink Jacqueline?" she asked.

"Most definitely Mary, trust me!" she replied.

"In thet case, it be fine for me!" stated Mary.

"Won't be long Jackie." muttered Mitch as he rose up from the chair offering his hand to Melissa. "Are you coming with me 'My lady?' he asked, as he bowed to her. "Would you like to help, let's see what we can whisk up?"

Melissa giggled, then said. "Yes please Father." The all importance of a task was too much for Melissa to refuse as she scrambled off her chair to take her Father's hand.

Jacqueline looked hard at Mary. "What is it Mary? What is upsetting you? It should be a happy day." she said.

"Me know Jacqueline but jus be scared thet's all, an am wonderin if me be doing the right thing, am talkin bout a new life an it be frightenin me. Also there be so much fuss jus for me, don't know if I deserve thet." she answered.

"Now you listen very carefully Mary!" Jacqueline said with a seriousness, and determination in her voice which urged Mary to sit up, and take notice. She knew that tone of voice, she had come to know it well, and also knew that nothing would change Jacqueline's mind either with her opinions. "You have done nothing but good, your whole life Mary, but for other people. Now it is time for you to have a life for yourself, and the happiness you deserve."

"Now, I am sorry about all the 'fuss' as you call it, but be assured Mary that is purely my fault, it is something I wanted for you on this special day, you deserve the 'fuss'.

"So just enjoy it please Mary, but I don't apologize for it at all. It is what I had to do for you! Also don't think for one minute I don't know how nervous you are! Don't you realize how nervous I was, the day I married Mitch? It is a natural reaction Mary. I cried most of the time that day! Sad, and happy tears, but it was the most, happiest day of my life, and always should be when you love someone."
"You do love Drew, don't you Mary?" Jacqueline asked.

Mary looked up from her lap as the tears filled her eyes. "Oh Miss Jacqueline… I mean Jacqueline… she corrected herself. "I love ya so much, hav done since ya was a baby, an I no ya be wantin something special for me, an I do thank ya. It jus means so much ta me, thets all. It be jus like ya to do things yor own way. So I be enjoyin it taday, thank ya, an I do love Drew so much." she said.

"Well!" stated Jacqueline. "Thank goodness for that! You have nothing to be nervous about after all, so let us celebrate now Mary Higgs!" said Jacqueline laughing, but then added more seriously. "But don't you dare say I am 'fussing,' when I give you, and Drew your present!"

Mary's face beamed, the absence of a smile returned to light it as she laughed for the first time that morning until Jacqueline's words sunk in. "What present ya mean? I be thinkin ya hav given me nough Jacqueline?" she said.

"We won't be arguing today Mary!" Jacqueline stated with conviction. "Oh look, here come Mitch, and Melissa. What good timing. It is good timing isn't it Mary? Are you alright now?" she asked, concerned. "Yea Jacqueline, I be fine now, ya no thet. Ya hav helped me heaps." she said.

Mitchell reached the balcony then strode over to the table, a big grin spread across his face as he looked at them. Melissa skipped along beside him, her face also lit up with a smile, then she rushed to her Mother's side.

"Mother!" she said excitedly. "We made drinks, it was so fun, and Marie is bringing them." she gushed "Oh that sounds fascinating Melissa, well done!" said Jacqueline.

Marie walked up beside Melissa, and placed the tray of drinks on the table. Her hair was long now, but gone was the hint of freckles from her face she used to have in her teens when she first was taught by her Mother May, to be a waitress, and housemaid at The Outback Gardens.

"Good morning Missus Coby-Stringer, good morning to you Mary, and best wishes to you, and Drew." she said.

"Good morning Marie, thank you" replied Jacqueline.

"That is fine Missus, your lunch is ready so I will bring that up now." she said. "Oh that is good." said Jacqueline, as Marie passed around their drinks, and turned to leave.

"Wait Marie!" said Mary. "I be wantin ta thank ya fer your wishes fer me, an fer Drew, an also fer ya service."

"You are most welcome Mary. I guess I will be serving you a lot more later today, and you deserve that. I hope you enjoy this day Mary. Congratulations!" she said.

"It be a happy day, an thank ya Marie." replied Mary.

"Well!" stated Mitch as he joined them. "There is that smile we have been missing Mary. Looks like everything is fine now, you look much happier, so that is good."

"Yea, me be ok now Mister Stringer. Hav bin talkin to Jacqueline, an she be set me on tha right track, me thinks." she said. "Good! Oh here is lunch." he said, as he spied the girls bringing up their food. Let's eat, I'm starving!"

Platters of food were placed in the center of the table, and the girls were arranging their place settings as May Jeffries their house cook, walked to their table, and spoke.

"Excuse me for the interruption everyone. I hope you enjoy your lunch. I just wanted to come up, and wish you, and Drew all the best Mary, in case I don't get a chance to later. I hope you will be very happy Mary!"

"Thank ya May, thet be meanin a lot ta me, but sorry I be causin ya, an tha girls more work taday. But I be make it up ta ya all when I be back at work." replied Mary.

"Nonsense Mary! We wouldn't hear of it. You deserve today, so you lap it all up girl. It is our pleasure. I must go so have a good day! If you have any further instructions for me Jacqueline, or Mitchell, just let me know." she said.

"Thank you May but everything is looking wonderful, we will see you before we leave." replied Jacqueline.

L unch was slowly consumed amidst their laughter as friendly banter seemed to dominate the conversation as old tales were told of their youth, and somehow to all of them it felt like they were saying goodbye. Uneasiness overcome Jacqueline abruptly, she had to speak her mind.

"Mary, sorry to interrupt your fun, but there are some things we need to talk about, and it has to be now I feel."

"It be ok Jacqueline. What ya need ta know?" asked Mary.

"Well firstly Mary. Would you mind telling me if you, and Drew have made any plans as to where you are going to stay tonight, and where you are going to live after that, have you made any arrangements?" asked Jacqueline.

"Yea! We be goin away for two weeks. Drew has got time off work ta take me away, but tonight we were goin ta stay in the bungalow at Shallow Downs where he lives, an I'm guessin thet when we come back maybe we hav ta stay there. It be very small, so we might hav ta look for a house in town. Tis a bit scary leavin here, but hav ta make plans for our future I guess. It be ok!" replied Mary.

Jacqueline looked at her fondly. "I am so pleased Drew is taking you on a trip Mary, it will be so good for you both. As for tonight I have an arrangement you may like.

"I want you to know that I have especially prepared a suite for you both upstairs for tonight, so discuss it with Drew, but I think that would be appropriate. It will give you a chance to enjoy your celebrations, relax a little with friends instead of driving out to Shallow Downs, and then after you have had breakfast with us in the morning, you could leave from here to go on your travels. What do you think Mary?" Jacqueline asked, with just a hint of a smile.

Mitch laughed. "Just look at the look upon Mary's face Jackie, she doesn't know if she is coming, or going. Mary, I think she has a point though, but you know Jacqueline, she leaves no stone unturned. What about you Melissa? Should Mary, and Drew stay here tonight?" he asked his Daughter. "Yes! Yes! Mary, stay here!" called Melissa.

"Then I guess that is settled then, as long as the couple agree. Your thoughts Mary?" he asked.

"Nothin would please me more Mister Stringer. I am sure Drew would agree ta thet too. Thank ya Jacqueline, thank ya both!" said Mary, as tears rolled down her face.

"Good, all is settled, but I suggest when you go to your room, you had better ring Drew just to confirm, and Mary you had better go after lunch so you can have a rest. I have the girls going up at 3pm to assist you in dressing, and to arrange your hair." said Jacqueline, smiling sweetly.

"So determined ya be Jacqueline Coby-Stringer, but I be lovin ya for it. This day, I will neva forget." said Mary.

"You are welcome Mary! But you had better leave, and rest now, you can't be late to the Chapel." said Jacqueline.

Mary lay upon the soft bed just staring at the ceiling. She had spoken to Drew, and all was organized for the night, and thoughts of her future filled her head, but suddenly other visions enveloped her of a time long ago.

She was a kid again. An aboriginal child reared in The Northern Territory, by her Mum, and Dad, Grandmother, and the rest of the clan. Vague memories of this life barely existed from her youth, but she remembered the car crash that took her parents. She had no idea then where they were, but she was left alone, and she remembered the face clearly of the lady who saved her. Missus Mel Coby from Shallow Downs, who took her in, gave her a home, and a job, but treated her like her own. How she had loved her. How sad she felt the day that Missus Coby was consumed in the fire that demolished her home at Shallow Downs.

Her thoughts turned to Miss Jacqueline. She had loved her from the day she was born. She always looked out for her, but couldn't shield her from the pain, and shame that consumed her when her life was in ruin, forcing her to be an outcast from her home when they left Shallow Downs.

Like in a dream, it washed over her. Flashbacks snow-balled to reveal their past life, their heartaches. She shuddered at the memories. So much pain, and grief Miss Jacqueline had lived through then. Mary remembered it so vividly, as she had lived through it with her.

Almost like being in a time warp they travelled across Australia endlessly, but the one thing Mary remembered most was when they went to The Northern Territory, and though it had been a stressful time for Jacqueline Coby, Mary had re-united with her Grandmother, and relatives for the first time since she was a child living at Tenna.

For years they travelled. Always searching, but never finding, then by chance they entered The Flinders Ranges. Mary remembered it well, as she had spent most of her life working there. For her, and Jacqueline Coby it became a place of sanction for them both at Waverley Downs.

Until one day a letter Jacqueline had received changed their lives again. Jacqueline decided to return to Shallow Siding leaving Mary behind, as she planned to return, but once again disaster struck her, and she almost lost her life.

When she recovered fully, and planned to stay she had made arrangements for Mary to return home where she resided at The Outback Gardens. Mary lived, and worked there, but also worked at Shallow Downs, her old home, where she met Drew Hargraves, the head stockman there.

For the first time in her life, Mary Higgs felt another type of love, a closeness for the first man she could relate to, feel close to. They fell in love, and became inseparable.

A soft knock on the door dragged her from her reverie, back into the world of reality. 'It was her Wedding Day.'

Chapter 6

Night was closing in fast when he finally crossed the border into South Australia, but a road sign alerted Cheyla of a Homestead providing Motel accommodation only 84km ahead so he pressed on. He had been travelling many hours, and it had been a long day so he was looking forward to a break, but though the drive was spectacular through the amazing Countryside, his attention became diverted as his senses tingled, his eyes just captivated by a spectacular view of the sinking sun, displaying a sunset in all its glory like no other he had seen, to spread colours across the land, and transform the scenery once again.

He knew he was bypassing many tourist attractions, he passed the signs, knowing that Uluru was just down one turnoff, and other tourist trails he could follow, and though he was on a road that was safe, but very, very long he would have liked it well enough to take the off-road adventure though the wilderness which appealed to him, and maybe even explore the Simpson Desert. It seemed huge out there, but he couldn't afford the luxury of that now. He was on an important mission, and nothing could deter him from that. 'Maybe some other time.' he thought.

Lights were the last thing that Cheyla expected to see out here in the wilderness, but there they were. 'Just up ahead, twinkling in the darkness.' he noticed.

He assumed that he must be close to whatever was out there, but once again was fooled by the deception of the straight, endless highway which continued on its never-ending, straight line into nothingness, so he persevered once again, and drove on towards the only signs of life.

Finally a big sign attracted his attention, and he pulled off the highway into civilization. Set back off the road was a Homestead. He could see up to the top balcony clearly in the lamplight as people moved about the verandah, but as an addition to the big building, bright lights suggested a Restaurant, and Bar which spilled out to a beer garden which was flooded with coloured lights.

On the outskirts, dimly lit buildings barely attracted his attention as he guessed they were smaller houses, but the one he relished, was a neon sign as it blinked. 'Motel,' and he drove into the reception area to park his 4WD.

Stiffly Cheyla climbed down. Stretched his neck, and back then headed for the front door. A bell jingled from above as he pushed the door open, ducked his head, and walked inside the dimly lit office where an elderly lady looked up to the ringing of the bell from her seat at the computer desk where she had been busily typing.

"Good evening young man." she uttered, straining to look up at Cheyla as she chuckled. "Here I was thinking I was going to have an early night, ya never can pick it!"

"So I've just made it, have I. Thank goodness, do you have a room?" he asked. "Yeah got one left!" she replied.

"You're kidding me right?" joked Cheyla. "So where is everyone then? I don't see any people around." he said.

"The ones that aren't tucked up in bed already will be over at the Restaurant, or Bar. You'll find the car park out back facing the room. I only have the six rooms anyway!" she chuckled then grinned up at him. "How long are ya staying?" she asked, as she handed him a room key.

"Oh I see!" he chuckled, to join in her joke "I'll be just staying tonight. I'm pretty bushed, but I might leave after your earliest breakfast tomorrow if that is alright, then hit the road. I thought no-one else was travelling this Highway! Haven't seen anyone all day, guess they're all here!"

"You would be surprised, there are so many travelers, lots of tourists about these days. You better fill out your breakfast menu before you go too." she said, handing him a menu. "Then I will lock up for the night." she added.

Cheyla bent to fill out the menu, and handed it to her. "I'll pay you now if you like." he said, as he pulled out his wallet to pay. "Ok! Thank you!" she stated, as she opened the register. "Have a good night, sleep well." she said.

Just to see that bed was a bonus to Cheyla as he entered the room. 'But not just yet.' he thought to himself.

'Tonight! I am going to eat like it's my last meal. Drink like there is no tomorrow. Chill out to shake cobwebs out of my brain. I will like that well enough. Sleep will come.'

He quickly showered, then changed, and left the room closing the door softly behind him. He ambled along the bitumen to cross the carpark, then onto the lawns of The Homestead, and headed towards the Bar, and Restaurant.

Cheyla noticed 'The Homestead' as it was called, was obviously home to the owners of the establishment.

It was in a good state, newly renovated, but cleverly designed to cater for a floating population of tourists from what he could see as he passed through an almost hidden archway groaning with the weight of flowers on the new extension leading to double doors, and he walked inside.

Wall lights, nestling in crevices bracketed on the walls, were dimmed creating a cozy atmosphere to a huge room servicing all needs, with a laid back Country feel about it.

He headed straight towards a central bar area where he slid onto a chunky timber bar stool, to order a drink.

"Nice place you have here." he said to the bartender as he served his drink. "A bit isolated though."

"Thanks! Yeah it is, but people seem to like it here, and it is a good stop-over. Have you travelled far?" he asked.

"Have been on the road for two days now, come down from the top end of the Territory, but have a long way to go yet. My destination is The Flinders Ranges." he said.

"Well, you need a break, and you've stopped here at a very good time, we have a band starting up later, so you can relax, and chill out a little." said the bartender.

"That will suit me well enough!" stated Cheyla. "It has been a long haul to get here. I need to relax a little."

He eyed the bar area of barrel tables, and chairs, as he sipped his scotch, and then out to an eatery of individual tables, and chairs, which were skirted by bench seats, and tables that sat in alcoves along opposite walls of the room. A neon sign that blinked 'Servery' attracted his attention on the back wall adjacent to the kitchen, and a chalk board displaying a 'Menu' brought him off his stool, with glass in hand, and heading towards it. He was famished, and ordered the biggest steak with the lot, from the menu.

He paid for his meal, grabbed his number from the counter, then headed towards the alcoves lining the far wall, and slid in behind the table along the bench seat.

The bartender was watching Cheyla, and his obvious empty glass, and he left the bar to walk across the room.

"Would you like another sir?" he asked, as he pointed.

"Ah! Good man, just keep them coming. My name is Cheyla by the way." he said, extending his hand.

"Pleased to meet you Cheyla. Just call me Woody." the bartender replied, as they shook hands, then he whisked the empty glass away saying. "I will get you a refill."

"Thanks!" Cheyla replied, then when Woody had left, his eyes scanned the room. He head-counted about ten people eating inside. He guessed they were travelers, but through the back sliding door where the coloured lights displayed an outdoor area he could hear the laughter, and shouts of some shenanigans going on. 'Must be locals.' he thought. 'Getting ready for a big night out.' He guessed the band would be playing out there in the courtyard.

Cheyla finished his meal, got a refill from the bar, and walked outside to the courtyard where he found a vacant seat in the corner. He set his drink down on the table, and looked around at what was happening. The band was set up in the far corner busily tuning their equipment, there were a few tables of couples waiting in anticipation for the first song to be played, but most of the noise seemed to be generated from five guys sitting at a table engrossed in some type of competition. He knew at once what they were doing, and he watched with interest as the next roar went up, and they all starting cheering.

Suddenly there was a lull at their table. Apart from the strumming of guitars, it became quiet in the courtyard as a couple of the competitors stood up looking around.

One burly guy pushed his chair back quickly when his eyes picked out Cheyla watching them, and he rose from his seat, and pointed towards him, then moved across the courtyard, egging his mates on to follow.

Three of them faced Cheyla, but the burly guy spoke out. "Hey big fella, seems to me that you are interested in our game. Just so happens we are one man short! Leaves me without a partner, but by the looks of you, it could be a good competition if you joined us. What do you say?"

Cheyla put his hands up as if in defense. "No, you've got the wrong bloke mate. I was just watching that's all. I'm happy having a quiet night because I have a long way to travel tomorrow." he replied.

As the burly guy braced the table, his muscles flexed, and rippled to knot like coils of rope as he spat a reply at Cheyla. That's no excuse! What are ya chicken? Or are ya frightened of getting beaten big guy?" he heckled.

"I don't arm-wrestle!" stated Cheyla calmly.

"I don't arm-wrestle!" mimicked the other guy, and he laughed. "I think you are just chicken shit mate!" Then his mate chimed in. "Yeah you're chicken alright, a coward is what you are! You're shit scared big fella, with no guts!"

CHEYLA

Hairs that began bristling at the back of Cheyla's neck seemed to engross his brain as the taunts sunk in. This was something he was not used to. No-one had ever spoke to him like that, but the words cut deep, and slowly he pushed his chair back, and towered above them when he stood. 'I will not back down to any man.' he thought.

"Seems like we have a competition after all!" he stated, as his eyes locked with, then stared hard into the burly man's face. "Lead on!" he said, as he rounded the table.

They were all laughing as they headed for their table, and as the burly guy sat down he flexed his huge muscles, and placed his huge forearms down, while he watched as Cheyla pulled out the seat, and sat down to face him.

Their eyes locked, and Cheyla's green eyes had a mean gleam that wiped the smile off his opponents face. He saw something deep in those eyes that he didn't like, and for the first time in his life he was unsure, until the green eyes clouded over, and he began to laugh again.

'What am I doing?' Cheyla asked himself, as he drifted away with thoughts of long ago. 'I promised myself that I would never arm-wrestle again, and here I am about to do it!' he thought, as he recalled the past. 'He was twelve again.' At that particular time, he was trying to come to terms with a growing body, and his increasing strength.

'They were all his friends, boys from the Aboriginal clan that he had grown up with, and they all joked, and decided this day to test their strength against each other.'

It was on the sand at Tenna Creek they selected teams, then in pairs began competing in an arm-wrestling match. There was a lot of laughter as the losers were outmatched.

However it was Cheyla's turn that soon stilled their laughter. He was drawn against Juba, who was one of his best friends. They laughed with a friendly banter as they lay belly down in the sand, and then locked arms.

Juba was older than Cheyla by two years. Lately he had filled out in the chest, and arms, though his legs were still thin. He was laughing, and telling Cheyla that he had no chance, then Jono spoke out to call the start. They both braced to lock wrists, starting to force each other's arms.

In one massive swoop Cheyla laid Juba's arm over. The crack, piercing as it echoed in the still creek-bed, cut off all sounds of laughter to complete silence.

No-one moved. No-one realized what had happened, but Cheyla knew, and for the first time in his life he cried. Juba screamed in pain, and Cheyla saw the bone sticking out of his forearm. He couldn't believe it. 'He had broken his friends arm, and, with not much force.' he thought.

It was the worst thing he had ever done, and though in time Juba's arm healed with help from the local Doctor, Cheyla made a vow that day, never to arm-wrestle again.

"Are ya going to start now, or not!" the voice yelled at him from close at hand to wrench him from his memories. Cheyla looked at the starter with glazed eyes. "Yeah I'm ready." he said, as he turned his eyes upon his opponent who was sitting there just leering at him, and he knew this guy wouldn't give in, but he asked anyway. "You know mate, we don't have to do this. Shall we call it quits?"

"You're kidding, right? My god you're yella mate! No, we start now!" he said, with a gleam in his eye. "Ok, your call!" said Cheyla. As the starter called, they locked arms.

CHEYLA

A transformation overcome the huge burly stockman, his face becoming stern, but twisted with a rictus of pure elation as he searched Cheyla's eyes for some sign of any disclosure. This was his game, and he was noted for being the best at it, an undefeated champion, and he reveled in the outcome of it. He knew initially it was a game of cat, and mouse, and looked for the signs on Cheyla's face, but there was none, only his deep green eyes staring blankly.

Cheyla sat quietly but with a sense of distaste, or anger even, at what he was doing. It showed in his eyes as they smoldered, and bore into his opponent's face, but not able to chance taking them off him, waiting for a first reaction.

"Hey Bull! When will we see some action?" called his mate, and they all cheered to get something started.

But Bull was in another world, and ignored them. 'It's just his eyes,' he thought to himself. He was always wary of the quite types also, but it was those eyes that unmaned him. They seemed to pierce his soul, mesmerizing him to a point of complete distraction, and confusion as a few beads of perspiration wet his brow, his face showing signs of stress. Suddenly he sensed a change, and he went for it, was waiting for it. 'Now he had him.' he thought.

Cheyla had lapsed into deep thought wondering how he could get out of this without hurting this man. He had dropped his guard, his concentration momentarily askew and only just recovered in time as his senses warned him of movement. Immediately he gripped hard, locking his wrist, and braced himself for what he knew was to come.

Sensing victory, the burly stockman summoned all his

strength, and went in for a quick kill. With huge force he attempted to push, but his hand jarred, his face displayed pure shock, as his hand was met solidly by a fist of steel.

His wrist twisted to an awkward angle as if it had hit a brick wall, and he immediately howled out in pain.

"I think my wrist is broken!" he uttered, as he looked up at Cheyla in agony, with disbelief written on his face.

He had never experienced fear before, but now sweat pored profusely from his brow as the pain was becoming intense. But more than that, was the shame of losing. He could just not believe it. He had always won, but now he was faced with the huge embarrassment of not being able to continue. 'Something he would never do.' he thought.

Cheyla looked at him sadly, and he felt bad. He looked at the man's hand, unlocked his, and sat back in the chair. "Are we done now?" he asked softly.

"No fear!" spat the stockman, looking at him squarely, his face lined with pain, his hand cradled into his chest.

"Yeah, you go Bull!" his mates urged. "Know you can take him Bull." they all said their piece, egging him on.

"Don't be a fool man, you need to get that hand looked at, straightened, and strapped up. If you continue on you will do more damage, and it won't be so easily repaired. Sometimes we just need to let go mate. Conceding doesn't make you less of a man, but a wiser one." Cheyla said.

Bull looked at him with defeat in his eyes, but in their depths lurked some other reaction. Something he was not used to. 'Respect for his opponent, and his compassion.'

Cheyla offered his hand. "Name is Cheyla." he said.

"Call me Bull." said the burly stockman, as he put out his left hand. "And yes! We are done!" he conceded, as he smirked. "Geez mate, just how strong are you?" he asked.

"Strong enough!" replied Cheyla, with a grin.

"More than enough! I've never seen the likes, and I've been around for quite some time." Bull chuckled. "Now I know why you didn't want to compete. Sorry we heckled you. I guess this has happened before, has it?" he asked.

He looked at the stockman, and suddenly he sensed they were on friendly terms as the others gathered round to congratulate Cheyla. So as they all shook hands, he decided to tell them what happened a long time ago.

"So you see!" he said, as he completed telling his tale. "I've learned to contain myself as the years have passed, and my strength is used for good purposes these days."

"Geez mate, you are a walking weapon!" declared one of the men, and they all laughed. "Yeah! A mate you need on your side, not against ya." offered Bull. "We are better people for having met you Cheyla, so I apologize for our beginning. You're a true champ in more ways than one."

"Thanks Bull, and guys, but I think someone ought to look at that hand. Is there anyone around to help out?" he asked. "Yeah! There's a nurse lives in a house over back. Me mates will take me over now, thanks Cheyla." he said.

As he watched them walk away, Cheyla pondered the ways of man. Their habits, and traits. 'What makes a man who he is?' he wondered. 'Is it his upbringing, or friends he associates with?' Then he thought of his own primitive upbringing, and his friends that he grew up with, but he knew that he was taught right from wrong. He shrugged. 'Guess there is good, and bad in everyone.' he mused. 'I guess you have to be your own person, and believe.'

Someone started singing as the band struck up a tune, but somehow Cheyla had lost his interest in any more entertainment, as the events of the evening had left a sour taste in his mouth. He knew in his heart at the beginning what would happen, but he couldn't prevent it. Now he felt remorseful, at blame, and so sorry he hurt someone.

He pushed his chair back to stand, and headed for the bar where he bought a bottle of scotch to take to his room.

Once inside his room he went to the bar-fridge, got out the ice trays, and a glass then made himself a stiff drink. He sat upon the lounge, and flicked the controls on for the TV. There was some documentary on about wildlife, so he watched it for a while, but thinking of the events of the day, and what lay ahead. He needed to make some plans.

'I must ring Jono.' he thought. 'I will do that first thing after breakfast, he should be in the office by then. He will be wondering where I am.' His thoughts turned to home. So much had happened since he had left there, he felt like he was a million miles away. He knew he had travelled a lot of miles, and immediately he thought of his 4WD.

'Might be best if I head to Port Augusta tomorrow.' he thought. 'Have a well-earned break, get my 4WD checked out then I won't have far to travel to The Flinders Ranges. 'Yep, good plan I think, though a seven hour trip. Should make it if I leave after I call Jono.' Now he had a plan in place, he craved sleep, so he stripped, and fell on the bed.

Morning came with a knock on the breakfast servery door, and a burst of sunshine lit the room when the door was opened, and his breakfast tray was slid inside.

"Breakfast!" called the voice outside, and a loud knock on the door stirred Cheyla from sleep. "Are you awake in there sir?" the voice called out again.

"Yeah I am up now!" Cheyla called out, as he donned his jeans then opened the front door, his eyes squinting to the burst of bright sunlight. "Thank you for breakfast!" he said to the young girl. "Your welcome!" she replied.

There was not a cloud in the sky, he noticed when he looked up to check the weather outside, only the bluest, clearest sky he had ever witnessed on a sunrise before. He closed the door, then walked across the room, and flicked the switch on the kettle. When it boiled, he made a coffee, then he settled down to eat his breakfast, and reflected on his journey so far. 'It certainly had not been un-eventful.' he recalled. 'It definitely had its moments.' he chuckled to himself, but the long driving with no-one else to converse with was wearing him thin. 'I might stay two days in Port Augusta if I like it there.' he thought. 'I'm worn out.'

His phone call was directed to message bank after his office number rang out back home on his Property. He left no message, but hit re-dial, and then waited. 'Jono should be up, and about by now, maybe I should call his mobile?' Cheyla thought, but then the line came alive, as he heard the voice he was wanting, and a chair being moved.

"Cheyla! It's me Jono!" he yelled out into the phone.

"Where ya bin? You be worryin me I hope ya know." he uttered breathlessly. "Where are ya now?" he asked.

Cheyla laughed. He could tell that Jono was gasping for breath. 'Probably running to answer the phone in time.' he guessed. "Slow down Jono! Don't yell." he said.

Immediately Jono calmed down, and this time when he spoke Cheyla could understand him much better.

"So good ta hear ya voice agin Cheyla. How ya bin, an where the hell are ya?" he asked.

"Hi Jono, it's good to hear you too. Thought I'd let you know that I am staying at a place called The Homestead, about 600kms or so, north of Port Augusta. I am going to try to make it there today, then stay there a couple of days I think. I need a break, so I will leave after we chat. From there it is not far into The Flinders Ranges. It has been one hell of a trip, and I've liked it well enough. Such beautiful Country, but wild, and untamed but I have met some nice people along the way, and I will have a few stories to tell when I get home no doubt. So, how is home?" he asked.

"Thet all sounds good ta me Cheyla. Everyone here be ok, an takin good care of ya Property, ya not ta worry ok. Oh! An the boys jus finished the cemetery fence yestaday. Looks good, an they even made a track in." Jono replied.

"Thanks Jono sounds like a job well done. Tell the boys it is greatly appreciated. You might want to check on the mare that's close to dropping her foal too." Cheyla said.

"Already be done thet!" said Jono. "She be at the inner stables now, an in the stall. So we hav bin watchin her. An Henry be takin good care of ya cattle. So all good here!"

"I'll have to go away more often, looks like you don't need me there, but next time Jono I will take you on a trip. You would love it out here. We might organize a camping trip, so we can rough it a bit. There is so much to see, but now I haven't got the time to be a tourist." said Cheyla.

"Me neva been on a trip afore Cheyla!" remarked Jono.

"Then that is a promise Jono, we will do it one day. It's about time you seen some of Australia too." Cheyla said.

"I be think bout thet first me thinks." said Jono.

Cheyla laughed. "You will be fine, besides, you will be with me!" he stated. Anyway Jono, take care. I'd better hit the road now, and put some more miles behind me. If you need me, just call my mobile. Will probably call you from The Finders Ranges when I hopefully meet up with Mary Higgs. Till then Jono! Have to hang up now." said Cheyla.

"Yeah see ya Cheyla. Ya take care too ya hear." replied Jono, then he heard a click, and the line went dead.

Once again the Highway stretched out before him to seemingly be an endless track seeking the horizon way out in the distance, as Cheyla settled in for his trip.

Surprisingly the air felt crisp, and a cool breeze blew, but he was not fooled into thinking of a reprieve when the offensive sun rose above the skyline, and settled its wrath upon the sunbaked land. 'There has been no rain here.' he thought. 'Just how bad did it get out here in a drought?'

He had travelled almost two hours when he drove into a small town where dust swirled about in the streets, and the earth was red, and dry. It looked like a mining town. He passed a Motel, and he slowed as he read the signage. "I don't believe it.' he chuckled. 'An underground Motel?' He wondered about that, trying to imagine it. 'If I had of kept driving, I could have stayed underground. What an experience that would have been, but it was late, and I was too tired.' he realized. He needed to re-fuel now, and up ahead he noticed a servo, so he drove on towards it.

Cheyla knew as he approached the servo, and drove in that he had to keep driving to reach his destination today, so he purchased fuel, a few necessities, grabbed some food to eat on the run, then hit the road again.

By mid-afternoon, the welcome sign on the approach into Port Augusta was a sight to behold for Cheyla as he sensed the milestone. It was a small city really, known as 'The crossroads of Australia' he noted reading the sign, but more important to him was the other sign which read, 'The Gateway to the Flinders Ranges.' He was close now, he could sense closure to his journey. Now all thoughts of his long trek through the red center was slowly receding, as feelings of excitement, but an uneasiness overtook him.

For the first time since he made a decision to search for his Mother, the doubts crept slowly into his mind. 'I really haven't thought this through.' he realized. 'Would he find Mary Higgs living in The Flinders Ranges?' he wondered. She was the vital key in his search. 'However, if she still resided there, then maybe my Mother was with her! What would I do then? What do I say to her?' he was thinking.

There would be no trouble for him to find the property where Mary worked, he noted as he drove on through the city. 'Waverley Downs' it was called, he knew that. 'It was the only address, the only link to Mary Higgs he had, but going on advertisement signs, and directions, it appeared to be a big tourist attraction in The Flinders Ranges area.

CHEYLA

Huge waves emerged, rolling in one after the other to reach their zenith, almost seemingly to defy gravity before tumbling, then surging into a surf which bore into the shore, flattening, as the white water rolled in to foam around his ankles. He felt the surge of the undercurrent, the tug on his legs, and looked down as his feet imbedded in the sand became visible as the water rushed to escape back out to sea, and he watched it with great interest.

Cheyla had never been as close to the ocean before, and he relished the feel of the sand, the smell of the ocean, and surf rushing through his feet. He had been to Darwin many times, but it was always for business. Either buying, or selling cattle, or attending meetings with his associates, never once going to the beach. Without another thought he stripped off his shirt, wrapped his wallet, and his keys inside it, then he raced out into the deeper water, diving under the first big wave that was rolling in. He surfaced snorting from the cold, but it was exhilarating so he swam out further. 'He was liking it well enough,' so he kept on going. He was a strong swimmer, churning through the water effortlessly until he finally stopped to tread water, then turned waiting for the next wave. He laughed as he experienced the thrill of riding each wave into the shore.

On the beach once again, he was felt more refreshed than he'd been for days, and smiled as a thought crossed his mind when he sat down to dry off. 'Yes I could do this for a couple of days.' The Motel he had checked into was a short walk away on the waterfront. He would get his car serviced tomorrow, chill out a while until his important trip to The Flinders Ranges, and in to Waverley Downs.

Chapter 7

Music filled the small Chapel as the wedding march was played by the organist from above them, and the congregation quickly turned their heads. Immediately there was whispers of oohs, and aahs to be heard, as the wedding party proceeded slowly down the aisle.

Showing great importance, but her instructions firmly set in her mind, and giving her face a rather serious look Melissa Anne Stringer stepped out, then looked down at the purple satin pillow she held protectively with the two rings pinned to it. Finally convinced they would not fall, she looked up with such relief on her face that she smiled at everyone as she led the way dressed in a lighter shade of purple, but a miniature replica of her Mother's dress.

Jacqueline Coby-Stringer looked at her daughter with pride. 'She looks like an angel in her beautiful purple dress, her golden locks bobbing around her glowing with a hint of sunshine from the windows, falling on her head as she walked.' she thought to herself. 'What a great job she is doing for one so young, she is so astute, determined too. But I know only too well where she inherits all that determination from. She has Coby blood in her veins.'

Jacqueline sensed Mary's need for her attention, though their arms were locked, she felt for her hand, and gave it a light squeeze for assurance, and Mary looked at her.

Nothing could prevent Mary's famous smile evolving, not even the fine netted veil that fell over her face. She felt so safe with her best friend walking beside her. Jacqueline had been everything to her in her life time, and rightly so, she was now giving her away, as Mary had no Mother, or Father living, no relatives she could contact anymore, so Jacqueline Coby-Stringer was adamant in this decision.

She looked at Mary dressed in a white lace gown with a long flowing train, and returned her smile as the hint of lilies filled her senses from the bouquet Mary held. 'How beautiful, and happy she looks.' she thought, and glanced behind at the two girls in different shades of purple.

Susan Stringer stepped out proudly as Mary's Matron of Honour, a band of lilies kept her long curls contained though they still bounced when she moved, and Margaret Hargraves who was Drew's youngest sister, was Mary's Bridesmaid. Her long blonde hair was caught up high then pinned at the side with a sprig of lilies, and her blue eyes sparkled as she smiled out at the congregation. They held the long train up from the floor proudly together as they followed Mary down the aisle. They looked identical dressed in similar gowns, but different shades of purple.

As they approached the alter Mary's smile widened as her eyes fell on the man she was about to marry, and her heart filled with love for him. She knew him so well, they were good together, and she realized that this day was the most special day in all her life. He stood side-on watching as she walked towards him, then their eyes locked, and a huge smile lit up his face, as he held out his hand to her.

"You made it." he said seriously, as their hands joined. Mary smiled. "There be neva any doubt!" she replied, as they looked longingly at one another.

Then the priest was speaking, the spell between them broken, and Jacqueline stepped forward to complete her task smiling at them both, then stepped back to sit in the front row with Melissa, and listened with intent. She just loved weddings. Memories were still fresh in her mind of her own wedding day. 'Such a wonderful happy day that was.' she remembered, then surprisingly there was Pete's wedding two years later 'No-one ever thought that would happen, but it had, and he was very happy.' she thought.

So they all had been blessed with so much joy over the years, but still the silent tears slipped slowly down her cheek. 'Tears of joy.' she thought. 'Just can't help myself.'

Drew Hargraves searched Mary's eyes, his own soft brown eyes shining with happiness as he spoke his vows. He was a little younger than Mary, but he knew in his heart from way back that he wanted her for his wife, even though their heritage was miles apart in every way, a natural attraction had formed between them. He knew that Mary Higgs was a very special person to everyone.

They first met when she returned to Shallow Siding, and started working at Shallow Downs, where Drew had been the head stockman there for over ten years.

He smiled fondly at her hoping to give her courage, he knew she was nervous, and she returned his smile.

Drew was known by those who knew him well for his gentle nature, he was a sturdily built man, his body toned from hard work though his friendly face appeared a little weather-beaten from long days in the brutal sun, and his blond hair was almost bleached white.

He had been raised in The Northern Territory, and still had family there, though his youngest sister had followed him when his quest for travel had brought him to Shallow Siding, and the Outback that he loved, and he wrote home telling them that is where he would stay when he got the job at Shallow Downs. His sister was a nurse so she had no trouble getting work at the Hospital, and lived in the nurse's quarters out back. Drew always thought that he would be forever a single man, never finding someone he could be close with, but now, here he was standing at the alter where his life was about to change dramatically.

As the congregation looked on, there was no thoughts of a miss-match between the couple about to be joined, as they knew them both well, and knew most decidedly they would be very happy together. Smiles lit all their faces as Melissa Anne Stringer stepped up beside Drew with her arms outstretched to proffer the all-important rings that balanced on the purple cushion she carried.

He looked down at her angelic face, and smiled at her. "Thank you Melissa." he whispered, as he then unclipped the rings, and a huge smile lit up her face, then she turned to return to her seat beside her Mother.

Jacqueline's face filled with such pride. "Very well done Melissa." she whispered, as the little body climbed up, and cuddled in close to her. "I know!" came the reply.

Jacqueline put a hand over her mouth to stifle a giggle which was threatening to escape, and she smiled down at this small person beside her. 'She has grown way beyond her years. Confident, so sure of herself, such knowledge for a little one.' she thought. 'Was I like that? I'm guessing I was, from what my Father, and Mother had told me.'

Pete Stringer could not keep the smile off his face as he watched them all walk down the aisle, though he was secretly seeking his wife Susan. He was sporting a well-kept secret they decided to share between themselves, so as not to upset all the wedding celebrations, as they had only just yesterday received news of. He was to become a Father, and the unreality of it was blowing his mind. His task as best man was important, but he was finding it very hard to concentrate, as he could think of nothing else.

'I want to be a Father just like my Father is for me!' he thought. 'I owe everything to him. Yes! So much love, and advice had emanated from Mitchell Stringer who was just a perfect Father in every way. He has been my rock all my life, always there when I needed him, and my best mate!'

He looked across to the aisle where his Father sat, and their eyes met. Pete almost felt he was reading his mind, as his Father's deep blue eyes searched his face. 'It would not surprise me at all.' he mused. 'He just knows me so well, always has!' There had been many times during his life he had been surprised when his Father had sensed his concern, and spoke out about something that was already uncertain in his mind.' he remembered. 'Yeah! Uncanny that, but true. Almost like a sixth-sense.' he thought.

'Guess that is a big part of being a Father. Getting to know your child so well that you almost sense what they are going to say, or do. Yep! I can do that.' he thought to himself. 'I will be the best Father ever, as I have so much knowledge to teach my child, and Susan will be a perfect Mother.' he realized. He thought of their own wedding day, and how much love they shared, then his thoughts ceased as his attention focused once again on the wedding procession, and knew that Mary, and Drew would be just gob-smacked with the celebrations to come for them that evening. Pete simply knew Jacqueline Coby-Stringer only too well, and he had come to love her just like a Mother.

'She has not held back on this celebration at all!' he thought, as he looked over her way, and smiled. Then she acknowledged him with a nod, and smiled back at him.

Coloured lights twinkled throughout the gardens that evening as darkness crept up, but closed in fast, as it descended upon them. Candles on the tables were aglow, and the pit fires were ignited, bringing the Marquee to life as it was cloaked in an array of subdued light.

Speeches had been long ago completed, presents were unwrapped, and now music filled the night as the Bride, and Groom stepped out onto the board dancefloor.
Mitch stood up to offer Jacqueline his hand. "Shall we?"

"We certainly shall Mister Stringer." was Jacqueline's reply, as he folded his arms around her, and as she melted into his embrace. Memories of a long time ago filled her senses of another time when his touch had sent shivers up her spine, and his warmth had consumed her.

Slowly they swayed to the music. But to feel his body, his closeness, just never ceased to amaze Jacqueline, and her own body trembled as she looked up at his face.

"You ok Jackie?" Mitch asked, and she giggled as their eyes met. "More than ok I would think!" she whispered. "But just know Mister Stringer! You sir, stir certain things inside me. Later I may not be responsible for my actions!"

His huge grin that she loved so much lit his face as he looked down at her. "Guess it's going to be an early night for us then!" he replied kissing her forehead, then rested his cheek against her hair. Just the smell of her made his senses go haywire. "God I love you Jackie." he whispered.

"I love you too Mitch, I always have. I am so proud to have you for my husband. You, and Melissa are my whole world." she said with seriousness, then suddenly looked for Melissa. "Oh look Mitch, Melissa has fallen asleep!"

Mitch looked over at Melissa curled up in the arms of her brother Pete. She was sound asleep, but as he looked at Pete he sensed something changed in him. 'But what?'

"Jackie, something is bugging me! Does Pete seem any different to you today?" he asked.

Jacqueline looked up at him quickly. "I am not quite sure what you mean Mitch." she replied.

"Oh nothing I guess, just a feeling I have, that is all. We had better get Melissa to bed though, it's late"

When they reached their table, Jacqueline bent down to take Melissa, but Pete stood up with her in his arms.

"Continue your dance Jackie, and Father. Susan, and I will put Melissa to bed." he offered. "Oh thank you Pete, thank you Susan. That is so thoughtful" said Jacqueline.

But as they walked off doting on Melissa, Pete cradling her close to his chest, Mitch just stared at them, convinced now that something new was in the wind.

Pete had always mucked around, and played with her, tousling her hair every time they met to torment her, but he also taught her things about horses just like a brother would do, expecting her to understand grown up things.

But now, Mitch seemed to think he was treating her like a baby…'A Baby?'… 'I wonder?' Mitch mused, as he watched them closely as they had reached the stairs.

Mitchell pulled Jacqueline back to the dancefloor. He had that look in his eye that Jacqueline knew only too well. "Ok, what is it, what is up?" she asked.

He laughed. "You know me too well Jackie, can I not keep anything to myself? Ok! Since you are so inquisitive. Answer this! How would you like to be a Grandmother?" his eyes twinkled with mischief, as he looked at her.

"Whatever are you rambling on about Mitch? No-one is going to turn me into a Grandmother in the for-seeable future, unless Pete, and Sus….Her voice trailed away, as she stared hard at Mitch. "Pete, and Susan! Are you sure Mitch? Did they tell you?" she asked earnestly.

"Wow! Hold on a sec, this is just premonition of mine Jackie, and no I haven't been told. Should we ask?"

"No! Definitely not Mitch, they will tell us in their own time if your thoughts prove to be true. Anyway if they are pregnant, it is not a good time to spring their news in the middle of a wedding. No, we wait Mitch!" she stated.

"Yeah, I guess you are right. You usually are!" he said.

As the music ended, they crossed the floor to resume their seats with Anne, and Jake Hardy.

"Why aren't you two up dancing?" Jacqueline asked, as she sat down. "Jake?" she questioned, as she looked into his warm, friendly brown eyes. "What's up?"

"Oh Jackie, we are both exhausted! We were dancing before, but we are just having a break." offered Jake.

"I see! What about you Anne? Are you enjoying the evening? You look lovely too I might add Anne."

"Thank you Jackie, you look as beautiful as ever also. All of you looked beautiful today, and Melissa was just so cute, she did a really great job. We have had a great day, and are having a wonderful time Jackie, it has been the loveliest wedding, and tonight is so special." said Anne.

"We are going to say our good-nights now, and go up. Did you manage to find your room alright Anne?"

"Yes Jackie, we have already checked it out when we first arrived. It is so beautiful, thank you."

"You are both so welcome. We will be coming down early for breakfast as we have a surprise for Mary, and Drew. Please join us, but you can just please yourselves when you come down if you don't want to get up early. May will look after you." replied Jacqueline.

"That sounds great Jackie. We may stay up tonight a little longer, we shall see. It's just like a mini holiday for us here. Thanks so much for asking us to stay," said Jake.

Jacqueline bent to kiss them both, then Mitch stepped up to say goodnight, then they moved towards Mary, and Drew's table to wish them well, and say good night, but also to give instructions for the all-important breakfast.

Except for the moonlight shining through the double doors, they were in darkness inside their room, and covers were stripped from the bed in haste as they groped blindly for each other. Their mouths seeking, and meeting in a yearning, a demanding, yet passionate kiss which set Jacqueline's body on fire, and her desire could barely be contained as Mitch pressed her close to him, and lifted her into his arms, and tenderly lay her upon the bed.

He kicked off his shoes, and quickly stripped from his clothes to stand naked before her, then lay down beside her to take her in his arms as he began the long process of undoing buttons from her clothing, then with her help, he whisked them away. His hands moved slowly over her body now to caress her, seeking out every part of her that sent her senses reeling with each touch as he nestled his head into her breast to take a nipple tenderly between his teeth. She gasped just with the thrill of it, and pulled him closer to her. How she loved this Country Cowboy whom she had known since their childhood. They had a special bond that had stood the test of time way back then, also during their marriage, and having a child. Melissa Anne.

"Please Mitch." she murmured softly. "Quickly now! Stop teasing!" she said, as she pulled at his hair to lift his head, and their lips met in a smoldering kiss. 'So soft, so sweet, so passionate.' she thought as their kiss endured.

Mitch covered her body with his own, and she could feel his arousal hard against her body, and instantly they were in a world of their own as he penetrated her deeply, and she moaned out loud with the pleasure of it, then she felt his body stiffen, and release, and her body shuddered.

They lay in each other's arms savouring the closeness, the love they felt for each other, then as the darkness filled the room Jacqueline turned to him, and spoke softly. "I am certain I will love you forever Mitchell Stringer!"

"I know that Jackie, and I have always loved you, and always will. Now sleep, we have a big morning planned."

Breakfast was a huge event. May had pre-arranged the tables as Jacqueline requested. All the tables were to be joined to run lengthwise so all the guests would be at one long table, except for a very special table which jutted out from the others, placed off the center with two chairs heading it, especially positioned to face the guests.

In the center of all the floral blooms stood the three tier wedding cake with purple ribboned icing as a decoration, it as Mary's favourite. But around the main table, Marie, and her sister Sandy were making the final touches, and fussed with decorations then selected appropriate seating arrangements for the all-important place-cards just when Mitchell, Jacqueline, and Melissa all walked through the doors to enter the breakfast room.

Jacqueline was captivated, and nodded her approval as she scrutinized the room, then immediately headed over to approach May Jefferies, their cook. Melissa broke the grip of her Mother's hand to skip along a whole length of the tables, and her eyes lit with pure delight with the flowers, and decorations, then raced back to her Mother's side to ask urgently, as she tugged on her skirt. "Where is my place Mother?" Jacqueline looked at May, and smiled.

"Excuse me May." she said. "Where's your manners?

Please Melissa! I am about to speak to Missus Jefferies. If you recognize your name on the cards, then that is where you will be seated, so you may go and look." she stressed.

"Sorry Mother, sorry Missus Jefferies." Melissa said as she looked at them abashed. "So! I guess I should do that now Mother!" she said decisively, in her childish chatter, then she was gone in a swirl of petticoats without another thought of reprisal to offer to her Mother's wrath.

Jacqueline turned to watch her daughter leave, but most of all to hide the hint of a smile which had escaped her lips. 'This child has been here before, in another time. I am sure.' she thought. Then she turned back to face May.

"She is growing up so fast Jacqueline, and certainly has a mind of her own." offered May, with a chuckle.

Jacqueline could not help it, but chuckled with her. "I guess I was the same at that age. The world is your oyster growing up. So much to see, and do, always something to learn, and every day is a new one to be explored. Being a child is a very special thing, but sadly you don't really get to appreciate that fact until you are much older, and have other responsibilities, and a family of your own."

"Yes I know exactly what you mean, having reared my two girls. I wouldn't want to miss a part of their growing up. You can't turn back time. Wouldn't it be nice though just to pause a while to reminisce Jacqueline, and see the world as if through the eyes of a child?" she inquired.

Jacqueline's smile disappeared as she stared up at this wise lady, and knew now why they had become friends. "You have a big point there May!" she replied absently.

Something inside her was churning, memories tugging at her heart of another child, at another time. She tried her utmost to discard the thoughts but they remained still after all this time inside her, and imprinted in her brain.

She forever asked of herself. 'Did the child survive to play with other children, is it a possibility? Was its gender male, or female?' She felt so disgusted to think she didn't even know that, or any of the things that plagued her.

"I wouldn't want to miss a part of their growing up!" echoed May's words in her head, to tear her apart.

Guilt seemed to rise like a living thing in her throat. She could feel the sensation, the heat of it coming from deep down like it always did, threatening to choke her. She tugged madly at her scarf to tear it from her neck, and gasped for air as May's words echoed in her head. "You can't turn back time." and she knew it would never stop.

She had made a point of telling her close friends, and those close to her of her well-kept secret that would haunt her all the days of her life, and to her grave no doubt. But that was way back when she returned to Shallow Siding, and somehow now in this day, and age. It just didn't seem right what she had done back then in her youth, though as she paused to re-think the circumstances…She shook her head sadly…Knowing she could not accept it then, and she couldn't accept it now…'Impossible' she thought.

"Are you feeling alright Jacqueline." asked May. "You are a little pale now, maybe you should sit, and rest a bit.

Jacqueline felt her body shaking, and she looked up at May with thanks as she pulled up a chair for her.

"I will be fine May, but I may take a moment, thank you!"

she answered, as she sank into the soft seat momentarily, until all of a sudden the room came alive with chatter as her guests began arriving, and all talking to one another.

'I will rest later' thought Jacqueline as she rose from the seat to look at May. Gone was the uneasiness with a shrug, her back rigid, and Jacqueline was in control again as she spoke. "Let's greet our guests May if you please!"

May just looked back with admiration deserving of her, as she had come to know this lady so very well over the years. 'If anything needed doing, she just done it with no qualms as she would expect anyone else to do the same. Her inner strength was her power, but her power was used with total respect for her employees, and other people. 'The reason why we all love her' thought May.

'Yes, she was a leader, but she also harbored an injury.' May knew of her childhood through Mitchell, who never stopped talking about her, and she also knew that she lost her Mother in the Shallow Downs fire when she was just a young girl. Though there was gossip, there seemed to be a side of Jacqueline that no-one talked of, from the time of her youth to when she returned to Shallow Siding. May knew from the very first moment she had met her, when Mitchell brought her to The Outback Gardens that this lady had been to hell, and back, she knew that Jacqueline had suffered grief beyond the telling of it. "But that's how it was, no-one talked of it!' thought May, as she replied.

"We shall indeed Jacqueline! Everything is prepared, and ready for your personal attention." she said proudly.

Jacqueline nodded, then smiled with a knowing smile.

They mingled just inside the entrance doors all talking at once. Jacqueline noticed that Mitch had Melissa's hand while in deep conversation with Pete, and Susan.

'Thank goodness for that' she thought. She had visions of the table being wrecked before they were even seated.

She acknowledged each one of her guests with a nod, and "Good Morning All!" as she glided effortlessly across the room towards Mitchell, and Melissa while she made a brief announcement. "Thank you all for coming, and for being prompt. May has breakfast ready, but we shall wait for the Bride, and Groom to grace us with their presence. Oh! So good to see you made it down this morning Anne, and Jake, thank you both. "We didn't want to miss all the fun Jackie, it has been such a special time." gushed Anne. "Yeah, the wedding has been a credit to you Jackie. Mary, and Drew will remember this for the rest of their lives." said Jake. "Thank you both, that is pleasing to hear, but now everyone give a special welcome to Dion, Margaret's friend who partnered her yesterday at the wedding. You must introduce him around please Margaret." "Yes I will Jackie." Margaret replied. "Thank you for the invitation Missus Coby-Stringer." said Dion. "You're most welcome Dion. Do call me Jackie that will suffice." she replied with a laugh. "Now if you would assume your places, the girls will serve beverages of juice, coffee, and tea as we wait." she announced as she reached Mitchell's side, and smiled up at Pete, and Susan. They were absolutely glowing this morning, she noticed. 'Hmm! I wonder' she thought.

"Morning Jackie! A great wedding you put on." said Pete in his country drawl not unlike his Father's. Pete was a legend in his own right. As a bushman, he was the best, and his expert tracking skills earned him all the accolades that were bestowed upon him, and people come from far, and wide just to go out on hunting trips with him. Over at The Bush Camp, and in the bush he was in his element, a true country man in every sense, but here in this setting, at a wedding, he was really a very quiet, modest person.

"Yes such a beautiful wedding Jackie! " Susan Stringer was saying. "We have had such a great time, and just now we were saying to Mitch that we would love it if you, and Mitch, and Melissa could come to dinner tonight over at our place, so maybe we can wait on you for a change."

Jacqueline smiled a knowing smile, and looked at Mitch who had a grin from ear to ear, then she replied. "What a lovely idea Susan, and Pete. We haven't been over for some time now, we've all been too busy. That would most definitely be a yes! Don't you agree Mitch?" she asked, as she looked to her husband for his response, but who now seemed miles away, lost deep in thought. "Your thoughts Mitch?" she queried. "Mitch, is tonight ok?" she repeated.

"What is it Jackie? Yes of course, dinner. That will be great." he muttered. "Sorry everyone I was just thinking."

"Good, that's settled then. Just let us know what time Susan, and now you had all better take your seats as I can see Mary, and Drew at the door, and I would like to greet them, and take them to their seats." stated Jacqueline.

Everyone busied themselves while finding their place settings, then proceeded to sit as Jacqueline left them, and made her way to the entrance doors to the dining room.

Drew, and Mary emerged in the doorway attentively, but instantly, both their faces lit up when they saw the decorations of the once normal dining area.

"Oh Drew! Just ya look what they hav done in here, is it not beautiful?" gushed Mary.

"It certainly is Mary, but I guess it shows how much you are loved by everyone, and why I love you so much!" he said, as he looked into her eyes, then pulled her close, and wrapped his arms around her. Their kiss was a long, and tender one, and it brought laughter from around the tables, and clapping filled the still room with joy. Mary, and Drew immediately sprang apart. In a world of their own, they had forgot about their guests, and were lost in that special moment. They both laughed together.

"Well that was quite an entrance!" offered Jacqueline, as she laughed with them. "Good Morning Drew, I trust everything has been to your liking with the wedding, and your accommodation?" she asked.

"Jacqueline I can't begin to thank you enough for what you have done for Mary, and myself with the wedding, and everything else. You are a very special person. So a big thank you from both of us." Drew replied. "Yea, thank ya Jacqueline, it be bit much though as usual." said Mary.

"Nonsense you two but thank you. Only now we have a very important part. Welcome Missus Hargraves!" she stated, as she took Mary in her arms, and they hugged. By this time Mary was crying. "Yea! I guess I be thet name now!" she said, but Jacqueline had already turned to face the guests, raising her voice above the chatter to be heard. "Attention all! I give you Mister, and Missus Hargraves!"

Everyone stood up, and clapped. Then a huge roar was heard as their voices became one.

"CONGRATULATIONS MARY AND DREW!!!!"

Mary blushed, and started crying again, and Drew put his arm around her, and spoke. "Thank you all so much! Mary is a little overwhelmed, but you all know how much your presence means to her, and myself. Thank you all for being here. Come on Missus Hargraves, let us be seated."

As they settled into the seats provided for them, Mary looked around the long table at all their smiling faces, and though tears ran down her cheeks, and through bouts of sobbing, she thanked them all with a heartfelt speech.

Laughter filled the room, as everyone clapped, and the chatter began, setting the mood for the morning. Old stories were told as breakfast was being served, and the table became abundant with food, and drinks. Some tales were so old that Mary had almost forgotten them, so for her it was a special time to reminisce.

Drew also got into the swing of things, and added his own escapades, and his sister told tales of him when they were growing up which made everyone laugh.

Mary looked at Jacqueline as a shadow clearly passed in her eyes, and there was something in those eyes which warned Mary not to disclose their travels, and Mary felt sad about that. 'What a secret she must bear forever.' she thought. However, she did decide to talk of their life on Shallow Downs when they were young, growing up, and how she had come to live there. Rescued by the Owner, a lady whom she loved like a Mother. Missus Mel Coby.

At the mention of her Mother, it was an opportunity for Jacqueline to move the proceedings along, so she stood to address her guests. "If you would all bear with me for just a moment there is something very important I must do that can't wait. Sorry to interrupt conversation, but you can resume over coffee, when we cut the cake."

Everyone looked intensely as Jacqueline left the table, and went over to the sideboard to retrieve a large purple envelope tied neatly with purple ribbons, and bows.

"Mary, and Drew, I am hoping that you will enjoy this gift as much as Mitch, and myself enjoy giving it to you both!" she uttered, as she handed over the large envelope.

Mary's eyes widened in surprise. "Oh no Jacqueline! It not be more presents? Ya hav given us nough." she said.

"Not like this present Mary, now open it please!"

Carefully unwrapping the envelope, Mary seemed to be a little puzzled by the contents before her. "What it be Jacqueline, som sort o drawins me thinks?" she asked.

"Read the contract please Mary!" offered Jacqueline.

Mary, and Drew read the letter, and Mary's face paled.

"No, oh no Jacqueline, it be too much." she sobbed.

"Nonsense Mary! As we speak, workers are at Shallow Downs building a bridge across the creek to the site I have chosen for a house paddock, and 35 hectares to be pegged of which will be yours, and Drew's to work as you wish, and to live out your life there. However I want you both to realize, and keep in mind that I cannot split the titles at Shallow Downs. So there is one stipulated rule that I have as per your contract, and that is that all Titles will always remain secured as Shallow Downs!" Jacqueline looked at them both hopefully, and then she added. "Are you both happy with that arrangement Mary, and Drew?"

"It be fine by me Jacqueline, ya giv me too much now!" replied Mary, as she looked up at Drew. "It is the best gift anyone would want Jacqueline, we both really appreciate it, and titles mean nothing to Mary, and I. We understand that situation, so I would like to thank you, and Mitch for your generosity." he said in earnest.

"Excellent! Just sign the contract, and we can all move forward. I will need to know before you leave here which house design you would like so we can start building. So the drawings you see, are two plans I chose that suit the property. It is only up to you both to choose which house plan you want to go with, then you may design it to suit your own lifestyle. I will pay for everything. Building will commence while you are on holidays, and you may stay here when you return until it is built." stated Jacqueline.

Their smiles was reward for Jacqueline Coby-Stringer. "We be let ya know bout tha house after lunch Jacqueline. Drew, an me go ta look at tha plans at lunch, then we be leavin ta go away!" said Mary. "Excellent, as then I need to prepare for an all-important dinner!" added Jacqueline.

Later that night on the drive home from dinner at Pete, and Susan's house Mitch was full of chatter. He was just so excited to be told the news that finally he would be a Grandfather, and Jackie a Grandmother. It was as they had guessed, so when they arrived home Mitch suggested a night cap. "Just a small a celebration drink to greet the coming baby." he said. Jacqueline laughed, as she looked at him, then replied with a twinkle in her eye. "This new baby is going to be one spoilt baby I fear Mitch Stringer!"

"Of course! Is there any other way Jackie?" he asked in a Country drawl that slipped so easily off his tongue, then he laughed, and Jacqueline laughed with him.

However, although Mitch's excitement was infectious, and Jacqueline was so happy for him, and so happy about Pete, and Susan's news, there were some things unsettled in her own mind that would not lay to rest as continuous thoughts hounded her of her own life she could not yet face. It was just so out of character for her, but she had so easily swept them under the mat to be dealt with another day. 'Out of sight, out of mind' she thought to herself.

Now everything was changing she had to step up, and attempt to face those fears as she finally realized she had unfinished business, and needed to address some issues.

Later in the comfort of her bedroom, Jacqueline could not sleep as concerning thoughts crept into her mind, to plague her. It seemed like a continuation of her mindset earlier as she tossed about, but sleep evaded her. Gently she eased the coverlet aside, careful not to wake Mitch as he snored softly beside her, and grabbed her nightgown, and shoes. She tip-toed across the floor, opened, and shut the door softly, then disappeared into the dark hallway.

Shunning the lights, she felt her way along the wall to the hallway cupboard, then opened the door, and reached inside for the torch. She wrapped her gown firmly around herself, and tied it tight, then slipped into her shoes, and walked softly down the carpeted hallway, on through the house quickly, but determinedly, guided by the beam of the torch light. She descended the stairs to the front door, turned the knob, and stepped through to close it softly.

It was chilly out, even though darkness still prevailed, she felt the fog hanging low around her so she pulled her gown closer, and headed towards the garages.

She paused outside the garage doors as apprehension overtook her, then gingerly, but determinedly she pushed against them, and swept the torch beam around inside the building. Her hands shook as the fear gripped her, but she rode the waves of uncertainty as she moved towards the back corner of the garage where she found what she was looking for, and very attentively, but nervously, grabbed at the tarpaulin edges that faced her, and slid them aside.

Her Jeep looked like it always had. Mitch had kept it in top condition from the onset of its arrival when she had organized to have it railed on the long trek from South Australia to Shallow Siding, but due to Jacqueline's past, she could not bear to drive it here, as it rekindled too many old fears. Now she wanted to quell all her fears, and also of going to the Shallow Downs Homestead especially now she was arranging things to be done there. 'It is time' she thought, as she reached out to grip the door handle.

Her hands trembled in trepidation as the door opened, then she slowly slid inside onto the seat, and gripped the steering wheel tightly. Immediately her thoughts were of another time she had gripped the steering wheel so tight as to turn her knuckles white from her fear, and rage was in her heart, as a storm raged, and lightning lit the sky.

CHEYLA

Mitchell sensed rather than knew Jacqueline was not beside him, and he jumped out of bed quickly to switch on the light. He scanned the room, then the en-suite, but no Jackie. 'Maybe she is downstairs' he thought, as he moved over to the window, to peer outside. It was just breaking day, but as he looked closer he spied a faint light in the garage. 'What the hell is she doing in there?' he wondered. Then he quickly dressed, and left the room.

Jacqueline was still sitting in the Jeep's driver's seat as the tears streamed down her face, and fell in huge drops to dampen her gown, and she started as the door opened.

"What the hell are you doing here at this hour Jackie?" asked Mitch, his head halfway in the door.

"Oh Mitch, you startled me! But the reason is simple! Some things have been worrying me, but now I have had a huge breakthrough. I feel that I can handle this now, and I have made a huge decision. Today is the day I will drive my Jeep for the first time since it was returned to me, and to add to that, I will be going to the Homestead at Shallow Downs, which I have avoided like the plague ever since I returned to Shallow Siding, to visit the Managers for the first time! We have things to discuss now!" she muttered, as she looked up at him through blurry eyes.

"Well, well!" stated Mitch. "You never cease to amaze me Jacqueline Coby-Stringer. However, I guessed that in your own time, you would get around to it all eventually, and I am very proud of you! Let's go up to the house, have breakfast, and celebrate." he said, as he wrapped his arms around her, then sort out her lips to kiss her tenderly.

"Sounds like a plan!" she said, when they had parted.

Chapter 8

South Australia's trek to the Outback the locals called it. 'But beautiful just the same' thought Cheyla, as the road meandered through valleys with scenery to behold against towering mountains. Activity was everywhere as wildlife scattered. Flowers seemed to bloom just to greet the sun as it appeared over The Flinders Rangers. There were many hills but The Range seemed to go on forever, some 400 km's he was told, and dominated the skyline.

For Cheyla it was a rewarding drive a great experience to witness this phenomenal part of Australia, and though he was determined to keep his mind on the task ahead, he allowed himself the luxury of enjoying it all as he drove the winding road through the smaller ranges where trails for tourists headed down to spots in the gorges below. It was a well-signed road. Anything of interest for visitors was well marked out, and so too was Waverley Downs well-advertised, he noted as he past the 20kms to go sign.

He had left the Motel early not sure what condition the road was in, but hoping to arrive at Waverley Downs for breakfast. He just knew he would find Mary Higgs there, and was hoping to talk to her before she started work.

Suddenly the countryside seemed to alter once again as patches of scrubby areas took over the scenery where low bushes grew in abundance, and created a spectacle of colour as they massed together seemingly leading a pathway into a dense forest of giant trees. This he noted, after driving through for some time, opened out once again to become a thick scrub line, then to undulating valleys that seemed to flatten out some-what to make way for rolling grassy plains where massive trees dotted the terrain of the scrub-line skirting the area, and he noted paddocks were defined. Then as small dwellings began to appear, Cheyla guessed he was in The South Australian Outback now.

Taken in by the scenery, he almost missed the turn-off, and had to brake, then reversed a little to read the sign at the grid. 'WELCOME TO WAVERLEY DOWNS & THE OUTBACK TOURIST RESORT.' it read.

'A Resort? That will be interesting.' he was thinking as he turned his 4WD to approach the grid, and according to the signage he noted it was only just 2 kms to go now, and breathed a sigh of relief. 'Thank goodness! It's been a long haul this trip, I need more rest.' he realized, as he drove slowly across, and onto the property of Waverley Downs.

It was soon evident to Cheyla as he drove through the paddocks boasting herds of cattle that this property was not only a place for tourists but a working cattle property as well, and just watching them reminded him of home.

He had driven from one end of Australia to the bottom end, such a long way from his home, and he missed it. He was hoping it would be worth his while. He slowed as he approached the next grid, and when he drove through he braked, coming to a sudden halt as his eyes widened, and he stared at the complex before him which seemed to take on at least three paddocks. From what he could see there were dwellings around everywhere, and activities galore to entertain. His interest was heightened once again.

Waverley Downs Homestead was a show case alone. Set off the main thoroughfare enclosed by its own house paddock. It stood majestic, a recently renovated old historic two-story weatherboard boasting verandahs all-around, which took in the scenery of the waterway below.

Cheyla could see it as he drove on through. A massive rock-lined gorge, with sun dancing on the rocks changing its colours in the early light. He could see the railings on the pathways going down to the water's edge as he pulled his 4WD into the carpark adjacent the Office Reception, where a huge billboard clearly stated everything on offer.

Eagerly he climbed from his vehicle and stretched as he read the billboard. It was obvious the place was large, everything well planned. Not only was it a working cattle station, but they had horse rides, and camel rides for the tourists. 'Camels?' mused Cheyla as he continued to read.

There were coloured signs pointing out the directions of the stables, holding yards, larger machinery sheds, and sheds where you could hire boats, and fishing gear from.

Cheyla looked around. From where he stood he could see many attractions. Taking the center of all the action was a common area with bar-be-ques, tables, and seating where guests could mingle just adjacent the grassed pool area. Coloured umbrella were scatted around the lawns, and pathways heading towards a Restaurant, and the Bar which was just adjacent to it. 'Looks like they have many, many cabins in the complex.' thought Cheyla as he locked his 4WD then walked over towards the Office Reception, took the two steps up to the entrance, then he opened the front door. He remembered to duck his head as he walked through the doorway, then a bell rang from somewhere inside when he crossed the threshold.

Almost immediately a tall, but well- built young man with dark brown hair walked through the adjoining door. His warm brown eyes softened as he smiled.

"Morning! An early traveler eh. How can I help sir?" he asked as he looked up at Cheyla. 'Not something I have to do usually, but this guy is huge' he thought.

"Morning to you also. My name is Cheyla Stone. I was hoping to get here for breakfast, hope it's still on? I am starving, and I guess seeing you have such a nice place here I might stick around for a while if you have a cabin available?" he asked, as he extended his hand.

"Name is Ed McKenzie!" he replied, as their hands met. "Pleased to meet you, and yep, I can accommodate you, the Restaurant's open for breakfast!" Then he turned in pretense of grabbing a room key off the peg, but was secretly giving his hand a moment to resume to normal after the hand-shake. "Cabin 12 has an en-suite, just down a bit on your left with access down to the gorge. Make sure you visit that while you are here, it is a treat." he said.

"Sounds perfect Ed however there is something rather important I need to discuss with you first." he stated.

Ed looked up into the big man's eyes, and something in those eyes had changed. Some emotion maybe, he wasn't sure, but he was becoming inquisitive now.

"Well you were lucky to catch me here. Just waiting for the reception girl to arrive, then I am heading out to the paddocks to check on all my cattle. I run Waverley Downs now since Dad retired, but he still helps quite a lot. I've only been back home for roughly two years, or so, prior to that I attended University in Adelaide studying agriculture, and learning all I can about cattle. We have a big cattle ranch here, so I wanted to be on top of things so I can help Dad, and maybe try some new things" he said.

"I'm into cattle myself!" replied Cheyla. "Have a big spread up in The Territory. That is where I have travelled from to here, so I am no tourist. There is a long overdue purpose for my visit, and finally am at Waverley Downs."

"Goodness me, you've seen half Australia almost!" Ed chuckled. "But you have me intrigued now. What brings you all that way to our Property, why here of all places?"

Cheyla laughed. "Yeah! I guess I have seen a fair piece of Australia, but there is still a lot of places out there. Why here? Well it is a simple explanation. Waverley Downs is the only address I have, the only contact I have written on some old letters from here, and this has directed me in my search for a lady who works here." he explained.

"Well I never!" said Ed. "Great to catch up with people isn't it? Bet she will get a surprise. What did you say her name was?" he asked, and hit some keys on the keyboard.

"Her name is Mary Higgs. Apparently she has worked here for many years." said Cheyla, as Ed scrolled down.

Silence was an oppressive thing for Cheyla to endure as Ed searched the files on his computer. Screen, after screen he scrolled through. It seemed to take forever, and Cheyla was becoming quite anxious, until finally Ed lifted his head, and looked into Cheyla's deep green eyes.

Cheyla's heart sank as he looked into Ed's concerned eyes, and knew the outcome even before he had spoken.

"Can't seem to find her on the current staff, and I have gone back two years. Still no sign of Mary Higgs. Are you sure she works here Cheyla?" asked Ed inquisitively.

"As I told you Ed, the only address I have is Waverley Downs. Her letters came from this address on the back, and stamped in Port Augusta on the front, so that is all I have to help you. Except maybe one thing. She was a full aboriginal lady, don't know her age though." he replied.

"Well in that case I shall look no further, because I am quite certain we haven't employed any aboriginal ladies, I only have a couple of young boys now in the camp that do some fencing, and they are aboriginal. It seems a bit of a mystery to me Cheyla, and I feel so sorry I cannot help you, seeing you have travelled so far!" he stated sadly.

Cheyla tried to ignore the knot in his gut, but nothing could stop the sadness from etching the lines on his brow as he reached out to grab up his room key, and he said.

"Thanks for trying anyway Ed. I think I might go, and get breakfast before checking into the cabin. Have a lot to dwell on, I will leave my 4WD in the carpark if that is ok?"

"Yeah, sure Cheyla!" Ed replied, as he looked up into his agonized face. "How long will you stay now Cheyla?"

"Not sure Ed! Have a lot to think on now, but I do need

a well-earnt rest so I will probably stay three days at least, that should give me plenty of time to recover, and try to relax a little, while I work out what my next movements will be. I will keep you posted, if that is ok!" he replied.

"That is fine with me. If you need me at all, just leave a note for me at reception, or if you want to talk to me, I will call your room when I get in. I'll leave my mobile number there for you anyway just in case." said Ed.

"All good thanks Ed." he replied then walked towards the reception door, and turned the knob just as Ed spoke.

"Forgot to mention! Run a tab in The Restaurant for your meals, or anything else here Cheyla. Just let them know your name, and Cabin number 12, so they can start an account, and you can settle for all when you leave!"

"Greatly appreciated Ed, thank you!" he replied, then opened the door, went outside to face the day with a heart heavy with sadness. 'I am too late!' he thought. 'Too late!'

Inside the Restaurant Cheyla looked around as he made his way to the counter to check in, but disappointment was overshadowing the true nature of the surroundings.

"Can I help you?" someone asked as he was jolted back to reality to look at the lady standing before him. She was in her late thirties, with brown hair. She strained to look up at him with eyes of the same colour. He noticed how sun-tanned her skin was from the outdoors.

"Ah yes, just want you to know I am having breakfast. Cabin 12, my name is Cheyla Stone." he muttered.

"Good morning Mister Stone, just help yourself to the buffet, and I will bring you some fresh coffee." she said.

He selected a table beside a large window with a view of the near surroundings, and the rolling hills of the property which boasted various paddocks in the distance where the cattle grazed. He threw his hat on the chair, and walked over to the buffet table to make his selections. He was starving as usual, and no platter was left untouched.

"Good to see a man with a hearty appetite!" offered the lady as she put the coffee pot down. "There you go Mister Stone, nice fresh coffee. My name is Jill McKenzie by the way. You would have met my husband Ed earlier."

"Thank you, and pleased to meet you Jill, and yeah Ed, and I have had a chat. You can call me Cheyla." he stated.

"Cheyla! An interesting name I haven't heard before."

He chuckled. "Yeah so they tell me. I owe thanks to a Grandmother for that! You probably won't hear it again."

"Well you enjoy your stay here Cheyla! Are you on a holiday, or just touring around?" she asked.

"Well I did come here looking for a lady called Mary Higgs who worked here, but she is not here apparently. Have you heard of her at all Jill?" he asked hopefully.

"Can't say that I have, I am sorry. I am usually pretty good with names too, but 'Mary Higgs.' It does not ring a bell. I am sure she hasn't been here since Ed, and I moved here about two years or so, ago. How very disheartening for you Cheyla." she said in a concerned voice.

"Yeah I am very disappointed but thanks anyway Jill." he said absently, as he poured coffee into a cup. I guess I will have breakfast now, see you later." Then he headed over to his table, set his plate, and cup at the end placing then wearily slumped down into the chair, and began to gaze forlornly out the window, his mind a turmoil. 'Why? Why couldn't I do this sooner, years ago even?' But sadly he knew the answer. He didn't have the information from Ol Mother that would have helped him earlier, until her very last breath. He guessed that she was only trying to protect him, but she had held that back until the very end.

'Ol Mother, you don't know what you have done!'

At the cabin he parked his 4WD under a tree, grabbed his gear out from the back, and locked the car, then walked across the grassed area to the little front porch to the front door, and inserted his cabin key.

Inside the cabin was nice enough, but his interest was not there. He dropped his bag on the bed, emptied out his pockets, picked up his keys to lock the cabin, and walked outside onto the pathway that headed down to the gorge, then began to stride out strongly. He was frustrated, and needed to blow off some steam, so soon the walk became a jog, even though it was slightly downhill he pushed on, exerting himself until the sweat trickled down from his face, and neck to his torso, and soaked through his shirt.

There was a landing down the bottom. Cheyla stood a while to survey the water before taking the steps down to a sandy bank where he stripped off his shirt, wrapped his key in it, discarded his shoes, and left them on the bank.

The water looked so inviting as it rushed along, so he waded in to the waist-band of his shorts. He was being cautious just to make sure there were no rocks, or big logs underneath. He learned at a young age in lessons of being raised with bush skills, not to dive into strange water.

Powerfully he pushed off, his huge arms reaching out in defiance of a strong current that he opposed, as his body surged through it towards the opposite bank.

There seemed to be a sandy bank down further so he allowed the force of the water to push him downstream a little, then he strove to make the bank as he stretched out strongly to swim into the bank, and dragged himself out.

'That feels more like it' thought Cheyla, as he sat in the sand, and took in the surroundings. He was beginning at last to feel his body relax, the previous tension releasing.

There were many rock formations the colours of which tended to change in the sun as sprays from the gorge of pure, clean water, wet the rocks in its continuous passing.

He lay back on the sand and let the beauty of the gorge engulf him, and as the sun played on his skin bringing its warmth, he slowly realized his predicament. He lay there for ages as his mind ticked over all his options.

'Should I leave, and go back home. Travel the way I just came from? Seems a bit pointless, but what else could I do. I can't travel all over Australia without a purpose.' he wondered. 'Maybe if I stay here three days, I might get to talk to someone here who knew Mary!' Suddenly, he sat upright. 'Yes!' he mused, that is as good a plan as any.

So now he had a plan, and eager to exercise it, he leapt to his feet in one bound, and did not hesitate as he entered the swirling water to push off with a grim determination to fight against the current, and strive for the other side.

He dragged himself from the water and ran to retrieve his belongings, climbed the steps, then faced the incline of the pathway with a vengeance as he ran up it strongly.

Back at his cabin, he was about to insert his key in the door when he looked up to notice the cleaning team at the cabins across the road, so he decided to approach them.

His questions to them all about Mary Higgs seemed to fall on deaf ears. No-one knew of her, or had even heard of her, and really, they weren't so interested in his plight at all, and seemed only to want to resume their workload.

Feeling dejected he thanked them all anyway, but then left. Back in his cabin he headed straight for the en-suite, and a hot shower as he re-assessed. 'His new plan wasn't working so well.' he thought. 'Damn! I need a drink, then some lunch, and maybe another, but I had better call Jono first. He will be wondering what is happening here.

Cheyla decided to call Jono's mobile for this call as he knew that he wouldn't be inside the house this time of day, and luckily the all-familiar voice called out loud, and clear when he picked up almost straight away.

"Hey Cheyla, tis me Jono!" he yelled.

"I know it's you Jono cause I called you, remember?" laughed Cheyla, as he held the phone way out away from his ear. "Now stop yelling!" he added.

"Yea sure, o course ya did!" laughed Jono, then spoke in a softer tone. "Bin missin ya. What be happenin there?"

"That's better Jono, you are not blasting my eardrum now." replied Cheyla, as he lifted the phone to his ear. "I am at Waverley Downs, but have no good news. No-one has even heard of Mary Higgs here. I am at a loss now as to what I should do. I am so disappointed, it has taken me forever to get here, and now, who knows what I'll do!"

"Am sorry ta here thet Cheyla, but things be happenin fer a reason. Maybe ya not meant ta find ya Mother, come home now. Ya bin gone too long. All is good here, an ya hav a new colt now from tha bay mare, they both be good, an ya property be all ok. Jus come back." he muttered.

"That's good to hear Jono. Finally I am receiving some good news today. But I'm not coming home yet Jono, I am not giving up that easily. I have come too far to quit now, and I have a plan to talk to as many people as I can while I am here so I have booked in to a cabin for three days. I will give you an update after that. In the meantime, if you need me, just call. I have to go now. Cheers Jono."

"Ok then Cheyla, guess ya no best. I be waitin fer ya call. Good luck, see ya." he said, and the line went dead.

It really looked like something from out of a movie with its weather-board exterior, a tin roof, barred windows, and chunky timber benches lining the front boardwalk as Cheyla stepped up onto it in his approach to the entrance of 'The Bar' where the double doors swung inwards at his touch, and brought a smile to his face as he stepped inside to a room that was dimly lit, the only natural light coming in through the limited space of the barred windows.

He looked around as he sidled onto a bar-stool at 'The Bar' situated in the center of the room. There was signage saying 'Restaurant.' above more double swing doors just adjacent to 'The Bar,' and a few couples having drinks as they chatted at their tables, briefly looked up when he sat down, then resumed their conversation. An old man sat in a corner engrossed in something on the big TV screen.

Abarman approached him, and stood waiting for his order as Cheyla scanned the room. "Excuse me Sir, can I help you, what will it be?" he asked.

Cheyla acknowledged the barman with a smile. "Oh hi, I am Cheyla Stone by the way, staying in Cabin 12. Just a Johnnie, and ice water thanks."

"Coming right up Cheyla." the barman replied.

'I guess I could try to speak to those people over there' thought Cheyla absently, as he waited for his drink to be served, someone may have heard of Mary.'

At that instant one of the men left the group of people to approach the bar to order a round of drinks. He had a friendly face, and a grin from ear to ear as he chuckled to himself still from the joke he just heard, as he breasted the bar beside Cheyla, and started up a conversation.

"Hi there! Sorry mate, just can't contain my laughter. I am with a group of friends over there. They are all a mad bunch, but good company, and there is no doubts about them, they have all seen some sights in their travels, and have some weird stories to tell. My name is Robert, how are you doing?" he asked, still with a big grin on his face.

Cheyla gave a chuckle. "So they are telling jokes over there! Good way to pass the time if you are all travelling around together? I am Cheyla by the way, pleased to meet you Robert." he replied, and they shook hands.

Robert placed his order with the barman who returned with Cheyla's drink, and he turned to face Cheyla. "Yeah, we are all tourists on a trip for about three months, and having heaps of fun. How about you Cheyla?" he asked.

"Well I am no tourist Robert. I have driven all the way

from The Territory to here, on the off-chance of meeting a lady called Mary Higgs who was supposed to work here, but no-one has heard of her, and I don't think you could help me either if you are all travelers." he said sadly.

"Gee I am so sorry Cheyla. That is a long way to travel, but best we get everyone's attention!" he said, and stood up to address all the customers. "Anyone here heard of a lady named Mary Higgs, this here guy has driven a long way to find her." he called to them all.

Just the mention of the name Mary Higgs was enough to alert the old man sitting in the corner. His ears pricked, and his interest in the big TV screen became waned, as he turned his head to listen to the conversation taking place at the bar, and he sat searching his brain for some inkling of recollection. He knew that name, he was so sure of it.

"Well I guess it was worth a try!" stated Cheyla, as he looked around the room at the shaking of heads. He felt devastated to note that no-one had heard of Mary Higgs, and it showed deeply on his face as the deep lines etched his brow. "Thanks anyway Robert." he said sadly.

Robert picked up his tray of drinks, and said. "Come over to our table Cheyla, and join in some fun. Might take your mind off your disappointment for a while."

"Thanks Robert but I am going to head into lunch so if you are still around later, I will join you all then." he said.

"Ok Cheyla, if you miss us, come down to Cabin 6, or Cabin 4. Later on we should be there." replied Robert.

As the old man's watery eyes settled on the saddened face of the big man at the bar, suddenly it came to him.

CHEYLA

Mary Higgs! 'Of course, how silly of me. I knew that name was familiar soon as I heard it.' The old man thought to himself. 'Damn it, I could never forget Mary.'

He looked across to the bar just as the big man slid off his stool, and stood eyeing off The Restaurant sign behind where he sat at his table, and started to walk towards him.

As Cheyla approached his table, he spoke.

"Eh Son, hold up a bit, something I need to talk to you about, but you may need to sit down, and join me at my table. I find it hard to look up to talk to you as you stand. Old neck aint what it used to be, it's a bit stiff you see."

Cheyla stopped. "Yeah sure, how can I help you Sir?" he asked, as he pulled a chair out, and sat down.

"Not so much as how you can help me, but how I might be able to help you Son!" replied the old man.

"My name is Jim. Jim McKenzie. I own this place here. My son Ed runs it now." he said, as he extended his hand.

Cheyla took his feeble hand in his, and tried hard not to squeeze, as their hands shook. "Cheyla Stone." he said. "So what do you mean Jim, and how could you help me?"

"Well you are looking for Mary Higgs, and so happens that I know her!" Jim replied, as he watched him closely.

Cheyla's eyes flew wide, and he grabbed the old man's hands in his, as he asked. "Mary! You know Mary Higgs Jim? Are you quite certain, don't kid me now."

"Yeah, I know Mary Higgs very well. She worked here for many, many years. Maybe fifteen, or twenty years, or more even, have lost count of the years over time. So what brings you here looking for Mary?" he asked.

"Now hang on a minute Jim, I just want to make sure

we are talking about the same person. The Mary Higgs I am looking for is a pure blood aboriginal, and I have come all the way from The Northern Territory to find her as her Grandmother had just passed away but she handed me some old letters prior to her death that Mary had written to her. That is where I got this address from Jim. Waverley Downs, off the back of the letters, it was all I had to go on.

"Yep, that is her Cheyla. Turned up looking for work. There was two of them travelling together, but the other one was a white girl. Mary was a pretty little thing for an aboriginal girl, gave her a job in the cabins, and part-time in the Restaurant. But the other one, the white girl, was so smart, but she wanted to work outdoors so I put her on a trial." he chuckled. "Shortest trial anyone ever had I think as she knew everything about cattle, could ride any horse like the wind, and apart from that. She would have to be the most beautiful looking girl I have ever seen. Beautiful deep green eyes she had that mesmerized you" he stated.

Jim looked up into Cheyla's eyes, and was startled as he spoke. "Not unlike your eyes Cheyla. How strange, but her eyes were just like yours. Thought I would never see that colour eyes again but yours are very close." he said.

Something in Cheyla's gut started churning. He knew in his heart that this man was describing his Mother, and somehow he felt an affinity with her, a sense of pride even for who she was, he knew not why, but just hearing about her in this way made him feel he knew a little something about her, but he tried very hard not to let it show on his face as he returned the conversation back to Mary Higgs.

He looked hard at Jim with a million questions on his mind, but only one that would really help him.

"Jim, about Mary! Do you know where she went when she left here, and how long ago it was?" his voice pleaded.

Jim chuckled. "Yeah remember well Cheyla. Took her to the airport myself. She left here about four, or five years ago, but the white girl left about one to two years before her. I remember Mary leaving because Ed my Son, was in College, and had two, and a half years to go, and that was when I was going to retire. However, I can't really forget Mary Higgs, as she sends me a Christmas card every year, god love her! So I guess the address is on the back of them where she's at. If you want to come for a walk with me to my office I think I know where I can put my hands on her Christmas cards. I've kept them all" he remarked.

Cheyla was gob smacked. "Jim, you don't realize how much this means to me. That is the best news I have had for quite a while!" he said excitedly. Suddenly things had changed. He had gone from having nothing to go on, to a possible chance. "Please show me the way Jim." he said.

Jim McKenzie rose from his seat, and walked across the room, went behind the bar, and grabbed a set of keys, and beckoned Cheyla to follow him.

Cheyla watched him in amazement. 'He is not that old at all.' he thought. 'Old, but still spritely in his step, and he still has an active brain to remember everything he has told me. I guess looks can be deceiving, because here is a man who has worked hard all his life to build an empire to be proud of. Long days toiling out in sun can alter the external appearance of a person, that's for sure.' he knew.

At the end of the bar there was a solid oak door. Jim paused as he felt for a key on the key- ring, inserted it, and then pushed the door open. Once through the door they both entered a long, narrow passageway where Jim felt for a light switch. Suddenly the hallway came to life, so he lead the way briskly, rambling on about his Son as he trudged along, and Cheyla followed closely behind.

"So you met my Son Ed" he stated. "I'm not too sure whether I done the right thing by sending him away to an agricultural College. Thought it would be good for him to learn about our property, and breading cattle, but now he comes home with these new-fangled ideas about planting crops! I told him I didn't want crops here as too much can go wrong. You have to rely a lot on the weather, so that is a gamble, and cost wise it's just not feasible, and too much labour is required. But he won't listen. He is just hell bent on his own ideas. I told him I was a Cattle Man, and have the tourist set-up, that's enough to look after, but if any-thing, I'd rather plant wattle trees than plant crops, but that didn't go down well with him either. I guess though at the end of the day, it will all be his one day, and I won't be here to see it all come to pass." he said sadly.

"Yes I met Ed when I arrived. Seems like a nice young fellow, and I'm sure that he has your best interest at heart, however just like you, I am strictly a Cattle Man also, and wouldn't want anything else out in my paddocks. I have a spread up in The Northern Territory." replied Cheyla.

"Oh, well damn me that's good to hear Cheyla, we will have to chat about that later, but right now the important thing is getting you some answers, and this is my office!"

he uttered as he stopped at the big Oak door, and inserted his key, and pushed the door wide so Cheyla could enter, then shut the door behind them, and headed inside.

"Yes that is for sure, but maybe we can lunch together, and have a chat when we are done here." offered Cheyla.

"Yes I would like that very much Cheyla!" replied Jim.

It was a large office Cheyla noted as he walked inside. Many large book shelves lined the walls, and a big oak desk stood adjacent a double window that looked out to the paddocks beyond. On one of the walls there was some art-work depicting Waverley Downs at different stages of its progression, and Cheyla commented on that, but it fell on deaf ears as Jim made a be-line for his filing cabinets.

He pulled out the third drawer, then flipped through the files, but almost instantly his face lit up as he retrieved a folder. "Yep, knew it!" he said with satisfaction. "This is all Mary's stuff. Christmas cards, tax information even a dossier about her. This here's the last card I got from her. Looks like the place you need to go to is Shallow Siding." he muttered, as he flipped it over, and read the back.

A knot creased his brow as he took the proffered card, but struggled to read it. "Says here she works! But where? Why is the town called a 'Siding' and where the hell is it?"

"Don't know for sure Cheyla! There must be a Railway there though! They used to call all the rail towns a 'Siding' back in the day. Here is a map, bring the card, and we will look at it over lunch." Jim beckoned, as he bustled away.

Cheyla knew how far he'd come, so didn't need a map to realize more agony was in store. But now he had hope.

Chapter 9

Mary walked across the wide verandah, and stood at the railing looking out over the paddocks. The sun, high in the north, seemed to caress her face, and although her smile widened as a feeling of contentment overtook her, tears silently slid down her face to fall on to her tunic.

'They be tears of joy I guess' she thought to herself. She had never known happiness like this before in her life. 'I be Missus Hargraves now, an so happy to be thet. Drew be tha perfect husband fer me, an this be my home, our home. This be my land, an our land, to do what we want fer as long as we be liven.' she thought. She found it just so hard to comprehend it all, but knew in her heart it was all due to her dearest friend, Jacqueline Coby-Stringer.

"Good Morning!" called Drew as he came through the doors, and strolled out onto the deck. Mary started as the sound of his voice interrupted her thoughts, and turned quickly to face him. "Oh good mornin Drew, you startled me! I be jus greetin the day." Mary replied.

"With tears?" he asked, as he slowly walked up to her, and pulled her close. "Why the tears Mary? I would have thought that this house would make you smile forever!"

She looked at him, then laughed. "No, silly! Tis cause I be so happy, not sad at all Drew. These be tha tears of joy ya see! Tis jus everythin Jacqueline be doin for me, fer us. Not only tha wedding, tha reception, but the land, an a new house built fer us. So much she be givin me!"

They had moved into the beautifully laid out weatherboard house enclosed by its own house paddock about four months ago. It had fire-places, and air-conditioning, double doors from the rooms on all sides that opened out to wide verandahs which took in the views of the rolling paddocks, the vegetation, and the huge gum trees. Inside every room of the house, a specific attention to detail had been showcased by artwork, furniture, and consumables in every nook, and cranny. Even a big pantry was full of food, and the fridge, and bar fully stocked. Compliments of Jacqueline Coby-Stringer who had spared no expense.

Neither one had much to bring, but that didn't seem to matter to Drew, and Mary, they had everything anyone could possibly need inside, and outside of the house. But they both knew most people would have to work so hard their whole entire life for what they were given as a gift.

Drew looked directly into Mary's eyes, then smiled at her fondly as he pulled her closer towards him, and spoke with such a special meaning in his tone of voice that even Mary was dumbfounded as she looked deep into his eyes.

"Now you listen to me Missus Hargraves! You are the most special person I've ever had the pleasure of meeting, and special people deserve to be treated accordingly. You, my lady, have been given all these things from Jacqueline Coby-Stringer because you have been a special person to her in her lifetime, throughout both your lives. So please don't take that away from her, let her give! It is her way of showing you how much you are loved, respected, and appreciated, beyond the call of friendship." he stressed.

Mary started to cry again. "Ya be so good ta me Drew Hargraves. I jus love ya fer explainin thet ta me, so I be understandin things a bit betta now. So I be cryin no more now! Will be only smilin." she said, as she sobbed.

Drew laughed. "That will be the day!" he uttered as he grinned. Then he became serious as he enclosed her in his arms, and leaned over to kiss her deeply, and longingly.

Mary responded with all the love she could muster for this husband of hers. As their kiss ended, she still stayed within the circle of his arms, smelling the man aroma of him that she loved, and feeling such contentment that she had never felt before. But he was off talking again so she had to look up into his face to try, and make out what he was talking about as he rambled on, and she missed the first few words, but now he was saying.

"I'll pick you up today when you've completed your work at Shallow Downs Mary! So don't walk home, just wait for me. There is something we have to do, and there is something I have to show you." he said mysteriously.

"Why thet be Drew, what we hav ta do?" Mary asked. "An, what ya hav ta show me! What thet be?"

"Too many questions Mary!" he laughed. "Besides, it's a surprise, and if I told you now, it would spoil it, so just be patient until this afternoon please. Can you do that?"

"Thet be too long ta wait, please tell Drew!" she pleaded.

Shallow Downs was all a buzz as people lined up, and paused outside the newly built gallery. They chatted as they waited to peruse the showcase of memorabilia of a long time ago local legend Clayton Coby, and what was promised as the first ever display of photos, and portraits of the initial property 'Shallow Downs,' which was built in the early 10's, and information on the lifestyle way back then, and the instigation of improvements which brought it to its hey-day in the 60's, and about people who worked at the property at the time to make it a legendary estate.

Mary was so excited. It was the first day of her new job, and as she looked upon all the people there she knew at once it was all going to be a great success. 'No doubt about her.' she thought. She had her instructions, and had arranged to meet Jacqueline inside the new complex prior to the Grand Opening, and so she made her way through the throng, speaking to each group of people politely as she passed them, and headed towards to entrance doors.

Meg Shaw stood in the wings inside the entrance of the bright, and airy Exhibition Gallery at The Historic Museum in which, after the Grand Opening formalities were over, the showing and auction was to take place.

She was making a mental note of the set-up, but also scrutinizing the building for any detail that was missing, but subconsciously from time to time, her eyes flicked to the entrance doors awaiting an important arrival.

'I think it is a safe bet that if anything is wrong or is out of order, then the owner would soon point it out to me.' mused Meg absently. She remembered only too well her first meeting with Jacqueline Coby-Stringer when she had arrived un-announced in her brightly-coloured Jeep, and they thought at The Homestead that a whirlwind had hit them. Jacqueline, they soon realized. Spoke her mind, and was very direct, with her own opinions. She spoke of things as they were, and straight up. A no fuss person.

'You really knew where you stood with her!' thought Meg, who had liked her instantly. She had a certain way about her that you could only admire. Her determination, and drive displayed purely in her actions was enthralling.

They had never met her in person, though Meg wasn't sure why, but had spoken to her on the phone. Jacqueline had been the existing owner of Shallow Downs for many years since Clayton Coby, being his youngest Daughter.

Flashes of their life returned in Meg's thoughts, and later events following of the first meeting on that morning with Jacqueline Coby-Stringer, and their conversation.

Meg, and her husband John both had been appointed Managers of the Property 'Shallow Downs' so long ago. Many, many years had passed by since the demise of the Owner Clayton Coby. The property had become their life, their home, and it was as Clayton Coby had left it.

After tea had been served they settled in the sitting room lounges to converse, and Jacqueline lost no time in updating them on the building of the house for Mary, and Drew that had taken place, and her ideas of future plans for Shallow Downs, as sadly she looked around the room.

'Yes it's time!' she thought. 'Her Father's presence was everywhere. In the choices of furniture, the outlay of the Homestead, and even in the paintings, and the artwork.

Suddenly her face altered, and lit up with a smile as she made her final decision, and she looked up directly in to the eyes of Meg, and John sitting with bated breath.

"Out with the old and in with the new!" were her exact words, Meg recalled. "I would like to make some changes to Shallow Downs, and the Homestead. I see too much of my Father in these rooms which creates a sadness, a loss inside me, and opens old wounds that I have to put aside, besides many things inside here should be available to the public. So I would like to strip it all bare, re-style the lot!"

John, and Meg had just gaped at her. They both knew of the catastrophe that had occurred so many, many years before they had arrived in Shallow Siding, and when the Shallow Downs Homestead was destroyed by a fire with Jacqueline's Mother trapped inside the burning house, so they understood Jacqueline's pain. Only now their whole world was to be turned upside down as they were under strict instructions from the Owner that the entire internal of the now existing property was to be re-furbished. They were about to voice their own opinions just as Jacqueline continued with an explanation that changed their minds.

"We shall build a Historic Museum! A Hub if you like, for Tourists, and locals to flock to. However, please keep in mind, that the majority of my Father's possessions in this Homestead will be auctioned if I don't require them to be used as a major attraction of the Exhibition Center, also the memorabilia I have access to will certainly create a lot of History for Shallow Siding by showcasing what a grand, prestigious property Shallow Downs used to be in it's era from the onset to this current date." she explained.

"Let us take on a new, a fresh, and inviting look for the Homestead, and surrounds that will appeal to all visitors when they arrive here! I want it to be prestigious, the first of its kind in Shallow Siding, but a great asset in possible income for Shallow Downs into the future." she added.

"I shall take total control of the design that I prefer for the layout of the outer buildings, and carpark, and will be responsible for hiring builders, and the appropriate staff for the areas when building is completed. However Meg, I shall leave the internal furnishings entirely up to you for The Homestead providing you run your ideas by me first for my approval. Then I shall arrange payment for all the renovations required. I have many ideas for the outdoors, and will keep you updated, and so as not to overload you, and John with extra work I will hire a Manager to operate it. However, if you both wish to be a part of it, and share in the Manager's role that would be ideal. So just say the word, and I will endeavor to hire a part-time Manager instead. I will instruct my accountant to make alterations to your contracts accordingly." Jacqueline had stated.

"What are your thoughts?" she had asked. Meg, and John had agreed to her terms, however that was not half of Jacqueline's plans Meg recalled. She just seemed to pull ideas out of a hat, and she was usually correct as well.

So, like her Father before her, the magic of Jacqueline Coby-Stringer unfolded. Her ideas extended not only from tours through the Exhibition Gallery at The Historic Museum with a set entrance fee to incorporate the display of the Walk-through Garden Center where her especially exotic orchards were in bloom, and although they were discreetly displayed in a separate enclosure away from all other plants, they were also for sale. As were the others.

However it did not stop there. It really all started at the carpark where an archway led through trellises laden with wisteria on a walk to the entrance of the new Historic Museum surrounded by gum trees, and fauna that was left specifically undisturbed to provide shade to the building, and surrounds of the buildings beyond.

Inside was a massive gallery of three adjoining rooms, each with high ceilings that provided spectacular scenery through the floor to ceiling windows, offering spectacular views over-looking the gardens beyond, and then further down the rooms, exiting through sliding glass doors to a massive display of the Walk-through Garden Center that flowed from the display of plants on offer to the Entrance of a completely new rustic log-cabin styled building.

In a sense. A Café, but aptly named. 'Coby's Retreat.' Offering indoor, and outdoor seating under shaded sails where breakfast, and lunch service would be available to guests as a respite for all customers visiting the complex.

'Yes! A very well thought-out plan' mused Meg, as she looked around with pride, and then to the entrance where Jacqueline Coby- Stringer stood looking immaculate.

Jacqueline stood inside the entrance, her eyes scanning the interior as she spied Meg walking over towards her.

"It looks great Meg!" she declared, when Meg reached her, and a smile lit Meg's face as she replied.

"Come with me Jacqueline! I will give you a mini tour."

Jacqueline was intrigued with the set-up of each room, and how the building provided views from every angle.

She looked directly at Meg, and smiled. "Meg, there is one special thing I would like to look closely at now if you don't mind, so a mini tour will suffice. We have not got time for more than that now before people start arriving."

She knew where she wanted to go, so Jacqueline led the way. Meg tried her best to stay in contact by her side.

Suddenly Jacqueline stopped dead in her tracks when she had entered the room she was seeking, and Meg could detect a gasp escaping her lips, as she then moved closer.

'1961' Cutting of the Wattle 'Garden Party'… Shallow Downs… was the plaque's headline, as Jacqueline read the text with great interest. It was lovingly enclosed in a glass cabinet just below the huge painting which took her breath away as her eyes lifted up to it. Delicately restored to its former glory, it looked immaculate encased within a massive timber frame which took up most of one wall.

'Yes it definitely does have its own place now forever!' thought Jacqueline. 'I should have paid Axel more for that original as now it's become cemented in a hall of History.' and she made a mental note to do just that. 'It was! After all, a Masterpiece! One, never to be replaced.' she mused.

As her eyes captured scenes within the painting, they misted over, then welled to form tears that softly fell upon her jacket, as memories of another day swamped her, and her life flashed before her to take her back in time to that special day. It was definitely one of the happiest times of her life. Not only did she earn a great achievement for her own part in the organization of 'The Garden Party,' but also working closely with her Father for the first time. To Jacqueline, that was her bonus, and a special time never to be forgotten nor could it ever be replaced. However she couldn't help remembering the feelings that stirred inside her as her love for Mitch blossomed at that time when he rode her most precious stallion 'Sailor' in the Mile Race.

"It is such a great piece of art!" declared Meg, bringing Jacqueline back to the present. "John, and I have always admired it, and now it is restored to new, it's even better. We couldn't bear to take it from the front entrance of The Property, but the new sign is so good also." Meg added.

"My goodness! Thank the lord you didn't do that Meg. It would have been a huge tragedy, and yes, I like the new sign also. Both done by Axel Hall, a great talent." replied Jacqueline, as she composed herself once again. "Let us head back now Meg shall we!" she stated, as she steered her to the Entrance. As they walked on she complimented her for her hard work. "I really could not fault anything in there Meg! A job well done! Oh there is Mary. That was good timing." she said, and Mary joined them both.

Meg was elated by the praise. "Thank you Jacqueline though I had a very good off-sider right there. Hi Mary! Are you ready for the big day today?" Meg asked.

"Mornin Jacqueline, mornin Meg. Me be jus so excited, an a bit nervous Meg, but seein it all finished now, looks ta be so good, an I can't wait ta start!" she said.

Jacqueline smiled at her. "Morning Mary! You will be just fine like you always are, no matter what you do, and I can't thank you enough for your hard work here also!"

"You and Meg make a great team!" she said. "But right this minute we have many people waiting outside, so let's greet them together for The Grand Opening!" she added.

Mary blushed from the praise bestowed on her but she replied. "Me thank ya too Jacqueline, an also fer tha new job too! An I want ya ta know I won't be letting ya down! An yea, we be both ready ta go outside now!" she stated.

"Good! Then let us get started, but please listen closely Mary Hargraves! Who better than you, should I think of hiring, to teach the young ones all you know about inside, and outside this Property? Of waiting on people, serving people, and maintaining a Homestead! So hold your head high girl, you have earnt this job! Now, enough!" she said.

They stood on the steps, as the hired staff joined them from both sides of the Entrance, as Jacqueline made the introductions to the people of her two Managers, and of their staff. There was a lot of clapping from the visitors, as two of the staff members held up a red ribbon across the Entrance, and handed Jacqueline the scissors.

As Jacqueline cut the red ribbon, and it floated to the floor she said loudly. "I now declare the Historic Museum 'Open!' In remembrance of my Father, Clayton Coby. A great pioneer out in this Outback Country, and of Shallow Siding. Please enter!" Then the public were allowed in.

From room to room, and through-out the gallery they admired the antique pieces, memorabilia, but especially the big art-work painting of 'The Garden Party,' which in remembering, a lot of them had attended, and all personal items were displayed of the great legend Clayton Coby.

Chapter 10

Jim McKenzie walked over to the windows of his living room in the down-stairs, self-contained, three bedroom area he had sectioned off to be renovated for himself to live within the Homestead, which had a front patio, and also a larger back verandah to entertain, and a car garage.

He parted the curtains to look outside. It was still dark out he noticed, and he nodded to himself, satisfied that he would not be too late, but he hurried just to make sure, as he grabbed a torch, and the carry bag he had packed, and quickly opened the door to his front patio, and shone the torch as he descended the three steps to the driveway.

All the cabins were in darkness as he ambled along, the occupants inside asleep in this darkest hour. However as he looked ahead he detected a faint light in one at the very end, and he hurried along until he reached the steps, and crossed to the front door where he rapped softly.

Cheyla sat inside the room sipping coffee, his thoughts so deep with concentration of the trip he had yet to make that he almost missed hearing a soft tapping on the door.

He stood then switched on the porch light, and opened the door, and was surprised to see Jim standing there.

They had gone over everything last night, he thought. When he settled his final bill late that prior afternoon in reception, Ed McKenzie, and his wife Jill invited him to join them, and Jim McKenzie for dinner that night.

So really the big topic of the evening was Cheyla's trip, and after pouring over the map in between courses, they all were adamant on which route he should take next day.

"Jim! Good morning! You are up early, come on in." he said, as he opened the door wide, and stepped aside.

"Morning Cheyla! Sorry for intruding but I won't keep you. I realize you want to get away early." Jim muttered, as he sat down, and placed his carry bag upon the table.

"I have inside this bag a thermos of coffee, and some sandwiches I made fresh this morning, so that should be enough food for when you have a break, and stop at first light." he said with conviction, as he smiled up at Cheyla.

"Can't thank you enough Jim! I was wondering where my next meal was coming from. I have a body that needs fuel for the fire." he said, as they both chuckled together.

"Really the food was so thoughtful of you, but keep in mind Jim. If it wasn't for you, I would be in dire straits, at a dead end, with no plan in sight. I really can't thank you enough for all your help! You have given me hope! Now I feel I will be on the right track. I will keep in touch, and you should come visit me at my place sometime Jim, you would love it, and I'll return your hospitality!" he stated.

"Pleased to be of help to you Cheyla!" he said, as their eyes met. "I may take you up on that offer one day, however now I have a request! When you meet up with Mary Higgs, would you give her the parcel I put in the bag?"

"Sure thing Jim my pleasure!" replied Cheyla, smiling. "It does seem strange to even think I will finally meet up with Mary Higgs, but now Jim I am feeling confident, and I owe it all to you. I will let you know if I do!" he said.

"That news I will look forward to hearing Cheyla. You have my mobile number, just call me anytime." said Jim.

Chatting came easily for Jim, and Cheyla, and before they knew it some time had passed. Jim looked at his watch, and rose from his seat. "I'd better let you get going Cheyla, you have a long day travelling ahead today. It has been a pleasure meeting you!" he stated, as he offered his hand, and Cheyla gripped it in a handshake.

"Thank you Jim, for everything. It has been a pleasure meeting you too!" Cheyla replied, as he opened the door, and watched Jim walk down the steps.

Jim turned once to wave and Cheyla waved back, then went inside, and closed the door. 'Now let's get this show on the road.' he thought, as he piled all his things together on the bed, then had a last final check of the room before he opened the door, grabbed his gear, and headed outside to his 4WD. It was still dark out, so he was thankful for that respite. It would be a scorcher later he knew for sure.

He unlocked his vehicle, stowed his gear, and climbed into the soft leather seats where he started the engine, and listened to its engine that throbbed away like a heartbeat, then slowly he drove through the complex of Waverley Downs, and out onto the main road. It was roughly about five hours to the border, so he wanted to make the most of today's travel, and would stop along the road to eat.

Travelling through the ranges in the dark was no easy task he soon realized when he was on the main road, where the road twisted, and turned around unbelievable bends. Some at right-angles, where, if you misjudged the angle, you would be hurled out into nothingness.

So unfortunately the trip was slow, but when the sun slowly began its climb over the mountain, for that instant, Cheyla was thankful for once of its presence, though he knew it would dictate his travel as the heat set in for the day. He was almost out of the mountain ranges, and the winding road, so he persevered to solely concentrate on the road until he noticed the land flattening out, and the road becoming straighter, so he started looking ahead for a place to stop, he was ready for a break.

Almost on que a sign read rest area ahead. Thankfully, he continued on towards the turn-off, and drove into the tree-studded rest area. It was well shaded, and there were amenities there as well, so he pulled into the car-park, and shut down the engine of his 4WD.

Grabbing the bag Jim had given him he climbed down, then walked over to a table with a bench, and set it down. He stretched, and realized the trip had his muscles tensed up from too much concentration, so he walked around his vehicle, but decided to stride out strongly down the track a little first before returning, and felt in a much better state as he opened the bag, and revealed its contents. He fell on the sandwiches with relish, then he sat pouring coffee into the thermos lid as he looked around at the deserted place.

'How this country changes so.' he thought to himself. 'Australia has so much to offer, and the only way to really

appreciate its beauty is by what I am doing…Driving.'
Where you could stop anywhere, at any time, and enjoy
it all. He finished his coffee, then gave Jono a quick call to
update him on his progress. All was good at home, so he
felt relieved about that, and his mind wandered to the trip
before him, and went to grab the map from the car seat.

From what he could work out, as he poured over the
map, was that his journey would take him into more
isolated areas throughout the Outback Country for many
miles, where towns were few, and great distances apart.

He had about at least two to three hours to the border,
and there was only one town just across that, so he would
have to stop there to re-fuel, and then continue on another
five hours to the next town, and after that one, one and a
half hours to a small town, where, he noticed, from there
the distances between towns was shortened somewhat.

'Looks like a very long day if I want to make it there,
it could be at least twelve hours and that is without stops.'
Cheyla thought. 'Better get on with it then!' So, with his
decision made, he climbed into the comfort of the 4WD,
and gunned the engine, engaged the gears, and drove out
to the main road, then settled in for the longest part of his
trip. His only concern being the condition of the road.

At the moment he drove on a single lane highway that
was bitumen, but he knew for certain he would run into
either dirt, or gravel along the way. He looked outside the
window at the countryside flashing past, and he noticed
the land taking on another form as it flattened out. Trees
became scarce where bushes, and scrub appeared instead.

Somehow, he felt pleased about a change anyhow. The winding mountain ranges had taken a lot more of his attention than the open road he was driving on now, and he could afford the luxury of looking out at the scenery.

It was certainly a different countryside now to what he had driven through from the Northern Territory, and he sat back enjoying the stillness of it, and the isolation of the bush, and his many thoughts seemed to pass the time.

'Will he succeed in finding Mary Higgs?' he thought. 'But more importantly would it lead him to his Mother?'

He felt so grateful to Jim McKenzie for his input, and he had made a real friend in Jim, and hoped he would see him again one day. Maybe he would come up to visit him.

His thoughts shifted at once to the town he was going to. 'Shallow Siding.' When he first heard it, when Jim told him that was where he had to go to, he was startled, and something stirred deep inside him. He remembered that he frowned in puzzlement, and Ol Mother's last words, though the story not completed, had come back to him.

'Tis in ya name Cheyla.' "What was in my name?' But she didn't get to tell him anymore, it was her last breath, her last words before she passed away. 'She was going to tell me more.' he thought. He was sure of it. 'But what?'

Now he lived with an unsolved mystery that nagged at him, and he hoped that this journey would unravel the pieces of the puzzle of his life, his beginning. But 'Shallow Siding,' the town, played a huge part in it, he felt that for sure. 'But what else could there be?' he wondered. He had been born near the shallows at Tenna Creek, not 'Shallow Siding,' but he was told that somehow his name referred to the shallows, or rather Ol Mothers interpretation when she named him. 'Or maybe it was the other way round.' he thought. 'Maybe the word 'Shallow' was only part of a word, but a significant clue to where his roots were, and the reason for his namesake. 'Just like the town's name!' he thought. It was called Shallow Siding, but who knows? That in itself might be part of the puzzle as well. It could be a sign that I have to go there. 'God damn it all, I've got nothing to go on. There just has to be something else.'

What-ever was Ol Mother thinking back then and who knows what went on in Ol Mother's thoughts?'

'Now I will never know.'

As he tossed possibilities about in his unsettled mind, unbeknown to him while he travelled, the miles had been slipping away, and was startled to suddenly notice the sign that read he was crossing the border.

'Good! There should be a small town coming up soon.' he thought, then almost instantly there was a signpost.

He drove on through the town. It was small but spread out, and the land flat. He continued until The Roadhouse sign caught his eye. 'Can't afford to waste time here, but I am starving. Maybe a meal, check the 4WD, and fill up with petrol, as this next leg of the trip is a long one.' he mused, as he pulled off the highway into the parking lot.

His vehicle was in good order he noticed when he checked it all. When he had filled it with petrol, he parked in a bay, and locked it, then walked over to the entrance.

Cheyla just wanted to relax for a while, so he ordered a quick meal, and coffee, then sat down in a window seat.

Chapter 11

Mary's face was lit up like a neon sign. She waved as she noticed Drew leaning against his land rover in the car park waiting for her, so she hurried towards him.

Drew smiled as she walked up to him. "No need to ask how your day went. You look mighty pleased!" he stated.

"However, I am sure you are about to tell me all about it, aren't you?" he chuckled, as he took her in his arms.

"Oh Drew! I be so happy. Ya won't believe everythin went jus like tha clock work. It be jus a beautiful thing thet Jacqueline bin doin there, an tha people be lovin it. Jus so much work bin done there, ya must hav a look som time!"

Drew chuckled. "I will, but not today. I knew that you would love it Mary. You had yourself so worked up about being a Manager, but what about now. Do you like it?"

"It be so strange ta me Drew. All me life I hav bin tha housemaid, an tha waitress an now I be teachin tha young ones what I no. What I be learnin all me life. Tis strange!"

"Well, you have earnt that right Missus Hargraves, so Congratulations." he said, and kissed her full on the lips. As the kiss ended Drew added. "What about The Outback Gardens, will you still work there as well?" he asked.

She looked up into his eyes, and replied earnestly.

"Bin thinkin a lot bout thet, so talked ta Jacqueline, an she set me right once agin. We be talk ta Meg, she be doin tha Management fer four days tha week, an I be doin the Management, an tha training three days tha week. So I be workin my ol job fer two days at The Outback Gardens. Tis what Jacqueline wants! She be wantin me ta look afta her house. Me be jus so pleased fer I hav lots of me friends workin there, an o course Jacqueline, Mitch, an Melissa."

"Good! That suits our purpose today well enough!" said Drew. "Come on, climb in, and let's get cracking."

"What ya mean Drew? What purpose thet be?"

"Why, the surprise I promised you! Don't tell me you have you forgotten about that?" he asked.

"Ya no Drew, I be forget bout thet, has bin tha busy day taday. So what be tha surprise?" she asked.

"Not telling! Only that we are driving to The Outback Gardens to meet up with Jacqueline, and Mitch for your surprise that they have organized for me." he replied.

"Ah no! I be havin no more presents from Jacqueline. It be nough now what she be givin me, and ya already." she stated most definitely, as she stared directly at Drew.

"Now, hold on just one minute!" said Drew. His hands raised up in defense as he spoke. "This is not a present from Jacqueline, and Mitch! This present is from me! They have only helped me acquire it after some conversation."

"Well if ya sure Drew, but ya promise me thet ya will take no more gifts! An what it be thet ya are gettin me?"

"Ah! Wouldn't you like to know, but you will have to wait my lady, and I do promise that this is from me, and

I won't be accepting any more gifts from Jacqueline, and Mitch if that pleases you. Can we leave now Mary, they will be waiting for us?" he asked in desperation.

Mary smiled up at him. "Of course Drew! I be pleased thet is settled. Now do hurry, I can't be waitin too much longer!" she said, as she climbed into his rover.

Drew laughed at her as he opened the door, then he climbed onto the seat, started the engine, then drove through the car park, and the portals of Shallow Downs.

The drive to Shallow Siding was pleasurable for Mary, as she looked out the window commenting profusely on the surroundings, and the bush. Then in no time at all, it seemed she noticed the crossing of the Shallow River, and was amazed to see the flowing river beneath the bridge.

"Four miles to go, and as you know, some of the best views of this Outback Country around Mary!" said Drew.

"Yea tis beautiful. Jus lov ta drive out this way Drew." she said, as they climbed the slopes, and she turned in her seat to witness the beauty of the valley they had just left behind them, where the township nestled near the river.

"Yea, be so beautiful." uttered Mary. "But ya no Drew, I be likin tha views at our home, an land well nough."

"I know exactly what you mean Mary. Home is where the heart is, and yes I too like the views at home." he said. "We have a beautiful area, and plenty of land to do what we like with, so we will choose things together. It will be a special time for us Mary, and you have two days a week off, so I will organize my days off to match yours!"

"Oh Drew, that be wonderful, we be so lucky an all!"

When they finally arrived at the gates to the entrance of The Outback Gardens they sat a while to admire the sign. "A bit weather-worn, but that sign is a classic!" uttered Drew, as he braked, and got out to open the gates.

"Yea, thet be tha great sign. Jus like tha one at Shallow Downs. Drew, do ya know thet one be worth lot o money now it's restored, an in tha Historic Museum? Jacqueline, be tellin me taday! Axel Hall be paintin both o them there signs, an I be guessin this one be valuable too!" she said.

"Well, I'll be!" uttered Drew. "Axel certainly does not look like an artist. You never can tell though, can you?"

"Yea, Axel gettin older now, but has bin paintin lots o signs in tha town. He be a great artist! Use ta do lots more, an still does tha odd paintin fer people, an artwork for tha Community Town Hall Committee." Mary replied.

They continued on into the property, and in no time at all they were at the crossroads, and Drew commented as he took the left hand route. "I like how the road into The Outback Bush Camp has a separate entrance than to The Homestead! Was it always like that Mary?" he asked.

"No! Tis a lot diffrent now Drew. It be changed when Pete, an Susan they build their house there by tha river, an he be havin a office next ta tha Restaurant, an there be a Bar there too now at the Bush Camp. So all traffic, an tha people fer tha Outback Bush Camp or tha Restaurant, go there now, but if they want ta visit tha Gardens, then they be go this way. There be tha signs. See!" she pointed out the huge signs. "Afore, all tha traffic be goin on past tha Homestead, so tis better now it bin changin." she said.

"Sounds like fun, may have a look around some time."

"Maybe we will come out for dinner one night at The Restaurant. What do you think of that idea Mary, would you like to do that sometime?" he asked.

"Yea I be likin thet idea. Hav lot o friends workin here, an I not be sure yet, but think Jacqueline be wantin me to Manage tha staff for there, an The Homestead. So be nice ta hav a night out with ya." replied Mary.

"Oh, guess that I miss-understood your job here Mary. Thought you were coming back to your old job." he said.

"No! Jacqueline don't be wantin me ta do any of tha hard work no more. Jus teach, an organize tha staff ta do it. Be strange ta me cause I still be fit, but she say thet she wants ta look afta me cause I be gettin older now, an she be wantin tha staff taught right, so that be what I be doin now here, an at Shallow Downs." Mary added.

"What a friend you have in Jacqueline, Mary. What a great job you have. Whatever happened between you two in your lives has cemented your friendship!" said Drew.

"Yea, I be no thet Drew. Maybe I be tellin ya one day!"

Conversation between them came to a halt as Drew pulled into the carpark at The Homestead. But then Mary spoke up as she looked at the vehicle parked beside. "Looks like Jacqueline havin a visitor. Nice car they hav!"

Drew raised his hand to hide the wry smile from Mary as he spoke. "Could be! But Jacqueline said they will be waiting out in the garden for us. She has organized some afternoon tea, so we are to go straight in." uttered Drew.

"Oh, thet's good. I be hungry now. Was too busy taday ta hav lunch. Cup o tea, an som food be good." she said.

Jacqueline and Mitchell were sitting in the garden. They both looked up when Drew called hello at the entrance.

"Oh good! Do come in Mary, and Drew, please take a seat!" Jacqueline said, as she added. "Mary, I have taken the liberty to arrange some food to be brought out to us. I take it, like me, you haven't eaten lunch today?"

Mary, and Drew offered greetings to them both, then Mary spoke as she sat down. "You be right Jacqueline! Jus too busy taday fer lunch, an me be starving, so thank ya!"

"Good! Oh here it is now. So good timing you two. We shall speak as we indulge." She turned in her seat to speak to the waitress bearing the large tray "Thank you Marie! Just set it down, we can help ourselves. It looks a treat."

"You're welcome Missus! Good to see you Mary, and Drew! Enjoy the food, mum made it especially." she said.

Drew, and Mary both smiled, and offered a thank you, then Mary added. "So good ta see ya Marie. Me be comin back here ta work soon, so we be catchin up agin then."

"Oh really? That's so great to hear Mary as we have all missed your smile, so will see you then. Enjoy your day!"

"Thet be so good ta hear Marie. I be lookin forward to thet, so say hello to everyone for me!" replied Mary.

"Will do!" said Marie as she retrieved the tray and left.

"Ok, let's dig in!" stated Mitchell in his country drawl.

They all laughed, and Jacqueline poured the tea as she spoke. "I suppose you could call this a celebration Mary. Drew has organized a special surprise for you today, and we have helped him in our own way with his venture by making it possible, so it is only fitting!"

Mary just stared at each of them, then made her reply.

"Jacqueline, afore ya goin on. Jus want ya ta know ya bin givin me nough now, an I be thankin ya so much, but please be stopping now, tis all too much ya done fer me!"

"You just let me be the judge of that my lady, however the surprise is not from Mitch, and myself, but from your husband, and I might say, a very loving husband to think of such a surprise. We have only assisted him." she said.

Mary looked into Drew's eyes. There was a twinkle there, and his grin was from ear to ear. "So tis only from ya after all, this surprise Drew?" she asked.

"Yes Mary!" he uttered and his laugh was so infectious that she had to laugh with him, and the others joined in.

"Now, if you are satisfied, when everyone is ready, we will all go and see it." Drew added.

"Oh, yes please Drew! I be lovin surprises." said Mary.

Jacqueline stood. "Well we have all finished eating, so now would be a good time. Lead the way Drew!"

Drew stood to take Mary's hand, and they all walked across the lawn towards the carpark.

"Where we be goin Drew, we bin drivin somewhere?" Mary asked as they entered the carpark.

"No Mary, this is it, we are here now, and there is your surprise." he said, as he pointed to the vehicle beside his. It was white with a spray of purple flowers up the side.

Mary's hands flew to her face. "This car is fer me? Ya not be serious Drew?" she asked, as she looked up at him, and tears flooded her eyes. Until she realized something.

"But I not be drivin it Drew. I neva be learnin ta drive!" she answered, as she looked desperately at him.

163

Drew looked at her, and answered with a chuckle. "I think between us all here, we have the perfect car for you. It is an older car but with 4WD, in case you get stuck on the dirt roads in the wet. Plus it is automatic, so it will be easier for you to learn how to drive, and that is where I come in. I will teach you how to drive at home."

"That be fine Drew, but what be the automatic?"

"It means Mary there will be no gears for you to worry about, just a shift lever, so it will be easier for you. Just keep in mind that it was Mitch who found the car at the right price, and he has done it up for you, and painted it."

"But Drew ya said…Mary started to complain. "I will be paying for the car, and Mitch's time Mary, if that is what you were going to ask!" he stated. "Is that ok?"

"Yea I be fine now. Jus can't believe I hav me very own car. Thank ya so much!" she said, as she hugged them all.

"Well, if that is settled we can move on Mary. We hope you enjoy your car. Congratulations!" Jacqueline stated.

"Yeah, congrats Mary. You'll be whizzing round soon enough. Drew, the car is registered to me, so when Mary is ready, just transfer the papers into her name. You will find the papers signed in the glove box." offered Mitch.

"Thank you Mitch, for everything you have done, and thank you Jacqueline." replied Drew earnestly.

Jacqueline spoke out then. "You are both so welcome! Now! I have to drive into town to visit Axel today, and Mitch has to get some stores from town, so he will drive your car home to your place, and I will follow to pick him up, if that is fine with you both?" she asked.

"Yes please, that is perfect Jacqueline." replied Drew.

"Oh, I jus be so excited! Thank ya Drew." said Mary, as she hugged him. "So we both be leavin fer home now!" she stated. "Will see ya out there Jacqueline, an Mitchell."

Jacqueline laughed at her, and said goodbye, then she looked at Mitch. "We did a good thing Mitchell Stringer, so thank you for all your help! You are just wonderful!"

"So are you Missus Coby-Stringer, and quite frankly I enjoyed doing that for Mary, and the old car has come up pretty good. It will last her a long time." he replied.

Axel Hall lived just one block from the hospital in a Housing Commission Unit. Jacqueline had dropped Mitch in town to get their stores, and she would pick him up after her visit with Axel. Now she parked her Jeep at the curb in front of his unit, and shut it down. She got out to lock it, then opened the wooden gate. It clicked behind her as she walked up the pathway towards the front door.

She rapped on the door and almost instantly Axel Hall appeared before her as he opened the door wide.

'He is much older now.' she mused. 'But still sprightly in step to get to the door so quickly.' However, there was one thing she noticed more about him that captivated her attention, and that was his flashing smile she had always loved. Such a genuine smile he had, which pulled his face into a huge grin, and his face lit up as he recognized her.

"Oh! It be Miss…."Sorry! I mean Missus Jacqueline!" he corrected himself quickly before she could reply. "Be so good ta see ya agin. Com in! Com in!" he stated, as he stepped aside to make room for her in the small entrance.

Jacqueline didn't bother correcting him. Axel Hall had

always called her Miss Jacqueline all her life. 'So Missus Jacqueline would suffice.' she thought, as she entered the room. Though small, it was neat, and clean, she noticed.

"Ya sit here Missus." he pointed to a chair. "I be puttin the kettle on, an we will hav tea if ya like?" he asked.

"I can't stay long Axel, but yes tea will be nice thank you. Mitch will be waiting in town for me to pick him up." However Axel was already starting to head for the door.

A xel disappeared, and when he returned he put two cups of tea on the table, and a plate of biscuits.

"Don't hav lot o visitors Missus Jacqueline. Tis good!"

"Thank you Axel, however there is a special reason for my visit today, but it is good to catch up. I trust you are well, and keeping in good health?" Jacqueline asked.

"Yea me be ok. Hav a girl from tha hospital thet checks on me, but am good. What of ya, an ya family?" he asked.

"We are all well also Axel, but I have news. I have just opened a Historic Museum at Shallow Downs. You must go out to have a look. Your painting is a show- stopper!"

Axel chuckled. "Yea I be so proud o thet there paintin. Tis so good! Even if I be sayin thet meself." he grinned.

"Which brings us to the main reason of my visit Axel." Jacqueline muttered, as she dug deep into her handbag.

"I have a cheque for you for the painting you done for the front gate. However for the restoration of the first one I have added a bonus to this cheque for its value. Call it a retirement fund if you like. You could go on a holiday, and set up a gallery displaying your paintings as they are priceless! I can also help you secure a location." she said.

Axel Hall stared hard at the cheque. His hands shook, then tears sprung immediately into his eyes, and for once he was lost for words, as he looked at Jacqueline, but before he had time to gather his wits, Jacqueline spoke up.

"Now you listen to me very, very carefully Axel Hall. You have earnt this money. So there will be no tears. Ok?"

Axel's voice was full of emotion when he spoke. "If ya say so Missus Jacqueline, but me dont deserve it. I hav me pension, an do som paintins fer cash, me jus can't hav me own gallery thet's all. Yea tha ocean, be wantin ta see thet. Plus Miss...sorry... Missus Jacqueline. I jus feel ya always be givin, an it be me who be owin ya more. I jus be feelin so sorry. Tis me fault fer what be happnen to ya, long......

Jacqueline looked so annoyed then cut him off quickly. "Do not ever say that again Axel! It was not your fault at all! I am still trying to bury the past behind me Axel, so I want you to do the same. Do you understand me? We will never speak of it again! Is that quite clear?" she asked.

"Yes Missus Jacqueline." Axel replied in a soft voice.

"Now! On a lighter note. If you have any paintings to show me I shall set up a gallery in the town for you, in my name, if you trust me to pay you for their sales." she said.

Once again the smile returned, and Axel beckoned her to follow to an outer lean-to where he worked on his art.

Jacqueline was captivated by his talent. "Just leave the gallery to me Axel as this work is magnificent. But why is this one covered?" she asked, as she removed a sheet, and stood rooted to the floor as an image of herself up upon the rearing back of her Stallion 'Sailor,' filled her vision.

"Oh how beautiful it is Axel! I was just sixteen." she said.

Chapter 12

As he drove slowly through the town, Cheyla became puzzled by the presence of barred windows which was quite obvious on the business establishments. He had never seen that before anywhere, it seemed quite odd.

He had travelled well and made good time during this stretch of the journey to reach his target for the day, so he was scanning the streets as he passed through searching for a Motel, with maybe a Restaurant that would suit him for the night's stay. It was that time of the afternoon just between sunset, and darkness, but the dusk almost made the streets seem eerie-like in the failing light.

'This town seems almost deserted as everything here is locked up and at the very least there should be someone walking the streets, but no!' he thought. He was starting to think that he wasn't going to detect a Motel that was open for business, but then finally he saw the sign ahead.

He realized that the Restaurant would close soon so he decided to eat first, so he took the turn-off into the carpark close to reception, and parked adjacent to the Restaurant.

He walked over, and grabbed a room key at Reception before approaching the entrance doors of the Restaurant.

It was the Motel Manager who greeted him at the desk, he realized, when he looked down at the business cards as they were introducing themselves. Then as they shook hands, they then became more acquainted as they spoke, and the conversation flowed between them.

"So Charles, tell me. Why is the town deserted like?" asked Cheyla. "Haven't seen a town quite like it in all my travels this last month or so. I was beginning to think that there was no bed or feed tonight until I saw your sign!"

Charles looked up at him to reply. "This is a sad town now Cheyla. Many white business owners have closed up shop, and left town, and the others still here have barred all their windows, but they all live here in fear. I guess the only reason why we are still here, is that I pay for security guards, but even that doesn't stop vandalism, and riots!"

"What vandalism? Who is causing these riots and why should people live here in fear?" asked Cheyla.

"It's the Aborigines! They have almost taken over the whole town. Even the police officers here turn a blind eye, they are scared of them too. So they pretty much have the run of the place now. Unless I sell, I'm not walking off like some have, but sometimes things can get rough here."

Cheyla's forehead creased into a deep frown as soon as he heard the Aboriginal people spoken about like that, and he really couldn't contemplate the reasoning.

"Are you sure they are Aboriginal people causing the problems here in town Charles?" he asked.

"Yeah Cheyla! No doubt about that! So if I was you, I would keep an eye on your vehicle while you eat. If you like, there is a spare garage you can lock it up for tonight."

CHEYLA

Cheyla was puzzled. He lived amongst the Aboriginal people. His best friend was Aboriginal and was raised by a clan of Aborigines or mainly Ol Mother whom he loved.

He looked Charles in the eye, and could detect that he was deadly serious, so he just replied. "Well, in that case Charles, I guess I will take you up on the offer of the lock up garage for tonight, thank you. However, right now I had better order dinner, or I will miss out. Sorry, I am not dressed accordingly but I haven't got time to shower, and change. I travelled about twelve hours today too."

"You look fine to me Cheyla. This here is a key for the garage." he said, as he pressed it into his hand. 'You can go in, and select a seat, then the waitresses will help you."

Finding a place to sit was not a problem for Cheyla as the dining room was almost deserted except for a few customers, but he took particular notice that he sat where he could see his 4WD in full view.

He picked up the menu just as a waiter arrived beside him. "Just a Johnnie with iced water thank you mate!" he said, and looked at the menu again to make his selection.

"Will do Sir!" said the waiter, and left him alone.

A waitress came to take his order of the largest steak he could order. So with that out of the way, and then with the arrival of his drink he sat in relaxation, as he sipped longingly at it, relishing the coolness, and the taste in his dry throat. 'It has been too long today. I will not be doing that again' were his thoughts, as his eyes glanced around the room, and then outside through the windows at his vehicle where, what he witnessed was unbelievable.

Cheyla pushed his chair back, and was running by the time he passed the front desk to rush for the doors.

"What is up Cheyla?" Charles called out as he passed.

"My car!" replied Cheyla over his shoulder as he burst out through the doors to the outside, with The Manager hot on his heels, just as the floodlights lit the carpark.

As Cheyla quickly took in the scene he yelled loudly.

"Hey! Get away from that 4WD you boys!" But his plea fell on deaf ears as they laughed, not even bothering to look up as they continued what they were intending.

There was four youths Cheyla noted, and the youngest two of them were letting his tyres down. One was trying to remove his number plates, but it was the older boy that Cheyla was watching carefully who had stepped up very calmly with a tyre lever lifted high, and Cheyla ran.

Charles was finding it hard to keep up the pace, but he actually stopped dead in his tracks as he watched Cheyla, then listened intently, as he heard a strange dialect, alien to his ears, suddenly erupt from Cheyla's mouth.

Cheyla was calling out wildly but to no avail. Though he was almost upon them, there was no response at all from them until subconsciously, and unintentionally, he switched into a language of their own tongue, then yelled.

Surprisingly all the youths reacted immediately to the familiar words. Now the silence fell over them like a veil, and they all became subdued, but more-so when Cheyla reached out then wrenched the tyre lever from the oldest Aboriginal boy's hand with such lightning speed that the boy stood amazed, and stumbled trying to step back from him when Cheyla towered over him, threatening like.

Now he stood back meekly as Cheyla began giving him a dressing down in his own language he understood so well. He was not used to someone telling him what to do, but when he looked the big man over his better sense prevailed, and he listened to what he was saying. 'He be just so damn huge, we won't escape him.' he thought.

Then surprisingly he noted that while at the exact time of his lecture, this guy had opened the boot to retrieve his tools, and a foot-pump, and was now giving out orders to the others in his gang in the same tongue, only they could understand. He just stared blankly up at Cheyla with total confusion as he detected the proficiency that he had in the knowledge of their language. 'How thet be?' he thought.

Charles was mesmerized as he ambled up just in time to witness the events. One youth was pumping tyres up, another replacing a number plate. But the leader of the gang, the oldest boy, he was just hanging back, afraid-like, but very much chastised as his face soon paled from the wrath that was emanating from Cheyla's mouth as he leaned in close to his face to make a point, his green eyes dark, fierce, and blazing with anger, and the boy cringed, and backed away, and Cheyla glared hard at him.

Cheyla walked around his car to check it out, then he spoke to them all, looked up to the leader of the gang, and waved his hand as if in dismissal, and stared them down.

Quickly, with a word from their leader, they all started to disperse, but very quietly, until Cheyla called to them, and they stopped in their tracks, and turned to listen.

To Charles, it seemed that Cheyla spoke his piece with

conviction though he wasn't sure, he couldn't understand a word of it. Then to his surprise, the youths replied, then turned, and walked away in silence. No-one looked back, but Cheyla stepped back to stand beside Charles. Then he stood tall to watch their departure until they had left the premises, and finally became out of sight down the street.

Charles strained his neck just to look up into Cheyla's face in admiration, then he spoke to him seriously.

"That was quite impressive Cheyla! We could use a man like you around here to deal with those Aboriginals, and others like them who roam the streets just to cause trouble here. Are you interested in staying?" he asked.

Cheyla laughed. "Would love to help out George, but I think I have done my bit, so you may see some changes here! However, I am on an important mission that is very personal to me, but as we speak time is getting away, and I have a long, long way to go yet." he replied.

"A shame Cheyla! Would love to see more of you, but changes you say, what changes?" George asked.

"I had a long talk to all of them, just to remind them of their Heritage, and what they learnt growing up, and that they are a disgrace to their forefathers who gave them the knowledge to survive the bush, and of their bush art, and dance that was passed down through the tribes, and also their ability of being the best trackers in the bush."

"These are the things they should be teaching white men. To work with them to introduce Aboriginal Culture instead of abusing it by their actions in this town, causing the Aboriginal name to dragged in the dirt." Cheyla said.

Charles gaped at him. "You told them all that and they listened? I find that hard to believe, though I guess I was there to witness you speaking to them, and in another tongue as well. I take it you can speak their own language Cheyla, but where did you learn that from?" he asked.

"Well, it is a long story Charles, and one of the reasons I am travelling. So I won't go into that personal stuff. I just learnt the Aboriginal tongue at an early age." he replied.

"As a matter of fact Charles, I have an Aboriginal man who is my best friend at home, but that's enough about that now, though I feel quite sure you will witness some changes here in the town now. At least I hope so, but you may have to help to get them moving Charles. Now can we go inside so I can finally eat dinner, I am starved."

"Yes, of course your dinner. I had forgotten about that. I am so sorry Cheyla, I will join you for dinner if you like, and rest assured now I know that these Aboriginals have some talent to share within the Community, I will be right there for them, and help to get them started." he said.

"Good man Charles. That's good to hear. You will find when you get to know them better that they will be quite timid, and might need some encouragement. Yes, please join me for dinner, and we can discuss some things then!"

"Very well! Come on then Cheyla." Charles urged him to walk with him, and added. "Let me re-order your food Cheyla, maybe I can come up with something special for you as a celebration for the occasion."

"Sounds good to me Charles." replied Cheyla as they approached the Restaurant doors, and walked inside.

"I will grab us a table George, and get some drinks. I

175

drink Johnnie with ice-water, what about you." he asked.

"No, no Cheyla! I shall order drinks, then the waiter will bring them over to our table. That is the least I can do, and dinner is on me as well, so you just make yourself comfortable Cheyla, I won't be long." he chuckled.

'Ok then, thanks Charles!' Cheyla was about to reply, but Charles was already on his way, hurrying towards the kitchen, so Cheyla selected a table, and sat down.

'What a day!' he thought to himself. 'I am bushed.'

Then his thoughts roved to the next day. 'Tomorrow I have to put in at least seven to eight hours driving. Then continue with a shorter trip the next day. That should get me to my destination about mid-morning. So on arrival, I should be able to look around Shallow Siding a little.'

Almost as soon as Charles arrived back at his table, the waiter arrived with their drinks, and they sat in deep conversation as to how he could help the Aboriginal people display their craft in shops, and also the possibility of getting them work on the properties out of town.

"This could be a big turn-around for this town Cheyla. If the Aboriginals will work with me, I will do all I can to make it happen. To get their culture recognized, get them appropriate jobs according to their skills." said Charles.

"Sounds like a good plan Charles! Just pleased I could help in a small way. I know that you will follow through to the best of your ability." replied Cheyla.

"Oh you have helped me heaps Cheyla, more than you know. I can't thank you enough and I have other people here that would only be too pleased to help out." he said.

Once again in the darkness of morning Cheyla left the Motel, and pulled out onto the highway. He set out in a northerly direction for his trip planned for the day.

Even though darkness hid the terrain, he could sense a difference in the countryside he was driving into. Then as day broke, the sun in its usual brilliance, soon became an oppressive heat bearing down on the earth. Though it was still only early in the morning then the real truth was revealed to him as he gazed out upon the bare paddocks dried out like rivulets from a long-term drought, and the bush country was like no other he had seen before.

'Sheep country' he realized. 'But what's here for them to eat?' he wondered, as he gazed forlornly at the pathetic animals trying to grab what little they could nibble from the cruel earth, and they left a trail of others behind them that had not been able to survive the harsh conditions.

'Poor beggars' he mused. 'They have no chance unless it rains. Rain, where was the rain? Didn't it rain out here like other places?' Cheyla felt like he was in another land.

Later in the day after he had stopped to grab food at a small town, he noted that now the earth had turned black. 'Black mud it would be in the wet.' he said to himself in a silent prayer as he noticed some of the road was untarred, and would have been a slippery journey in the wet.

For the first time the Countryside depressed him, and he felt sorrow for the animals out there living in this harsh bush of The Outback, and was thankful at the close of the day when he came upon a small town which was his stop, his target for the day, where he could relax for the night.

'Thank the lord. Just a short trip tomorrow.' he mused.

Chapter 13

Shallow Siding was not at all what he expected it to be. Especially not like some of the towns, or Countryside he had driven through the previous day. On the approach into town, the main road seemed to imitate the railway line, which snaked its way around the hills. He drove past paddocks of lush pastures, which deviated somewhat as he entered a beautiful valley where the township nestled.

Then he noted a deep flowing river under the timbers as he crossed the bridge into town, which at first glance, seemed to throw you back in history of by-gone years.

It was a town alive with expectations, and promise, as activity was everywhere he looked. 'It is a typical Railway Town, a last link to The Outback.' he guessed, from what he was told about it. He noticed that The Historic Railway Station in all its glory, seemed to dictate a certain type of mood, setting a Historic theme, for this neatly organized Outback Country Town, spreading up through the valley.

Cheyla drove slowly into town. A Hotel-Motel sign caught his attention, and he veered off the road to park at the curb in front. 'Well I am finally here at last, but I have covered almost half of Australia getting here.' he thought.

He gathered his thoughts together. 'What now? What would be my best option in my search for Mary?'

Shutting the engine down, he sat to ponder. 'Maybe I should try to find someone who knows her. But where?'

Slowly he opened the door to climb out from his 4WD, then locked it as he stepped on a path in front of the Hotel.

'Please let it be that I find everything I am seeking here in this town. I desperately need a rest, but that can wait until tonight. First things first, then I will check this town out. This trip has taken its toll, but I will bounce back.'

However, tomorrow…Let the real search begin…

He ducked his head down as he pushed inwards on the entrance doors. Then he walked across the dimly-lit room to the bar, pulled up a stool, and sat down.

"Hi mate, what will it be?" asked the bartender.

"Hi there! I will have a Johnnie with iced water, thank you mate, and is there any lunch on?" added Cheyla.

"Yeah sure, lunch is on now! My name is Tom by the way. We have lunch served in the dining room, or if you prefer you can order here for a bar meal, and sit anywhere here!" was his reply, as he handed a menu to Cheyla.

"Hi Tom! Name's Cheyla." he said taking the menu to momentarily glance at it. "Well the lamb roast sounds ok to me Tom, and with some coffee will do fine!"

As they shook hands Tom asked. "So are you passing through town Cheyla, or staying? You will find we have great accommodation here, the best in town!" he boasted.

"That is good to hear. Yeah, I am staying, so I will need to book a room. Say a week at a time until further notice."

"No problem Cheyla! I will get it sorted for you now!"

"Better order your lunch first. Just need your last name for the room booking. Then after your lunch, you can go into reception to sign, and get your key." offered Tom.

"Sounds good Tom, thanks. My last name is Stone!"

Tom gave him the thumbs up, and Cheyla watched as he walked down towards the end of the bar to cross the room, and disappeared through the kitchen door.

Cheyla used the respite to take in the surroundings. Though the room had very little lighting turned on, there was also arched windows that let in natural light, making the mood very cosy, and comfortable, and presence of the Historic theme was evident in paintwork, and furniture.

There were two men deep in conversation at the end of the bar, an older aboriginal lady sat alone in a corner cradling her drink. Apart from them the room was empty.

'Well it is a week day, and lunch-time.' mused Cheyla.

Tom's voice alerted him as he placed his drink on the bar top. "There you go Cheyla, enjoy! Lunch shouldn't take long, and your room is all sorted. Got you a good one off the back deck overlooking the pool, and close to the laundry, seeing you are staying a while. So you just need to see Veronica at reception at some point after lunch."

"Good man, thank you Tom." replied Cheyla.

"So what brings you to Shallow Siding Cheyla? Have you got friends here, or are you looking for work. I may be able to help with some names if you are?" he asked.

"Tom, I have travelled half way around Australia to get here but not to visit or work. I'm seeking an aboriginal lady named Mary Higgs. Do you know her?" he queried.

O ver at the corner table, the lady lifted her head to the mention of the name 'Mary Higgs.' Her ears pricked as she listened closely to the conversation over at the bar.

She looked hard at the man asking the questions. 'Thet face be familya me thinks, why thet be?' she thought. 'But maybe not, would be rememberin thet there body. He be jus so big! I be neva forgit thet huge man if I be no'in him.'

Suddenly as to make no noise, she eased her chair back to stand up, then she left her table quickly, but quietly to walk across the room to disappear through a side door.

"Can't say that I know a lady by that name Cheyla, but I'm still to meet a lot of the locals here as I haven't worked here long enough to know them all. However I know that Vera over there is an Agoriginal, she may know her!" he pointed to the corner table, as he strained to look around Cheyla. "Oh! She's gone. She was there only a minute ago. Well maybe you will run into her at some time. She works here, and does the laundry for the Hotel Motel." he said.

Cheyla remembered seeing a woman earlier sitting in the corner. He thought nothing of it, but replied to Tom.

"Never mind Tom, it is only my first day, but thank you for your help." he said, as his buzzer rang. "Oh lunch! Excuse me while I get that. We will talk again Tom."

"Yeah sure Cheyla, enjoy your lunch!" replied Tom.

Cheyla went to the servery, collected his lunch, then sat at a table near the window where he could look out at the street, and observe his surroundings.

'Only a small town really.' he noted. 'Surely it couldn't be that hard to find one person.' he thought, as he poured coffee into his cup, added milk, and relished the taste.

He fell on the roast dinner with a vengeance, realizing he hadn't eaten a roast meal since he left home. 'Home.' he thought. 'So far away. He should call Jono tonight.'

With lunch over, Cheyla decided that he had plenty of time to check the town out, but he wanted to get his key from reception so he approached the bar, and rang a bell.

Tom appeared from the back room, and stood before him. "Hope you enjoyed lunch Cheyla?" he asked.

"You bet Tom! Good home cooking, just like home."

"I have some info about meal times Cheyla. Breakfast, dinner, and lunch is served in the dining room, or you can order in room service delivered to your room. Lunch, and dinner is also available in the Bar. The laundry near your room is available for use any time after 11am daily, and there is a car park at the rear of the Hotel for guests, with access to your room. Now if you want to go to reception, the entrance is to the side of The Hotel off the boardwalk from the front. From in here just use the exit to a hallway to get you there." he pointed the exit door out to him.

"All good, thanks Tom. I will have a little look around this town this afternoon, see you later." he said.

"Yeah, see you Cheyla, and good luck!" replied Tom.

"Thanks Tom, but I hope luck doesn't come into it!"

Cheyla walked across to the exit then took the hallway along to reception where he wasted no time there. He just paid a deposit for the booking, grabbed his room key, and left through the entrance door to step onto the boardwalk, then strolled out towards the pathway of the main street.

He was eager to explore now, and strode out strongly.

Shallow Siding had everything on offer, he noted, for a Small Country Town. He took a particular interest in The Community Town Hall building built of sandstone in a Heritage theme set back off the street, but an additional building fronted the street, so he crossed the street to read the articles in the window. He noticed artwork displayed that he thought was very well done, and being interested in art, he noted the local artist's name on the paintings on the shelves, so he strolled inside to look around.

There was a billboard, and brochures of 'Things to do' in Shallow Siding, and he plucked one from the shelf.

'Looks like the properties in this area have a lot to offer also' he thought. 'The Outback Bush Camp' operated, and owned by renowned tracker, and hunter Pete Stringer' he read. 'Wouldn't mind seeing that place, and meeting that guy.' thought Cheyla. But then one other advertisement caught his eye, captivating his attention. He paled as his gut churned when he read the name of the property. Re-discover 'Shallow Downs' it read. Newly opened Center. The Historic Museum at 'Shallow Downs' which portrays memorabilia of A Legend of the Outback. 'Clayton Coby.'

"Why is it that the name 'Shallow' strikes such a chord with me?' he wondered. 'I may never know.' he stressed, as he recalled his Ol Mothers' final words of his naming.

'Only thing I know is… I have to go to this place too, as this particular property 'Shallow Downs' seems to be calling me I feel. But why? Though somehow I just feel at last that I am in the right place to find my Mother because there is just too much familiar to me in this town. It is uncanny, and I will find Mary Higgs. I just know I will!'

Deep in thought he moved over to where the paintings were displayed. Smaller ones sat upon the shelves, but the larger Artwork, mainly of Landscapes, dressed the walls. Local Artist, 'Axel Hall' the caption read.

'Very talented artist,' were Cheyla's thoughts. He had a liking for art, and had come to appreciate fine art, but especially art with scenes of The Australian Outback, and he was thinking of his own property, and his art collection when the voice beside him interrupted his thoughts.

"Do you need any help Sir?" the voice uttered.

Anne Hardy walked briskly through the front door of display center for The Community Town Hall , then headed towards the section near the Billboard displaying 'Things to do in Shallow Siding,' and began restacking the shelves with brochures. It was an honorary job she done in her spare time to get the artwork from Axel, scan them, and add text, and then print up all the brochures at home. She even served in the 'For Sale' section when she was in.

She glanced across to the back wall where she noticed a very huge, but young man standing there looking at the paintings. She knew he was a stranger in town, so when she was finished her brochure drop she then moved over closer to him, and asked. "Do you need any help Sir?"

Cheyla was suddenly startled, then spun around to face the person who had spoken. His golden hair fell long, and loosely across his forehead, but his green eyes met hers squarely at a short distance, and he heard her gasp.

Confused, but so uncertain, he replied. "Oh, afternoon Missus! I'm interested in the paintings. Are any for sale?"

Anne Hardy stood rooted to the spot. Her hand flew to her mouth as she gasped. Then she shivered, as if someone had just walked over her grave, and she almost felt like she was staring at a ghost from the past.

Only trouble was, when she finally came to her senses, Anne knew deep in her gut who she was looking at as she gazed into those trademark eyes of the deepest green.

She composed herself quickly to reply. "I'm so sorry!" she apologized. "For a moment there, I thought you were someone else. Please excuse me for being startled." but to herself, she vowed. 'There was no way she would disclose anything to this beautiful looking person, though secretly she longed to hug him. Oh no Anne! That pact with Jackie was done and dusted so long ago but unfortunately now the sands of time have turned. But who will speak up?'

"Oh! The paintings? Yes the paintings are all for sale young man." she finally said. "Anything you like there?"

Cheyla chuckled at the thought of maybe having a double. "Oh, no worries Missus, and the paintings...Well I love them all...But I will take this one if that is ok?" he asked, as he removed one from the wall.

"You know what young man you certainly know your art." laughed Anne, and I am sorry to say, but this one is the most expensive." she pleaded to those beautiful eyes.

Cheyla laughed. "That is ok Missus, I can afford it."

Anne looked up, and smiled. "Please call me Anne!"

He put out his hand. "Pleased to meet you Anne. My name is Cheyla Stone." he replied, as their hands met.

'Cheyla?' she mused. Her smile was a knowing smile, as she knew the name's meaning, as she gripped his hand.

'It was a name Aboriginals used for Shallow Downs a long time ago. But 'Stone,' was a mystery.' she thought.

'Oh my god Jacqueline!' she stressed. She was so sure of her thoughts, but she needed more to convince herself.

'What will Jacqueline do about this?' she wondered.

Cheyla looked at her as he paid by card, then she was wrapping his painting. 'She looks a little frazzled.' he thought, but put those thoughts aside when he asked.

"Can I leave the painting here for a while Anne? I was about to check out the town, but got waylaid here."

Anne looked up at him. "Oh a traveler! So you're new in town Cheyla, where do you hail from? So if you plan on staying in Shallow Siding long, where will you stay?"

"Just arrived today. I drove all the way from Tenna in the Northern Territory Anne! But, no! I'm not a traveler, but I have travelled far. I came here specifically to search for a lady. An aboriginal woman named Mary Higgs! You may have heard of her, have you?" he asked hopefully.

Anne nearly passed out, as she swayed on her feet, but Cheyla put out a hand to steady her. "Are you feeling ok Anne?" he asked in concerned voice.

"I will be okay Cheyla, it has been a long day. Guess I have done a little too much today!" she tried to laugh it off. 'Where was it you said you were staying?' she asked, trying to change the subject to avoid his question. "If you like, I could drop your painting off there." she suggested.

"I am booked in at The Heritage Hotel Motel over on the corner Anne. Room 9 at the back." he replied.

"I am leaving soon, so I will drop it at reception." she said.

Cheyla thanked her for her trouble, then walked out to stand on the front pavement deep in thought.

'Was she avoiding my question just then? No of course not! Why would she anyway?' he pondered, as he took in the beauty of the Jacaranda's in bloom all along the center of the wide street adding colour, and life to it.

'They should flower right through to almost summer!' he thought, then he looked to the sky. For the first time he thought about the weather. 'It's hot here, but not the same heat I felt when driving through the Outback bush towns yesterday. It is only early October, but for some unknown reason, this town nestled in the valley, seems almost to be protected from the elements a little. Maybe by those big mountains.' he thought, as he looked up at them.

Convinced of his theory, he looked around then at the buildings all painted in Historic colours, and silently he commended the owners for all their input. However, one sign captured his attention that was more to his liking.

'Shallow Siding Saddler' the sign read, so immediately he stepped off the path, and crossed the road once again.

Anne was watching him standing on the footpath, then she noticed he was crossing the road. She felt sick to her stomach knowing what she had to do, but her questions were all answered, so there was no way out of it now. She must go to Jacqueline, and warn her of her findings. That would mean a drive out to The Outback Gardens, but she knew what she had to say couldn't be said in a phone call.

Cheyla strode to a cobblestone path leading down the alleyway beside the shops, where behind sat the Saddler's shop with a frontage of at least two shops wide, and there was yards, stables, and a big shed out back. 'Looks like this guy has the monopoly around this area by the size of his shop.' thought Cheyla, when he approached the front doors. He ducked as he pushed them aside, and went in.

A young girl maned the reception desk, but it was the saddler that addressed Cheyla first.

"Mornin mate! Jed Owens is me name. I be tha Owner here. I guess ya must be new in tha town, I haven't seen ya afore. Can I help ya with anythin?" he asked.

Cheyla had been reading the sign on the counter, then he looked up to reply. "Hi Jed. Yes I have only just arrived here. I was just going to have a look around, but I see now you have horses out back for hire, and that would suit me well enough. My name is Cheyla Stone!"

"Well Cheyla, tha most times we be takin bookins for horse hire. That is if I hav one thet fits you!" he chuckled.

Cheyla smiled, letting him have his joke, then replied.

"Oh I don't mean right now! I was thinking of early tomorrow morning. Say 7am if that is ok?" he asked. "Feel I need to relax a little, have been driving a long way, so a horse ride is just the ticket. However, I would like to hire your horse for most of the day if that is possible?"

"Hope ya don't mind me joke Cheyla? Don't ofen hav customers your size, but it be all good. So I be bookin ya in fer tomorra. I hav a big chestnut stallion thet would suit ya purpose. Yea, a good ride thet one. If ya want ta hav a wander out tha back ta tha stables, ya will see me horses in tha yards. So ya be jus travellin, are ya. How long ya be stayin here in Shallow Siding Cheyla?" he asked.

"Oh, that is great, thanks Jed! Well I am not sure how long I am staying yet. I came here in search of a lady. Her name is Mary Higgs, she is an Aboriginal woman. Maybe you have heard of her Jed?" Cheyla queried, as he looked at him, just in time to see a shadow pass across Jed's eyes.

He thought Jed paled a little, and that his reply was a touch spasmodic, and he wondered why.

"Sorry. Me can't say thet I do no her Cheyla. This here lady be a friend of yours, is she?" he asked.

"Well let's say she is a friend, of a friend. Never mind Jed! I might go outside now, see you tomorrow." he said.

"Yea, ta be sure Cheyla. Be seein ya tomorra mornin!" came the reply and he watched as Cheyla walked outside.

'Wonder what he be wantin with Mary?' he thought.

Cheyla was confused, and his thoughts roamed, as he absently noted the stable doors, and pushed them in hard.

'That guy was holding back something, but what?'

As he flung the doors back he started to barge through.

In that same instant Tarryn Westley was about to walk through from the other side carrying a saddle, the saddle cloth, and bridle, until he sent her flying into the dust.

Cheyla looked down in disbelief as he noticed the girl sprawling in the dust. "God damn it! I'm so sorry Miss! It is my fault entirely. I was so deep in thought, and wasn't thinking!" he stuttered, holding out a hand to help her up.

Shunning his hand she rose up in a blanket of thick, jet black hair. Her eyes glared up at him. "Was I just hit by a truck?" she jested, as she gathered her riding gear. "Like hitting a brick wall!" she quipped, then turned and left.

CHEYLA

Cheyla put a hand up in attempt to stop her, or at least explain, but he was left standing there with not even one word uttered, and he just gaped as she walked away.

'Her fury was understandable. I was at fault! Though, she did try to laugh it off!' he thought. However, he knew it was in that instant as their eyes met, that the real beauty of her engulfed him. He felt it wrenching, deep in his gut.

He had never seen a woman as beautiful as she was at that moment. She seemed so wild, so carefree, as her thick black hair floated like a cloud about her. He felt a shock like electricity clash between them, and something passed across her dark stormy eyes, as they bored into his own.

'Was she flirting with him?' he wondered. 'Or? Much worse! Was she chastising him in more sinister way?'

He only knew that something unusual just took place between the two of them, and some affinity with her was happening. Something that Cheyla had never, felt before.

Quickly he shook off the strange feelings like a spaniel shedding water, then resumed his senses to immediately head around the corner, and walk out to the back yards.

'She was tall.' he noticed. Her mount was saddled, and ready. Her leg muscles flexed showing strength in those long, beautifully shaped legs clad in tight-fitting riding pants, as she lifted her leg to the stirrup of the huge horse.

"Wait!" he called. "I will help you!" he added.

She paused. Her long thick jet black hair flared around her when she spun her head back to face him. "Well, if it isn't the big, strong man!" she mocked. "Do I look like I need your help?" she chuckled, her scorn evident, as she jumped to sit astride then kicked the horse to a full canter.

He felt embarrassed, intimidated even. Something he was not used to, especially from a woman. Women usually chased him, not the other way around. 'Damn her then!' he thought. But as he watched her galloping away across the paddock, her black hair flying out behind her, he could not restrain the constricting feeling in his chest.

'I wonder who she is?' he mused. 'I must meet her, she obviously comes here to ride so that is something we have in common. We are bound to meet again. Well hopefully we do. I just have to know her name and speak to her!'

Strange as it was, suddenly he felt dejected and turned to walk back to the main street, where he stood to ponder his next movements. 'I think I should just go back to the Motel now.' he decided. 'I have just about had enough for one day, though today has been an interesting one, and eventfull not to say the least. But I am getting no-where with my search for Mary, the people around here are just closing up. I wonder why? But now, I have just bumped into this girl, a total stranger who has affected me in a way that I never felt was possible before. So now here I stand in strange territory, not knowing how to re-act to her. But I would like to know her a little more.' he thought. 'I guess tomorrow is another day! Who knows what will happen?'

Cheyla couldn't get the girl off his mind, so he grabbed a bottle of Johnnie at the bottle-o, picked up his painting from reception, and ordered his dinner to eat in his room.

As soon as he entered his room he started to unwrap the painting, then he sat it up on a shelf on the wall so he could study it while he was having a stiff drink.

'This artist is tops his painting is priceless!' he thought.

CHEYLA

'From the gum trees in the foreground, to purple hues of shaded mountains beyond, and of Jacaranda's in town. This Landscape of Shallow Siding in the Valley had it all.'

Anne Hardy gathered her belongings ready to leave the Center, so she went to retrieve Cheyla's artwork to deliver it for him, but struggled with the huge painting.

She couldn't even get it to the front door, let alone out to her car, so she decided to phone Jake, her husband who was at The Historic Railway Station where he worked as The Station Master, to explain her dilemma.

Jake braked out front of The Display Center. He shut the car off, then got out to walk inside, where he instantly noticed Anne standing at the counter shaking like a leaf.

"What is wrong pumpkin?" he asked when he noticed what state she was in. "Why are you shaking?"

"Oh Jake, thank god you are here! Can we talk at home please? Just not here in case someone overhears me, but I have the worst news, so distressing you won't believe it!"

"Yes of course Anne!" Jake replied as he looked at her.

"There is just one thing I have to do. I have promised to deliver this painting but I'm struggling to lift it. Would you deliver it to the pub on the corner at reception?" she asked. "I will follow you home then in my car."

"Ok, no problems!" Jake replied, then gave a chuckle. "So who is the painting for Anne?' he queried.

Anne passed him a note. "Jake I've written the man's name down for you. It is Cheyla Stone in room 9!"

"Yes, sure pumpkin." he replied. "But you drive safe!"

"I'll be fine Jake, I will meet you at home!" said Anne.

Chapter 14

Mary heard the whispered reports. Phone calls were coming thick, and fast, to send chills up her spine.

It was her day off. She took the first call having her first cuppa, and walked out to the deck with her mobile.

It was Vera whispering at the other end of the line as if someone was listening to her important conversation.

"Mary! It be me Vera. Someone be lookin fer ya child!" she said softly. "Me not tell, jus snuck away afore he could talk ta me, but me heard him askin fer ya child at tha bar. He be big, big man Mary, but a youngin an fer som reason I be feelin I be knowin him afore. Why thet be child?"

*****

Then come the call from Jed, even before breakfast.

"Mary! Hi, it be Jed here, tha saddla here in tha town. Hav ta tell ya Mary, someone be askin for ya in me shop. Big guy, but me tell him nuthin, so ya take care ya here!"

*****

But it was Anne's call that put fear in Mary's heart. Her voice was shaky as she mumbled. "Mary. It's Anne! Be prepared for the worst. He is here! I am sure it is him, so I am going out to warn Jackie, but he is asking for you!"

*****

Mary's hand shook as she snapped the phone shut.

195

Drew walked out on the deck. "Breakfast!" he called, as he struggled out with the large tray, upon which sat two plates of bacon, and eggs, and two coffees.

"Mary?" he stated in a concerned voice, as he noticed she was curled up into a ball upon the settee, and sobbing her heart out. "Whatever is wrong?" he asked, as he set the tray down, and went to sit at her side.

Mary just put her arms around his neck, and her tears soaked his shirt, as she buried her face close into his body, and she sobbed into his chest. Deep, heart wrenching sobs that took him totally by surprise. He had never seen Mary as upset about anything before, and in response, his voice became choked with emotion, as he tried to speak to her.

"Mary please stop crying. You will make yourself sick. Whatever is wrong Mary? Please talk to me!" he said.

Her head lifted, but her eyes swimming with tears met his, and in a voice choked with despair, she finally spoke.

"I be havin three phonecalls jus this mornin warnin me thet someone be lookin fer me in tha town Drew. Last one be from Anne, so no fer sure it be no mistake now!"

"Whatever do you mean by that Mary? Who would be looking for you, and do you know who it is?" he asked.

Mary wiped her eyes on her sleeve, and sat up in the chair, trying to be as serious as she could when she spoke.

"There be something I hav ta tell ya now Drew, so ya will no why me be so upset. An we spoke o this not long ago, but now be tha time ta tell ya bout Jacqueline, an me when we was young, an why she be so protectin of me!"

Drew feared the worst, and really thought that Mary was about to reveal something of dread from her past.

196

However she continued in a calm voice so he listened intently, hoping he wouldn't hear anything too bad.

"This be a story bout Miss Jacqueline Coby, youngest daughter of Mel, and Clayton Coby from Shallow Downs, an what be happenin ta ha when she be only eighteen, ta make ha leave ha Father, ha friends, ha home at Shallow Downs, an tha town Shallow Siding. Neva ta return agin fer thirty-one years. An be also bout ha servant, an friend Mary Higgs, who be leavin all ahind ta leave with ha, care fer ha, share ha pain, till she return, an bring ha back.

Mary looked up sadly at him, and he could tell this was going to be a very long story, so he responded.

"Mary, you need your strength! I can tell this has taken a huge toll on you, whatever it is that has happened now, and I know I haven't heard your full story as yet. But, first things first. How about we relax a little, have some coffee, and eat our breakfast, then you can continue?"

"Yea, guess ya be right Drew. I be feelin bit sick. So we be doin as ya say. This here story be a long one, an ya have ta know thet, afore I be tellin ya what be happenin now!"

After the break Mary looked at Drew decidedly. "I be startin now Drew. Tis way back when we was young, an me bein Miss Jacqueline's servant. I be startin when she be eighteen, she said, as the tears rolled down her cheek.

Drew watched Mary's face closely as the unbelievable words tumbled from her mouth of the anguish they had been through together, and he could not comprehend the plight of these two young girls in their flight, as they both strived for normality together, and tears filled his eyes.

197

He shook his head in total shock as her story ended.

"Are you ok Mary?" he asked, in a soft voice.

"Yea me be ok Drew. It be bringin back bad memories fer Jacqueline, an me, thet we be tryin ta forgit. Now it be startin agin. Poor Jacqueline!" she sobbed. "What she be doin now? Tis tha worst news fer ha, I be thinkin."

"After hearing that heart-breaking story Mary, believe me, I do understand what you mean! There were a lot of unexplained things that are quite obvious to me now, so please forgive my ignorance. However, I just cannot stop thinking of Jacqueline Coby-Stringer, who she is now. She comes across to me as a rock solid personality, so full of determination, to be that other person seems outlandish!"

"How that poor girl ever coped is beyond me? Or even you, for that matter? What a true friend you have been to her Mary, to each other, and what a bond you two have!"

Mary looked at his sad face. "Ya no Drew, don't be sad fer Jacqueline! She be comin outer this. Ya hav no idea the determination thet there lady hav. Even when tha worst things be happenin to ha, she be jus takin it. Ya see Drew! It be ha determination thet got ha through!"

"An so we hav ta face up ta tha real truth here now!"

"What real truth is that Mary? What has happened?"

Mary's face was set like stone with her reply. "Ya see Drew. Thet there child be a boy, an he grow ta be a man! Now he be here in Shallow Siding lookin fer me, an I be guessin thet he be hopin I be noin where his Mother is at!"

"Oh no!" fretted Drew. "Are you going to Jacqueline?"

"No Drew! I be waitin here til he be findin me!"

Anne sat stone- faced on the seat beside Jake, as they drove out to The Outback Gardens next morning.

She looked at his pale face, his knuckles turning white on the steering wheel, and she felt his stress.

"God damn it!" he cursed, as he thumped the steering wheel. "God, please give this poor woman a break! How much pain does one have to suffer in a lifetime?" he said.

"Are you sure you're right pumpkin? We could stir up something for nothing here!" he stressed, staring at her.

"Trust me Jake. There can be no mistake and if you get to see him, then you will know what I mean. But for now, I have asked all the questions. I just know it in my heart!"

"So be it then, but we tread very carefully with Jackie. Who knows how she will react to this." he cautioned.

"You don't need to tell me that Jake. I know her like a sister, so whatever way she turns I will understand!"

Anne had called Jacqueline to tell her they were both coming out, and they found her sitting out in the garden.

"Oh Anne, Jake. What a lovely surprise to see you both come out. It has been a while!" Jacqueline rose to embrace them, then directed them both to the settees. Come, take a seat you two, and let us catch up on all the gossip. I have ordered some morning tea, so good timing on your part."

"Thanks Jackie! But this is not a social call in a sense, rather more like something we have to tell you, and must tell you!" stuttered Anne, as she sat down with relief.

"Really how interesting. Please tell...Oh here is our tea. Thank you Marie, I shall pour it!" Jacqueline said to the waitress. "Now do go on Anne, I'm all ears." she laughed.

"Jacqueline please be serious!" said Anne desperately.

"This is serious talk Jacqueline. Please give me all your attention. There is someone in Shallow Siding asking for Mary Higgs! I met him yesterday. He is a big man, about Pete's age I guess but something about him is so familiar!"

Jacqueline felt the hairs rising at the back of her neck, a warning maybe, or a sense of doom. But something was not right here. Anne never, ever called her Jacqueline.

"Please stop waffling on Anne, and get on with it. Just give it to me straight, so I know what it is that I am dealing with here. Is Mary in some sort of trouble?" she asked.

"Oh Jacqueline! Forgive me, but I don't know how…. Her voice trailed off….and her eyes smarted with tears, her hand shook as she lifted the tea to her lips in respite.

Jacqueline was so baffled. 'What is going on here?' she wondered as she looked to Jake. "Jake?" she demanded.

"Jackie we are both in shock but if you want it straight! Then here it is! Anne went to the display center yesterday to do her brochure drop and she met a young man there, he was a huge man named Cheyla Stone, and before you ask! She went to great depths in conversation with him! Where he came from, what he was doing here etcetera."

"He told her he came from The Northern Territory, a place called Tenna, just to find Mary Higgs. But it wasn't just answered questions that convinced Anne! It was how he looked! His face, but especially his eyes Jackie. If you meet him, then you too will know who he is, as we do!"

Jacqueline's face paled as if blood was being drained from it. She just stared at them with a vacant expression then she opened her mouth to speak, but no words came.

Her whole life flashed before her and her body reeled on the seat as she relived her secret past. A past that had finally caught up with her as the memories surfaced.

She was a young girl on the verge of breakdown when she lost her Mother to a raging house fire but it was shame that forced her to leave home at Shallow Downs deserting the one person she loved more than life itself. Her Father.

With her heart broken, a child was abandoned.
So deep was her sorrow for the decision she made so long ago, but there had been no options then, and maybe there still weren't. She was torn between a heart that ached for that child and realization of how it would affect her loved ones, it was too much to bear as she swayed side wards.

Jake reached out a hand to steady her. "Are you alright Jackie? I am so sorry. What can we do to help?" he asked.

Suddenly the heat rose up in Jaqueline's throat almost suffocating her. Then her face turned a crimson colour as she gasped to breathe and then screamed out with such a pathetic sound of anguish that she knocked the table over in her haste to escape. "Get out! Go home! Its lies, all lies!" she cursed them in fury. "No-one can help!"

Anne rose quickly to grab her arm, then she wrapped her arms around her friend, and pulled her close. "Listen to me now Jackie!" she said. "I will not be going anywhere until I know you are going to be alright, so whatever you decide, Jake and I will support you! You know that!"

"Remember Jacqueline Coby-Stringer that we have all been down that road before! So it will not be happening again. You have friends! Just settle down now and discuss it with us so we will know how to help you!" she pleaded.

Jacqueline paused as the words hit home. A memory of that time of events seemed like it was only yesterday.

As she looked at Anne her dearest friend, silent tears ran down her face to wet Anne's dress as she pressed her head into her chest then she began to sob heart-wrenching sobs that racked her whole body, and tore Anne apart.

"Oh poor Mitch, this will break his heart!" she sobbed.

"Well Jackie, it's not as if he doesn't know of your past. So you really don't know what his reaction will be, but if I know Mitch he will support your decision!" said Anne.

"Then there is Melissa!" sobbed Jacqueline.

"You are grabbing at straws now Jackie!" offered Jake. "Melissa is just a baby so she wouldn't even need to know yet, besides you should be concentrating on what is best for you! So you need to tell Mitch and discuss it!" he said.

"I think Jake is right Jackie. You have to talk to Mitch first before you do anything. Who knows what this young man wants from you? But you knew in your heart that it was bound to happen sometime. We just don't know how genuine this man is. Though I have to say when I met him, he was most polite. As a matter of fact, he was so beautiful I felt like hugging him because I felt he was a part of you!"

"So Jackie, I would suggest that you stay here at home and let Mary handle it. He is looking for her you know so Mary will tell you what she thinks, I am sure. So until you know some of these things it is pointless worrying."

Jacqueline lifted her head, and grabbed a handkerchief from her pocket to dry her eyes then spoke sincerely. "Thank you both, once again you've saved me from doing something stupid. I'll be ok I just need time alone now!"

Chapter 15

Cheyla was up before sun-up. He had ordered the first breakfast available of the morning to his room, along with some cut sandwiches, and bottles of water.

He showered, shaved, then tied his long wet hair with a leather throng at the back, and donned a scarf, and hat.

Dressing in clothes specifically for a long ride, he sat on the bed to pull on his boots. As an afterthought, he put a change of clothes, and a pair of shoes into a carry bag just as the knock, knock, on the slide window, alerted him of breakfast arriving, so he flicked the switch on the kettle.

Then he made coffee, and as he sat eating his breakfast his eyes drifted to the painting up on the shelf. He looked hard at it. 'So much talent.' he thought. 'Those colours are so life-like.' Then he detected that for the Artist to capture that particular angle, he would have to be above the scene that he was sketching, and he thought of the lay-out of the town. 'He must have been up on the mountain, maybe on the hillside somewhere, at least.' he thought absently.

'Time to go.' he mused, so he packed the food, and the drink into a canvas bag. Grabbed his gear, turned off the lights, locked his door, and started out for the saddlers'.

Jed looked up when Cheyla rapped on the door outside. "Come in, doors open!" he yelled, and beckoned Cheyla inside. Jed had a thriving business, but it was not due to his hard work, but his Father's. Jed's Mother was a pure Aboriginal woman, his skin had darkened just like hers, but his Father was a white man who had toiled for many years to build up the business to what it was now, and he taught Jed the art of being a saddler, as well as running a business. So when he passed on, naturally the business was handed down to Jed in his Father's will.

Cheyla ducked his head, and pushed the doors in as he entered. "Morning Jed, looks like it will be a nice day!"

"Mornin Cheyla. Yea its sure ta be a beauty. Good day fer a ride. Hav ya decided where ya be goin?" he asked.

"Yes Jed! I decided to ride out to The Outback Bush Camp. I would like to meet the Owner, and maybe look around a little. Any information, or some directions you can give me, would be mighty handy." replied Cheyla.

"Well it be bout a four mile trip Cheyla!" Jed said.

"That's fine, I am looking forward to going for a ride, plus I did say I would need the horse for most of the day!"

"Yea I be rememberin thet! So hav bin out ta bring in tha big Chestnut Stallion I be tellin ya bout. He be tied up at tha railin in tha yard. Jus get what bridle, saddle, an tha blanket ya be wantin out o tha stables shed, an there be saddle bags there too if ya want em." he added.

"Thanks heaps Jed!" replied Cheyla.

"Now, best way ta go by horseback is ta take the track along tha river, not tha road it be goin over tha hills. So be stayin this side o tha river, an ya will meet up with tha road on tha other side o them there hills, an then there be signs ta show ya tha way. Jus ride down ta tha river, an turn right at tha end. Ya can't be missin it. Take this here book too!" he offered, as he handed Cheyla a brochure.

"Well, looks like I am all set then!" Cheyla laughed. "I will be seeing you maybe late this afternoon Jed, thanks."

"Thet be fine by me Cheyla, I be chargin ya by tha hour ya know! If ya be real late, here be me card. Ring me, an I will come ta tha shop fer ya." then Jed gave him a card.

"Ok!" chuckled Cheyla. "Thanks for everything Jed. I will get going now!" he said, as he walked to the door, gave a wave, and went outside, and over to the stables.

Cheyla got what he needed from the shed, then went to the yards out back where the big stallion stood.

He opened the gate, then went inside to stack his gear on the ground, as he approached the big horse. Tenderly he stroked his muzzle, and let his other hand slide across his shoulder, and along his back. 'Well! I guess it is just you, and me big red." he muttered, and the horse snorted.

Cheyla laughed as he picked up the blanket to place it on his back. "Don't get too cocky big red, we are going on a long ride, let's hope you have stamina for it?" he added, as he threw the saddle up, then began to tighten up the buckles. He put his belongings in the saddlebags. Food, and drink, on one side, and his clothes, and shoes, on the other, then he secured it to the saddle. He patted the horse again, as he picked up the bridle, and fitted it snugly.

He led the horse out of the yards, then closed the gate behind, as he placed his foot in a stirrup, and mounted.

He rode slowly towards the river, and had no trouble finding the well-worn track along its bank that he was advised to follow around the escarpment.

'Now, let's see what you've got!' he said to himself.

Firstly he took particular notice of the horses' gait, and with particular interest he found that even at the slightest demand from him, this stallion responded immediately.

'A well-trained horse!' he thought. So then as the track widened he tested him out. He pressed him into a slow trot, and then into a slow canter, and he was pleasantly surprised of the smooth ride. 'Jed was spot on about this horse.' he mused. 'He will suit my purpose well enough!'

His plan was to follow the track until he met up with the main road, but if he noticed the river veering away from him, he would stop to let his mount eat, and drink.

After about an hour, this particular event occurred as he noticed the big bend in the river looming, and he found a shady tree close to the river where he dismounted, and led the horse down to a sandy bank where he could lead him out to drink. Then he tied the reins to a tree where the grass grew thickest. He grabbed his food, and water from the saddlebag, and sat on a log while the horse ate, and found he had worked up a huge appetite himself.

When Cheyla had rested, and ate his fill, his horse was also rested. So he mounted the stallion, and then resumed his trek along the track which was definitely winding its way away from the river now, and seemed to be heading inland. It seemed no time at all when he joined the main road to The Outback Gardens, so thankfully he urged the stallion into a canter, and he rode beside the tarred road.

Cheyla was enjoying the ride immensely. He noticed in stretches that the dirt track each side of the main road had been recently graded, and he had plenty of room to push his mount along. He was making good time now. It was beautiful country, and relished the feel of the breeze in his face as he took in the scenery as he rode. 'Different to home.' he mused. 'But still beautiful Outback Country!'

Then finally he arrived at the gated entrance to The Outback Gardens Estate, and he had to stop, not only to open the gates, but to look closely at the sign there. 'This has to be this same artist Axel Hall's work!' he thought.

'He seems to have left his mark on this town.'

He led his mount through the gates, then mounted to resume his trip. He realized that he must be getting close when he noticed signage up ahead, so was not surprised.

It was the crossroads where one road veered left to the Outback Gardens Homestead, he noted when reading the signs, taking particular notice of the spectacular art-work, then took the right fork to The Outback Bush Camp.

His first impression of the complex which came from The Restaurant, Bar, and Office area as he rode in, reminded him a little of Waverley Downs. Though this place was huge, it was purely an Outback Bush Camp.

He could see the massive tents, marquees, and the out-buildings in the background, and was interested to have a look, but first he wanted to locate Pete Stringer. So he stopped at the Office to dismount, tied the reins to a post, then ducked his head as he walked inside the doors to the ring of a bell somewhere within, and stood waiting.

Ayoung girl came waltzing through the door. "Good afternoon Sir, do you have a booking?" she asked.

"Hi there!" Cheyla replied. "No, I am not staying. I just rode out to have a look around, maybe meet up with the Owner. I think I may come out and stay another time!"

"Oh that will be good Sir, just take our card so you can ring to make a booking whenever!" she stated. "If you are looking for Pete, you have only just missed him. He had to go down to his house, something came up. But you are welcome to go there, his wife Susan is home if he is out in the paddocks. Just follow the road down past the stables until you see the river, then take the first right turn."

"Thank you so much miss! Your name is?" he asked.

"Belinda!" the girl said.

"Thank you Belinda! My name is Cheyla, and we will meet again no doubt. Pleased to meet you!"

"You too Cheyla! If you want anything for your horse, you will find someone at the stables." she said.

"Ok, that is good to know. I will call in, we have had a long ride." replied Cheyla as he waved, and went outside.

He rode slowly through the complex trying to take it all in. There was so much to look at, so he started to think.

'Yeah, I might come back, and stay a couple of nights.'

Down at the stables, he reined in to stop at the gates. He walked inside, and was greeted by a young boy who was only too pleased to get him some oats for his horse, then after the horse had eaten his fill, they continued on.

Cheyla could just make out the Homestead sitting up on a high embankment overlooking the river, but to get there he had to go through the entrance gates, and across the larger paddock before the house paddock. 'Beautiful spot!' he thought, as he negotiated the gates, then rode on a well-worn track through the lush paddock.

Suddenly he sighted the large dam ahead at the bottom of the escarpment not far from the house, and he then noticed a Land Rover parked at the base of its hill.

Cheyla was interested to see who was there, so he rode around the huge dam then to the back of the Rover, where he dismounted to tie the horse's reins to bars at the back.

He climbed up the steep bank of the massive dam with ease then stood a while on the top to look down upon the expanse of it. It was then that he noticed the man waist deep in water trying to pull a heifer out. He had situated a girth strap behind its forelegs with a double rope each side that he was attempting to heave on. Even though he was a well-built big man his efforts were to no avail. 'That heifer is not budging.' thought Cheyla, then he called out.

"Hello down there! Need any help there mate?"

Pete Stringer's head lifted in response to the voice and as he looked up he shaded his eyes from the sun with one hand. Someone massive was standing on the crest of the dam. Pete couldn't believe the size of him. 'He could pass for a giant easily enough standing up there.' he thought.

"Hi there! Yeah I'm in need of help for sure, but don't know whether you can help. I was thinking about calling in some more men. Can't get the Rover down as the bank is too steep, just don't want to damage my cow." he said.

But as he spoke Cheyla had already begun his descent down the slope, then finally slid to a stop at the bottom.

Cheyla took in the situation quickly and come up with the best option when he surveyed the surroundings.

"Just bear with me!" he said as he strode to the water's edge and immediately without hesitation walked straight into the water boots and all. Then as he planted his boots firmly in the mud behind the heifer he looked up to speak.

"Hi! I came out to meet Pete Stringer. Was told he lives here. I am Cheyla Stone, and you are mighty lucky I did!"

Pete gasped when he looked into those familiar eyes. He knew those eyes so well, but that face was legendary.

He was shaking as he made an effort to reply.

"You've found Pete Stringer!" he muttered in shock.

"Oh good, well met Pete! We will talk soon, we won't be long here. But now we have work to do!" said Cheyla, as he settled his boots in the mud and squatted down.

"Are you sure you know what you are doing Cheyla? This is one of my prized heifers." said Pete in defense.

Cheyla detected Pete's country accent that seemed to roll off his tongue effortlessly when he spoke. It sounded different, almost alien to his ears. Not something Cheyla had ever been familiar with in The Territory, but he liked it well enough. "Don't worry Pete! I am a Cattle Man too, and I have done this many times before. It will be fine! I have to free the back legs first, then raise her forelegs. This is a tough job so I'll do this twice to make sure she is free before you pull on the ropes. You ok with that?" he asked.

Pete looked at him. 'He really seems to know what he is doing.' he thought. 'But there is no way he is going to lift that heifer. I couldn't budge it, and I am fairly strong.'

"Yeah, sounds like a plan Cheyla, go for it" he replied.

Cheyla's face was set in concentration as he adjusted his footing then wrapped his huge powerful arms around the back legs of the heifer. He heaved once, then again to lift it up, and the heifer was released from its muddy grip.

Pete stood back watching. He was totally amazed with the feat he was witnessing. Then as Cheyla repeated the effort with the forelegs then the back legs again, Pete stepped forward in admiration to congratulate him.

He just couldn't believe this show of pure strength and had forgotten all about the ropes until Cheyla spoke up.

"Ok Pete, get ready to pull now! She should be free but go gently! I will push from the back on the count of three."

In surprise Pete looked down at his feet, then regained the ropes he had dropped as he answered Cheyla.

"Ready when you are Cheyla!" Then Cheyla counted.

On the count of three the heifer, though very wobbly, made her first steps forward as Pete urged her with the ropes and then slowly but surely she was out on the bank.

For the first time Pete looked into Cheyla's eyes as he finally left the water to edge towards him along the bank.

'I know those eyes, and that familiar face.' he thought.

'God help us all, but it just has to be him!'

Suddenly they were shaking hands and Pete could feel power in the strength of his grip, and they both laughed.

He slapped Cheyla on his back. "I can't tell you how amazing that was Cheyla, and thank you. Man you are so strong it is frightening!" he said, and Cheyla chuckled.

"But first things first Cheyla. I will call the men to pick up the heifer and get her into a yard to recuperate a little!"

"Excuse me one minute, I won't be long!" he stated as he pulled out his mobile to dial a number then began to speak. "Ok all sorted!" he said snapping the phone shut.

"They'll be here soon. Let's try to get her up that lower bank over there!" he pointed. "I will tie her there to graze. Stupid beast has been here all night so she is very weak!"

"Then you my friend shall come up home to meet my wife, then we will celebrate. Would you like to join us for lunch Cheyla!" asked Pete. "I would like to talk to you!"

Cheyla looked down at his dripping-wet clothes and at his muddy boots, and a frown creased his brow.

"Somehow I don't think I am dressed too well to meet a lady, or to join your table for lunch Pete!" he chuckled.

Pete laughed. "That is no problem Cheyla! I have just the solution up at the Homestead being with the existence of an outdoor shower shed that I use specifically for these one-off times. However having said that, I don't think I'll have clothes or boots big enough to fit you!" he chuckled.

Cheyla laughed too. "Well that is good to hear because I happen to have spare clothes and shoes luckily so in that case I would like it well enough to join you for lunch!"

"Good man! Ok let's get this heifer up and we will go!"

Cheyla followed Pete's rover to his Homestead, taking particular interest as he rode. 'Huge place!' he thought, as he noticed the river view beyond. Pete braked at the gate. "Cheyla I'll just grab you a towel and soap, and tell Susan we have a guest then meet you at the showers out back!"

"Will do!" said Cheyla and led his horse into the shady yard, tied the reins to a trough and slipped the saddle off.

CHEYLA

As he walked towards the verandah where they were sitting Cheyla looked up and smiled.

Once again Pete seen a flash of those deep green eyes and he smiled back. He looked hard at him. He looked so different now, but he had the most magnificent physique he had ever seen. Pete had warned Susan of his suspicions but had asked her to swear to secrecy until he learnt more about this man who suddenly materialized in their lives, and he would speak in privacy with him during lunch.

A very pregnant Susan Stringer rose and walked to the railing in expectation of their arriving lunch guest.

His golden hair was wet, but shone in the sunshine as it fell to his shoulders. His jeans were cut low and muscles bulged in his forelegs. A tight fitting T-shirt barely hid the massive abs bulging beneath the fine thread, and the cut-off sleeves revealed solid muscle in his arms and his chest.

Susan just stared at him, then gasped. Now she knew exactly what Pete was talking about and she could barely contain herself to act normal as he approached. 'He is just so beautiful. He even looks god-like almost!' she thought.

Pete rose and stood beside her as Cheyla walked up.

"Come on up Cheyla and meet my lovely wife Susan!

Susan this is Cheyla Stone, and do I have a story to tell you of him! Cheyla please meet my wife Susan!" he said.

Cheyla assessed them. 'Both beautiful looking people.' 'Pete very handsome with the bluest eyes Cheyla had ever seen, and he was a big solid man who looked like he could handle himself in any situation.' Cheyla was thinking to himself. 'Guess he is not called a legend for no reason! But this man just oozes Country, a typical Country Cowboy!'

'Then there was Susan. Somehow he felt there was a special something about a pregnant woman. She had that glow about her, and her long, brown curly hair bounced as she moved, but her eyes captivated him. Such genuine friendship emanated from them framed by a pretty face.'

"Welcome to our home Cheyla!" she was saying as she interrupted his thoughts. "I am so pleased to meet you!"

"Thank you for your welcome Susan. I too am pleased to meet you also! Thank you for inviting me on such short notice. You both live in a lovely place here, and from what I have seen so far of The Outback Bush Camp, it is a huge complex I would like to see more of!" replied Cheyla.

Pete stood impatiently as they chatted then suddenly interrupted. "Hey you two! What say we sit down to be comfortable as well while we talk? I'm so damn thirsty I am having a beer. What about you Cheyla?" he asked.

"Beer will be fine for me also thanks Pete, and like you I have worked up a thirst." he chuckled.

"Ok come this way and pull up a seat Cheyla and I will get the drinks!" he pointed to the settee. "What about you Susan?" "Just juice for me thanks Pete, and I'll just duck in to get you both some nibbles' for starters." she replied.

'Talk about Country hospitality.' thought Cheyla.

When they returned Pete immediately started with the details to explain to Susan what Cheyla had done earlier.

They were laughing and joking, each giving their own version of the events that made Susan laugh. "I can't help but admire your efforts Cheyla, thank you! I might leave you both to talk now and I will make lunch." she said.

L eft alone the two men looked at each other. "Cheers Cheyla!" said Pete raising his glass. "I just can't seem to thank you enough. What you done today was special!"

They clinked glasses as Cheyla said. "Thanks Pete!"

"So tell me more Cheyla? You said you're a Cattleman, and a good one too, I can tell! Where do you hail from?"

"Got my own spread way to the north. 'Tenungeri' I named it. Five hundred acres of the best cattle country in The Territory. I run a cattle ranch with thirty employees."

"Hmm! The name sounds Aboriginal! A massive place you have. What did you do, win the lottery?" Pete jested.

"Yes it is Aboriginal!" Cheyla chuckled. "I guess you could say that. I struck gold at age seventeen at my birth place 'Tenna!' So I not only own the largest cattle property in The Northern Territory, but I have my own gold mine."

Hairs stood erect on Pete's neck. It wasn't the fact that this man was loaded, it was the names of those places he had heard many years ago that shook him to the core. He knew who he was looking at now. 'What should I do?' he wondered. "I have to delve a little further, just to be sure!' he decided. 'My god, poor Jackie. Whatever will she do?'

"Sounds like you have left a lot behind to go travelling Cheyla! But why Shallow Siding, why here?" asked Pete.

Cheyla sensed Pete's sudden change of mood. 'Why is it that people here seem to be hiding things from me, and questioning me? What is it about me?' he wondered.

He shrugged it off and replied. "Well I have come here in search of an Aboriginal lady named Mary Higgs. I have vital information for her and also a parcel from the owner of Waverley Downs S.A.! Would you know of her Pete?"

Pete had heard enough. He had his answer now and he looked directly into Cheyla's eyes. He decided to be honest as he didn't want Cheyla walking in on Jackie.

"I do know Mary Higgs very well Cheyla, but Mary is now married. Her name is Mary Hargraves."

Cheyla's face beamed. "I don't believe it! Finally I have met someone who knows Mary Higgs. But are you certain it's her Pete? Please be serious, are you sure. Don't kid me now. I couldn't bare that! So please tell me where she lives Pete, I have come a long way to see her!" he pleaded.

Pete looked hard at him before he replied.

"It seems to me Cheyla that there is more to this visit than meets the eye. More than what you are telling me! I find it hard to believe you have travelled half way around Australia just to give Mary a message and a parcel."

"What else is it you want here Cheyla? I would expect an honest answer seeing I have been honest with you!"

Cheyla felt trapped. 'I dare not tell Pete my reason to be here!' he knew. 'Mary was a key, a link to his Mother!'

"Just wanted to see the Country Pete but events forced my hand to finding Mary and to give her some sad news."

"And what else Cheyla?" asked Pete persistently as he stared into those deep green eyes, his own eyes darkening as he began making his statement obstinately.

"You know Cheyla! My Father has a famous saying! I learnt it from him at a young age and this is what he said."

"Pete! Give a man worth when he proves his worth!"

"Wise words that have helped me many times!"

"So now Cheyla if there is anything you should tell me do it now, and prove your worth, if you want my help!"

Cheyla could feel those deep blue eyes searching his face. For that precise moment as he looked up, he seemed to face the demeanor of a Hunter. Only one that possessed those skills could un-man someone to the state he was in now, and suddenly he understood only too well why Pete was such a Legendary Hunter in this Outback Country.

Momentarily he got a reprieve when Susan appeared.

"Excuse me you two so sorry for interrupting, but I am cooking large steaks Pete. So I just need to know how you like yours cooked Cheyla?" she asked, then she smiled.

Cheyla smiled back. "Don't trouble yourself too much Susan, but thank you. Just medium-rare for me!" he said, and as she disappeared, he turned back to face Pete.

Cheyla knew Pete would be waiting for his reply so he looked straight at him and started to speak.

Pete could sense his emotion, his eyes even seemed to glaze over as he choked out the words, and Pete felt deep compassion for this poor lost soul as he listened.

"Pete it is no lie that I need to contact Mary, however you are right there is a greater need in my heart that has hounded me all the days of my life, and Mary is my only link to fulfil that ambition of finding my natural Mother!"

"You see Pete! I was abandoned at birth by my natural Mother, left to be raised by an Aboriginal clan. Mary was at my birth as she was with my natural Mother, but she is also the Granddaughter of the Ol Mother who raised me!"

"Which brings me to another truth! I have to tell Mary her Grandmother died and with her dying breath she told me to go find my roots, and gave me letters from Mary!"

"So I began my search for Mary with only a few letters, and one only address in S.A. where the letters were sent from and Waverly Downs Property where Mary worked.

I drove there in hope this would lead me to my Mother but when I got there Mary had long gone. But luckily the semi-retired Owner had kept in contact with her. Hence the package I have for her, from him! 'Another truth!' But that led me half way around Australia to Shallow Siding!"

"I'm worn out from a constant fire in my gut, my need to see my Mother. But I won't stop now! My name 'Stone,' is concocted, as I have no identity. I must find Mary, she's my only hope!" Cheyla sighed as he completed his story.

Pete could hardly contain his remorse for what he had to do but he had to! He had to stay strong for the sake of the others. Though subconsciously he couldn't help but imagine himself being in the same position as this gentle giant of a man who sat before him, pouring his heart out.

"Cheyla I can't begin to say how sorry I feel. I hope it works out. However I do have certain responsibilities to two very dear people I love. Heed me well as I say this!"

"If you make a promise not to look for your Mother in this town while you are seeking information, then I shall give you the details you need to find Mary. I could inform you of certain things of your past that may not be exactly true. Only Mary knows those details and I will rely on her judgement as to where you should go to from here. Please keep in mind she will be protecting your Mother also!"

"Just keep in mind Cheyla! If you harm Mary or your Mother, I'll hunt you down like a wild animal!" he added.

CHEYLA

Cheyla could not believe his ears. But as he stared at Pete Stringer, he knew that he was deadly serious.

"So you not only know Mary Higgs but you also know my Mother! Why not just tell me where she is?" he asked.

"Lunch is ready!" commented Susan as she carried the huge tray out to the table and set it down. "I hope you are hungry Cheyla. I made extra!" she added, as she laughed.

Thankful for the respite, Cheyla laughed with her, and Pete seemed to assume his usual manner.

"Thank you so much for your trouble Susan! If I may say it looks so good but I could eat the leg off this table!"

"Then dig in Cheyla! I do so like a man who has a good appetite. I guess I am just used to Pete, he is the same!"

Pete laughed. "You have outdone yourself my love, so thank you. Help yourself, and eat up Cheyla!" he added.

"Thank you kind sirs' I hope you enjoy. Maybe Cheyla can tell us a little about his life while we eat." Susan said.

"Well Cheyla has already told me he has a huge Cattle Property in the Territory, so let me tell you Susan he knew exactly what he was doing at the dam today!" said Pete.

"Oh really, do tell me more Cheyla!" replied Susan.

"Adding to that Susan, he owns his own gold mine as well. So I'd say this guy is pretty well set up!" said Pete.

Cheyla felt embarrassed. Here he was receiving their Country hospitality and eating their food when he could really afford to buy their whole place, so he interrupted.

"If I could just add something. I really appreciate your hospitality, so as a favour in return I'd like it well enough if you would both join me for dinner one evening. Either in town, or at your fine Restaurant. My shout of course!"

A shadow passed over Pete's eyes and his reply was matter of fact as he looked hard at Cheyla.

"Guess we might take a rain check on that Cheyla! You did say you had some things to sort out first didn't you?"

Cheyla directed his attention to Pete who had that look on his face again, so he replied. "Yes sure Pete!"

"Oh, whatever you both decide is fine with me Cheyla. But now tell me, as I am very curious to know what made you come out riding to our Property today?" she asked.

"Funny you should ask that Susan! I arrived in town yesterday. It was my intention to look around when I got way-laid at the front building of The Community Center that displayed art in the window, so I went inside. I ended up buying a work of art by Axel Hall. A great landscape painting of the town and area. So it was there I picked up a brochure of your Outback Bush Camp, and with interest in the Outback I had to meet the man who runs it, to find out what type of man makes a Legendary Hunter. So now I've met Pete, I guess I know the answer to that." he said.

"Oh how interesting! You know that Axel Hall is quite famous here and I guess my husband is too." she laughed.

"Yes I deducted that! But now though unfortunately, I must be back in town before dark. Thanks again for lunch, we will meet again no doubt." he said, as he rose to leave.

"So pleased to meet you Cheyla, do come back!" she said.

"I'll walk you out Cheyla." said Pete. But out at the yards Cheyla turned. "Trust me Pete! I will keep the promise!"

"Very well but mark my words! Mary lives at Shallow Downs, heed what she says Cheyla! Then get back to me."

"Can't thank you enough Pete. I won't betray your trust!"

Chapter 16

Just a hint of sunshine remained above the skyline when Cheyla returned by the back-street entrance to the yards and he could see a light still shining in the saddlers shop.

On the ride back he had plenty of time to reflect on the day's events and now, though he was thankful to actually find someone who knew Mary, any further plans seemed somewhat difficult. His thoughts clouded with emotions, seemed to go haywire to a point where his muddled brain couldn't cope, as Pete Stringer's words hounded him.

He could still feel those deep blue eyes upon him and floating before him to darken with the ultimate threat that would not leave him in peace. He had not been expecting a response like that at all. 'Who would have imagined that I would encounter a secret service arrangement here.' he puzzled. But deep down, his gut knew one certain thing. 'To actually find his Mother would not be an easy task.'

He had been told that everyone would be protecting her. 'But why? What happened to her in this little town?'

Quickly, so as not to miss Jed, he dismounted to tie the reins to the railing where he unsaddled, and left his gear on the ground while he went to grab up a bucket of water nearby to wash the stallion down. When he was done he led him into the warmth of one of the stables.

He removed the bridle then as he caressed his muzzle the stallion snorted, and Cheyla chuckled as he patted his shoulder. "Thanks big red it was a great day. We must do it again one day!" he said, as he reached for some hay.

He was hurrying as he picked up his gear and headed towards the shed to stow it away. His mind was in turmoil, decidedly in another place and his concentration was awry, but he managed to get one hand out ready to push on the doors, but was startled when they flew open before him, and Tarryn Westley stepped through.

Cheyla was flustered. Not only to be surprised, but to see the beautiful woman again, and once again he froze.

She laughed. "Ahh! It's you again. Guess it's my turn to startle you mister strong man though you are not in the dirt like I was. I was wondering who took the big red out today, so now I know! You are starting to encroach on my territory." she remarked, as a tinkle of laughter escaped her lips. Then she turned on her heel and walked off.

Cheyla gathered his wits to call out. "Sorry I didn't… but his voice trailed off as he gaped at her. 'What is with this woman?' he wondered. The tinkling of her laughter and her voice so seductive and husky-like tantalized him as he walked determinedly after her towards the shop.

"Oh Cheyla ya made it back!" called Jed as he walked through the doors.

"Hi Jed, yeah all good! I washed the Stallion, he's in a stable. Yeah a good ride!" he said, as he looked at the girl.

CHEYLA

Jed looked from one to the other. Cheyla was just glaring at the girl, looking frustrated. But Jed knew Tarryn well, and he detected a smile on her face that she just hid.

"Told ya he be a goodin, didn't I? Hope ya bin havin a good day an thank ya fer washin him Cheyla but there be no need fer ya ta do thet!" said Jed.

"Yeah good day thanks Jed! Take what I owe you out of this!" replied Cheyla absently as he handed over a card.

Jed sensed his opportunity so he spoke loudly. "Looks ta me like yar goin ta be a good customer Cheyla seein ya be stayin a while. Like ta look afta me customers! Don't I Tarryn?" he asked the girl who stood at the counter.

Tarryn spun around to face Jed as the mention of her name alerted her, her long black hair swished about her. "Beg your pardon Jed, what did you say?" she asked.

"I be sayin thet I look afta me customers! Ta this here new person in tha town. Aint thet tha truth? Oh! Ya may not hav met as yet! So me be sorry!" he exclaimed.

Cheyla chuckled as he spoke. "Well we have bumped into each other a couple of times! But no! We don't know each other, and haven't been introduced proper yet Jed!"

A tinkle of laughter escaped Tarryn's lips at his jest but then Jed spoke out and a huge smile remained on her face.

"Well then Cheyla. We be not havin thet, I be doin this proper! So Cheyla please meet Miss Tarryn Westley! She be a good customer ta me too, an helps me out sometimes. Tarryn, please meet a newcomer ta town, Cheyla Stone!"

Cheyla had her full attention now and he returned the smile that spread across her face but when he looked into those dark smokey eyes, his heart almost missed a beat.

223

'Get a grip Cheyla! This is no time to get tongue-tied.' he thought. So determinedly he stepped closer to her, his hand outstretched and a huge grin on his face as he spoke.

"Well, well!" he chuckled. "The mysterious lady has a name, and a beautiful one too. I am pleased to finally meet you Tarryn! I have been trying to talk to you a few times to apologize for knocking you over yesterday out back at the storeroom shed. My only excuse, though petty as it seems is that I was just pre-occupied and deep in thought. So I guess that I wasn't really paying attention to what I was doing at the time. I am really very sorry about that!"

Their hands molded in a hand shake and Tarryn could not ignore the tingling that emanated just from that one touch. However she turned to face him squarely, her eyes turned a dark smokey colour as she spoke out softly.

"Apology accepted Cheyla! But can you please tell me why I am the mysterious one?" she asked.

Cheyla chuckled. I thought of you as mysterious, only because you wouldn't stay still long enough for me to talk to you! You are a hard girl to attract the attention of! But now we have finally met, and I have apologized, I realize we may have things in common. Don't you agree?"

Tarryn for once was lost for words. She had never met anyone quite like this man who could match her word for word. 'He is not just a pretty face.' she mused, laughing it off with a quip. "Well I am not so sure about that Cheyla Stone! I rather think you may be the mysterious one with a name like Cheyla! Don't you think? Also I am struggling to find something in common, we just met." she laughed.

CHEYLA

Cheyla's brow creased, his green eyes darkening with annoyance, and irritation which resulted in his reply being curt, as he looked at her very seriously.

"What I would really like to do Tarryn Westley, if you would really like to know! Is just simply to converse and get to know you! So if you think my name strange then so be it. However there is good reason for it, and if you were at least interested to hear my story, then I would tell you! As for having things in common! Well! I was referring to horses, horse riding or enjoying the outdoors for starters."

Her smile immediately disappeared, then her face too was serious. 'Oh no! I've hurt his feelings.' she thought.

"Oh Cheyla please forgive me for my outburst! I was really having a joke with you. I certainly didn't mean any bad reference to your name. It is an unusual name, but a beautiful one, so I didn't mean to be so rude!" she uttered.

"All good, no harm done!" he replied. But his manner was aloof now. She had come too close to his hurt and yes, her words stung, his feelings were wounded. Something he had carried with him for a long, long time.

"Well I best get going now, nice to meet you Tarryn Westley!" he said as he backed away from her then turned to face Jed. "Thank you for all your help Jed!"

Jed had heard the whole conversation and he felt bad. 'There be no need ta insult tha man Tarryn.' he mused.

"No worries Cheyla! Ya no ya be welcome ta com here any time. Here be ya card, com agin ya hear!" he stated.

"Yeah sure thing Jed! Thanks again." Cheyla replied, then he turned to walk away.

Jed, and Tarryn stood side by side to watch him leave.

Tarryn looked at Jed with a very concerned look upon her face. "Oh dear I do feel so bad! I am so sorry Jed but I think I may have upset your new customer!" she stressed.

"Don ya be worryin Tarryn, ya was only jokin! He be noin thet. Mus be somthin touchy ta do bout his name thet worries him ta hav thet there reaction!"

"I just feel so regretful and really ashamed. He is really very nice too and I love his unusual name. That is the sad part. Oh how embarrassing, I guess now I shan't be seeing him again. Typical of me and my big mouth!" she stated.

Jed looked at her and spoke. "Tarryn ya don fret now ya hear. I be seein tha way he be lookin at ya, an he could barely speak ta ya. I be guessin ya will be seein him agin.

"Really! Do you think so Jed? I fear the horse has just bolted and I have lost my chance of getting to know him."

"Trus me Tarryn. I no tha look he bin givin ya. Jus next time ya treat him right ya hear!" stated Jed.

"Yeah I guess I was a bit too cheeky with him but I was actually flirting with him you know Jed!"

"Ya no Tarryn, som men don't be likin too much flirtin if they wan ta be serious. An he seems ta be tha honest an decent type an I'm guessin expects tha same back ya no!"

"You know Uncle Jed sometimes you surprise me!"

"Now jus a minit young lady. Since ya Father died an ya came here with ya mama ta live, I now guessin why ya still single is thet ya fool too much with tha men ya see. I know ya be educated an all but ya should be settlin down Tarryn, havin a family an all with somone nice. Ya be very beautiful girl but me thinks ya be ya own worst enemy!"

226

A frown creased Tarryn's brow as she flicked her hair over her shoulder and stared at Jed.

"You know what Uncle Jed? This is one time you are completely wrong. I am not my own worst enemy at all! I do know what I expect in a man, and what interests me."

"If I am flippant it is probably because he interests me. That is how I am! Besides I haven't met the right person yet!" she stated. "Or have I?" she added, as she paused in the doorway. "I must say Cheyla Stone seems one hunk of a man, but I may not get a chance to find that out now!"

"I not be arguing with ya no more Tarryn, ya always hav a answer fer everythin. Too smart ya problem be!"

"Hmm! Maybe I am but that's just how it is. Especially when it comes to men. I am very particular with my taste, and I like a challenge! Who knows what a new day will bring! Are we friends?" she asked, as a smile lit her face.

"Cause we be friends, silly girl. Jus tryin ta help is all!"

"And you have! Thank you Uncle. Do you want me to come in on my day off and help you out back?" she asked.

"Only if ya hav som spare time Tarryn, com if ya can."

Tarryn looked at him, then walked back to the counter where she leaned over it to kiss his cheek. "Will do! I do like working with horses. I guess Cheyla was right about that too!" she said. 'He predicted that from one meeting with me!' she thought to herself. 'Hmm! Maybe there is more to learn about this man.' "Give my love to Mother please Jed, I must rush!" she called as she left the counter.

"Will do Tarryn an good luck be with ya. Jus rememba what me bin tellin ya bout Cheyla. Me thinks he be one o tha good ones! So ya do tha right thing ya hear!" he said.

Cheyla walked back to his Hotel feeling confused, and disillusioned with all the day's events. Everywhere he went he felt a brick wall was being put up in front of him, secrets held back, and he felt the walls closing in.

Even though it should have been a day of celebration for him to eventually find out the whereabouts of Mary Higgs, it had come with a huge price tag. So celebrating was not on his to-do list. Instead there was a sour taste in his mouth like a bitter feeling of defeat threatening, as his ultimate goal seemed many light years away because the people here were not letting him any closer.

Though somehow, some way he knew that deep down inside he would persist until he achieved what he set out to do. He had come this far so he was not about to let other people stand in his way, but at the same time he realized that he did need their help.

'Baby steps!' he thought. 'That is what I need to do. So, one step at a time, starting with Mary Higgs.' But now as he reached The Hotel and inserted the key to his room his immediate interest wasn't exactly the company of people, he had enough of that for one day. What he really needed was a hot shower, a good meal and maybe a few drinks.'

He dialed reception to put in an order for his dinner to be served in his room, accompanied by a bottle of Scotch.

As he sat waiting he looked at the painting on the shelf and his mind drifted to the girl. This girl was blowing his mind. Just by thinking about her made his stomach churn. Something he had never experienced in his life before. He knew his own feelings only too well, but hers remained a mystery. 'But I may have ruined my chances!' he thought.

Chapter 17

Mitchell Stringer had aged well with a distinguished hint of white at the temples of his loose sandy hair. Only a few lines surrounded his deep blue eyes, but now a deep furrow was obvious creasing his brow, causing his eyes to darken as he replaced the phone receiver gently.

'So the time has finally come!' he stressed to himself. Something in his gut churned. 'He knew it would happen, he just knew it!' Then the memories came flooding back.

His thoughts turned to his wife. 'Poor Jackie! So much she has been through.' he thought. 'Whatever will she do now?' he asked himself. 'It is an impossible situation, but if I know Jackie she will handle it with finesse, just as she does with everything! However it's hard to pick exactly which way Jackie will turn in this crisis, this is different. I better go and find her to break it to her.' he thought sadly.

Melissa was tugging at his pants in urgency in her best effort to seek his attention. "Father can we eat now, I am sinking!" she exclaimed in a rush. Mitch looked down at her angelic face and laughed. "Well we can't have that can we? Mother is upstairs so let's surprise her. You may help Missus Jefferies make lunch to bring it up to the balcony!"

Jacqueline was sitting in her favourite chair looking out towards the river. She turned her head as she heard the footfalls on the balcony behind her.

Mitchell looked at her tenderly and his heart went out to her. 'She will be devastated!' he thought. 'Just look at her! Still as beautiful as she was in her teens. These long years had treated her kindly but there was more to her. Maturity and unbridled determination combined, made Jacqueline Coby-Stringer a force to be reckoned with.'

Her short cropped blonde hair fell in wisps about her beautiful face as she raised her head to stare at him with those beautiful deep green eyes that he loved. Only now they were misted over as she looked at him, and he stared.

"Oh Mitch, thank goodness you are here!' she cried in definite stress. Something unforeseen has evolved. I must talk to you rather urgently I fear. Where is Melissa at? We have to talk in private, I don't want her hearing us!"

'She knows!' thought Mitch straight away.

"Melissa is down in the kitchen no doubt driving May crazy helping her with our lunch. I left her there as I have something urgent to tell you also after Pete's phone call, but it sounds like you may already know what I am about to say. Shall I go first just in case?" he asked.

Jacqueline looked puzzled. "What phone call could be more important? I have something drastic to talk about. But yes do go on if you wish Mitch though I don't see how I would know what you were talking about!" she said.

"Because my love I do think we are talking of the same topic. Someone new in town looking for Mary Higgs!"

Jacqueline just stared at him. "Go on!" she muttered.

Mitchell looked hard at her. "Ok then, if you are sure! Well like I said before. I just got off the phone with Pete, and have been struggling with the message I need to tell you, however I do think somehow you already know. But there can be no doubt about who is looking for Mary!"

"Yes I do know what you have to tell me Mitch! Anne and Jake came out to see me especially to tell me, as Anne met this person called Cheyla Stone in Shallow Siding, so she is quite adamant she knows his identity. But just the name Cheyla was enough to convince me!" she said.

Mitchell looked puzzled. "I'm not too sure what you mean by that Jackie! How would you even know that particular name Cheyla is his, if you never saw him?"

"Many years ago Mitch in Father's rein of the original 'Shallow Downs' we employed aboriginal people to work for us. Mary was one of them, so Mary would know also that The Aboriginals found it hard to pronounce 'Shallow Downs' so to them it became 'Cheyla-D.' So it is him!"

"Well I never! But one more question! Why would he be given that name Jacki, who named him?" asked Mitch.

"Good question Mitch. I can only think the name came from Mary. She must have mentioned 'Shallow Downs' to the Ol Mother who delivered Cheyla, I am not sure. But she was after all, Mary's Grandmother, and very clever to give him the name Cheyla, but what puzzles me though, is why it took him so long to look for Mary, and for me!"

"Yes it's much clearer now, an amazing story. Though there's still some unanswered questions that maybe only Mary would know! Now I need to tell you about Pete!"

Pete has stressed that it is imperative we come over to his house tonight. There has been some new updates to what you know already, but facts about Cheyla Stone that you must hear. "He said it was too much to go into on the phone and wants us to go over for dinner tonight!"

Jacqueline stared at Mitchell. "Pete knows more? How could that be Mitch?" she asked.

"Apparently, according to Pete, Cheyla Stone rode out to The Outback Bush camp today. So Pete met him face to face also and he even had lunch with Pete and Susan. That is all Pete would tell me. So I am in the dark too!" he said.

Jacqueline put a hand to her mouth as a gasp escaped her lips. "He was here! So close to me!" she stressed. "It's becoming frightening how everyone is getting involved."

"Oh my god Mitch. Please forgive me for what I done. I am so embarrassed to even think of involving you, and our baby Melissa with my past. I really didn't ever think it would come to this. However will I cope?" she asked.

"Nothing to forgive Jackie! What will be, will be! Just for the record. I know you will cope just fine, so whatever way you turn, remember I will be by your side!" he said.

"What a special man you are Mitchell Stringer! I know how hard this must be for you! I am just so sorry about it. Does nothing ever faze you?" asked Jacqueline.

"Well I could answer that with a statement. I know of someone very dear to me who is of the same ilk! Don't I? Missus Jacqueline Coby-Stringer!" he questioned, and his chuckle, and huge grin made Jacqueline laugh.

"You do have a way with words Mitchell Stringer! Though, now that you mention it, I guess that is correct!"

Jacqueline replied, and they both laughed together.

"Oh! That's better. It is so good to see you laugh Jackie. Now let us be positive about this. Will you agree that we should go over to Pete and Susan's tonight for dinner, just to see what he has to say?" he asked inquisitively.

Jacqueline looked at him squarely before she replied. "I would have to agree Mitch. I need as much information as I can get. Maybe Pete can shed a new light on this!"

"Ok then! We will leave about 5.00pm. I did confirm! But I told Pete I would call if we weren't coming." he said.

"There is only just one small problem Mitch! I don't want Melissa to be there. Any suggestions?" she asked.

"Don't worry. I will go down and speak to May. I am sure she will give Melissa her dinner, and get her to bed for us. We won't have a late night I shouldn't think, but May will be fine here until we get back!" replied Mitch.

They had barely just finished speaking when Melissa came rushing up the stairs to join them.

"Mother, Father! Lunch is ready!" she called. "Missus Jefferies is coming up the stairs." she gushed, then busied herself finding her place, and climbed up on the chair."

"You are so clever for helping Missus Jefferies Melissa! Well done!" said Jacqueline, pulling her daughter closer.

May crossed the balcony and set the lunch tray down. "Enjoy your lunch Jacqueline, Mitchell and Melissa thank you for your help!" she said as she winked at Jacqueline.

"Thank you so much May!" said Jacqueline.

"My pleasure Jacqueline." said May turning to go.

"Hold up for a sec May. I'd like a word?" stated Mitch.

Susan stood on the verandah while Pete walked down to open the gates for their guests as they had spotted the land rover approaching their Homestead.

He opened the gates wide when they stopped, then he beckoned them on as he called out a hello, and waved.

Jacqueline wound down the window to speak as the Land- Rover passed through. "Hi Pete! Thank you for the invite. I hope we are not too late?" she asked.

"Hi Mother no all good. Hi Father, go up to the house and I will walk up!" he said, starting to close the gates.

At the Homestead they parked in an accolated parking area then got out of the Rover. They walked hand-in hand over to the verandah where Susan greeted them.

"Come on up Jackie, and Mitch. It is so good to have you over for dinner, welcome to you both!" she said.

"Hello Susan!" said Jacqueline as she reached the top stair, then stepped forward to wrap her arms around her.

"I hope you are feeling well Susan, and up for a visit. Please don't go to any trouble but thank you for the invite, I only wish it was under different circumstances!"

Susan was glowing she noticed, as she replied.

"Jackie, I feel absolutely marvelous, so this pregnancy is agreeing with me obviously, but don't you worry I have everything under control. It is my absolute pleasure to be catering for you. Yes! I do know what you must be going through, so I hope that Pete can offer some help to you."

"Thank you for that Susan. You can't imagine what it means to me to be able to talk freely about my problems, usually I tend to keep them to myself." replied Jacqueline.

"Yes, we all know that Jackie! But no more!" she said.

"You are looking just great Susan!" offered Mitch as he reached over to give her a hug.

"Thanks Mitch. I've never felt better surprisingly, but Pete is fussing over me 24/7." and she laughed.

They both gave a chuckle and Susan added. "Please sit down and I will bring out some punch that I made. Non-alcoholic, so if you want a beer Mitch, I know Pete will!"

"Yes I'll have a beer thanks Susan. Jackie?" he asked.

"I will join you with the punch thank you Susan!"

"Good. I'll get that now. Pete is coming up the path."

Pete's eyes told the tale as he stared at them both when he stepped onto the verandah. He looked like he was carrying a burden as his face was set in a serious manner.

He slumped down in the chair as he greeted them and his voice filled with emotion when he spoke to Jacqueline.

"Jackie I am so sorry to be the bearer of this latest news so thank you for coming over to talk about it."

"Pete, sorry to interrupt, but I already knew in a way! Anne, and Jake came out to warn me. So don't feel bad. I for one should feel bad for getting you all involved." said Jacqueline, as she added. "But any information you have for me I would appreciate as I have no idea what to do!"

"Oh thank goodness you know, it really takes the load off. However I have lots to tell you about Cheyla Stone! I got to know him well enough in a short space of time over lunch here, to enforce my opinion of him." said Pete.

"Which is?" asked Jacqueline immediately.

Susan had just arrived with the drinks. "Oh Jackie, he is just beautiful and so very polite. He looks exactly like…

Pete put a finger to his lips, then stared at Susan, and her voice trailed off as he spoke up. "Susan, I thought we had an agreement! Remember?" he questioned.

"Yes I do remember Pete, I am sorry. I won't interrupt again, or say more. However from one woman to another, I felt Jackie needed to know that!" she said.

"Well Jackie now it seems I need to clarify a pact Susan and I made about revealing Cheyla's demeanor. I thought it would be more appropriate for you to experience something yourself if you chance to meet him. However with a reply to your question, and to voice my opinion, is this!"

"Susan is correct, he is very good looking and he is the most pleasant, upstanding person I have ever met, and I do not say that lightly. I have had him under scrutiny here for some time so I believe what he has told me!" said Pete.

"That is all very well in hindsight Pete!" remarked Jacqueline. "But to get right down to it, what has he told you Pete? What does he really want with me? Is it money? Is he violent, maybe it is revenge for abandoning him?"

"Before I answer that Jackie, there is more you should know about Cheyla Stone. He is also the largest, strongest man I've ever seen, and I don't mean that in a casual way either. He is super-strong. He is bigger and stronger than your own Father ever was Jackie!" answered Pete.

"My own Father?" appealed Jacqueline. "Are you very sure Pete? Father was a gentle giant though you wouldn't chance to get on the wrong side of him! But his bark was worse than his bite. However, he was very, very strong!"

"So too is this person Jackie, and I guess you could say he is a gentle giant also. Please just listen to my story!"

So Pete went on with his tale to tell them what Cheyla Stone had done to help him out at the dam the day before.

"That performance was beyond normal!" said Pete.

"You're kidding Pete?" questioned Mitchell.

"I fear not Father, that is exactly how it happened, and there is much more about this person that I learnt. Which brings me to your question Jackie. 'What does he want?'

Jacqueline looked impatiently at Pete. "Do get on with it please Pete. I am finding it hard to comprehend all this, and now you say there is more. Just tell me the worst!"

"That's just it Jackie there is no worst that I can foresee! I genuinely believe that Cheyla Stone travelled to Shallow Siding from The Northern Territory just to find Mary who was his only link to you. Mary's Grandmother just passed away. She had given him a few letters she had received of Mary's sent from Waverly Downs. It was the beginning of Cheyla's long, long search. 'What does he want? You ask. He just wants to find you! He is a lost soul with no identity. The name 'Stone' he made up in his teens! He is not looking for trouble, but I don't think that he is of that type anyway. As I said. I think he is a gentle giant!"

Pete took a reprieve to have a drink as Mitchell spoke.

"Some story! Are you quite sure you believe him Pete? Or maybe Jackie is correct. He may be seeking revenge or wants money from her."

Pete looked up, his eyes darkening. "You know I can detect a man's worth Father. I have judged this man and have told him to prove his worth in no uncertain terms!"

"I am sorry Pete, but I had to ask!" replied Mitchell.

Jacqueline gaped at Pete, and her body sat rigid on the seat. She placed her trembling hands in her lap and she attempted to speak with a voice choked with emotion.

"Just how is he to prove his worth Pete?" she asked.

"I'm so sorry Mother. I know how this is affecting you, but bear with me, there is one more important issue!"

"Just tell me Pete!" said Jacqueline, her anger rising.

"Ok, I will be quick. If what he says is true Jackie, then he is definitely not after your money either. On the other hand, he could buy us all, because he owns a gold mine."

"Oh that's a bit much!" interrupted Mitchell angrily.

"I thought so too Father, but I do believe him!"

"But why devise such a belief in only his words to you Pete?" questioned Jacqueline in dispute.

"Trust me Jackie! I will check him out. In the meantime I have set conditions for him to promise me he would not search for you, or harm you or Mary or he faces my wrath, as I threatened to hunt him down like a wild animal if he did. He knows I well mean it! So I told him where to find Mary! I have pre-warned her, but you stay home Jackie!"

"You did what?" screamed Jacqueline in disbelief.

"Jackie, stay calm now! I think the man has a right to know his identity, and who better to tell him than Mary!"

"Pete can we stop please, it's too much for Jackie." said Susan, as she rounded the table. "Come with me Jackie!" she coaxed her. "Dinner is ready everyone!" she called, as she led Jackie to the dining table where she already had a sherry poured for her. "Have a sip Jackie, it will help!"

Quiet words were spoken over dinner then Jacqueline spoke. "Ok, I will agree with your terms for now Pete!"

Chapter 18

Mary's hands shook uncontrollably and she fumbled with the phone to finally drop it in its cradle. With Pete's words still ringing in her ears, she put out a hand to steady herself on the lounge, and sat down wearily.

'God be helpin us all, so now it be beginin!' she prayed to herself. 'He be noin where I be workin at now. So I be guessin he no I be livin here too! I would hav thought I be havin plenty o time to git ready fer when he be findin me but now it could be soon, like tomorra.' she shuddered. 'I jus hope Pete be noin what he be stirrin up!'

Pete had given her instructions on how he wanted this handled, so Mary's part was a vital one to play. 'I jus be hopin I don break down. I hav ta be strong fer Jacqueline!'

"Mary what are you doing?" Drew's voice startled her back to reality as he came in the room. "I am just about to start dinner, but maybe I will put that on hold!" he stated as he looked at Mary in distress. "Whatever is going on Mary, who were you talking to on the phone?" he asked.

Mary looked at Drew. "It be Pete warnin me o what he bin doin. An, It seems I can be expectin tha man lookin fer me ta turn up any time, he be noin where ta look now!"

Drew looked at Mary in disbelief. "Who is this man?"
"His name be Cheyla Stone!" said Mary.

"Why did Pete reveal you Mary, what happened?"

"Pete be likin him, he trustin him Drew! But he thinks thet Cheyla should be knowin tha truth bout hisself, so he be thinkin he deserves tha right ta no!" answered Mary.

"Is he dangerous this Cheyla Stone?" asked Drew.

"Won't be now thet Pete is involved. Pete be tellin im thet he be hunt im down like a wild animal if he be lookin fer his Mother, or hurtin me an Jacqueline!" said Mary.

"Yes, but Mary! Pete might not be in the right place at the right time. He should be with you for this meeting!"

"No! Pete offer ta me. But me be tellin him no! Pete be noin what he doin. An I hav too much ta say ta Cheyla!"

"But how can you know for sure Mary?" stated Drew.

"Caus Pete be huntin down Cheyla's Dad a long time ago when he be murderin two people, but Pete tracked an caught him afore he be killin Jacqueline too ya no! Pete be tha great hunter, an tracker, an no one messes with Pete!"

"Murder in Shallow Siding? My god! This is sounding worse as it goes along Mary. Are you quite certain you aren't in danger? Maybe I should be with you?" he stated.

"I be fine Drew! I be more upset then in tha danger, jus trust me ok! An. I will be ok me thinks." replied Mary.

"But you don't even know this person Mary. He could be violent, or worse maybe!" persisted Drew.

"No I guess me not no thet fer sure Drew! But I be noin his roots an his blood be Jacqueline's! Thet be good nough fer me! So if thet there man be havin half Coby blood in his veins, then he hasta be tha good person!" Mary stated.

"Only now me havta go see Axel Hall urgently. An, it has ta be right now. I can't waste time, hav ta warn Axel!" Mary added, as she looked up at Drew.

"Now you have lost me completely Mary! Why do you need to rush out now especially just to warn Axel Hall? Of all people, what has Axel got to do with this? Can't it wait for another time?" asked Drew in bewilderment.

Mary looked at him earnestly before giving a reply. "Fraid not Drew. Axel be tha most importin person me hav ta visit, jus cause I be sendin Cheyla Stone ta see him when he be findin me, so me must warn Axel afore tomorra. Don't want ta give ta Axel tha heart attack."

"Please explain further Mary I cannot see the link."

"Sorry Drew. I guess ya hav ta no me thinks. Axel Hall be Cheyla's Grandfather, so me be hopin he will be tellin Cheyla bout his Dad. Anyways thet be somethin I not be noin bout too much, so will be askin him ta do thet."

"My god Mary this is unbelievable. I can't help but feel for Jacqueline. She must be in a state. Her whole life will be turned upside down. Can she take that?" he asked.

"Jacqueline be takin anything this here life be handin out, but how she be decidin what ta do, me not no thet! Only thet Pete be helpin ha now! He be tellin ha jus ta stay home. I be doin what he wants, but so is she." said Mary.

"Now I must go afore it gets ta be too late, so I will hav dinner with ya when I get home Drew."

"Ok, you are stubborn. Let me walk you out." he said.

Drew stood to watch the little car until it disappeared around the bend. 'She drives good now.' he thought.

Axel Hall's front yard was lit up by a front porch light Mary noticed as she pulled up at the curb out front.

She walked quickly through the gate then up the path to the front steps and knocked on the door. She called out as well because light was fading fast, and she didn't want to startle him. Axel didn't get many visitors especially this late in the day, so she wanted him to know who it was.

"You be there Axel? Tis me Mary out here." she called.

She could hear the shuffling behind the door as Axel approached to open it, then he called out. "Me be comin now Mary. Hold ya horses!"

A huge grin graced his face as the door opened wide. His teeth flashed white as he greeted Mary. "Big surprise fer me Mary ya com visitin. Come on in girl! Come in! He said in jubilation, and pointed to the couch. "Ya sit there!"

"Me be thankin ya so much Axel!" offered Mary as she entered the room, and took her place on the couch.

"So sorry bout tha late visit Axel but me hav somethin importin ta talk ta ya bout now. Somethin thet can't wait!"

Axel's brow creased in thought wondering what could be so important. "Ya be gettin me worryin Mary! What be thet importin fer ya ta race out this late?" he asked.

"Betta brace yerself and sit down Axel cause what I be sayin tis goin ta hit ya hard. Jus don't want ya gettin tha shock. Ya tell me quick if ya not feelin ok!" she stated.

"Mary jus git on with it, me startin ta stress now!"

"Ok Axel, but jus had ta warn ya! Now do ya remomba back when Jacqueline be comin home ta Shallow Siding? Then what be happenin ta ha here?" she asked.

"Be neva forgettin thet Mary! Thet be somethin I hav bin sorry fer all me life. So sorry fer Missus Jacqueline thet be happenin ta her. Am so ashamed thet it be me son thet be assaultin ha. Jus thankful Pete got ta her in time!"

"Axel I be so sorry fer ya loss. I be noin ya son died in tha jail, but can I take ya back ta when Miss Jacqueline be jus eighteen. Do ya no tha real reason thet she had ta leave her home, also her family, an why I be goin with her afta tha fire? Answer true, it be importin Axel!" stressed Mary.

A xel looked at her sadly as he remembered, and tears sprung into his eyes as he croaked out his reply.

"Firstly Mary, ya dont hav ta be sorry fer me loss cause I aren't. Me son be a bad, bad person. Was bad nine years old. He be causin lots o deaths here in this here town, an when I rememba what he be doin ta poor Miss Jacqueline I jus be feelin so ashamed, so he get what he deserved!"

"An, yea Mary I do rememba tha time Miss Jacqueline be jus eighteen, an why youse both leavin Shallow Downs way back then! Twas so, so bad I be neva forgettin. All me life I be suffa cause it be me son bin doin terrible things ta ha! Thet be why she go! An, it be him thet lit tha fire thet burnt Shallow Downs Homestead ta be killin ha Mother. Jus be so ashamed Mary!" his head hung in recollection.

Mary looked hard at him. "Look at me Axel!" she said.

Axel lifted his head slowly, and she could see this was upsetting him as the tears ran down his face.

"Me be so sorry Axel but there be more ya should no! Especially now! Thet be why I comin ta see ya!"

Axel just stared at her. "What more there be Mary?"

Mary could see that Axel knew no more of that time and it saddened her to have to bring it up now.

"Please be forgivin me Axel but ya hav ta no thet when we bin leavin here Miss Jacqueline was with child!"

It took a while for that to register in Axel's brain, but when it did his face crumbled and he cried out in anguish.

"No! Oh Noooo…. Poor Miss Jacqueline!" he wailed.

"Please be tellin me tis not true Mary!" he pleaded. "An, please be tellin me it wasn't my son's doing!"

"I be so sorry Axel but it was him, tis so true! I swear!"

"I'll be tellin ya now what be happenin when we left Shallow Downs after the fire. Miss Jacqueline be distraut! I had ta be with ha to help ha. Had bin with ha all me life. Grew up with ha afta Missus Coby be findin me when me parents was killed in tha car crash! So she be takin me in ta give me a home, but she be killed in thet there fire, an I hav no home then no more, jus like Miss Jacqueline too!"

"Mary I be so sorry fer ya! Me didn't no bout ya family. So not no how ya com ta be livin out at Shallow Downs. Jus no ya be a true friend ta Miss Jacqueline all ha life!"

"Thank ya Axel, but it be long time ago now, but I did get ta see some o me family later in the N.T. Afta we left!"

"Ya see our main problem be thet Miss Jacqueline be carryin a child. She be only eighteen an nowhere ta go an she be not wantin thet there child. She be hatin that there child at tha time! Then I be rememberin thet I hav family in the N.T. So we be startin the long trip ta there ta see if we be findin them!" related Mary.

"My god, ya poor girls. Poor Miss Jacqueline. I jus feel so bad bout this, more ashamed now Mary!" Axel cried.

"Don't be feelin bad Axel. Tis not ya fault at all. Ya jus remember, it not be ya fault Axel!" consoled Mary.

"Missus Jacqueline be tellin me thet too!" he replied.

"So ya listen ta ha Axel when she be tellin ya thet! Ya jus can't be blamed fer what ya son bin doin back then. He be tha bad one, not ya Axel!" stated Mary.

"So he be deservin all he be gettin fer goin ta thet there jail. Thet's where he belonged ta be Axel. He bin doin lots o real bad things, not jus ta Miss Jacqueline ta ruin ha life, but murder thet this town aint neva seen!"

Axel lifted his head and the tears were quite obvious to Mary as they streamed down his face.

"I no Mary, jus so hard is all!" he said, totally dejected.

"I jus can't believe it thet a son o mine could hav done tha bad things he done. Things thet ya only hear o others doin, an other families be sufferin, but we be havin people hurt thet we all be lovin, an look up too. Jus so sad!"

"Yea it is Axel. I hav lived Jacqueline's pain! So now I be noin how this will affect ha afta all this time!"

"I be so sorry Axel fer puttin ya through this, but mus tell ya what be happenin then." she said, and continued.

"It be afta a long time travellin we get ta where I be from, an we be findin me family at Tenna in the N.T."

"Or rather they be findin us at our campfire out in tha bush, an I meet up with me Ol Grandmother, me Aunts, Uncles, me Nieces an Nephews who still be where I use ta live long time afore when I be a kid."

"It be a great time fer me ta meet em all agin, but fer Miss Jacqueline Coby, it be tha worst time in ha life!"

"Miss Jacqueline gave birth there beside Tenna Creek with tha help o me Ol Grandmother. But Miss Jacqueline, she not even want ta see thet there baby! She no want thet there baby! So Ol Grandmother talk ta tha elders. So they say she can hav tha child, an she offa ta raise thet child!"

"Keep in ya mind thou Axel! But I no fer sure thet Miss Jacqueline she be sufferin fer makin thet there decision all tha days of ha life! I be watchin her struggle fer years."

"So thet is what be happenin. We left tha child behind an began tha long time o travellin till we found Waverley Downs, a cattle property in S.A. Thet be where we live an worked for many long years till Jacqueline get letter from Reagan Chase, tha man thet she be meanin ta marry afore, so she decide ta go back ta Shallow Siding!" Mary said.

"Ya no the rest Axel! An ya no thet there man, Reagan Chase be murdered by ya son on tha train out of Shallow Siding, an thet ya son would hav murdered Jacqueline if Pete Stringer not be savin ha jus in time!" added Mary.

"Yea rememba it all Mary. It be worse fer me now ya told the rest, but I be wonderin why ya tellin me now?"

There was anguish in his teary eyes and Mary tried her best to get on with the real problem.

"Axel you be noin I not put ya through this if it not be serious. Tha reason I hav ta tell ya everythin now be this."

"Jacqueline's child thet she left be a male child, an thet there male child now bein a man. An right now he be here in Shallow Siding lookin fer me, an fer his Mother. I be his only link ta his Mother. Me Ol Grandmother who raise im name im Cheyla. He be ya Grandson Axel!" Mary added.

Slowly Axel raised his head and Mary detected a new light now visible now in his eyes. "Me Grandson! Ya sure me be havin a Grandson Mary?" he asked.

"Yea, as sure as I be standin here Axel!" replied Mary.

"Missus Jacqueline be havin me a Grandson? Tis jus thet me thinks it be too hard ta believe Mary!" he stated.

"Believe Axel! Ya be ok?" questioned Mary in concern.

"Yea Mary, don ya be worryin bout me. I be ok. Jus too much ta take in. We all bin tryin ta forget all thet past stuff, now there be more I not no. Poor Missus Jacqueline! What she goin ta do bout this now?" he asked.

"Not sure Axel! Ya jus can neva pick Jacqueline's mind but it be in Pete's hands now, so we hav ta folla his there orders. Pete be thinkin Cheyla be havin tha right ta no his roots, so I hav ta tell Cheyla all I no when he comes lookin fer me. So I be tellin him things jus afore tha fire an afta!"

"But Axel all tha things thet I not no bout his Dad be when he be young an why he got sent off Shallow Downs. I need ya ta tell him bout his Dad, an all tha bad things he bin doin. Will ya do thet if I send him ta see ya Axel?"

Axel looked ta Mary's eyes. "It be hard fer me Mary, but I promise ya ta be tellin Cheyla tha truth! When he be comin? An do ya no Cheyla be meanin Shallow Downs?"

"I do no what his name be meanin Axel! An he may be here tomorra, I not be noin thet fer sure. Jus had ta warn ya thet's all. Jus one most importan thing be Axel. Don't tell im where Jacqueline be livin, or who she be marryin!"

"We not want im ta turn up at The Outback Gardens!"

"I be keepin thet secret Mary! Ya not ta worry now, I be knowin what ya want! So I will be waitin fer him!"

Chapter 19

Mitchell watched Jacqueline closely as she saddled the stallion. She just wasn't herself this morning.

She seemed very restless last night as she tossed and turned in bed trying to sleep, but when she announced at breakfast she was taking the stallion out, that concerned Mitchell. To choose 'Rain' out of all the other mounts, that confirmed his fear that she was unsettled, as she usually rode him very hard when she wanted to let off steam, and he was thinking that was the mood she was in today.

"Which way are you heading Jackie?" he asked as he reached up a hand to help her mount, but keeping a tight grip on his daughters hand with the other.

"Why can't I go for a ride?" protested Melissa.

Mitchell looked fondly at his daughter and chuckled. "Because Miss Sunshine, we are going on a special trip. A drive in the car to Shallow Downs and then into town. I bet you would like an ice-cream at the milk bar." he said.

"Oh Father!" Melissa giggled at the name he called her then all of a sudden her attitude changed. "Well, maybe I can ride Rain another time!" she decided.

"That's my girl!" he said, then questioned Jackie again.

Jacqueline looked blankly at him. She sensed Mitch was worried as a frown creased his brow, but so eager to get away now she replied quickly. "I think I shall head down the river-road. I will see you both later. I hope you enjoy your day Melissa!" But before either of them could reply she sunk her boots into Rain and he bounded forward.

Mitchell wasted no time as he pulled his mobile from his jacket and dialed.

"Yeah, what's up?" came the reply at the other end.

Thankful to hear Pete's voice, Mitchell spoke.

"Pete! Thanks for picking up so quickly, but I think I may have a situation. Jackie is on Rain and she is in a bad state of mind. I think she is hell-bent on trying to blow off steam so you know only too well how she rides with that attitude. She just left, heading your way on the river-road, but riding fast. Can you saddle up quickly to head her off further down the track somewhere? Just stop her Pete as quick as you like! I have to go into town, Melissa is with me. Call me and let me know what is happening!" he said.

"On my way now!' said Pete, and snapped the phone shut as he raced across the verandah, jumped down the stairs and headed for the stables. He whistled and out in the first paddock the chestnut stallion's head was thrown up. He whinnied and started at full gallop towards him.

Pete grabbed a saddle, his gear and as an afterthought picked up a blanket a water bag and opened the gates to where his big horse stood patiently. "Good stuff Amigo!" he said as he patted him and dug deep in his pocket for a sugar cube. He saddled quickly and was on his back in no time deciding to take the back-track to the river road.

He was at full gallop by the time the back boundary gates came into view, so he eased the stallion down and slipped off his back at the gates. He dug into his saddle bags and pulled out his binoculars then he led his horse through the gates and over to the river where he tied the reins to a tree, and shimmied up to the higher branches.

Pete noticed the dust swirling clearly in the lens, then he picked out Jackie lying low on the Stallions back, but riding hard just like she was racing, and urging Rain on, pushing him to an even greater speed.

'Guess Father was right!' he thought. 'But he usually is and Jackie is hell bent for a disaster happening here. To cover the ground she has in such a short time tells it all.' Though secretly he couldn't help but to admire her talent as he watched her. 'She is one hell of a rider.' he thought. 'She is glued to that saddle and in total control but I guess accidents can happen, and realized his Father's concern.

He had heard tales of her when she was younger from his Father, but he really hadn't personally witnessed her riding skills at this level and he was awestruck and totally mesmerized for a moment forgetting his purpose.

Then reality struck him as Jackie loomed closer in the lens so very hastily he slid down from the tree, grabbed the reins and led his mount to the center of the road where Jackie would have a clear view of them as she rode closer.

Pete was a big man and when mounted on his Stallion he became a formidable figure for Jackie to notice quickly as he guided the Stallion sideways to block the road and raised his muscled arms, then waved her down.

Jacqueline was in a zone of total concentration. She was in her element, and just loving it. There was no time for thoughts of her predicament or worries to enter her head.

She knew exactly what she was doing and the thrill of it excited her. Her surroundings became just a blur as they thundered down the track, but she had no interest or time to look at the scenery, this was serious business. This was racing and she yearned to go faster still, but as she raised her head to see further ahead disappointment overcame her immediately as she spied the imposing figure of Pete Stringer on his favourite horse almost blocking the track.

'Damn!' she cursed. 'I bet I know what he's doing here. Why can't they leave me alone to deal with my problems myself like I've always done all of my life? I just have too many people fussing over me these days. But realistically, at the end of it all at the final curtain when push comes to shove, I know in my heart I will do exactly what I think is best for all concerned, just like I've always done, and I will be telling Mister Pete Stringer exactly that.' she mused.

'It will be my decision, and my decision only. No one else's that is for sure! I will decide my own fate as always, and live with the consequences!' she promised herself.

Casually she eased back on the reins and Rain altered his step to pace himself accordingly at a slow canter, then as they covered the ground towards Pete, he slowed again to her command, and Jacqueline trotted up to Pete.

"Well Pete, fancy meeting you here! Where might you be going Son?" she asked as she reined in beside him.

"Hi Mother! Well Jackie I… He looked at her green eyes searching his face but couldn't lie so he mumbled on.

But as he tried to continue with some excuse he noted the look in her eyes and he realized that he could keep no secrets from this lady, she was much too switched on, and besides he really didn't know what excuse he could give anyway. 'Better confess, tell the truth!" he thought.

However it was Jacqueline who spoke to interrupt his pathetic attempt to reply to her question.

"So it was Mitch, wasn't it Pete? He put you up to this! No need to deny it, I realized that the minute I saw you!"

"Sorry Mother! Was about to tell you just that, but you beat me to it! Father was just so concerned about you, and rang me to ask if I would check on you. So I have, and all is good, but accidents can happen to the best of riders!'

"Yes, I know Pete and I do know that Mitch is worried about me, but I am not made of eggshells. I am not going to break and I will survive. I am a Coby after all!" she said.

Jackie you are not telling me anything I don't already know except this. You! Missus Coby-Stringer are one hell of a rider. I had you in focus with my binoculars. I have never seen you ride like that ever before. You seemed free from the reality around. Though Father has told me many a story of you when you were both younger. I guess there is a lot I don't know about your young lives." he stated.

"Well I will have to enlighten you won't I?" she said. She took out a water bottle from her saddle bag and took a long drink, then looked directly into Pete's blue eyes as she began speaking. "Racing used to be a huge passion of mine when I was a very young girl, so I guess you could say I was enjoying that ride until you interfered Pete!"

253

"I am so sorry Jackie but I was under orders you know. How about we ride back to the house and have morning tea. I did bring a water bag for you but I noticed you have water, but a cup of tea would be better and seeing we are talking about your youth I am interested to hear more!"

Jacqueline laughed as she turned her horse around. "Yes I guess Mitch can be so persuasive so I shall forgive you Pete, however tea, and a chat sounds good." she replied.

"Excellent!" said Pete as he maneuvered his mount to join her. "But continue what you were saying as we ride."

"Your Father gave me a gift of a racing saddle as I used to compete in all the races around the area on my beloved Sailor. He was the most beautiful Black Stallion that you would ever lay eyes on, and Sailor was well known as the fastest horse in the district. Your Father won a race on him once. I was organizing The Gala Event of The Cutting of the Wattle Party so I couldn't compete! But it wasn't only the race that astounded me, it was the prelude to it! "

"You see no-one could ever ride my Sailor. He used to throw anyone who tried, but Mitch mastered my Stallion and had him eating out of his hand so to speak. So that is how he came to ride Sailor in the Gala race. I must admit that at the time I was a little jealous of their bond, but also so very proud of Mitch!" she chuckled in remembrance.

"Father done that, and raced also?" questioned Pete.

"You didn't know? If you think I ride well, then think about this Pete. Your Father was the King! He had such a special way with horses. I called him the horse whisperer, for how he broke them to claim them, then rode them!"

"His talent was far more superior to any rider I had ever seen, myself included Pete. He was a typical Country Cowboy who excelled in horse sports. He won everything he entered into, and was Camp-drafting Champion also!"

"Wow! I wish I had of known that Jackie, but Father is not one to boast you know that. He taught me everything I know about horses, and how to handle them and other animals. He is a legend at that, but I never imagined him in horse events. Come to think of it he never talked about his young life much! I guess there is much more I should know!" he replied with hint of regret in his voice.

His eyes clouded over, and a knot creased his brow. 'He is craving knowledge.' thought Jacqueline with utter astonishment as she looked hard at him.

"Well this could be an eventful morning tea Pete. I have lots to tell about Mitch!" she joked.

Pete looked quickly at Jacqueline. "Could you Mother? I mean."…he stumbled on… "Can we talk about yourself and Father's youth?" he asked.

"Of course Pete!" replied Jacqueline. "You only had to ask you know but you never have. Why now?" she asked.

"I did not think it was proper Jackie, prying into your private lives though there were things I wanted to know, besides the subject never came up before." Pete replied.

"I am an open book Pete! You learnt that the first day we met. You know the absolute worst about me, so I am guessing now you should know some good things! Not only about me, but about your Father also!" she stated.

"I would like that a lot Jackie!" he answered earnestly.

They rode along side by side, their stirrup irons almost touching. Jacqueline could see The Homestead now up on the ridge ahead, and secretly she was thankful for that because the silence seemed to be oppressive now as Pete was a closed book all of a sudden lost in his thoughts.

"I just had a thought Pete!" Jacqueline said, trying to lighten the mood a little. "I bet you didn't know Rain is a descendant of Sailor's, who sired many, many foals in his time. When I left Shallow Downs I left instructions for My Father to give Sailor to Mitch, who then started a breeding program, and bred all Sailors foals for many, many years, trying to imitate the beautiful Black Stallion. He says Rain is the best one he ever had that was a close resemblance.

Pete's head turned and he seemed to be remembering something as his eyes lit up in awareness. "Black horses! It was always only the Black horses which Father kept, he just sold the rest. I always wondered about that Jackie! So now I know! Even then he was thinking of you Jackie!"

Jacqueline felt embarrassed and tried to explain.

"Pete, your Father and I, go back a long, long way, we grew up together! We were the same age even sharing the same birthday date. We were inseparable, and loved the same things. We did everything together with our group of friends. So I guess even back in those days there was a special bond developing between us that always drew us together. When my Father bred Sailor just for me, he then became a big part of both our lives. Mitch loved him too, I knew that for sure! It's the main reason why I had to give Sailor to Mitch. Oh look! There is your Homestead, that didn't take us long really. Race you Pete!" she challenged.

Not really wanting to hear his reply, she put her heels into Rain, and he responded immediately. "Catch me if you can!" she urged Pete on as they bounded away.

Pete Stringer just loved a challenge, but to be bettered by a female rider was unthinkable so he kicked his mount hard and the big chestnut responded and lunged forward to soon reach a full gallop with his big strides.

They covered the ground effortlessly to reach the flank of Rain, and Pete called out. "Got you now Jackie!"

Jacqueline laughed. Pete smiled. He had not seen her laugh out loud like that for a long time. Her face lit up with pure excitement so he laughed too as she called out.

"Ah! Ah! But you are forgetting one thing Mister Pete Stringer. This horse has the genes of a past Champion!" she chuckled, looking back at him as Rain seemed to find another gear at her command, and they drew away.

Pete looked on in amazement. 'No one ever beats me at anything, especially a woman!' he thought dejectedly, but his spirits were soon restored when his gaze drifted to Jackie up ahead. Just to see the elation on her face was something to behold, and he cherished that one moment. She was in her element as if re-born and he realized now what made her tick. 'She knows her own best medicine.'

Finally, much later at Pete's Homestead they were in a more relaxed state as they sat on the verandah at the dining setting though a few jokes and friendly banter was tossed across the table about their race. "I will never live this down when people hear!" stated Pete, as he placed a plate of sandwiches down he had made and looked at her.

Jacqueline chuckled as she poured the tea, but looked at him tenderly as she spoke. "There is no shame in losing Pete, but I guess you are not used to that, are you?"

"You can say that again Jacqueline Coby-Stringer, but I will survive the humiliation. You are a legend!" he said.

"You know what Pete, you are more like your Father than you realize. I am so very proud of you, and of Mitch too, for the way he has raised you. So let us keep this our little secret. We don't have to tell anyone that I beat you!"

Pete stared at her with admiration. "No! No way. We won't be doing that Jackie! There need be no secret. I can accept defeat though I must admit it feels different!" he chuckled. "Besides you have earnt all the accolades for a great ride "But I won't say no to your promised stories!"

"Ok Pete! But where to start?" puzzled Jacqueline.

"Try at the beginning!" offered Pete, and she laughed.

"So be it then! You sure want your two cents worth!"

Pete watched her face closely as her story of her young life unfolded, and the love she bared for her parents and family. Her home at Shallow Downs and the prestige that surrounded it. He could only imagine what that life was like with servants always at your beck and call. Then her Mother and Father at the center of it all creating an empire with the parties they catered for, un-heard of for that era.

Jackie had a special glow about her, especially at the mention of his Father which was often in things they used to do. He tried not to interrupt, but couldn't help himself.

"It sounds like to me that you and Father were in love with each other all your life, even when you were kids!"

"Young love is never forgotten. It goes too deep Pete!"

"What a great life you have lived Jackie. I wish that I had witnessed Shallow Downs in its heyday!" he said.

"Maybe you should visit the New Museum at Shallow Downs Pete. There is much memorabilia there. " she said.

"Now, that is an idea. I will do that! I know it is only recently built, but I haven't had spare time to go and see what you have done out there Jackie. Maybe I'll see some old photos of you and Father. I just can't believe you have done all those things together. So sorry to interrupt your story Jackie but I am enjoying our chat. These things you are saying I have never heard before, so please continue.

Jacqueline looked hard at him. He genuinely seemed to be interested in their youth. She knew probably because his Mother died young, there was no one to tell him any past history. Mitch wasn't one to talk of the past much.

She tried her hardest. Even though at times it proved a difficult task for her to bring up the past, and the pain that surfaced with it, but she thought it was important for Pete to know about it, so she left nothing out.

"Pete, from the instant I walked and talked Mitch was there for me. Of course we loved each other. Even though our love was not spoken about, it was assumed, especially from Mitch who joked and fooled around, but took little time with words that he was too shy to speak of. He could compliment or surprise me with touching gestures but he was so young, still learning, and feeling his way and very, shy to speak out, but love was our special bond growing up, he was forever in my heart!" explained Jacqueline.

Pete frowned. "Father shy in his younger years? I can't imagine Father being shy about anything, so forgive me for finding that hard to comprehend Jackie! He is not shy now, and I have never known him to be! Though that shines a light on unanswered questions bugging me!"

"Well you can take my word for it Pete. Your Father was very shy in his young years! Now what is this about unanswered questions bugging you?" Jacqueline asked.

"I shouldn't ask, but could you explain why you were going to marry someone else when you loved my Father!"

Jacqueline drew in a breath as the undeniable question was asked. 'There it was!' she thought. No-one had ever asked her that question, and she searched her soul for the best response. "Pete I will try my best to explain to you!"

"I was the biggest tom-boy growing up. I reveled in things that men loved to do. Everything my Father taught me of the land, about shooting or driving, were the things Mitch loved too, and why we connected so well. It was in our blood, our Country upbringing was our bond. I learnt ways of survival on our Property, how to raise cattle, and tend a wattle plantation as I was to run it all one day, but there was something else Pete, something important."

Jacqueline looked directly at Pete before she went on.

"Can you keep a personal secret Pete?" she asked.

"Of course I can Mother! What is it?" he asked.

"Then I will say this to you Pete. My Parents and Mary were the only ones who knew this about me, though now you must know that I have never told another living soul of my dilemma back then, not even Mitch. So it must be our secret! I would like it to be kept that way!" she stated.

Pete was puzzled, but he replied earnestly. "Mother you can trust me to keep your personal secret in tact. I will not disclose our conversation to anyone, not even Susan!"

Jacqueline knew by the serious look on Pete's face that he would keep her words safe, and keep his promise to her, so she continued on.

"You may find this strange, but a reality none the less."

"I was devastated to make the transition in my life to become a woman at fourteen. I detested the thought even of trying to be a woman! I hated it with a vengeance, this invasion of my body, and I could even go as far as saying that my resentment was quite obvious to my family, the household, and our family doctor at the time."

Pete gaped at her. This was not what he was expecting. He never imagined this beautiful woman could not accept her birthright as a woman. "Go on Jackie!" he stammered.

Jacqueline smiled. "But as time passed, so too did my childish ways. But it took a young man like Reagan Chase who was much older and wiser who taught me that being a woman was a very special thing, and that I was special. It was what my Mother had been telling me all along!"

"So I guess you could say that I was swept off my feet by Reagan Chase, and I was introduced to romance in an innocent way I didn't think possible. He openly loved me, and said words of love, and finally an offer of marriage."

"So you see my dilema Pete? I loved two completely different young men, in completely different ways!"

"My god Jackie, what did Father do?" asked Pete.

Jacqueline chuckled as she looked at Pete, then smiled.

She didn't have the heart to say that Mitchell Stringer didn't even recognize, or realize what she was going through back then. Especially that she was going through a crisis in her teens, so she tried to explain it to him.

"Just to put it simply Pete. Mitch confused me with his actions. In his Country way he was very laid back. So he accepted that life was what it was, and that is what we got. Our future seemed all mapped out to him where we would end up together like most Country folk, so words were irrelevant and didn't need to be said when we were so young he assumed! So that suited him well enough, as he was far too shy to say them!" Jacqueline disclosed.

Pete opened his mouth to speak, but closed it quickly. His face was in anguish, not really knowing what to say.

"He just couldn't say the words I desperately needed to hear Pete!" she cried. "There was no, I love you Jackie! Instead only unspoken words of love by loving gestures, and such niceties' towards me. He teased with a manner of assuming our relationship as someone who knows you deep down, someone who you have a deep bond with, is the one you will end up with in your life. Someone you will marry one day. 'Mitch's philosophy.' One day! Pete."
"He didn't think to ask me to marry him Pete!" she said.

"Oh Jackie I am shattered, and so sorry I can't speak, only to say. Thank god you found each other again! You were meant to be together from the start!" he stressed.

At that remark a tear slid down Jacqueline's cheek.

"I thank god for that every day too Pete!" she replied.

"So sorry to upset you Mother! I really didn't mean to pry so much, will you be ok?" Pete asked with concern.

"Yes Pete I will be fine. Now you know my life story!" she laughed. "I must get home now, but before I go. May I just say a little about Cheyla Stone please?" she asked.

"Sure Jackie, what did you want to say?" he asked.

"After our dinner I have thought a lot and most things you have done are fine by me. I know you are just trying to protect me, and I do need that, which was undoubtably proven when you saved me before. Mostly I tend to go it alone, so no one else gets hurt or tied up in my mistakes!"

"Now hold on one minute Jackie!" Pete interrupted. "I didn't take this upon myself for any other reason but to protect you from harm, just in case this Cheyla was a bad egg! But Jackie it wouldn't embarrass, or hurt me at all to be involved in your mistakes. Mother you are my family!"

"Pete I do appreciate everything you've done, and the relationship, and understanding you have with Cheyla is good. So as I am family like you said, then please listen to me. I want you to back off!" she said with determination.

"Back off! I can't back off Jackie, this has to be handled with certainty, so I know for sure you are safe!" he stated.

"You must Pete! I just have to act on my own decisions when, and if I make them, and only I can do that! But it is nice to know that you are here if I need you." she said.

In surprise Pete offered. "He checks out you know! All he said is true. He is a wealthy land and mine owner!"

"Still, I have to do it my way Pete, please understand! It is all I really know is how to rely on my instincts."

He held up his hands in defence. "Your call Mother!"

"But I sure as hell hope your instincts are correct in this."

Chapter 20

Cheyla parted the curtains to look out the window. It was just breaking day. 'Thank goodness this night is over.' he thought, as he let the curtain drop and turned to pace the floor. 'But what now? How do I fill in time before I can leave, the waiting is going to be the worst today.'

His nights sleep seemed somewhat non-existant as he had tossed and turned all night, with thoughts of rejection plaguing him, and sleep would not come.

'Finally!' he thought. 'What an important day.' But his excitement was overshadowed by doubts of his decision to seek out Mary Higgs, a vital link and reason for his trip, but now the day was suddenly here, his gut churned.

'Will I be shunned, and fobbed off with some excuse?' he wondered. 'Will a secret service protecting his Mother continue to shield her? There has to be a way to find her?'

His mobile phone ringing startled him as it broke the silence in the room and shattered his thoughts. He moved over to grab it up from the desk, and looked down at the all-familiar number on the screen of his private office.

In relief he took the call, and with mixed emotion he acknowledged the voice at the other end, but felt guilty.

It had been quite some time since he had called home, but now as he listened to the all-familiar screeching voice of his friend Jono he laughed. "Not so loud Jono, you will wake the whole household! Milly won't like that!" he said in jest. However now he was feeling that finally after all this time away he had something important to report.

Cheyla was pleased to hear all was good at home, that was a load off his mind. Then immediately he started telling Jono his news. What he had been doing since last time they spoke, but more importantly of his imminent meeting with Mary Higgs finally happening today.

They chatted for sometime until Cheyla could hear the rattle of the breakfast tray on the shelf outside his room, so he ended his conversation by promising Jono he would call him after he had met with Mary, and had something more positive to tell him. He detected the silence at the other end. "What is it Jono?" he asked with concern.

"Jus missin ya thets all Cheyla. Ya bin gone too long now. It jus not be tha same here without ya!" said Jono.

"Jono, all this time away I have had nothing to go on, but now I do have hope. This is very important to me and I promise to come home after I meet my Mother, and Jono, she is in this town! I know that now so please be patient. I do thank you for taking care of everything at home so I can do this. It won't be for much longer!" he replied. Jono replied and Cheyla ended the call, then hurried to get his breakfast. He made coffee, and ate leisurely. His plan was to leave about 9.30am so he had plenty of time. He only had to shower and dress then drive out to the property.

Shallow Downs was well marked on the map inside of the brochure so Cheyla easily found the right road out of town, but he need not have worried because the road out was well signed by billboards, and indicating the new aditions and Tourist attractions to the Property.

As he neared the turn off he could see the paddocks of rows, and rows of wattle trees climbing the slopes, and he immediately thought of Jim McKenzie and his quip to his son about growing wattle instead of crops. He chuckled at the memory, and turned off the main road.

'It is just huge this place!' he thought to himself, as the wattle paddocks soon made way for a different aspect of the Property where the ghost gums grew high and alongside the road a creek flowed. He passed a timber mill then paddock, after paddock of cattle country at its best, where prime cattle grazed in contentment, to remind him of his home, as he reached the front portals of Shallow Downs.

He remembered a feeling he had at the Display Centre in town when he first picked up the brochure of Shallow Downs, and now as he braked at the entrance that same feeling returned. 'Strange!' he thought. 'But I just knew I had to come here!' He admired the painted sign, and the artist 'Axel Hall! 'He has art everywhere.' he thought.

Cheyla drove slowly through the complex, noting all the new buildings and the signs to the carpark, but it was the main Homestead he wanted, and he looked at it now.

'Not at all what I thought it would be! A little mediocre for the size of the property. I wonder why?' he mused.

He parked his 4WD in shade, walked along pavers to the stairs, then up across the porch, and rang the doorbell.

Mary was unsettled. She was sitting in the office at the Homestead doing the book work, and ordering for the café. She didn't have to do the hard yards anymore now that she was a Manager, but it still felt strange to her to be doing book-work, and giving directions to the staff.

Melissa Stringer sat quietly, but very importantly, next to her, as she busily coloured in the figures of her book.

Mitchell Stringer had called earlier to ask Mary to care for Melissa while he drove over to the timber mill to order some timber for his property. He didn't expect to be long.

But it wasn't her work at all that was keeping Mary on edge. She knew quite well what was bothering her. Lately she seemed to be walking on eggshells and seemingly she was just waiting for disaster to happen as her nerves were stretched to breaking point. So the sound of the doorbell ringing made her start, and she jumped in her seat.

"Daddy!" yelled Melissa, as she bounced from the seat knocking her pencil cup off the table, as she raced for the door, then out down the hallway to the front door.

"Wait Melissa!" Mary called, as she bent to pick up the pencils, and as she was putting them back on the table she could hear Melissa speaking in her childish chatter.

Melissa reached the front door, and while standing on her tip-toes she turned the big knob eagerly expecting her Father to be there, and opened the door wide.

"Oh!" she exclaimed. Suddenly aware that a stranger was standing there. "Yes please Mister, may I help you?" she asked in her childish chatter. A cheeky smile altered her mouth but as she tilted her head sideways waiting for a reply, her golden curls fell about her face in a cascade.

Her eyes sparkled as she raised her head to look up at the huge man standing there. Suddenly though, she felt a little scared and stepped back a little poised for flight, and was about to close the door when he knelt before her.

Cheyla smiled down at her angelic face, but it was the eyes that captivated him. They were an imitation of his own, and he felt an affinity towards her.

Then he realized he was too tall for her to see into his eyes, so he knelt down on one knee before her, a big grin spread across his face, and he laughed as he spoke to her.

"Well now my ladyship, that is better. We can see each other now. My name is Cheyla. What is yours?" he asked.

Melissa at once giggled at the name that he called her. It was just like her Father did by calling her special names.

"Cheyla!" she repeated, stumbling a little on the name.

"Yes Cheyla!" he smiled down at her, then they both laughed at her pronunciation.

"My name is Melissa!" she stated boldly.

"Well that is a lovely name! What a pleasure it is to meet you Melissa!' Cheyla said, as he extended his hand. "It's a nice place you have here my ladyship!" he jested.

Melissa laughed at his jest. "It is not my place Cheyla." she said between fits of giggles, but she put out a hand.

Cheyla took her small hand in his large one. He smiled as they shook hands, then Melissa spoke again.
Her head turned with that way she had in question. "Why are you here Cheyla, who did you want to see?"

"Well seeing you asked Melissa. I travelled a long way just to come here looking for a lady named Mary Higgs!"

Mary could hear Melissa talking to someone at the front door, but she couldn't believe her ears as she overheard the conversation, and she raced down the hall.

At the front door, she pulled the door wide to chastise Melissa severely. "Melissa!" she said sternly. "Jus what ya think ya bin doin there answerin tha door? An talkin ta a stranger too! Ya be comin inside with me young lady!" she said as she took Melissa's hand then looked at Cheyla.

She stifled a gasp as she looked at him and recognition was no mistake in her mind. 'He be jus like…her thoughts were going to over-rule her and she immediately wanted to just hug him as tears smarted her eyes. But she steeled herself and instead she looked at him sternly, then spoke severely to him. 'Please be goin ta tha end o tha verandah Cheyla Stone there be a seat there an I be comin out ta talk ta ya when I get Melissa something ta play with. An also! Ya should be noin betta then ta talk ta a little baby!"

Cheyla just stared at her in confusion. 'She knows my name. Who is this woman?' he wondered, as he gaped at her. "Yes maam!" he muttered, but she was already half-way through the door tugging at Melissa's hand. Cheyla's reply was lost as the door shut but he heard Melissa call.

"Bye, bye Cheyla!"

"Bye Melissa!" he called, then he heard her complaint.

"You do know Mary that I am not a baby, don't you?" Melissa asked Mary in anguish.

'Mary?' 'Melissa has just called that woman Mary! It couldn't be, could it?' he wondered. 'In all the time I have spent searching for Mary Higgs, I didn't think that a baby would find her for me!' he chuckled to himself.

He laughed as he heard this child speak. Even though in a little childish chatter, it was said with such authority.

'This little lady is well bred.' he thought to himself.

He stared at the closed door then slowly he moved and walked to the end of the verandah as he was told and took a seat overlooking gardens to glance over the property.

He had a great view of the grounds from where he was sitting, and could even see the new buildings across the carpark. No doubt they were the tourist attractions.

As he looked out over the paddocks he noted it was a large property, though not as extensive as Tenungeri, so once again he found himself counting his blessings for the fruits in life he had obtained. 'Now there seemed only one thing he lacked in his life that was most important to him, and that was to have someone to share it all with him.'

Cheyla was deep in thought so he didn't notice that he had company. Mary took advantage of the respite as she stood back a little just to study him.

'He be so handsome, an so much like Jacqueline's side o tha family.' she thought to herself, and immediately she knew what she had to do, and she spoke.

"I hear ya bin lookin fer me Cheyla Stone, so now ya be findin me, an me thinks I be noin what ya want!"

Cheyla's head turned and his green eyes softened, but flashed his interest as they caressed her face.

"So! Would you be Mary Higgs?" he asked.

"No! Tis no more Cheyla, since me be married ta Drew Hargraves. Now me name be Mary Hargraves. But yea I be Mary Higgs afore, an fer a long time!" she laughed.

He could barely contain his excitement. His breathing became rapid to a point where he could feel the rise and fall of it, and his heart thumped in his chest.

Cheyla searched Mary's face for any animosity there, but found none, but he choked up when he tried to speak.

"My go...odness I can..not believe it. I have actually found you at last, and do you know Mary Hargraves that I...I have travelled half way around Australia to find you, and as you suggested before. What I want? Yes it's true. I am seeking my Mother, my birth Mother. You see Mary I was raised... His voice trailed off as Mary interrupted.

"I be noin ya past Cheyla, so I be one person ya don't hav ta tell anythin ta bout ya past life. Except maybe ya own Mother. If ya eva get ta see ha!"

"You know my past? How come Mary?" he asked.

"Cause I be at ya birth Cheyla, an I be left here Shallow Downs ta travel to tha N.T. with ya Mother as I hav family there. Me Old Grandmother, uncles, aunts and cousins!"

"Hell you were at my birth Mary? Then you will know what happened more than anyone else! Will you tell me all you know, and where my Mother is?" he pleaded.

"I be tellin ya jus one thing now Cheyla, an thet be this. Ya name Cheyla! It be meanin 'Shallow Downs' cause me Old Grandmother be so cunnin by namin ya afta I be tellin ha where I be comin from. Ya see! Long ago tha aborigines worked the fields here an non o them could say 'Shallow Downs' so they be callin it Cheyla-D, so thet be where ya name be comin from!" Mary stared at his gaping face.

'So there it was finally! One piggy off my back.' Cheyla thought in bewilderment. 'All my life it has hounded me!'

'Others always questioned him about it endlessly, but it only fueled the fire within him. Anger would take over to stress him, and he would shake his head in confusion, not knowing what to tell them. His name was an unusual one, but to be named after a property, that he had never been to, was not what he was expecting to hear?'

It was very clear to Mary that this bit of information had shocked Cheyla as he still stood gaping at her.

"Ya be ok Cheyla?" she asked in concern.

His look was of one who was stunned, but slowly his eyes focused again and he looked at Mary when he spoke.

"It is a great shock to me Mary to hear the meaning of my name and it is something that has always haunted me. But why Mary? What has this property to do with me?"

"Cause Cheyla, your Mother be ownin it. Twas where she be raised, an me too, where I be her servant." she said.

"My Mother owns this place?"Cheyla said in wonder. "And you her servant? Mary are you serious?" he asked.

"I be very serious! I be tellin ya no lies. Ya see, back in them years Shallow Downs be known fer bein tha richest property, an twas tha most beautiful Homestead here of thet there era. 'How do ya say it?' Prestigious twas!" Mary struggled with the word. "Thet be cause tha Owner be a mighty man name Clayton Coby who only had tha best!"

"I not be tellin ya no more Cheyla. There be two things I be wantin ya ta do, then ya will know more. I hav ta get back ta Melissa now so I be wantin ya ta go ta The Historic Museum first, an then ya will see fer yourself. Here be an address o Axel Hall's." she said, as she passed him a note.

273

"Why Axel Hall? He is the artist who painted the land-scape I brought. What has he to do with this?" he asked.

"He be ya only livin Grandfather Cheyla!" she replied.

Cheyla opened his mouth, then closed it again. Mere words could not describe what he was feeling. He wanted answers, but the truth was hitting him hard.

"So Cheyla, I be wantin ya ta go talk ta Axel. I be callin him ta say ya comin, an he be waitin fer ya. Then ya com ta see me. I be finishin me work at 4pm. Ya com out ta me house an then we talk Cheyla. Jus folla tha road near tha creek up toward tha mountin, then ya cross tha creek over a new bridge an folla tha road. It be a mile in to me house! An I be waitin fer ya Cheyla!" stated Mary.

Cheyla could sense he would hear no more from Mary now so he rose from the seat, and held out his hand.

"Ok Mary! I will do what you wish for now! I will see you this afternoon at your home, and who knows? Maybe that will be when you tell me where my Mother is!"

Mary shuddered with dread of that outcome, but took his hand in a handshake. His hand was warm, but so large that her small hand seemed to disappear. She shook, as she tried to summon up a reply for him, but he turned on his heel, and walked down the verandah to the stairs. She watched him walk out to the carpark, and get in his 4WD.

Then something was squeezing her chest so tightly she could hardly breathe, and she grabbed for the seat to sit down, then sobbed her heart out. 'This be takin lot out o me!' she thought. 'Tis too hard. Oh poor Jacqueline!' She sat a while to calm down, then went inside to ring Axel.

CHEYLA

There were many tourists heading over to The Historic Museum as Cheyla slowly drove around the visitor's car-park. He was lucky to find one park near a shady tree, so he shut the engine down and climbed out of his 4WD.

He idly walked through a trellised archway of wisteria in full bloom to the entrance of The Historic Museum and somehow felt nostalgic as he climbed the stairs where he dug deep for a wad of notes to go in the box provided.

Visitors moved slowly along the exhibits, so he hung back a little as something attracted his eye, and he wanted to get a closer, private viewing. Just inside of the entance a showcase of framed coloured pictures dressed the wall.

As he moved in closer he stopped dead in his tracks as the massive man dominating the photo stared back at him with those deep green eyes… But the face… His face was a mirror image of his own, and Cheyla gasped. He knew now why people he had met in this town had re-acted so strangely toward him, so he didn't need the caption at the bottom of the photo to recognize his Grandfather, or even the lady near him dwarfed by his size, his Grandmother.

'How perfect they look together! Such pride emanates in their faces.' he thought, as a longing twisted inside him.

However it was the eyes of a beautiful girl sitting on a Black Stallion that captivated him, and his attention was diverted momentarily, but especially when he gazed into her beautiful face. It took his breath away, and he gasped. 'She has my eyes!' he realized.'My exact colour eyes!'

With great sadness in his heart for a life missed out on, Cheyla realized at once that he was looking at his Mother. 'My Mother, I am certain! 'Also with My Grandparents.'

He was finding it hard to tear himself away from the photographs of these three people, people who were very real to him now, but there were so many others begging.

There was just so much to look at, and to read, that it made him realize the reality of it as it came to him.

Here was a record of someone's entire life, and well worthy of these multiple exhibits in a museum.

Someone who had the foresight to build an empire in an era when it was un-heard of to do so. It took someone like Clayton Coby who stood out as a mountain of a man proudly beside his wife Mel, and his youngest daughter Jacqueline Coby, and he done it with prestige and finesse. 'He was my Grandfather after all. I would expect no less!'

Now Cheyla knew his Mother's name. 'It may help my search, but I am guessing otherwise.' But to see her in a past life was beyond his wildest dreams. His heart filled with love, and pride just by knowing that he was a part of her. Every picture of her portrayed a particular trait as her innerself shone through with a deep pride, not unlike her Fathers, and pure determination was etched upon her beautiful face. Something Cheyla was yet to witness in a young girl, but now that he had seen her he realized.

'She is just beautiful, inside and out!' he thought.

He moved slowly to the next exhibit and stood staring at it in awe. It was a picture of a Grand Homestead which stood proudly amidst the masses of colourful, manicured gardens. 'Wow, now that is just some Homestead!' and he thought of the one he had just seen. 'Why?' he wondered.

'What happened to the Grand Original Homestead?'

Then huge fires filled his vision as he looked upon the following picture, and his heart saddened as he read the caption, and the section of his Grandmother's fate. So now he knew what fate be-fell the Grand Homestead.

He read articles, saw memorabilia in the halls, but in a final room before the exit out to The Gardens, he paused in awe just to appreciate the fine artwork of Axel Hall's piece which covered most of the wall. 'The Cutting of the wattle Garden Party.' It was captioned, year 1961.

This masterpiece of art made him aware once again of a bygone era, and all the prestige of Shallow Downs, and he was named after it. 'This was his roots.' he thought.

Finally he walked through to admire The Gardens and then into 'Coby's Retreat' where he sat drinking coffee.

There had been so much to take in and so much to hear as he listened to the tourists speaking about the exhibition gallery, and of Clayton Coby who appeared to be a legend of a man in his time that his mind was in turmoil as he sat there to ponder on the information that he had acquired.

It was not the riches or wealth of Shallow Downs, or all the functions they held back in the day that had got to him, but he could only surmise or read between the lines to its demise. 'What really happened to bring down this most prestigious property that flourished in another era?'

So by the time he left Shallow Downs he knew that no mere words could describe the feelings he had got by just looking at all those photographs, and he couldn't help but wonder why Mary Higgs was so anxious for him to meet Axel Hall. 'He was his Grandfather she had said, but what else could he add to all this?' he wondered.

Chapter 21

As he drove down the main street of Shallow Siding Cheyla's brow furrowed, and his gut churned as he tried to digest all he had heard and seen that morning.

To finally meet Mary Higgs had been a huge plus for him, but now he understood her reason for limiting their conversation to instead send him to the Historic Museum.

He had left no stone unturned there, and what he saw would remain with him always, and dear to his heart.

He took the hospital road after he had driven through town, then peered down on the seat where a small street map was scrawled on the note Mary had given him for Axel's address. It was quite accurate he detected, as all too soon he was to veer off the road to the right as per her instructions. A street sign confirmed he was on the correct street so he drove on slowly down the street, then noticed the street number of a small unit with a wooden gate.

As he parked and unlatched the gate to go through, he happened to look up as he walked along the pathway and realized he didn't even have to knock on the door because the front door opened wide as he watched a wiry little old man, who was smiling broadly, appear in the doorway.

279

Axel's palms were sweating and he wrung his hands anxiously as he sat on the couch to wait patiently for his visitor to arrive after he had the phonecall from Mary.

He was so nervous because he had no happy events to tell of. It was all bad, and he shuddered to think of it. Stuff he had tried for years to push to the back of his mind. He was ashamed, and now he wondered what effect it would have on his Grandson. 'Their first meeting was doomed.'

'Whateva will I say? An how I be startin ta tell tha poor boy bout tha bad stuff, an there be so much!' he thought.

He was startled, and rose quickly when he heard a car pull up out front, and peaked through a slit in the blinds.

His heart seemed to jump in his chest as the huge man climbed out of his 4WD, and Axel watched him closely.

'Well this be it!' he cautioned himself, then hurried to open the door, and flashed his best smile while waiting in the doorway. Then suddenly he recoiled in shock.

It wasn't only one factor that the man he watched now walking up the path had appeared to be more enormous as he got closer. It was his face…Axel Hall knew that face so well…Then when the man spoke and their eyes met it was more than Axel could bare and he swayed on his feet.

Cheyla looked up at the smiling old man. Suddenly he thought. 'Finally I feel at least someone wants to see me!' and as their eyes met, he smiled. "Hi there! Would you be Axel Hall?" he asked, just as Axel's face crumbled, and he was falling. Just one leap it took Cheyla to grab him before he hit the floor. He bundled him in his arms, and took him inside to lay him down on the sofa. He grabbed a cushion to put under his head, and stared at him with concern.

He noticed that Axel's breathing was heavy. His eyes were a little weird, but he was conscious so he spoke.

"Axel! My name is Cheyla Stone. Please tell me what is wrong, and how I can help you?" he said in a concerned voice. 'Just don't you die on me Axel Hall, as we haven't even met yet!' he thought to himself as he leaned closer.

"Me pills!" Came a whispered reply, but when he tried to point Axel's hand fell to his side.

Cheyla looked around the small room. There was an oval table set in the corner, and on it was what he thought looked like a pill bottle so he went across to pick them up and read the label. He knew those pills as his Ol Mother used to take them for her heart so he took them over to Axel and asked. "Are these what you need Axel?"

Axel's eyes opened and he recognizised the bottle. 'Jus be needin one under me tongue Cheyla.' he rasped.

Cheyla opened the bottle to get one, and popped it into his mouth, then pulled a chair in to sit down.

At that precise moment a female voice called out from the back rooms to startle him. It was voice that was music to his ears, and one that he thought he would never hear again for some time, and it sent chills up his spine.

"Axel? Axel where are you? I thought you would be out painting, but you weren't there! I am finished….Her voice trailed off as she poked her head in the doorway, then she took in the scene. "Axel whatever is wrong?" she asked, as she stood staring at them both, her eyes blazing, then she rushed to the sofa."You!" she said, as she stared at Cheyla. "Just what have you done? Why are you here?"

281

Her hair was plaited and contained by a ribbon at the base of her head, but still it fell over her shoulder in a long plait, and at that moment Cheyla had never seen her look more beautiful. Her face was flushed. 'Was it a blush?' he wondered. 'I think not!' he realized as he looked deep into those dark smouldering eyes, but in that instant, for some reason she reminded him of a lioness protecting her cub.

He could hardly breathe as his chest tightened, then there was that all too familiar ache deep inside that he was getting accustomed to, but could not fathom.

Just the sight of her was enough to make him tongue-tied, but as he looked at her he realized she was waiting for a reply, so he tried his best to answer her. "Well…We ah… meet again Tarryn Westley! What a nice surprise!"

"It is not a pleasant surprise at all Cheyla Stone! Just what do you think you are doing here?" she quipped.

"Ah, well…I ah, came to visit Axel! You see…He did not finish what he was saying as she interrupted him.

"But, you are a stranger here. Do you know him?"

"Ah…Not really." He looked to Axel who seemed to be recovered a little now, and he detected a hidden smile passing his lips as he looked from one to the other.

'What is going on here?" Axel wondered. He was the forgotten patient, and he was witnessing a fiery debate.

Cheyla acknowledged Axel with a plea in his eye, then he winked. "Well, you see Tarryn, Axel is going to show me some of his art!" replied Cheyla, though the lie did not sit right with him, but he could not say why he was there.

"Oh really? I am sorry. I didn't think!" she mumbled.

CHEYLA

Axel looked at them both and immediately sensed the tension, and something else going on between them both so he didn't have to be a genius to work that one out.

'Ah, yes!' he rubbed his chin as he thought. 'Me art be jus tha thing I be needin ta talk with me Grandson a bit ta get ta no him afore we bin getting inta bad conversations bout his Dad. Jus should hav thought o thet. Seems ta me thet Cheyla he bin likin art, so tis lucky thet we be havin somethin in common ta talk bout.'

He was feeling much better so he rose to sit up.

Tarryn looked at him, and then went to sit beside him.

"Oh Axel, I am so sorry. Can I help you at all? What is the problem? Is something wrong with you?" she asked.

"Tarryn don't ya be worryin, I be ok now. I be takin a turn. Twas shock me thinks, an Cheyla he be helpin me! He be jus at tha door as I be fallin, so he grab me ta help me inside. He give ta me one pill, an I be fine now. Hav a weak heart ya no thet Tarryn" he said.

"Yes I know, but will you be alright if I leave you now. I was about to say before that I finished your washing and cleaning, but I have to go back to work now" she replied.

"I be fine Tarryn, off ya go! An thank ya fer all ya help, though ya don't need ta be doin it ya no!" said Axel.

"Oh rubbish Axel! I am just only too pleased to help you. Now, I will come back in two days for your elbow treatment. If you are not well, call me at the hospital!"

Axel looked at Cheyla who had a puzzled look on his face. "Sorry Cheyla fer not includin ya as we bin keeping ya in tha dark, but Tarryn be workin at tha Hospital as a Physiotherapist, so she be comin here ta treat me elbow!"

"Be damn arthritis in me joint so she bin treatin thet as it hurts ta do me paintins now. But all tha time she come, she has ta do other work fer me. I tell her not to, but thet be Tarryn ya jus can't stop ha. Tis determined is Tarryn!"

Cheyla looked at Tarryn, and his teeth flashed white as a smile lit his face, and he chuckled. "Yes Axel, I have noticed! Though we don't know many details about one another at all really. We've bumped into each other a couple of times at Jed's saddlery, so we haven't got into small talk yet. But if she would stand still long enough to talk, I would like that well enough!" his grin widened as he looked at her but he was sure her eyes changed colour.

"Oh Jed! He be Tarryn's Uncle, a good friend o mine. Guess thet be why Tarryn has takin ta lookin out fer me." You no what Cheyla! You an Tarryn, ya should be gettin ta talk more me thinks!" ya should hav a lot in common!"

"Just what I was was thinking Axel!" replied Cheyla.

But Tarryn's eyes sent daggers to him as she rose, and her plaited hair fell forward to her waist as she spoke.

"Let me tell you both something gentlemen. I shall be the one who decides who I will talk more with thank you, and now if you will both excuse me, that is if you are sure you have finished talking about me, then I shall leave for work! See you in two days Axel! Without another word she headed for the front door, opened it, and was gone.

Cheyla's face fell as he stared at Axel in question.

Axel could feel his distress. "Go! Go now!" he pointed.

"Thank you Grandfather. I will be back!" and he ran. As the words sunk in he shed a tear. 'Grandfather!' he say.

CHEYLA

Tarryn stomped down the pathway in total annoyance by the conversations. 'How dare he make a mockery of our meetings, or rather, the lack of them?' she thought.

"Tarryn wait! Wait up!" Cheyla called to interrupt her anger. She couldn't believe the gall he had to follow her.

Then she heard the footfalls close behind her as Cheyla was calling her name, so she stopped and whirled around quickly to face him. 'This time she would set him right!'

But this time she turned right into his path as he closed in on her, and he could not stop, so she fell sprawling into his arms. He grabbed for her to stop her fall, then his huge arms closed around her and tenderly he pulled her closer.

"Please don't go Tarryn!" he whispered into her ear as his lips leant against hair so fragrant it made him giddy.

She lifted her head, and stared up into his eyes. Those beautiful green eyes were consuming her, but something else was in them that was all too obvious to her, and her heart seemed to melt and miss a beat. She saw a yearning in his eyes that she had never experienced before, but the strange thing was, she herself felt the same yearning.

Time seemed to stand still as they looked at each other. No-one spoke as Cheyla drew her closer and wrapped her in an embrace. His head slowly moved down and his lips ever so softly brushed hers then he showered her face and neck with feather-like kisses until Tarryn could bear it no more, then she grabbed a fistful of his hair and pulled him down to her, and their lips came together with such force from her urgency that their teeth gnashed.

"Oh my goodness!" she uttered when their kiss finally ended, lips still apart. 'Cheyla Stone you do surprise me!"

Cheyla looked longingly at her. "I am ever so pleased to hear you say that, so I like it well enough! But you Miss Tarryn Westley! You don't surprise me, not at all! I just knew from the first moment I saw you that we would be good together! I wanted that so much. Just getting you to see it was my problem!" he said, as he claimed her lips yet again, and she shivered as she thrilled to his touch.

Their mouths were searching, bruised lips unfelt in the heat of their desire as tongues entwined, and each shared a similar passion to vent their emotions. So it was a long, tender, but smoldering kiss as Cheyla released his pent-up emotions upon her. Tarryn's response was immediate as if she couldn't get enough of him, and she pressed her body closer to him still, drinking in his desire and power.

As they parted he held her at arms length, as his eyes searched hers as they smoldered with desire as she spoke.

"I too, Mister Cheyla Stone, have had feelings for you from day one if you must know. Just couldn't make it too easy for you!" she chuckled. "That is a man's job to seek out the lady then prove his intentions, don't you think?"

"Ah! So the truth is finally out. I hope you realize that you made my life miserable with your taunts!" he replied.

"Oh! But you don't know how miserable I have been also Cheyla as I too knew we would be good together. I've been waiting a long time in my life for this moment when the right person came along, and it was worth the wait!"

"Well, so we finally agree on something!" he chuckled. "Though I must add. There are many ways I dreamed of kissing you but never on a pathway of someone's house!" Tarryn laughed out loud, and Cheyla laughed with her.

286

"What say we start again Tarryn? We could start right now, so we can learn more about each other and get... His voice trailed off as she interrupted him.

"Nothing would please me more Cheyla! So I have to say with feeling. 'Yes please! Let us start again!' However, right now I am afraid that is not possible, or convenient. I have to go to work remember, a late shift too. But as from tomorrow, and the next day, I have a whole two days off!"

He at first looked dejected but then as Cheyla thought about it he realized he had important things still to do today, so he agreed by saying. "Excellent Tarryn, that suits my plans anyway now I have thought about it. But! Tomorrow at first light. We begin! I shall pick you up for breakfast and we will see what the day unfolds! Agreed?"

Tarryn looked at him instantly. 'Cheyla appears to be very much a man of purpose, and knows what he wants, as if he is used to taking control. I like that in a man, so I guess I'll find out more about this Cheyla Stone in time.'

"Sounds like a great plan Cheyla. I live in the Hospital nurses quarters around back, room 6. I will be waiting!"

"Great, then I guess you could say that is a date then? So not to mention it is our first date either!" he chuckled.

Tarryn laughed. "Yes Cheyla it is, and I am so looking forward to it. Got to rush now though, see you in the early hours!" she raised her head to kiss him on the cheek, and then she was away, walking briskly down the path. At the gate she turned to wave, and blew him a kiss.

Cheyla watched her leave, but he couldn't believe the feelings he had inside. He felt he was on top of the world.

Axel Hall let the blind close as he moved away from the window where he had been secretly spying on the events that were happening outside, and a huge smile spread his mouth wide, but he stifled a chuckle as he went to the front door to open it wide. 'Jus new it!' he mused.

As Tarryn's car pulled away from the curb and Cheyla turned to walk up the path, he too supported a huge grin as he reached the stairs and looked at Axel standing there.

"Me thinks ya be lot happier now Cheyla!" joked Axel.

"Can't thank you enough Grandfather for giving me a push, but now I have an actual date in the morning with Miss Tarryn Westley. This girl has been bugging me since the first day we met." he chuckled. "Or I should say from the first time that I sent her sprawling into the dust!"

Axel laughed. "You pushed her over?" he questioned.

"It was accidental! It was over at Jed's back shed when I pushed the doors out I didn't know she was on the other side!" he laughed. "But she went sprawling in the dirt!"

They both laughed together.

"Com, com up Cheyla. Ya wanted ta see me art didn't ya?" asked Axel, hoping to start the visit on a happy note.

"Oh! I just told Tarryn that because I couldn't tell her the real reason why I was here! I didn't want her to know that yet, so it seemed a good excuse at the time. You see Axel, Mary Higgs sent me to see you. My name is Cheyla Stone! Oh! No, not really! Stone is the name I gave myself as I have no roots, no real identity. So that is the reason why I am here in Shallow Siding. I am trying to find my birth Mother, but Mary told me that you had things to tell me, and also that you were my Grand…. His words were interrupted as Axel raised a hand to stop him talking.

"I no who ya be Cheyla so ya don't hav ta explain. I be knowin Mary be sendin ya, an yes I hav a lot ta tell ya, but first can we jus get ta no each other, an later afta I be tellin ya me story. Well then ya can tell me if ya still want ta call me ya Grandfather! You do like art, don't ya?" he asked.

Cheyla looked puzzled at the old man's words, but he decided to let it slide and replied in earnest. "You bet I like art! I have a lot of artwork at home, and as a matter of fact I purchased one of your paintings while in town. It was of a landscape, captured from the hills, looking down into the valley and the town. Great piece of art that is!"

Axel scratched his head. "Ah yep, I be rememerin thet one now. I sat way up on tha hillside thet time jus ta get me sketches!" he laughed, as he recalled that time. "Hav bin in som strange places doin sketches Cheyla! But now thet I think of it, I hav com a long way I guess. Use ta jus use charcoal ta sketch on ol tin cans!" he chuckled. Com out tha back Cheyla, an I be tellin ya bout it, an show ya me work. We can talk there!" he said, as he beckoned.

Cheyla laughed with him as he followed him through the tiny unit towards the back stairs. "Charcoal sketches? I can just picture you doing that, but why do that? Why not get the proper equipment for your art?" he asked.

Axel laughed, then sighed. "I hav so much ta tell ya I don't no where ta start, but me be guessin this will do. So will tell ya how I be startin ta paint." he chuckled. "Go on down!" he pointed. "Thet down there be me art room!"

It was more like a lean-to rather than an art room. 'A make-shift building built out from a rear section of the unit!' was Cheyla's thoughts, but as he stepped down to the ground which was a dirt floor he did notice that it was quite large. It was almost all covered in on the three sides with big windows allowing light to spread to Axel's work area, and all around the walls and on the floor stood rows and rows of all sizes of paintings, and Cheyla just gaped.

"Great guns! This is so amazing Grandfather. You are sitting on a fortune, but really you need somewhere safer to store and to display all this work properly!" he said.

Axel chuckled. "Yea me no, I will get ta thet in a sec! Cheyla strolled along the rows admiring each one with a comment, recognizing the skill, but he let Axel continue.

"Ya see Cheyla I didn't no nothin bout art, so was jus foolin round drawin leaves on ol cans with som charcoal from the fire, an then I be doin som charcoal scenes o tha property Shallow Downs cause thet be where I be livin in a hut there an workin at tha time fer Mister Clayton Coby.

Cheyla's ears pricked as he heard the familiar name.

"He was tha best man, an fairest man I eva meet in me life. He be a great boss, an yes, a legend in thet time. They use ta say o him. 'Clayton Coby could move mountains ta be sure.' An in them times he be doin som amazin things!"

"But strangely it be his daughter Miss Jacqueline Coby who praised my art an then convinced me I could sketch.

She jus loved me sketches, an urged me ta paint proper an it was cause o her thet I be an artist now. I be poor back then an I had a son ta raise afta tha death o me wife when he be born, so I not hav money left over fer art!"

"Yea I owe a lot ta Miss Jacqueline Coby! She bought everythin fer me. Paints, an easels, brushes, timber, ah jus everythin. She even teach me how ta mix colours an paint in tha colour. So much like ha Father thet Miss Jacqueline be! She even be gettin me a place in town fer me paintins, so I no need ta worry no more cause she bin doin it all in ha name, an be hirin someone ta sell me paintins!" Axel paused and searched Cheyla's face. "You know thet name now don't ya Cheyla? But do ya no who she is?" he asked.

Cheyla frowned as he stared at Axel's face. "Yes! I was at The Historic Museum and I found her name with some photos of her and her family. There was no mistake to who the huge man in the photo was, his face is my own, so he was my Grandfather I guess?"

"Now ya no why I took tha turn when I see ya!" said Axel. "Neva seen two people more alike then you two!"

"Ah, I see! Though now I think about it, I realize a lot of people have had that same reaction, and it is all starting to make sense now. So yes! I think the girl in the photo is my Mother, and her family long gone it seems! I just know it. But until someone confirms it with me for sure I am in the dark, and no closer to finding her unless you tell me!"

Axel shook his head. "Yes Cheyla! Miss Jacqueline she be ya Mother. I no thet fer sure, but I not say how ya be findin ha, so tis a no from me! Ya hav ta talk ta Mary. Me not gettin involved in thet. But I will show ya a paintin I jus finished o her if ya like. I be so proud o it, think it may be me best work yet!" he said with pride. "So what ya say Cheyla? Ya want ta see tha paintin?" he asked.

Cheyla's heart raced as he heard the confirmation that the girl in the photographs was really his Mother but his face fell in a heap when Axel refused to help him find her. 'I just can't believe this!' he thought to himself. 'Why are so many people protecting her? I don't understand.'

Axel could tell that Cheyla was upset so he put a hand on his arm. "I be so sorry Cheyla, are ya ok?" he asked in concern, and Cheyla looked down at him standing there.

"Yes Grandfather! It has been a rough day, but if you say you can't help me then that is ok. I will speak to Mary later! Having said that, now I will say on a happier note I would be greatly honoured to view your painting. I guess it is of my favourite subject after all." he chuckled.

Axel chuckled too. "Yea I be sure it is Cheyla!" He was liking this boy so much, and his heart felt heavy because he knew that what he had to tell him would break him.

"Ok folla me!' he said trying to lighten the mood. "Tis jus separate from tha others cause I bin workin on it."

Cheyla trailed along, and asked. "Maybe you can clear something up for me Grandfather?"

"What thet be?" questioned Axel.

"You called her Miss Jacqueline, tell me why that is?"

"Well thet be how it was way back then Cheyla. Twas respect fer yer employer, an tha family. Coloured folk and white folk speak o them same way. Jus what we be used ta be doin! We all be servants an employees ya could say!"

"I see! Didn't think anyone had servants back then!"

"Ah yea, tha whole Homestead be run by servants. But som people hav permanent jobs ta run tha property."

"Twas a big staff they bin havin then, an when we was cuttin wattle Mister Coby hire bout one hundred people!"

"Oh! I just wished I could have seen it. There is really nothing like that anymore, and I noticed in some photos they used to have some big parties at Shallow Downs!"

"Yea fer sure Cheyla! Mister Clayton Coby was a man of many missions, an important man in this town. There even be a plaque in tha hospital fer him, cause he be tha instigator of thet there hospital. They be namin a wing o tha hospital afta him. He be a great boss, was real good ta me. Gave me a hut ta live in, an gave us food, an we got paid too. He be known round here fer his entertainin, an I don't mean jus a few friends. Everythin he do was done on tha big scale, an in style too, so lots o people come!"

Cheyla laughed. "He sounds like my kind of man. Just wish I had of known him!" he said sadly.

"Yea tis a shame, but life be goin on Cheyla. Here take a look at this." he said proudly, as he paused to draw the covers off a large painting in the far corner.

Cheyla just stopped dead in his tracks to stare as the cover slowly revealed a flash of purple, then little by little the painting was revealed, and he drew a breath.

"My god Grandfather, this is stunning! You must be so proud to have painted this. He moved in to study it.

"Yep I be mighty proud o thet there one!" said Axel.

Purple, the first colour he noticed, was of the outfit she wore with prestige and finesse of a by-gone era. But also clearly an indication of her personality, her determination and pride etched on her face simply depicted by the artist.

He stared, unable to take his eyes away, but he then looked longingly at the beautiful black Stallion. He reared high beneath his exquisite rider who sat him like a true professional. Axel captured the pure essence of her.

'She was such a beautiful looking girl then, and what a magnificent beast. What a pair the two make! What an exquisite painting this is!' he thought as he then noted the Stallion too was clad in purple on the saddle cloth, bridle and the plaits of purple ribbon in his mane. I just have to have this painting. I must take it home with me!' he plead.

He turned around, and stared at Axel. "I want to buy it Grandfather. Will you please sell it to me?" he asked, as he quickly dived in his jacket pocket for his cheque book.

"I jus think thet no other person should be havin this paintin Cheyla, cept maybe ya Mother, so yea. I will give it to ya fer sale" replied Axel as he flashed his best smile.

Cheyla bent to write a cheque and handed it to him. "I think this should just about cover it Grandfather, and the cover because I will need to wrap it. Plus I have given you enough to set up a new gallery, or maybe you could teach painting to the kids in town." said Cheyla earnestly.

Axel looked vaguely at the cheque, and then his eyes popped. "This here be a real lot o money Cheyla! I can't be takin thet from ya!" he said, a frown creasing his brow.

"Grandfather, I am a very rich man. Believe me when I say. I won't even miss that money, and besides I want that painting badly, and just as importantly I want you to be able to decide on whatever you want to where your art is concerned. Your art is magnificent and needs a proper home, it should be passed on like a legacy to this town!"

"Then I be leavin it to ya if I take ya money ta do it. Ya be me only livin relative, an me Grandson!" replied Axel.

Cheyla noted it was the first time Axel had called him his Grandson, and it felt good. But he looked at him stubbornly to reply. "I won't ever need it Grandfather!"

"I own a cattle Property that is three times the size of Shallow Downs and I also own a gold mine. Why don't you leave it to the town as a rememberance to you? I am sure my Mother will help you with the final details. Just instead of renting a building, you will have enough to buy one, and set up a teaching school for kids. The community will love you for it Grandfather. You will love doing it!"

"I can't be thankin ya enough Cheyla. Yea I think I be havin enough energy ta do thet fer a few years, an ya right I be lovin ta do thet. Can we hug?" he asked sheepishly.

Cheyla reached down and he wrapped his huge arms around Axel, and then the tears sprung into Axel's eyes. He loved this boy that was of his blood, but now he had to cause him grief. "Come Cheyla!" he beckoned. "We be goin upstairs now, bring ya paintin, an I put the kettle on. We be havin a chicken sandwich I make. Have ya eaten?"

"Well, no I haven't. I only had a coffee at the Historic Museum, so yes a sandwich sounds good to me!"

"Ok, ya wrap ya paintin and meet me upstairs."

"Will do Grandfather!" said Cheyla with a smile. 'It is just so good to finally have a family.' he thought.

They sat, and chatted while Axel poured the tea, and then produced a platter of sandwiches which Cheyla fell upon. He hadn't realized just how hungry he was.

He sat back in his seat when he had eaten his fill, and looked at Axel squarely before he spoke.

"So tell me Grandfather. How is it that I have heard all about everyone else, but not my Father! Why is that?"

Axel gulped, and almost choked on his tea. 'Well this is it.' he thought sadly. 'This is where I lose him.'

"Well Cheyla. I be puttin this off fer too long now, but Mary be wantin me ta tell ya bout ya Dad, an what I hav ta say is not good Cheyla, so steel yaself fer the worst. I be jus so sorry I hav ta tell ya bout it all. It be grievin me. Ya Mother an me bin tryin ta forgit all thet past stuff! So I tell ya first thet ya Dad no longer livin, he be dyin in prison!"

Cheyla's back straightened and his mouth widened as he gaped at Axel. "Did you say prison Grandfather? What was he doing in there?" he asked solemnly.

"Yea twas prison he be go Cheyla fer lots o things thet I hav ta tell ya. I be jus so ashamed an so sorry, but ya Dad be bad from bout age 9 an it got thet way I hav no control. He bin doin bad bad things in this here town an Shallow Downs,so I be tellin ya now me story but afore I do, please will be back ta see me Grandson? I be so fond o ya now!"

"Of couse I will Grandfather!" stated Cheyla.

Axel tried to smile as he started the story. Problems his son had with the Coby's, and Cheyla's Mother. Chills shot through Cheyla as things were revealed. Things he never in his life could have imagined. He shook uncontrolably as he listened to the pure hatred his Father had for others, and his face paled under the onslaught of Axel's telling of it, but he didn't interrupt. Instead he sat stolid on his seat, his heart heavy with grief of this revelation that this was

296

about his Father, his blood, and he felt ashamed. He knew he could never be like that to anyone. 'But could he? He had this person's genes! He was feeling sick inside.'

He heard of his youth, his rebelliousness, his outright anger. Then came the worst things like arson, and more.

His first thoughts were of the pictures he had perused at the Historic Museum of the outstanding Homestead at Shallow Downs. Now he knew what the downfall was of the great property from back in that era, and the fire that caused the death of his Grandmother who was consumed in the flames, and it was his Father that was to blame.

He just couldn't believe it, and his breathing felt harsh in his chest, but hearing of the cold-blooded murders was what brought him to his feet, and shocked him to the core, and he couldn't help but burst out his questions in shock.

Cheyla gaped at Axel, his mouth open wide. "Are you sure Grandfather?" he just had to ask, hoping that he had made a mistake but Axel's sorrowful reply was all the proof he needed, and he could tell just by looking at him that this was taking a lot out of his Grandfather.

"Are you alright Grandfather?" he questioned. "You can stop you know! Besides, I think I have heard enough anyway for one day to know my Father was no good!"

Axel looked sadly at him. "Sorry Cheyla, but I be ok. Tis jus thet I promise Mary I be tellin ya all thet I no, but I be nowhere finish yet, an ya haven't heard tha main part yet, tha part thet tis bout yaself an ya Mother. Axel sighed heavily. Tis no other way but ta tell ya straight." he said.

"There is more?" Cheyla asked in bewilderment.

Axel looked into Cheyla's eyes, his own eyes starting to mist over as he stammered, and stuttered.

"Yea, be a lot more Cheyla! Forgive me fer hurtin ya? This be so hard fer me ta say ta ya, but swear it be true!"

As the story continued Cheyla was at a stage where he just couldn't comprehend all the vivid, violent scenes that he was visualizing as Axel skirted around the main issue.

Then very quickly Axel spoke of his Mother and what had befallen her that forced her to become a self-declared outcast, to leave her home, her family and friends forever.

When Cheyla heard mention of his Mother, Jacqueline Coby, and what had befallen her in these unmentionable terms when she was so young, and pure, he could bare it no more. He could see visions as Axel described it, and he knocked the chair over behind him as he backed away in defense from Axel, trying to get away from the words that were tearing him apart, and he screamed out in pain.

"Stop! Please stop Grandfather! I will hear no more!"

His whole reason for this visit to Shallow Siding was to re-connect with his Mother, but now he realized maybe that could never be. His face was livid with anger, and felt such sorrow for what happened to ruin his Mother's life. His look to Axel was pure grief on his handsome features.

"I have to go Grandfather excuse me please." he stated with a voice choked with emotion, and turned to go.

Axel put a hand on his arm. "Jus rememba Cheyla, ya be a good person, a gentle person, nothin like ya Dad. I be proud ta call ya me Grandson, so ya stay strong ya here! Now take your paintin, an try to put this behind ya!"

"I can try!" said Cheyla with head bowed, then he left.

Chapter 22

Axel moved to the doorway. He clutched his chest as he watched his only Grandson walk away so slowly along the path. His shoulders drooped to a sag as he hung his head in sorrow, and tears sprung into Axel's eyes.

'Tis all me fault. He be jus gutted! An it be me thet be doin this ta him. This here be a great young man, an with a pure heart that be now hurtin. He be me Grandson, me only Grandson, an he be such a good boy. We jus met, an I hav bin lovin his company taday, but now I hav ruined him with tha cruel words. He will neva be tha same agin! Maybe he be gone forever! An I won't get ta see im agin!'

Tears streamed down Axel's face as he turned to rush to a table where the phone was, but he was so upset, and sobbing now, that he couldn't see to dial the number.

'Please be home Mary! Please!' he prayed as he sat on the chair, and tried to calm himself down for a phonecall, but he was past all hopes of that. His grief was as deep as his Grandson's. His heart heavy, and fresh tears flooded his eyes. 'Oh Mary! Ya don't know what ya bin askin me ta do! It be done now, an I can't take tha cruel words back. He finally dialed, but it rang out, so he sat back, and cried.

Mary left work early. She couldn't concentrate on the most simplest of tasks. Even to think about work was an ordeal as her mind was elsewhere.

'Might be thet I be givin Cheyla jus too much ta take in taday!' she thought as she put her things into her car.

'Won't no til this arvo when he be comin ta see me. Tis a bad thing ta hav ta tell a boy bout his Dad, an me should o thought bit more bout Axel too. Fer im ta tell it, tis bad!' 'An fer Cheyla ta hear tha story bout his Mother, an what be happenin ta ha tis bad nough, but there be tha rest. Yea tis too much! Me should hav thought o thet. Oh no!'

As she drove home her mind wandered. 'I wonda if I should be callin Jacqueline? Seems ta me thet we be doin all tha bad stuff, an she should be noin thet. No! She be through nough. We be handlin it now! Be ok me hopes!'

When she arrived home, she grabbed her things from the car but as she reached the font landing and walked up the steps she could hear the phone ringing inside, so she hurried inside but missed the call. When she looked at the number she knew who it was, and she was concerned.

Axel answered straight away when Mary returned his call. She could tell that he was very upset, and crying too.

"Oh Axel! Be forgivin me please. I be so sorry, an I jus realized thet I hav asked too much o ya. I be not leavin ya alone tonight so ya go pack a over tha night bag an ya will be stayin at me house tonight. I be askin Drew ta pick ya up bout 5pm. Thet be ok?" she asked hopefully.

"Thet be fine Mary. Yea feelin so bad! So guess ta stay at ya place be good, thank ya!" he said, feeling relieved.

"Cheyla be comin out ta see me soon so we may talk a little afore ya get here, but me not goin inta no more bad stuff taday. Instead we may hav som laughs. How bout a family bar-be-que fer tea. What ya say Axel?" she asked.

"Thet soundin good ta me Mary. An would like ta see Cheyla agin, he be in tha bad way when he be leavin me, so me guessin he could use som laughs too!" he said.

"Good, so it be all settled then. Jus be expectin Drew ta get ya at 5pm!' replied Mary, and just when they ended their conversation she put the phone down Drew arrived.

"Talking about me?" he asked, as he bent to give Mary a kiss. Then he grabbed her, and gathered her in his arms.

"Oh Drew, thank goodness ya be home. Me be doin a silly thing, an now everyone be upset!" she cried.

"Wow! Just back up there a little bit, and tell me who is upset, and what you have done." he asked.

Drew had a way of always calming Mary down. Now she looked at him with admiration in her eyes as she related her instructions she had givin to Axel, and Cheyla.

"So now I have Axel so upset cause he be tellin Cheyla all bad stuff bout his Dad and bout his Mother. So Cheyla be devastated Axel be tellin me an I feel so bad!" she cried.

"Now hold up a little Mary, there is not much point in getting all upset yourself as well. There must be a solution Mary, there usually is. We'll talk about it!' he said calmly.

"Thank ya Drew. Was jus talkin ta Axel, an don't want ta leave him alone tonight. He hav a heart thing ya know, an I think he be havin rough time tellin Cheyla thet stuff. So I told him ta com out, hav tea an stay with us tonight!"

He looked at Mary fondly. "See? You didn't need me at all. You have almost sorted it out yourself Mary. You must have faith in your decisions, sometimes gut feelings are the best ones. So what ever you told Axel, and Cheyla, it had to be told sometime. So now it is done, and we only have to make sure they are both ok. Savvy?"

Mary laughed for the first time that day. "Yea savvy!"

"You jus be best medicine fer me Drew Hargraves!"

"You lady, are my best medicine Missus Hargraves!" he chuckled, as he bent to kiss her.

"What bout Cheyla? He goin ta be so upset he may not com. He was ta com out here an talk ta me bout 4pm, but now I'm guessin he be hearin nough taday!" stated Mary.

"What did you have in mind for dinner Mary?" asked Drew. "Have you thought about that yet?" he asked.

"Was thinkin of a family bar-be-que where we can hav som laughs ta make up fer what I done!" said Mary sadly.

"Don't be so hard on yourself Mary. It will be ok, you will see. We will make it ok! I think the bar-be- que is just what we need to lighten the mood. I will pick Axel up and grab some more food while I am in town if you like. What time did you tell him we would be there?" asked Drew.

Mary looked relieved. "Thank ya Drew. I be tellin Axel bout 5pm, an yes we need ta buy some more things."

"So why don't you ring Cheyla to inform him there is a change of plans, and ask him to stay for dinner. That just might sway him to still come out at 4pm. It will give you some time alone to have a chat before I bring Axel out."

Mary smiled. "Ya be jus a genius Drew, only there be one problem. Me don't know where he be stayin at!"

"He will be staying at The Hotel-Motel Mary. I bet my bottom dollar on it, but you could ring, and find out."

Mary got up quickly. "I be doin thet right now Drew!" she said as picked up the phone, and dialed. She spoke to someone in reception, then gave Drew the thumbs up.

Mary smiled, and spoke to Drew briefly as she waited. "You be right, he be stayin there Drew, an they be puttin me through ta his room now. Man say he com back ta the Hotel jus afore. Her hand shot up, a pause to take the call.

Cheyla sat on the bed staring at the two paintings on the shelf. His eyes were automatically drawn to the girl's eyes as she rode high on the Black Stallion's back.

'I am so sorry for your pain Mother!' he whispered to her. 'You gave me life! For that I thank you. But really, I was never meant to be! I know that now. So how do I deal with it? I have no idea, and it hurts so much inside!'

Absently he ran his fingers through his hair, and felt like pulling it out by the roots as stress racked his body.

He felt numb, and was totally drained. What he hoped would be a successful trip was turning into a nightmare as he re-lived the conversation with his Grandfather.

'My Grandfather! My only living relative that wants to know me. Cheyla had liked him so much, and now he was wondering if he was ok as he knew that his talk had taken a lot out of him. It was a huge toll for an older man. Maybe I should go back to see if he is alright!' he pondered.

'I don't think I should go out to Mary's house. I have heard enough for one day. I don't know what else she has to tell me but I'm starting to realize that it won't be good!'

303

Suddenly the phone rang to interrupt his thoughts, so he reached across to release it from its cradle, but then to recognize the voice at the other end came as a surprise.

Mary spoke loud and clear. He winced as he held the phone out from his ear, her voice reminding him of Jono.

"Ya be ok Cheyla?" she was asking.

"I am just ok Mary! So confused and totally devastated by what I know now. I will survive I guess!" he replied.

"Oh Cheyla, ya don't no how sorry I be now ya no, but we be workin it out Cheyla. So we hav tha change o plans fer later. Maybe afta ya rough day ya can com out here an relax, an hav som fun. We be havin a Family bar-be-ue an you an Axel be tha main guests, but ya still com out at tha 4pm time. Will ya please Cheyla? Thet be ok?" she asked.

He thought about it. Tossing it over in his mind, then he conceded as he heard the plea in her voice. 'Maybe that is just what I need, a bit of fun to cheer me up. She did say a Family bar-be-que, and he liked that well enough.'

"Then how can I refuse. That sounds good to me Mary, so thank you. I will see you later!" he said to end the call.

When he eased the phone back into its cradle, for the first time he thought of Tarryn, and he jumped up.

'My god, I forgot breakfast! I need to go and speak to the Chef. So he grabbed his keys, and rushed out the door then headed towards the kitchen. 'He wanted something special, not just breakfast delivered to his room. So he was hoping what he had in mind, they could do for him.'

He asked to speak to the Chef, and was told to go inside. As he approached the Chef, he seemed busy at that moment, but took the time to listen to Cheyla's request.

"It is short notice Cheyla, but I have plenty of staff, so I will be only too pleased to accommodate you. Here, just write it all out so we don't forget anything, and the time!" he stated as he pushed his notebook towards Cheyla, then handed him a pen. "My name is Geoff Owens, Cheyla. Special occasion is it?" he asked, as he raised an eyebrow.

"Well met Geoff! I can't thank you enough, and yes it is a very special occasion. A First date!" replied Cheyla. "So don't hold back, I can afford it. I want it to be perfect."

"It will be for sure!" answered Geoff.

Then Cheyla had an idea. "Geoff, I might be pushing boundries, but I have just been invited to a bar-be-que this afternoon and don't want to turn up empty-handed. Any chance of you whipping up a salad platter for me?"

"Do you like prawns?" asked Geoff. "Fresh in today!"

"Sure do!" came the reply.

"Well how about a prawn salad, a nice big one!"

"Sounds fantastic Geoff thank you, but I will have to leave about 3.40pm. Is that ok?" he asked hopefully.

"Consider it done Cheyla. Just collect it as you leave."

"Can't thank you enough Geoff. You are a good man!"

Cheyla felt pleased with himself as he left and hurried over to the bottle-shop where he brought four bottles of wine. Two bottles of red, and two of white just in case. He took the boardwalk across the deck to his room. Then once inside, he started looking for carry bags. He looked at his own bag, then as he quickly emptied it to fit everything inside his hand fell on a small package. "Well I'll be, I had forgotten all about Jim's gift to Mary!" he thought.

Mary jumped in the air with excitement as the call ended with Cheyla, and she turned to face Drew.

"He be comin Drew! He be comin bout 4pm. Me gotta rush now, an get shower an dress!" gushed Mary.

Drew laughed. "You look mighty pleased with yourself Mary, so go ahead, get ready! I hope it all works out!"

"Oh Drew! This be meanin lot ta me, an ya will see thet when ya meet Cheyla, jus what I be meanin. He be jus tha nicest person. I hope ya find thet too, an he be me family!"

"Off you go then. I will set up tables and chairs for the deck and clean up. But just rest assured Missus Hargraves that if he is part of your family, he'll be part of mine too!"

As she raced across the floor she called. "Tis why I be lovin ya Drew Hargraves!" and she laughed.

Drew shook his head. 'How he loved this woman who was his wife.' What she was attempting now was out of pure love for Jacqueline Coby-Stringer, who was her best friend since childhood. Only now, he had the feeling of a new vibe in her manner, and sensed her connection with Cheyla Stone was going to be a permanent arrangement.

He would of course deduce his own opinion, but if he knew Mary, he knew she couldn't be wrong to mis-judge.

If she thought this Cheyla Stone was a good, decent person, then he would be. 'He would bet anything on it.'

His thoughts drifted from one thing to another, and he hoped for Mary's sake that the evening went well. Then he heard her in the kitchen, and went inside to join her.

"Wow, you look beautiful Mary. I must say you scrub up well. Special occasion is it?" he asked jokingly.

Mary gave him a push and laughed. "Ya be noin thet!"

"Yes, I do. Just teasing you!" He took the opportunity to pull her close, and they kissed.

"Tis nice! But let me go now Drew Hargraves, so I can be gettin som things done inside an be ready fer when me guests com!" Mary said, as she pushed him away gently.

Drew laughed. "Off you go then. But don't you worry about outside. I will have it in ship-shape." he said.

"Thank ya Drew!" said Mary in relief.

Cheyla parked his 4WD under a tree, and retrieved his bag from the back seat when he alighted. He looked up at the couple on the deck in conversation as he walked towards the house. 'Well, here goes. I just hope I won't be getting more of what I had today.' he thought to himself.

Mary jumped up from her seat as she noticed the big 4WD pulling into the parking area, and she walked to the railings, and she stood there patiently waiting for Cheyla to come up to the house, a huge smile upon her face.

Cheyla climbed the stairs, and decided to speak first. "Afternoon Mary, thank you for the invite. I must say you look great in that outfit." he smiled, as he looked up.

Mary had been studying him, and trying to assess his demeanor as to what state of mind he was in, but on the outside he looked fine to her, well more than fine. He was the most beautiful man she had ever seen, and the closer he came the bigger he become, but as he smiled her heart melted, however it was the eyes that projected the pain he was trying to conceal as they clouded over, so she felt bad.

"Aftanoon Cheyla, an thank ya fer a compliment. Am so pleased ya com out. Com up an meet me husband!"

307

Drew stood when he heard his name mentioned, and took in the sight of this young man Cheyla Stone.

'My god but he's huge, good looking too. Exact image of his Grandfather Clayton Coby when he was younger. No wonder Mary has a soft spot for him.' he pondered, as he walked towards him with his hand outstretched.

"I am guessing you must be Cheyla Stone. Welcome to our home Cheyla, so pleased you could come out and stay for dinner. Just between you, and I." he chuckled. "Mary hasn't stopped talking about you, so I guess I know a little about you. They shook hands when Cheyla extended his.

It was at that instant Drew felt the enormous power generating from those huge forearms and shoulders but surprisingly the hand-shake from his huge hands seemed somewhat gentle in comparison. He looked into sad eyes, and felt so sorry for him. "Come Cheyla, come in and help me with the drinks. These trying times will pass you will find my friend, so let's enjoy ourselves." offered Drew.

"Thank you Drew. I am pleased to meet you also, and yes I will help you get drinks and I have a bag here to un-pack in the kitchen, and thank you for inviting me out."

Drew noticed how polite he was. "All good!" he said.

Cheyla was thankful there had been no fifty questions. He too wanted to put today behind him, so he smiled at Drew then at Mary and he asked if she was coming inside.

"Course I be comin in Cheyla!" she answered.

He smiled, then followed Drew into the kitchen.

It was so good to see him smile, so Mary followed them, hoping this time together would create an understanding between them, and make up for the things she had done.

She hoped that he would soon realize she had done what she had to do to make things right, and the way she done it may have been cruel, but at some point he had to know those things. Deep in her heart she longed to make things right, and hopefully cement their relationship, but as to Jacqueline, she had no idea how she would react.

Mary looked at Cheyla as he was unzipping his bag. He seemed calm, but she knew deep down he was hurting, but there was no undoing the past. 'It is what it is!' she thought. 'An there be nothin we can do ta change it. Somehow, some way Cheyla hav ta live with thet now.'

Cheyla was lifting a big dish out of the bag, and Mary peered around his physique to look. "Oh! Me goodness, they be prawns, an big ones too. Com hav a look Drew at tha biggest prawns ya eva see, but why ya bringin im here Cheyla. Ya didn't need ta ya no, I be havin lots o food?"

Cheyla smiled. "I couldn't just come out with nothing Mary!" he said, as he started pulling the wine out of the duffle bag. "So you see the Chef at The Hotel made it for me. I thought it may go towards your bar-be-que. I hope you drink wine? I wasn't too sure about that." he stated.

Drew looked at the prawn and salad plate. "Sure looks good to me Cheyla, thank you. I will have one drink with you both, and yes we both love wine. A good choice too!" he said, as he picked up a bottle of red. "Then I have to go and pick Axel up so I am guessing now some huge steaks might be on the list for me to purchase while I am in town. What do you think Cheyla?" he asked.

"What-ever you decide on is fine with me Drew!"

Cheyla's hand rummaged around in the bag, then he smiled as he lifted out a package, and looked straight at Mary. "This is for you Mary, it travelled many miles!"

Mary looked up at at Cheyla in surprise. "Fer me?" she asked, as she took it from his hand. "Who it be from?" she asked, as she turned the package over, and read the name.

Her hand flew to her mouth when she recognized the name, then she gasped. "Oh geez! It be Jim McKenzie. Its bin so long since I be seein im, but we send ta each other Christmas Cards. Oh Cheyla, this be jus tha best. A lovely surprise!" she uttered as she ripped open the paper.

"Oh! Look Drew, it be a small phota album an jus look! This be Miss Jacqueline an me when we be young. So long ago! So many years past since thet there time." Tears filled her eyes, then rolled down her face to drop on the plastic, and she quickly wiped them away.

Drew came over to her. "You ok Mary?" he asked.

"Oh Drew! I be ok. It jus brings back tha old memories o long ago thets all. Twas not tha happy times back then, but I will be lovin tha photas, an I be guessin Jacqueline will too when I be showin them to ha!" she replied. "Let's be goin outside so I can show ya both. Thank ya so much Cheyla. So ya bin ta Waverley an ya met Jim?" she asked.

"Didn't mean to upset you Mary, but yes Jim and I got on real well. He is a source of information. Nice guy, and because of him I have found you. I had almost given up hope until he approached me. I have travelled across half of Australia trying to find you. You were my only link to my Mother, and I was going on only a hope that the letters you sent to your Grandmother would lead me to her."

Drew looked from one to the other as they spoke, both deep in conversation, and he knew it was only starting.

"I don't mean to interrupt Mary, but I have to go into town now to get Axel, time is getting away." said Drew.

"Thet be fine Drew, we jus talkin now." replied Mary.

"Catch you later Drew." replied Cheyla.

"Yeah, all good. I won't be too long." Drew called over his shoulder. "Ok." said Mary, and started talking again.

"Oh, my Grandmother! She be raisin ya, an be doin a good job too I see. So that be makin us kin Cheyla! Maybe we be brother an sister ya no. How is Grandmother? An do I hav Aunties, Uncles and cousins thet ya no Cheyla?"

Cheyla smiled. "Well you could say we are at least kin Mary, but Brother? I like that well enough, so be it!" he chuckled. "I am not too sure just who your relatives were but rest assured if there were any of them remaining at Tenna, then they work for me, and live at Tenungeri."

Mary's face lit up as she spoke. "Really? But Tenungeri where thet be Cheyla? I not rememberin thet there place."

"Tenungeri is the name I called my Property which is rather a large cattle station incorporating a big part, well all of Tenna actually. So when I purchased the property everyone from the tribe came with me. They work for me and I have provided houses for them all." he chuckled.

"Oh, so ya be ownin property, an all o Tenna too! An me family there. Thet be amazin me Cheyla!" said Mary.

Then Cheyla became very serious as he looked at her.

"There is something else you should know Mary!"

311

Suddenly his eyes clouded over with grief. He looked deep into Mary's eyes. "I am so sorry to bear sad news Mary, but I have to tell you that Ol Mother passed away."

"Oh no!" cried Mary. "I should hav bin there fer her!" her shoulders shook, and Cheyla laid a hand on one.

"Don't upset yourself Mary. Ol Mother wouldn't want that, and Tenna is a long way from here. She lived a very, very long life, more than most I knew, and at the end she was happy. She was back home at Tenna again. No-one really knew her age, but she was ancient. She was an old woman even when she started raising me. So don't feel sad, instead celebrate her long life." Cheyla advised.

Mary looked up at him, tears still streaming down her face but she knew what Cheyla was saying was true.

"Yea ya be right Cheyla. Twas a long life she be livin!"

"You know Mary, it was Ol Mother who urged me to search for my roots. She had held back all the letters you wrote to her until her dying breath, then she gave them to me and said. 'You go find!' "They were her last words!"

"I built a graveyard at Tenungeri and buried her close to the waterfall. Many people attended her funeral, then after it was over I left home in search of you and Mother!"

Mary cried. "I be jus thankin tha lord thet I be seein ha when ya was born Cheyla. Twas tha last time I see ha! An want ya ta no thet no matta what Jacqueline be decidin ya should no thet back in tha time o these here photos, an all ha life, she suffa fer leavin ya. An I be lovin ya Cheyla!"

"Thank you Mary! But I am not thinking straight now, and uncertain what to do. I think it is pointless to pursue Mother, she wouldn't want me under the circumstances."

"I can understand that now, after hearing of her past."

"No Cheyla! Don't ya giv up now. Ya be travellin long way ta find ha. Ya go see Pete, he be tellin ya what ta do."

"Mary after today I just have to put my search aside. I just can't bear any more. I need to settle, then try to accept things as they are so I can come to terms with it. Besides I have met a special girl now who I just have to get to know more about, and spend time with her. We are having our first date starting at breakfast in the morning, so it might be just the distraction I need at the moment!" he stated.

Drew startled them when he spoke. Neither of them had heard the car pull up during their conversation, or even heard them approach, and Mary jumped up.

"Still talking you two? I'll get us all a drink."

Cheyla stood as well. "Grandfather, it is so good to see you. I was worried about you. What is the bag for?"

Axel flashed his favourite smile. 'Grandfather, he say!' So he went to hug Cheyla. "Mary puttin me up fer tha night Cheyla. Taday not be a happy day, but be so pleased ta see ya, so I can see if ya gonna be ok." replied Axel.

Mary stood. "A toast all! To Axel and Cheyla. My new-found brother!" They cheered as Mary added. "Cheyla has news of a girlfriend. Tell us about her Cheyla!"
Cheyla grinned. "Just promise to keep it quite, it is Tarryn Westley. Jed Owens, niece. I think he knows all of you!"

"We be doin thet Cheyla! Ah! Ya no there be special place o ya Mothers ya should take Tarryn to, jus down the road turn right. Ya be me guest ta tha waterfall, an pool!"

"Now you are talking Mary, great idea. So thank you!"

Chapter 23

Jacqueline road slowly home, and the stallion picked his way confidently along the track. She noticed that the big horse 'Rain' was well rested now after the grueling ordeal that she had put him through earlier, but the rest at Pete's house had fully revived him. She bent down, and leaned over to pat his shoulder. "You're a legend Rain. It was one great ride, I needed that." Rain snorted, and she laughed.

She felt as if a weight had been lifted off her shoulders. It wasn't only the ride on Rain that had thrilled her, but the conversation she ended up having with Pete.

For some unknown reason she felt as if she had turned a full circle. Talking about her youth with Pete had some-how rekindled many old thoughts, and usually when that happened her thoughts spiraled as she went haywire, but now for some unknown reason she finally felt in control.

Her past had caught up with her. But now, for the first time in many years, she was ready to face it head on.

Her mobile phone rang, and she dug into her pocket to retrieve it, and answered to the all-too familiar drawl.

"Thank god! Where the hell are you Jackie? I've been worried sick. You could have called at least!" said Mitch.

Jacqueline smiled to herself as she replied. "Hello my darling husband! Checking up on me I see, but there was no need, I am just fine and all in one piece." she joked.

"Very funny Jackie!" Mitch tried to say, but she added.

"I am coming up to the stables now. Rain, and I have enjoyed our morning out and I had a great ride. Since then I have been over at Pete's house. Obviously someone was eager for him to find me! Don't know who that could be?"

Mitch detected the little dig at him in her voice, but he had to laugh. 'This woman is impossible.' he thought. 'So damn determined she is.' Then he spoke out to her. "Yeah well someone has to be sensible Jackie as you sure as hell weren't this morning! So yes I acquired a little detective."

"Thought so!" she laughed, and he laughed with her.

"I'll drive over to pick you up at the stables, and deal with you later, much later." he drawled, then chuckled.

"Ooh! I can hardly wait. So I'll take that as a promise shall I? Don't you disappoint Cowboy!" came her reply.

Mitch grinned to himself, and chuckled as he hung up the phone. 'Saucy wench!" he thought to himself. She had a unique way of getting to him, and his loins stirred.

Jacqueline rode into the stable yard and stopped at the railings. She slipped off Rain's back, and tied his reins to the railing. She gave him a hug, and patted his shoulder, then quickly released the girth strap to pull the saddle off.

"Hey Missus Jacqueline!" called the voice beside her. "I will look after Rain!" said the stable-hand.

"Oh! Thank you Jimmy. That was one excellent ride!" Jacqueline replied as she looked around. 'The land-rover was parked there. But where was Mitch?' she wondered.

She laughed when she noticed him almost hidden by the over-hanging branches of the huge gum tree, and her heart leapt in her chest, just like it had always done when it came to her attention that he was in her presence.

Mitch was leaning against the gum tree sporting the huge grin she always loved so much. His hat sat at a jaunty angle over those beautiful blue eyes, which, even from the short distance, seemed to twinkle with mischief.

"Ah! So the missing person emerges." he spoke in that Country drawl that was so typically Mitch, the Country Cowboy as usual. It done things to her to send tingles up, and down her spine, and her heart beat faster.

He stepped out from his cover, and slowly sauntered towards her. It took Jacqueline all her restraint to pause, and not run to him, but she waited patiently to see what he was going to do, he had a menacing look in his eyes.

Mitch laughed as he got closer. "Someone may need a lesson I am thinking my love! Not exactly sure who that would be! Do you Jackie?" he asked, as he swept her into his arms, and lifted her. His lips came crashing down on hers like he was a man on a mean mission, but suddenly they were both lost in a magical embrace of their love, and she responded to the tenderness he was now bestowing.

"So that's it then?" she asked as the long kiss ended.

"Umm, maybe not! So let's see what I have in store for you?" he laughed and his jest proving to Jacqueline what-ever it was, it wouldn't be good. "But Mitch, I'm sorry!"

"Shush my love!" he chuckled as he walked away with her cradled in his arms to the paddock behind the stables.

He took the descent of the dam like a pro. His strong legs giving him purchase on the rocks, and gravel, then the sand, as he strode stoutly towards the water, and walked straight in boots and all, and he grinned that grin.

"Oh! No you don't Mitchell Stringer. Just stop now!" Jacqueline yelled as she realized her fate, and twisted her body trying to release his grip on her, but she was locked in strong arms. "My phone!" she cried, as she dug for it.

Mitch grabbed it from her to throw it on the sand, and then he plunged under the water with her in his arms.

They both came up gasping from the cold water, but Mitch was in his element as he listened to Jackie cursing.

"Oh! How could you Mitch? Really this is uncalled for! I just hate you now Mitch Stringer!" her screams became a splutter as he put a hand on her head to duck her under.

But this time when she surfaced, and before she could speak, his mouth covered hers, and his passion surpassed any previous engagement they had encountered, and she relaxed in his arms to revel in the pure pleasure of it.

"Oh, god I love you Mitch!" she stuttered as a mouthful of water almost choked her and burst from her mouth.

"You hated me a moment ago my love!" he replied.

"Please forgive me, you know I lied. I could never hate you Mitch Stringer, you are my world!" Jacqueline said.

"Even if you get the same treatment again? Because it will happen again I just bet if I know you Jackie! How you must love freezing water. So you get used to it, you may spend a lot of time here unless you tell me if you're upset, or where you are going. It'll be your place!" he said in jest. "You are so mean Mitch! Laters then?" she asked sweetly.

Mitch shook his head in disbelief. 'She simply thinks I am joking with her.' 'Is there no chastising this woman?' he wondered. 'She is just so stubborn, and determined. It would take a mine field to alter that, but I wouldn't have it any other way. I love everything about her, everything!'

He lifted her, just loving the closeness of her, then he carried her in his arms, and placed her on the sand where she grabbed up her phone in haste.

"If that had of got wet Mister Stringer then the sparks would be flying right about now!" she giggled.

"Tell me about it. It is the story of my life Jackie!"

'Surely it is not that bad, is it?" she asked seriously.

Mitch laughed. "Let's just say, with you there is never a dull moment Jackie. Now listen, I have a plan." he said.

As they started the climb up the hill Jacqueline asked.

"What plan is that Mitch?" she inquired inquisitively.

"How about when we get back, we have a swim in the pool? How does that sound, we are already wet anyway."

As they reached the top of the hill and walked towards the Land-rover Jacqueline looked down at her clothes.

"Oh Mitch, we just can't get in the rover. Have a look at us. We are covered in mud, and my hair smells so bad. No, I have a much better idea. We shall walk home, then have a hot shower downstairs. Maybe we can swim after that if you like. We can drive back to get the rover later!"

Mitch's mind was already taking in the scene, and to him that was a very good plan. "Jackie, have I ever told you what a genius you are? That is a great plan my love!"

"You tell me most day's beloved husband!" she joked.

They walked hand in hand towards the Homestead and chatted casually. "So where is Melissa? What is she doing this morning Mitch?" Jacqueline asked.

"Well, at breakfast May mentioned that she was going down to the gardens later to pick fuit, and vegetables, and as an afterthought she asked Melissa if she would like to help her! Melissa was excited, and I had to find a special hat for her, gloves and a basket for her all her goodies."

"So I guess you will know how the rest pans out. By now Melissa will be telling May how best to pick them!" he laughed, and Jacqueline looked at him, and burst out laughing too. This child of theirs had outgrown her years.

When they reached the Homestead Jacqueline headed straight for the showers downstairs. She quickly grabbed some towels, soap and shampoo, then rummaged in the drawers for some togs for them to wear in the pool.

She discarded her muddy clothes where she stood as she stepped from them and set the temperature very hot at the shower head to let the hot steamy water caress her.

Mitch on the other hand quickly discarded his clothes and bundled them all up and put them in the laundry tub.

"Oh yes! But that feels so..oo good!" Jacqueline's voice echoed from inside the shower, as Mitch quietly stepped in behind her, and grabbed her breasts in his hands.

"Umm! Yeah it shore as hell does!" he said as he rolled her nipples between his fingers ever so gently.

"I meant the hot water Mitch!" Jacqueline answered.

"Yeah, me too!" he replied absently as he nuzzled her neck, and turned her to face him. Their lips came together in a second of urgency, as the hot water engulfed them.

He lifted her easily. She felt his hands firmly gripping her bottom and pulling her closer still so she wrapped her legs tightly around him. Instantly she felt the hardness of him against her tummy, and she wriggled to help him.

Passion felt in the heat of that moment consumed them both, and she could feel him slip inside her as he laid her back against the wall, so she gripped him firmly.

Squeezing him tightly until she could feel the throb of his manhood deep inside her, and she screamed loudly, unable to still her feelings for any longer, and she moaned with pleasure as he joined her in his release to match her.

They clung together desperately as one, though there was two bodies entwined and totally spent in exhaustion.

Mitch was the first to move. "I'm getting a cramp!" he laughed at the cruelty of it. "Must be getting old."

Jacqueline laughed. "You will never be old my love!"

"Oh, yes I will my lady, one day! But not for now, and I give thanks for that. So we may be able to enjoy a little more of the same ilk for quite a while yet!" he chuckled.

"Thank goodness for that small token, but get dressed now Mitch. Melissa will be back any moment." she said.

They both needed to relax so they swam for a while, then sat on the steps in the heated pool and chatted.

"So did you get your timber order in this morning?"

"Yeah, all good! Will be ready in three days, so good timing. They run a good shop over there." said Mitch.

"So, how is Mary? I hope she didn't mind watching Melissa for you at such short notice?" asked Jacqueline.

Mitch thought about that for a while before he replied.

Mary! "Well seeing you asked. I really think Mary was in some sort of state. She seemed like a cat on a hot tin roof! Couldn't sit still, and looked very anxious!"

Jacqueline sat up so straight. "Mary? Are you certain? Whatever is wrong with her Mitch?" she asked anxiously.

"Seems she is to expect a visitor any day. One, Mister Cheyla Stone! So I am guessing she is worried about that."

Just the name was enough to make Jacqueline stiffen, but her main concern was Mary. 'Too much had been put on her shoulders. She was wishing now she had told Pete to back off sooner. It must have been him who done this.'

"So what was she going to do or talk about to Cheyla?"

"Well! Seems she has a sort of plan for him to visit The Museum first, and then it will be Axel who will tell him all the bad things about you, this town and his Dad. Can't say I would like to be in Axel's shoes!" stressed Mitch.

"Oh no! What have they done? Are they crazy? Axel is getting old now, and we both have been trying to forget all those bad things. How could they do this to him?" said Jacqueline furiously. She got up to grab a towel, then she paced the pool tiles in anger as she cursed herself and the others. Mitch got out of the pool, and grabbed her hand.

"It's not your fault Jackie, so don't get upset!" he said.

"How can I help it? Look what I have done by giving Pete the reins?" she cried. I finally told Pete today to back off, and let me handle my own mess. But now? Oh no! I'm too late! I just have to fix this! Poor Mary, and Axel. This is just too much for them to handle. I should have been in control. I knew it all along, but Pete kept persisting when I was vulnerable, but not any more. I'll face this head on!"

"What are you thinking of doing Jackie? I am starting to worry you will do something outlandish." said Mitch.

"I have no idea how to fix this Mitch, but as sure as the sun rises, I know it will come to me, then I will re-act. But until I have made a decision Mitch, rest assured you will be the first person I tell of what I will do about Cheyla!"

Jacqueline stiffened as her daughter spoke from behind. "Cheyla!" she said as clear as day. "He is Mary's friend, Cheyla is. I met Cheyla today when I opened up the door Mother and Father!" came the angelic voice of Melissa's.

Jacqueline gaped openly at Mitch as if a silent question posed upon her lips, then her mouth widened in disbelief, but he shrugged his shoulders as if it was news to him.

So instead Jacqueline turned angrily to face Melissa.

"You done what, young lady? You opened a door to a stranger? You know you don't do that Melissa!' she said with a voice so raised that it made Melissa frown.

"I am sorry Mother, but Mary already told me that, but I don't know why because he was so nice." she replied.

"You do know Melissa you're not allowed to open the door to strangers here!" said Jacqueline, chastising her.

"But he was so funny! Just like Father when he called me "My Ladyship." came the childish reply.

"Just you never do it again young lady. It is dangerous when you don't know who the person is!" she said.

'But this one is your brother.' thought Jacqueline.

She raised her arms up in a plea. "When will this ever end?" she asked above. "Come on, lets all go upstairs!"

Mitch eyed her closely. "Right behind you Jackie."

323

Chapter 24

Cheyla woke instantly as the sun crept in through the gap in the curtains. It was just breaking day he noted and jumped out of bed to throw the door open just as the sun began to rise and he wanted to go outside to watch it.

As he sat on a bench seat staring into its brilliance, he could feel the warmth already on his skin, and he knew it would be a magic day. He was hoping for good weather, so now he had his wish. There was no-one around, and it was quiet around the pool. Not even one ripple broke the surface of the water. It was still and peaceful, and looked like transparent glass as he could see right to the bottom.

He went inside to have a shower so that this important day could commence. He was up too early he knew, but he didn't want to be rushed today. He wanted to savour every moment. He felt so much more relaxed today after last night's bar-be-que at Mary's place, and he had slept like a baby last night. Through all the disappointments of yesterday he was hoping to stay positive by thinking only of the good things, and pushing the bad things to the back of his mind. Only now he was approaching a new phase in his life. At least he hoped so, but a lot depended on it.

He just knew in his gut that this girl had to be special. Cheyla had never felt so mixed up before, and his feelings had gone haywire, sometimes it even hurt. 'They say love hurts.' he thought. 'I just wonder? But when you know deep down something is different and your insides ache, there has to be a reason for that surely?'

'I often thought there had to be more to a relationship than just physical contact, but somehow for me that had never happened. I guess I never met the right girl before, but now I am experiencing a new type of relationship.'

Something set her apart from the others he had been associated with before so Cheyla was hell-bent on finding out what that was. His heart couldn't be so wrong. It was doing flip-flops ever since he had met her. This was a new feeling he was experiencing, one he had never had in his life, so he couldn't wait to see her for their first date.

As hot water cascaded over his body, he relished the feel of it on his skin, but his mind, it was everywhere else.

Visions of what the day would bring, and scenes from yesterday at Mary's. Then came the dark thoughts of his conversation with his Grandfather they were all mixed in.

He turned off the water, then he shook his head just to clear his mind. 'No dark thoughts!' he reminded himself. 'Today is going to be a happy day, a day filled with love.'

He laughed as he quickly dressed, and realized he was over-reacting. 'It may not pan out she may not be the one!' he thought. 'I have to find that out, don't I? This day is so crucial and could be. I say could be, a vital time in my life.'

Happily he grabbed his keys eager to greet the day, so he opened the door of his room, and walked outside.

To his surprise there was activity everywhere. 'Looks to me as if Geoff is holding up his end of the bargin!' he thought as he noticed trestle tables being brought outside.

A unique table with two lavish chairs were being set up down the bottom end of the pool area where a grass-clad cabana hut stood but the list went on and he laughed.

'Sometimes it just pays to have money, and this is one of those times!' he thought, as he tried to imagine the bill.

Cheyla walked briskly to the car-park at the rear of the Hotel-Motel feeling mighty pleased with himself.

'Now to collect the little lady!' he thought as he looked at the time. 'It is 6.30 am so all is good, breakfast is at 7am, so that will be perfect for time, and it looks to me that all will be ready when we come back!'

He drove slowly out of town, and veered off onto the hospital road then took a turn-off leading him to the back nurse's quarters, and parked in a space near Room 6.

Excitedly he jumped out of the 4WD and walked up a pathway. Tarryn Westley stood in the doorway watching him. 'My god, but he is a hunk of a man!' she thought.

Cheyla looked up to see her standing there. He waved, and she waved back. Then, there it was again. That lurch in his stomach that he was becoming so familiar with.

As he reached her, and their eyes met, he spoke first.

"Good morning Tarryn! You have no idea what is in store for you today. So let the games begin!" he laughed.

He just loved her reply, and the way her laughter was music to his ears. "Games? Umm interesting!" said in jest.

"I am up for anything you can dish out Cheyla Stone!"

His smile showed teeth of white, and he chuckled. He just loved her sense of humour. 'Just like my own!' he thought, as he then looked at what she was wearing.

"In that case Tarryn, I will give you a list of things you may need at some point today. You wouldn't want to ruin that beautiful dress, and speaking of beautiful, is just how you look today. You are a vision to look upon!"

"Now. Your list! You will need walking shoes, maybe joggers would be best, shorts, and tops. Swimming gear and towels, and maybe a change of clothes just in case I throw you in the pool!" he laughed, but he could see that she took his joke as a joke, and not a threat.

"Well! Whatever are we doing? But don't tell me, I just love surprises. Just give me five." she said, then laughed.

"Plus, thank you for the compliment Cheyla but I must say you look beautiful too! However if I am being thrown in the pool Cheyla Stone, then know, you will be coming with me!" she joked, and disappeared through the door.

He just loved her quips, and smiled to himself as he waited. 'I will get even Tarryn Westley.' he thought.

In no time at all she was back at his side, and laughing like a school girl as she toted a canvas bag.

Cheyla leant over to relieve her of the bag, and quickly she slipped her arms around his neck as she moved closer still and her body pressed against him. Cheyla reacted to drop the bag and his arms enclosed her in an embrace, his mouth searching hers, and there on the steps they kissed.

Her lips felt soft and moist, and he was lost in a place of exquisite seduction, and fighting to respond with such pure feelings, with his own lips seeking the opportunity to consume her with his pent-up emotions and passion.

He was in another world as he gently released her, his eyes boring into hers. He held her at arms length to speak.

"You do know that we have done it again, don't you?"

"Done what again?" asked Tarryn inquisitively.

"Tarryn, we have kissed on the pavement again. It is becoming a habit, but I like it well enough!" he chuckled.

"Don't you like privacy at all young lady?" he added.

Tarryn laughed that throaty, sexy laugh she had as she replied. "I am rather a 'In the moment type of person.' So you Cheyla Stone have a way of creating my moment, and when I want something I usually react instantly. But just like you however. 'I liked it well enough!' Privacy is not an issue with me, I am an open book!" she giggled.

Cheyla's grin spread to a huge smile. He had no reply. She just picked up his favourite saying and used it in a way that was cheeky, and as if it was hers alone.

They looked at each other and laughed together. It was almost like she had read his mind, and he couldn't help but feel an affinity towards her at that moment.

"Come on miss mischief maker, let's go, or we will be late. He picked up her bag, and grabbed her hand.

"Late for what Cheyla? I didn't imagine we had any schedule to keep today!" she stated.

"I have a little surprise for you." he responded.

"Oh I do love surprises! What is it Cheyla?" she asked.

"Ah! But that would be telling, and then it would be a surprise no more. No lady! You have to wait." he replied.

The carpark at the rear of the Hotel-Motel seemed almost deserted, and all was quiet, but as they got out of the 4WD they both heard soft music playing.

"Some people are rejoicing early!' Tarryn exclaimed.

"Yeah, I guess so!" replied Cheyla, as he hid a smile.

As they cornered the building Tarryn paused. "Oh no! I thought you were joking about the pool, but there it is. Please don't Cheyla!" she cried, and then as they reached the edge of the grass cabana she laughed, and said.

"Looks like I was right, someone is having a party. Oh! How cool. Look how they have set it up Cheyla!"

He steered her towards the exquisite table which was now set up like something out of a magazine, with a pure white tablecloth with all the trimmings, and even candles already lit providing a scent drifting on the soft breeze.

Cheyla pulled out a chair for her, and smiled.

"This is your surprise Tarryn!" he said, as he gestured for her to sit. "We will be the ones rejoicing, to celebrate our first date, but at home we call it breakfast!" he joked.

She looked at him in astonishment for the trouble he had gone to. "Oh Cheyla, this is just so special. How can I thank you enough? It is perfect but maybe a little costly!"

"I can think of a way you can thank me!" he said as he bent over to find her lips. But at that time he was thinking. 'Maybe I have gone overboard. I want her to learn to love me, for me, not for my money. Better tone it down a liitle!'

He laughed, then tried to change tack. "Well I think a little splurge is well worth it just to see your face Tarryn, so money well spent! But it is our first date after-all. Now! Juice? Or coffee?" he asked, accepting the role of waiter.

CHEYLA

Tarryn laughed at him standing there with the napkin over his arm just like a proper waiter. "I would like both please Cheyla if I may?" she asked politely.

Cheyla looked at her with the surprise obvious upon his face, and he laughed.

"What?" she asked.

"Just the same as me Tarryn! I like to have both also!" He shook his head as he went to get their drinks.

"Croissants with jam and cream first, or cereal? Muesli Cornflakes, fruit?" he asked, as he poured their coffee.

"Sounds like it will be a long breakfast, but I will have muesli and fruit please. I like to leave the sweet things to the very end." she replied.

"Ah! Just a girl after my own heart." he laughed, as he placed their drinks on a tray, and set them on the table, then quickly served up two plates of cereal and sat down.

She looked long and hard at him, captured by his eyes.

"So tell me? Who is Cheyla Stone, and where is home to someone who says, when he is home that this is called breakfast? This is way beyond breakfast, it is a huge feast. So what does Cheyla Stone do for a living? I was thinking you could always take up waiting tables if you lost your job." her laugh was a tinkle, but her questions serious.

Cheyla laughed at her joke, but then his brow creased.

"So many questions, and even before coffee! But I will do my best Tarryn, just bear with me, I am starving."

"Which answers one question. Where ever I may be, at home or out I like to eat big, but at home? Yes it is pretty much like this. I have a body that demands it you know!"

331

Tarryn knew he was speaking the truth. His physique was massive, but well contained for his height.

"So your home? Where is that Cheyla?" she asked.

He took a big mouthful of coffee to help digest his food and he laughed at her. "You are so persistant! But when do I get to hear about you Tarryn Westley?" he asked.

"I shall have my turn!" she answered. "But I also need to know what brought you to Shallow Siding?"

His eyes clouded over, then he looked at her seriously.

"Tarryn today is our first date so I don't want anything to interfere with that. I want it to be a happy day with lots of laughs, and I really want to get to know you more!"

"I want to get to know you more also Cheyla, so that is why I asked you the basic questions first!" she replied.

"I understand that, and I will tell you some things, but firstly I will say just once. Yesterday was the worst day of my life, and the only way for me to get past that for now is to concentrate on other things so I can try and put it out of my mind. I don't feel I could talk about it now, or even think about it even, as there are things I still don't know, or understand myself, but when I decide what to do, you will be the first person I speak to about it. Your life maybe simple or basic as you say, but mine is not Tarryn! It is so complicated, it is ridiculous! Please try to understand that I need time. So can we please make a pact! Until that time, you won't ask any more questions? I'm so sorry!" he said.

Tarryn could tell that deep in his heart he was hurting, so she had to acknowledge the fact something was tearing him apart. She could see it was quite obvious in his eyes. "Don't worry Cheyla I'll respect your wishes!" she said.

His relief was obvious to her as he tried to smile, but instead his mouth pulled out of shape into a meager grin, and her heart went out to him. 'Whatever this is, it has to be so bad to rock a man like Cheyla Stone!' she thought.

"Well, you just tell me what you are comfortable with Cheyla, and that is good enough for me. Besides, you are right. This is our first date, and I too want it to be special. You will find in me Cheyla a trust that you can rely on!"

He looked squarely at her. 'Understanding was a rare trait in a woman! That he knew. But to have someone's complete trust was just so important to him, and he knew now her values were part of his attraction to her.

"You have no idea how much I appreciate hearing you say that Tarryn, and I do see in you as someone whom I could talk to about anything, that pleases me also, so keep in mind when the time is right, we will discuss it all, ok?"

"You just take your time Cheyla. Do what your heart says, and you can't go wrong, so let's enjoy today!"

He smiled that smile she loved, then spoke out. "We will do that Tarryn! I have a full day planned for you my lady, but firstly. I must tell you a little about myself. I live on the land in the Northern Territory. I am The Owner of a spread there, or cattle ranch you might say. I named it Tenungeri mainly because part of the name is where I was born at Tenna within an aboriginal tribe. The only Mother I ever knew was to me 'Ol Mother' who raised me and she has just passed away. With her final breath she told me.

'Ya go find ya roots!' She gave me some letters she had with-held from me written to her from a Mary Higgs!"

Tarryn opened her mouth, but said nothing when he raised a hand for her to pause, as he then continued.

"So I have travelled half way around Australia trying to find her because Mary was the only link to my natural Mother, and as it turns out I found Mary here in Shallow Siding. After the rough day I had yesterday I ended up at her place for a bar-be-dinner last night, she is kind of my sister. Her Grandmother was Ol Mother, who raised me."

"Her name is now Mary Hargraves, and Axel Hall was there as well. Turns out he is my Grandfather. But please Tarryn, do not tell anyone this information as it will spoil my search. You see my Mother lives in this town so I now know, but don't know where to find her, or even if I want to as yet. These are the things I can't talk about yet. I know your Uncle Jed would know these two people, so can you please keep my secret for now Tarryn?" he asked.

Wide eyed, and spellbound, Tarryn realized she was supposed to answer, and her voice come out croaky with emotion as his story had her on the edge of her seat. This was something she hadn't expected at all, and as Cheyla had explained, it was complicated, but there was more?

"Cheyla, your secret is safe, I'm so sorry!" she croaked, to clear her throat and continue. "I can read between the lines, so that is enough for now! I can see you are upset. Only please don't be! Let's try to forget the world around us, and just live for today! So now! Please sir, or should I call you waiter? May I be served my next course please?" she uttered, and there was that tinkle in her voice again.

A smile lit Cheyla's face suddenly as he looked fondly at her to say. "That sure would please me well enough!"

Breakfast became rather a long indulgence of not only food, but laughter, and friendly banter as the two people Tarryn and Cheyla shared experiences, and explored each others minds to discover their similarities were endless.

Even though it was a first date they had covered a lot of ground, and discussed many different situations, but when it came down to knowledge, and understanding of their fellow man, they were on the same page.

Cheyla reached across the table and took her hand in his. She immediately linked their fingers, and slowly he eased her forward as he bent over to kiss her fully on the lips with a passion he never felt for anyone before.

Tarryn responded instantly to his touch. Cheyla Stone had reached her heart and her mind, in a way that no-one had ever done. When he released her, she felt cheated by his absence, but a lot was going through her mind.

She had waltzed through life on a whim that one day she would eventually meet her match. 'Is there no-one out there for me, or even like me?' she used to ask herself. As she looked at him with smokey eyes, suddenly it came to her, and she slowly realized, she had met her soul mate.

She thought of past relationships and what had lacked in them, but with Cheyla Stone, though for only this short time, she felt at home, and she just knew he was the one.

'Though in truth surely it would only happen in a fairy tale?' she mused. 'If I waited so long to find the perfect man, then I think it was worth the wait!' she smiled.

"What is it Tarryn? What is funny?" asked Cheyla.

"Cheyla Stone. I think I have an affinity with you!"

Suddenly Cheyla reacted by pushing his chair back as he then rounded the table to take her in his arms.

He pulled her closer, his face so close to hers now, then his lips touched hers only briefly before he moved a lock of her long, thick, black hair, and whispered in her ear.

"I like it well enough to hear you say that Tarryn, as I too have an affinity towards you, so you could say, without a doubt, that the feeling is mutual! Might I add that I have never had feelings like this about anyone in my life!"

He faced her now and their eyes locked as his lips sort hers, and once again they kissed, a long smoldering kiss.

Then they both laughed for the only reason being, just the joy of being together, then he grabbed her hand.

"Come on Tarryn, we have much to do. Did you enjoy your breakfast surprise?" he asked.

"Absolutely Cheyla, but I think I may have over-done it!" she chuckled, as she touched her tummy.

"I have just the solution, though it was part of my plan anyway. Do you feel up to a trail walk?" he asked.

"Sounds perfect! I do need to walk off that breakfast."

"Excellent! Then come over to my room." he pointed. "We can change there, and you will need joggers, maybe shorts, and top, and a hat, and sunnies if you have them, otherwise you can wear a pair of mine. Remind me to get the water bottles out of my fridge before we go, but while we are in the room I will show you something special!"

"Oh! Sounds exciting Cheyla. Where shall we start our walk from, and where will be be walking to?" she asked.

"Maybe I won't tell you that just yet, but we will drive to the base of the mountain. You will understand later."

"Come on, let's get started!" he said pulling her along. "Well we are lucky to have such a beautiful morning to go walking, the heat will set in later though." said Tarryn. "Yeah I know. That's why I want to get started." he said.

Cheyla opened the door to his room for Tarryn, and they both went inside. "You may change in the bathroom Tarryn." he said, pointing it out. "I will change out here!"

Quickly Cheyla dressed with care, then started to roll the covers off the paintings, and stood looking at them.

As Tarryn opened the door and came in, the paintings were the first thing that attracted her eye. She stood staring at them. "They are so, so beautiful!" she said.

"Come closer Tarryn." beckoned Cheyla. "I want you to study this landscape carefully, because I am going to take you to the place that it was sketched from." These are both works of Axel Hall's, my Grandfather, and he told me where he went to sketch this particular painting."

"Oh, I will Cheyla, but the second painting is riveting. I just can't seem to take my eyes off it. Just take a look at that Stallion! What a magnificent horse. I would just love to own him, but it is the girl who draws you in with those deep green eyes. Axel really captivated her personality in this magnificent piece of Art. It is quite amazing! Such a very, very beautiful young girl too! Who is she Cheyla?"

"She is Jacqueline Coby! Grandfather's very last piece of work. Great art, I just had to buy it. You see Tarryn the girl in the painting is my Mother when she was sixteen!"

"So if I never get to see her, she will always be with me now, and will have a special place in my home." he said.

Tarryn looked at him so sadly. She felt such sorrow for him. She only knew part of his story, but she realized the worst was yet to come. 'But whatever it was she steeled herself to stand by him. Already her feelings suggested that is where she belonged. Standing by him.'

"Ok Cheyla! Let's cheer up now. How about for these next two days you put those thoughts aside, and then I will discuss it with you. Keep in mind Cheyla that I want to help you if I can. But for now, let's go on this adventure you have planned for us, and have some fun!" she said.

"Cheyla looked at her, then smiled. "Exactly Tarryn, thank you for being the girl who has my back. So I agree, I'll just grab our water bottles, and we will be off!"

When they arrived at the base of the mountain, Cheyla was surprised to see a proper parking area, and he could see a track winding up the hill with railings on both sides.

"Looks like this is a popular spot Tarryn." he said. He grabbed the water bottles that he had in a bag and jumped out, then went to open her door, and helped her down.

"Oh! This looks just perfect Cheyla, and well shaded too. The trail does look as if it is a well-used tourist area."

"Yes I agree, it does look like it's been frequently used. Now just remember Grandfather's landscape, we have to find the exact place he was sketching from. I just have to see that. That painting is just so good, and for him to climb a mountain just to get his sketch is something so unique."

"Yes, I must agree. Axel has a real sense of personality in his paintings, but he has so many, and no-where to put them. He really needs a shed or something." Tarryn said.

"I think I have solved that problem for him Tarryn!"

Tarryn looked at him as he grabbed her hand. "What do you mean Cheyla?" she asked, looking up at him.

"Well yesterday when I was at his place, I too noticed the same thing about all his Art, so I wrote him a cheque so he could purchase a building to maybe set up a display center. My idea of incorporating an 'Art Teaching School for Juniors' he liked that well enough, and is excited about it. I told him that this town needs his legacy to live on, so Grandfather is set up now once he finds the right place."

"Cheyla, that is brilliant! A wonderful thing for you to do for him, and you are right, it will give him a new lease on life! Exactly what he needs. I bet he is over the moon!"

"Yes! You could say that!" he chuckled. "Last night as he was telling everyone his plans I noticed the gleam in his eyes! So yes, I'm happy with what I have done, and suggested. He wanted to leave it to me in a will you know, but I told him I'd rather see him donate to the town as a legacy for art so he will live on in that building." he said.

Tarryn looked up at him in surprise. "You are not only handsome, and talented Mister Cheyla Stone, and do put on a good breakfast, but you are also very generous!" Cheyla chuckled. "Good one! I might have to read a joke book just to compete with you I think. Come on! Let's see how smart you are walking up this mountain!" he said.

They found it wasn't such a steep climb as anticipated, but rather a criss-cross of wide, flat steps that took away the shape incline. Cheyla laughed out loud.

"Looks to me as if you have charmed this mountain too my lady! It is not that difficult a climb!" he remarked.

They walked hand in hand admiring the view, and the higher they climbed, the more spectacular it became.

"Keep close to the railing now Tarryn, and just focus on looking for the scene in the landscape of Grandfather's painting. Picture it in your mind, as we should be getting close, he gave me a rough idea of where he was sitting!"

"Stop!" called Tarryn. "Look down there Cheyla at the town nestled in the valley. I think that is it!" she stated.

Cheyla looked over the railing. "Yeah, no doubt about it. Just looking at that particular scene makes me realize how realistic Grandfather's painting really is. It's exactly the same, and look down there!" he pointed. "See them rocks just over there. That is where he sat to capture the sunlight for his sketch. What a cunning old bugger he is!"

Tarryn laughed. "For him to go to that extent just to get a sketch, is a sign of a true Artist. I am so pleased you brought me up here Cheyla, it is really beautiful. I will be sure to mention it to Axel he will be proud we came here."

As they left the mountain Cheyla had an arm wrapped around her waist as they chatted, and laughed together.

"Now what would like to do for the rest of the day? I have two options for you suggested by Mary last night."

"You told Mary about me?" Tarryn asked.

"Yes, I did. I was pretty stoked to be having a first date so I had to tell someone, but Mary will keep it a secret."

"Now would you like to see another spectacular place, or would you prefer a swim in an almost equal setting?"

"Well, it is warming up, and this view here is hard to beat so what say we leave the other spectacular view until tomorrow, and go where we can swim." replied Tarryn.

"Excellent choice Tarryn. I will just pull up in town to get us some food, and drinks, and we can have a picnic."

"Where will we be going?" she asked.

"Well we have to go to Shallow Downs turn-off first, then go towards Mary's house, she gave me instructions."

"Just to let you know Cheyla, that I think my Uncle Jed may know Mary Hargraves, so are you sure she will keep our dating a secret?" Tarryn asked.

"Yes, Mary does know him very well however she will keep our secret, so that will give me time to decide what I will do about seeing my Mother. I may have to visit Pete again just to see what he advises. He was the one who told me where to find Mary" replied Cheyla.

"Pete who?" may I ask Cheyla.

"Pete Stringer! He runs a tourist resort at The Outback Gardens Bush Camp. Great bloke too!" said Cheyla.

Tarryn stared at him unable to express her thoughts in case it wasn't true, but warning bells were ringing in her head, as she was thinking. 'She was starting to put the puzzle pieces together, so now she realized who Cheyla's Mother might be, but more importantly, where she lived.'

Tarryn hadn't lived in Shallow Siding long, only a few months, but names of 'Stringer' at 'The Outback Gardens' and the Property, 'Shallow Downs,' steeped in history on display at The Historic Museum, was owned by Coby's.

'Jacqueline Coby-Stringer!' to be exact. So both names linked had alerted her. Both were legendary names in this town. Shallow Downs had been left to Jacqueline by her Father, the late Clayton Coby. Her uncle had told her that.

So she knew for certain who Jacqueline Coby Stringer was now, but also that someone else calls her Mother.

Her step-son named Pete Stringer. 'I guess that would make Pete Stringer Cheyla's half brother!' But something else bothered her. 'Why would Jacqueline Coby abandon her first born child?' That child, Tarryn had just realized, was Cheyla. So that remained a mystery though she knew of stories told when Jacqueline left her home, family and friends. Oh dear! What should I do?' she wondered.

'Should I tell him what I know and what I am thinking, and lead him to his Mother? No! I'd better let him find out himself, he is not too far away from finding out anyway!'

Cheyla regarded her silence just as if she was digesting information, and thought nothing of it, but he asked.

"Penny for them Tarryn?"

Tarryn started at the question, but composed herself for her reply. "Oh! Nothing really. Just trying to imagine this place we are going to, and what you have in mind!"

"Well, I haven't been there, but Mary tells me it was a special place my Mother used to go to, so we will see!"

Cheyla grabbed some food, and drinks on their way through town and put them in his esky.

Tarryn watched through the window at the scenery as they passed, but her thoughts still remained.

In no time at all it seemed that they were at the turn-off to the property Shallow Downs, then Cheyla veered right, and followed the road along the creek.

"Do know where to go Cheyla, are we allowed here?"

"I am only going on instructions from Mary, and yes I have her authority to go through Shallow Downs Tarryn!"

Cheyla took a sandy track over a causeway to cross the creek, then headed bush. They emerged out onto a flat, rocky area where the river gums dominated, and before them a track leading down to a sandy bank bordering a deep pool of crystal clear water, and up above a waterfall cascaded down over the rocks to tumble into it.

"Oh this is magnificent Cheyla! It is so beautiful here!"

"Let's go swimming first." Tarryn said eagerly, when Cheyla parked the car and they had placed a large blanket and towels down in the shade, and unpacked their things.

It was under the waterfall, standing high on the rocks, when Cheyla lifted her up from the pool laughing with pleasure, and held her, that he fell deeply in love with her.

He had heard of love, though it hadn't eventuated in his life before, but now as he looked upon her beautiful face, he knew that he had to have this woman for his own.

'Am I thinking marriage?' he asked himself. That had never entered his head before. "But now, though they had done no more than kiss, or cuddle. He hadn't touched her body, though the urge surged through him. However he just knew deep down he could not still all the feelings she always created inside him, and just how special she made him feel. They were as one, on the same wave-length.

'Yes this lady is definitely a keeper!' he thought.

She was amazed at the little effort it took him to lift her high up onto the rocks where a waterfall cascaded down upon them. "He is so strong!" she thought, and lifted her head to reach him as his lips took hers in a kiss of passion. 'Cheyla's thoughts were how, or when to propose to her.'

Chapter 25

Jacqueline drove straight though Shallow Siding to then take the road to the property Shallow Downs. She was in the Jeep and driving fast, but as she reached the portals she slowed and drove to The Historic Museum car-park.

She got out to walk briskly along the path, through the Museum, then on out to the Café named 'Coby's Retreat.'

Jacqueline was on a mission after her talk with Mitch.

'I'll get this sorted quick smart so help me!' she mused.

She knew Mary was at work in The Café today so she walked in, and noticed her sitting at the back table. "Good Morning Mary we must talk." she said as she sat opposite.

"Mornin Jacqueline, ya lookin well, but are ya tense?"

"You can bet I am tense Mary, after what you and Axel done. I told Pete to back off, so I am taking over. Where is this Cheyla Stone staying Mary? Have you met him yet?"

"Ya he be comin out fer a bar-be-que. Axel he stay tha night, so all good, but ya dont need Pete agin. Cheyla not be lookin fer ya no more, he too upset! An Jacqueline I not be noin where he stayin!" said Mary as her head lowered.

Jacqueline gaped at her, not believing a word."Umm! So that is how it is Mary?" She knew Mary only too well.

Cheyla had driven Tarryn home to her unit after they spent the night having dinner at the hotel, and now he sat in the bar thinking over the events of the day, and what a day it was. There was no doubt in his mind at all.

He looked up just as the chef walked into the bar.

"Hi Geoff, finished for the night are you?" he asked.

"If you have time I would like to buy you a drink, and thank you for a great breakfast and maybe give you a tip!"

Geoff chuckled as he pulled up a stool beside Cheyla.

"I don't need any tip from you Cheyla. Just so pleased you enjoyed what we done. The bill I put into reception is more than enough, but I won't say no to a drink!" he said.

"So, tell me. How did the first date go? Was it worth all the effort? You went all out you know." he laughed.

"Well, thanks to you, and your staff, it was a breakfast fit for a queen. So yes, I find it was well worth it, so much so that I want to marry her, and that is not like me at all!"

"Wow! Congrats Cheyla I'm pleased for you." he said.

"Whoa, hold on. I haven't even asked her yet, so keep that under your hat. I want to do it proper, but I have no idea where to buy an engagement ring in this town."

"Ah! That is where I can help you my friend. We have the best jeweller this side of the city, in Shallow Siding, and he works from home. He lives in a small place with a shop front just the next lane down just past the saddlery.

He would be still working as he tends to his animals during the day, and does his jewellery making at night."

"Amazing Geoff, thanks for the information! Cheers for good luck so drink up Geoff. I hope you don't mind if I head off then, I have to talk to this man." said Cheyla.

"Yeah sure! Best of luck Cheyla. His name is Joe Burns, and Cheyla, you're secret is safe with me!" said Geoff.

Cheyla smiled. "I know it is Geoff, so thanks again."

"You keep me posted though Cheyla." replied Geoff.

"I will!" said Cheyla as he slipped of the stool and left.

There was porch light on, and as Cheyla peered in the window he could see an old man, head bent over his work bench, and a light shinning on the table.

Cheyla knocked on the door, and immediately from inside a voice bellowed. "Come in, doors open!"

"Hi, I am looking for Joe Burns, would you be Joe? I have been sent by Geoff, the chef at The Hotel-Motel?

"Yep, you are looking at him." laughed Joe. Ah, Geoff, a good friend, and you are?" he asked.

Cheyla put out his hand as he approached the bench.

"Hi Joe! My name is Cheyla Stone, I am new to town." he said as they shook hands.

"Yeah, I know that Cheyla. I do know all the people in this here town. So how can I help you?" he asked.

"Geoff seems to think you are just the person I need to speak to, and rather urgently too I might add. I have met a wonderful girl, and I want to ask her to marry me, so I am in need of an engagement ring, can you help?"

"Sure can. I don't usually boast, but I do make the best jewellery this town has ever seen. His pot-belly wobbled as he laughed. As a matter of fact I have just completed a new edition, but I must warn you son, it won't be cheap.

"I don't want cheap, I want the best!" replied Cheyla.

The old man smiled."Well feast your eyes on this!"

Quickly he placed a red cloth on the bench, and turned to a cupboard behind him, inserted a key in the lock, then pulled out a glass case, and placed it on the bench.

His brow wrinkled as he chuckled. "I have to be proud of this ring Cheyla!" he said, as he lifted it from the case. "I have worked many hours on this, and it is perfection, but I was planning on making a wedding ring to match it. That would be the ultimate set. See how I have etched the sides and set two more diamonds of value each side."

He gave Cheyla his eye glass to look at it.

In the light it gleamed like nothing Cheyla had ever seen before. As he looked into the stone, he could tell that it had been cut with precision, as were the smaller ones.

"Is this ring completed now, and how long will it take you to make the matching wedding ring?" asked Cheyla.

"This ring is fully completed. Platinum and diamonds, I just have to give it a final polish, and the wedding ring I am working on at the moment, should take until Saturday to finish constructing the ring." said Joe, as he looked up.

"Platinum I like that well enough, and these diamonds are just perfect. I will take both rings. When can I collect the Engagement ring?" asked Cheyla excitedly.

"Don't you want a price first young man?" asked Joe.

"You look like an honest man to me Joe, so whatever your asking price is. I will pay." replied Cheyla.

Joe looked at him. "It is as you say, and what a lucky girl I have to say. So you may collect the Engagement ring tomorrow at 6.30 a.m if that suits you!" said Joe.

"Just perfect, thank you Joe. You don't realize just how lucky I am feeling right now to have met you." he said.

CHEYLA

Cheyla walked briskly back to The Hotel-Motel, then straight into the bar. He was hoping Geoff was still there.

He smiled as he noticed he was in converstion with the bartender. Geoff Evans laughed at a joke. His sandy hair fell loosely on his forehead, and he looked a slim figure sitting upon the stool, his long legs touching the floor. He turned as Cheyla pull up a stool beside him.

Geoff looked up at him, and smiled. He had taken a liking to Cheyla, even though he was many years his senior, and he laughed. "Well that didn't take long!"

"You won't believe the ring that Joe had just finished making Geoff. I can't thank you enough. I snapped it up real quick, and I collect it in the morning, which is why I was hoping that you would still be here as I have another favour to ask of you?" he looked at him in question.

"Ah! Let me guess. You would like breakfast for two?"

Cheyla laughed. "Am I that transparent?" he asked.

Geoff laughed. "It's getting that way, but no problem Cheyla, what is it you need this time?" he asked.

"Well I was thinking of a basket, because I don't have one. Filled with goodies, juice and coffee, pancakes and maybe bacon and egg rolls or whatever else you can come up with. Could you do that for 6.45am tomorrow?"

"So it's the big day is it?" Geoff asked.

"I think so Geoff! Anyway it's too late to second guess it now. I am committed, I just hope that she doesn't turn me down. I really hadn't thought of that!" he stressed.

"You'll be fine Cheyla, just be confident." he advised.

"Besides Cheyla, I think the girl is the lucky one!"

Geoff looked at him squarely. "Just don't sell yourself short Cheyla, you have a lot to offer. I wish you all the best of luck, and I will have your basket ready for you to collect early in the morning" he said.

"Thanks Geoff! So you think she's the lucky one. Ah! But Geoff, you haven't met my girl yet." declared Cheyla.

"True! But I will meet her some time. How about we organize a night out on Friday. I will bring my wife too!"

"Ok that's fine by me. I will have to see if Tarryn can make it that night, I will get back to you." replied Cheyla.

"Ok, I had better head off, another big day tomorrow, and another early start. Thanks Geoff!" said Cheyla, as he reached out, and they shook hands.

Back in his room once more Cheyla made preparations for the morning, and packed a few things to put in his car for the next day. Excitement overtook him that night as he realized he was embarking on a cross-road of his life that he thought he would never be taking, but sure as the sun would rise, here he was about to propose marriage.

It was still dark when he woke up, so he showered and dressed before making a coffee, then as the sun began to rise, he picked up his room key, and slipped out the door and started the walk down to the Jeweller's.

At the first knock on the door, Joe called from within. "Come on in Cheyla!" so he opened the door and entered.

"Morning Cheyla, all set for you. I am guessing if you leave it until Saturday evening about 7pm, then I should be finished the other ring. Just take a look at this though!" he said with pride, as he opened a petite box and revealed the Engagement ring. She sure is a beauty!" he added.

Cheyla took it from him, then he smiled. "Never seen anything so beautiful Joe, except maybe the woman I plan to give it to. You've done a great job, and yes, Saturday will be fine. I have made out a cheque for you for this as a down-payment. Just let me know the balance when I see you Saturday night." Cheyla said, as he gave it to him.

Joe looked at the cheque, then gulped. Wow! That's a mighty big cheque Cheyla. I think maybe we will call it quits, and say you have paid for both rings!" he chuckled.

"Are you sure? You can let me know later if it is not, but right now I have to go, so thank you Joe."

Back in his room again, Cheyla took one more peek at the ring and shook his head. Then he was wondering where he could hide it when his eyes fell on a vest on the chair. 'Perfect, it has a large inside pocket.' he thought.

He donned the vest, then slipped the box inside the deep pocket. He grabbed his gear in haste, locked his door and walked across to the kitchen to collect his hamper. Then walked out to the 4WD, and then set off.

Tarryn was waiting as before, and he smiled when he saw her standing there outside her door. He jumped from the 4WD and closed the space between them quickly with long strides to wrap her gently in his embrace. His mouth covered hers to become a smouldering kiss. She smelt like flowers in the spring, and his head spun.

"God, I've missed you!" he whispered in her ear when he released her. "You live too far away." he joked.

"Good morning Cheyla. I have missed you also but we still managed to reserve our spot here." she looked down.

He looked at her straight face, and had to laugh as he knew she was referring to kissing on the pavement again. "It must be a thing for us two I like it well enough!"

She laughed at his retort, and then gave him a friendly shove, but he didn't budge, and she looked puzzled.

'I just hurt my hand trying to shove him, but it is like hitting a brick wall! So much muscle he has!' she mused.

"Are you ok Tarryn?" asked Cheyla when he noticed she was shaking her hand, and in pain.

Tarryn laughed. "I must remember not to get into an argument with you Cheyla, your body is made of rock!"

He laughed. "Yes, I know! Sorry about that, but come on now we have something special to see!" he uttered.

They scrambed into the 4WD and Cheyla gunned the engine, and drove through Shallow Siding.

"Where to today Cheyla?" Tarryn asked.

"Well! Mary told me of another place to go, and I think it sounds like a must see, but she said you have to be there in the early sunlight, so I am in a hurry right now to get to Shallow Downs in time for this phenomenon!"

"Shallow Downs again?" asked Tarryn.

"Yep, but a different place to yesterday. It appears that property has a lot of special places to see so Mary said."

They drove closer towards the mountain, and took the gradual slopes that meandered through the hillside, and as they climbed the last rise a natural phenomenon was displayed in full brilliance in the early morning rising sun where huge formations of ochre-coloured rocks bunched together glistened in sun, and water sprayed from above a crest where a waterfall tumbled into the creek below.

"Oh, my god! Take a look at that Cheyla." said Tarryn. "Just look at all the colours!" she cried. As they drove onto level ground Tarryn could barely stand the wait for the vehicle to stop, then she was out and running to the crest.

Cheyla laughed as he fed off her excitement. Then he grabbed a blanket off the back seat, and his hamper, and strode over to join her, and spread the blanket down.

They sat close together with legs entwined and Cheyla wrapped her in his arms as they watched the display.

"Pretty special Tarryn, and worth coming early for."

"Oh, it's just so magical Cheyla. See that there!" she pointed. "Just the way the sun is playing on the coloured boulders as the water tumbles on them, they almost seem to be alive or bouncing as they glisten, so pretty!"

"Just look at the creek below. Have you ever witnessed such pure water? I know I have at Tenna. It has a waterfall just like this one. I was born there beside that creek." said Cheyla, and then went quiet, as if thinking.

"It must be beautiful Cheyla. I would love you to show it to me some day Cheyla." Tarryn replied.

Something seemed to clearly focus in Cheyla's eyes as he replied. "It is a long, long way to that place Tarryn. But I would like it well enough if you were by my side there!"

As if distracted he pulled the hamper closer, then he flipped the lid off. "We better have breakfast while this display is on Tarryn, or else it will be cold, and he got out some plates, and offered her to look at what was there.

"My good friend Geoff excells again!" he laughed.

"Certainly knows his way around food." said Tarryn.

Sitting there in, and amongst such splendor of the colours of rock formations, the waterfall, and pure water below and the stillness of it all they both fell quiet.

Tarryn's voice broke that silence, and Cheyla gulped, and almost choked on his coffee at her question.

Since yesterday Tarryn was unsure just how to handle her newly-found information that she realized she knew, and it was bugging her, so she decided to be upfront.

"So what have you decided to do about your Mother Cheyla, will you still search for her?" she asked bluntly.

She felt his body stiffen and she sensed that he seemed to be stuggling with something unknown to her.

Suddendly he spun her around to face him.

"Tarryn, there are two important things I have to get off my chest. So this is it! I have bad news, and good news, so just tell me straight which one you prefer to hear about first, as we must talk now while it is on my mind." he said.

She was actually surprised to hear that he now wanted to talk about it, and she knew what the bad news was, but good news? What could that be about?" she wondered.

"Well I always say. Leave the best until last, so I guess it has to be the bad news first Cheyla." was her reply.

"So be it then! But just prepare yourself Tarryn, as you may not want to know me anymore after I tell you what I have learnt. Now to answer your question. No! I will not be looking for my Mother anymore, and the reason being, is that she will not want to know me. You see Tarryn, she abandoned me at birth. Didn't even want to see me, she didn't want me, but she had good reason for that. This is the part I find hard to live with. I was never meant to be!"

354

"She gave me life that was all, but because of me, her young life was ruined. This is how Grandfather told it!"

Cheyla frowned, and creases appeared in his forehead that were not there before, as he choked trying to go on, but he started to continue, and when he looked at her she could see the raw pain of it in those beautiful eyes.

Tarryn's scream echoed loudly in his ears. "Enough!" she cried. "I don't want to hear the sordid details, so stop! Please stop Cheyla! You are only hurting yourself, and you don't deserve this burden. She grabbed his face, and pulled him close. Her lips were moist on his, but felt savage too with a force of vengeance. "It is not your fault Cheyla! Not your fault! Do you understand?" she asked, when their lips parted, and she stared hard into his eyes.

"I don't need you to spell it out for me Cheyla! I can read between the lines, so the words you were just about to utter can be buried for-ever more! We will not speak of it again, because it was in another life Cheyla. It was your Mother's life. That is what she chose to do. You can't go through life blaming yourself, because you had no say in the matter Cheyla. Do you hear me?" she screamed.

"I can't help but hear you because you are yelling!"

"I am yelling because I am so angry. I love you deeply Cheyla. I don't care who made you, or why? I don't care if your Mother doesn't want to know you! Because there are plenty of people that do. You are a good, honest and decent person Cheyla. Believe in yourself, you don't need this to screw you up. You are perfect the way you are. If they don't see that then they don't deserve you!" she said.

Cheyla stared at her in wonder. "Wow! You certainly speak your mind frankly when you want to Tarryn, and with a vengeance too. So much spirit you have in you Tarryn that I have to admire in any woman. There are so many things about you that I love dearly Tarryn, and you have captured my heart. I never thought I would say that to anyone, but I want you for my own! I want to cherish you, and love you as you deserve to be loved, and like you just said. I also love you deeply Tarryn, and want you to be my wife. Can you find it in your heart to overlook where I have come from, and start a new life with me?"

He looked seriously at her, his handsome face so close.

"I am asking you to marry me Tarryn, to be my wife? Come home with me to Tenungeri, and live our life to the fullest, with the love we share we can conquer all!"

"So is that the good news?" she asked, with a cheeky grin on her face. 'I may like it well enough!' she quipped.

He could not believe it. Here he was fretting about the things he had to tell her, and asking her to marry him was a big thing for him, but Tarryn used his favourite saying to answer him, or not answer him would be a better way of explaining it, so all he could do was laugh at her cheek.

"You taunt me too much lady!" he said, as he grabbed her, and rolled her onto her back, and covered her body with his own, and his lips claimed hers with brute force.

"If I wasn't a gentleman, I would take you now for not replying to my question that I have been stressing over."

"Then why don't you?" she asked.

"Are you kidding me?" Cheyla almost freaked out.

"No! Cheyla. I love you. Of course I will marry you!"

He jumped up. 'You will? You will marry me, be my wife? Come home with me?" he was beside himself, and she grabbed a lock of his hair, and pulled him back down.

"Quite Cheyla. Yes all those things I will do, but more importantly. What was it you were going to do to me?" her smile was so cheeky when she asked, that he laughed.

So, one by one. Each piece of her clothing disappeared, until she lay completely naked upon the blanket, and Cheyla looked at her in awe of something so perfect.

"Umm! Now it's my turn. First we need to get rid of that vest. Why have it on anyway, it is a warm morning!" she stated then tried to free it from his massive shoulders, but it wasn't budging. "You need to be prepared Cheyla!" she laughed, but then felt something hard in the pocket.

"What do you have here?" she asked.

"Never you mind my lady, but now I am prepared!" said Cheyla with urgency, as he whisked his vest off and dropped his pants to take her ever so quickly, she didn't have time to reply, only gape at what was to befall her.

Her screams seemed to echo high above them, and all around the rockface of the cliffs. Cheyla held back to give her that pleasure until he could bare it no longer, and he gasped with the release of his pent-up emotions, then he showered her body with kisses until her screams abated. She lay lifeless, but with eyes displaying her love for him.

He raised himself to take her lips, and she responded to his touch, and their kiss was one of confirmation.

'He has taken my heart and soul!' Tarryn thought. 'I knew I loved him but now I will walk beside him always!'

They smiled at each other as lovers do, then Cheyla said off-handedly. "You will be Missus Tarryn Stone! Is that ok with you my lady?" he asked.

"When that day comes, it will be be the proudest day of my life Cheyla Stone. I will stand beside you through thick, and thin, and love you forever!" she said earnestly.

"Oh! Just let me jot that down. They can be your vows Tarryn, just in case you forget! I'll just grab a pen." Cheyla chuckled at his own jest as he grabbed for his vest, and dug into the pockets, and Tarryn was going to shove him, but had second thoughts in case she hurt her hand again.

Then there he was with hand outstretched and a pretty box sat in his palm. "For you my love, my future wife!"

Tarryn snatched it quickly thinking it was a necklace or bracelet, and she flipped the lid.

"Oh no! Oh no! Look at it. That is the most beautiful bracelet I have ever seen Cheyla!" she rolled around on the blanket laughing, her thick, black hair fell all around her to hide her nakedness, and Cheyla's heart swelled.

"You cheeky wench, just give that back!" he said, as they wrestled each other playfully. So the tiny box fell out of her grasp to land between them as he claimed her lips.

Cheyla rose to take the ring from the box, and took her left hand in his to slip it on her finger. "Now, you are mine to do with what I want lady, but more importantly! When I want!" he chuckled, and kissed the ring on her finger.

"Ah! Promises, promises! We shall see!" she chuckled. Then she became serious for a second only. "Thank you Cheyla I will be proud to wear this beautiful engagement ring and of course to be at your beck and call." she smiled.

"Great! Seeing that is all settled, we have work to do young lady! Let's get moving and get organized." he said.

"What do you mean by organized?" Tarryn asked.

"Well, we just got engaged! So you know what comes next? The Engagement party! I have a plan!" he stated.

She looked at him with her quirky smile still evident. "So do you always have a plan Cheyla?" she asked, as she propped herself up on her elbow, and rested her head on her hand, at the same time flashed her diamond at him.

Cheyla chuckled. "Yeah mostly. But they are sort of on the spot type of plans, just like this one. Have you been to The Restaurant at The Outback Bush Camp?" he asked.

"No, I haven't, but I hear it is good!" Tarryn answered.

"Ok, so here is our first priority! I have to call them to make a booking for tonight with our special requests for an engagement party, so that will take up time. I can leave you at your Mother's place. You can tell her our news and invite her and Uncle Jed to our party. I'll have to meet her later when I pick you up. Now, other invites! Mary, and Drew Hargraves, Grandfather, Pete, and Susan Stringer, Geoff and his wife at the Hotel-Motel, so I have a few calls to make. What about your friends from work?" he asked.

"No not really Cheyla. I have only lived here for a few months, so I haven't any concrete friends." she replied.

As they drove through Shallow Downs Cheyla said.

"Remember you were asking about my name? Well I was named after this property by my cunning Ol Mother, as the aborigines could only pronounce it as 'Cheyla-D.' Tarryn, stared at him. "Well I never! How cool!" she said.

Chapter 26

It was as Cheyla hoped it would be as they entered the reserved room of The Outback Gardens Restaurant.

Lights were dimmed, candles were placed already lit, upon a huge table which centered the room with placings for eleven guests. Colours of his choice in different shades of purple, not only dressed the massive table, but in every area of the room, and there were flowers everywhere.

He nodded his head in approval as The Manager met them inside the entrance, and they shook hands.

"You must be Cheyla Stone! Welcome to The Outback Bush Camp Restaurant. Thank you for your booking, I do hope this setting is to your satisfaction Cheyla?" he asked.

"Yes Sir! I am pleased to meet you, and thank you for doing this at such short notice. It all looks just great!"

My name is Hank Sargent, I am The Manager of our establishment, and your beautiful fiancé is?" he asked.

"Please meet Tarryn Westley my beautiful bride-to-be. Tarryn, Hank is looking after us tonight!" Cheyla said.

"Oh, thank you so much, it is beautiful." said Tarryn.

"My pleasure Tarryn, we are here to serve you, so you will expect canapes in the lounge area before the buffet!"

Tarryn looked around the room. "Oh Cheyla, just look at all the flowers, and the table. All are my favourite colours too. I can't believe you did all this, thank you!"

"You are welcome my love, but another thing we have in common is colours apparently. He looked down at her dress. You look stunning Tarryn, and purple suits you so much, and how did you get your hair up like that? It is so beautiful. You will make a beautiful bride!" Cheyla said.

"Thank you Cheyla! Well my Mother braided my hair for me. Because I have so much of it, I wanted something a little different, and you too look immaculate my love."

Cheyla chuckled. It had been a last minute rush to the shops to buy his outfit as nothing in his bag was special.

Oh! Look there is a separate table with a cake. Oh! We have a cake Cheyla. You must give Mother your phone so she can take photos for us. I'm sure she would do that."

"Great idea Tarryn!" said Cheyla, as he grabbed two glasses of champagne off the waiter's tray standing near, and gave one to Tarryn. "To us Tarryn!" he toasted.

She raised her glass to clink with his. "To us Cheyla!"

They moved to the lounge area and Cheyla could see the first of their guests arriving. He seated Tarryn. "If you don't mind my love, I would like to greet everyone at the door, and tell them where you are sitting. When they all arrive I will introduce you then. Are you ok with that?"

"Yes please do that Cheyla. I am fine here." she smiled.

Mary, Drew and his Grandfather were the first ones to arrive. They all hugged, and congratulated him, but they didn't go to be seated, and as it turned out everyone had arrived by then, and he was directing them to the lounge.

In the private setting of the lounge area it was easy for Cheyla, and Tarryn to talk freely amongst their guests as everyone knew each other. As they drank champagne the canapés were served, so it was a great start to the night.

They were all laughing and making jokes, and then Pete started telling them about how he met Cheyla, and Tarryn's eyes opened wide at the close of the story.

"I knew you were made of rock!" she said to Cheyla.

Cheyla laughed. "I have more stories to tell my love."

She laughed at him."I just bet you do Cheyla Stone!"

Then they were called for dinner, and the buffet table groaned from the weight of food. A selection of hot, and cold. Seafood, and three meats. It was impressive.

They all took their places. Cheyla, and Tarryn sat at the head of the table, and as Cheyla looked to the other end, he noticed it was Pete, and Susan who faced them.

He whispered to Tarryn. "I need to ask you Tarryn as I have to make a speech at the cutting of the cake. "Could you be ready to leave Shallow Siding on Sunday, as that is what I would like to tell everyone here, and also are you happy if I invite them all to our wedding?" he asked.

"Sunday? That is short notice, but yes I could manage that, and by all means, I would love everyone here to be with us on our wedding day." so go ahead Cheyla.

"Oh that is perfect! I will move you into my room at The Hotel-Motel until we go. But just to add! I intend to tell all these people I will pay for their fares to Darwin and car hire if they are coming. Is that ok with you Tarryn?"

"Cheyla you just do what you want. It is your money."

So it was after the cutting of the cake, when Cheyla had made his speech, and everyone cheered in response, that Pete Stringer walked up to him, and whispered.

"Can I drag you away just for a few minutes Cheyla? I would like to have a private word, maybe outside on the balcony if that is ok with you?" he asked earnestly.

"You bet Pete!" replied Cheyla. "Can you just grab us both a drink, and I will meet you out there in a second?"

"Will do Cheyla!" replied Pete.

"Tarryn would you excuse me for a while? Pete wants to talk in private, and I did want to see him before we go."

"Yes Cheyla, you go ahead. I will be fine!" said Tarryn.

Pete was sitting in a small private alcove, and Cheyla slid into the bench seat opposite him. "Great idea Pete. I was hoping to chat with you before I left!" said Cheyla.

"So it's definitely this coming Sunday that you plan on travelling back home then Cheyla?" he asked.

Cheyla noticed his eyes were a little clouded, and saw the frown upon his brow. "Yes Pete, there is nothing more for me here now! I just thank my lucky stars that I have met Tarryn, she is the highlight of this trip, and I have no other plans to pursue, but I want you to know it has been a pleasure getting to know both you, and Susan. I hope you will come to our wedding! But I wanted to thank you personally for all your help, and for having my back!"

"That's what brothers do Cheyla!" Pete said as he then stared into Cheyla's eyes, his own now a liitle misty.

Cheyla felt like he had just been hit. "Brothers! I don't understand Pete? What do you mean by that?" he asked.

"It's just that we call the same person Mother Cheyla!"

CHEYLA

Cheyla's face said it all. He was dumbfounded by this statement, and his words tumbled out in a rush.

"My M...mother is...Your M...mother. Are you sure?"

"I am so sorry Cheyla for not telling you before, but I had to protect her, and make sure she was safe until I got to know you. You see, she is the only Mother I have ever known. My natural Mother passed away when I was only a child, and Father raised me. So Jacqueline Coby-Stringer has been Mother and friend to me for many years, and she is without a doubt, the most outstanding woman I have ever known in my life. I know now why my Father loved her so much all his life, since when they were only kids!"

"You see her problem is she has a fierce pride. Passed on from her Father Clayton. It was what ruined her life when she declared herself a self-made outcast to leave her home, her family, and friends so long ago, and it is pride that keeps her from you now. Unless you know her, then you will never understand." Pete said regretfully.

"Oh! I have seen that pride in her. It is etched clearly in her beautiful face in every painting that I have seen of her. Axel Hall is my Grandfather, and such a great Artist that he has managed to capture the pure essence of her in such a way on canvas, that I feel I know her! I purchased a painting of her on a black stallion. Such a great piece of art that will take pride of place in my home!" said Cheyla.

Pete looked forlornly at him. 'Oh my god! What have we all done?' he asked himself miserably. "What are you going to do about Mother Cheyla?" he asked.

"Nothing Pete! I know her story. I was never meant to be, I was a mistake. I understand that she will not want me!"

Sadly Pete looked up at Cheyla as the tears brimmed his deep blue eyes, then toppled to slide down his cheeks. Quickly he wiped them away in annoyance. He shook his head. He had never been brought to tears that he could remember, so now he sobbed. "I'm so very sorry Cheyla!" Cheyla reacted to go and sit beside him. He grabbed him in a hug, and that is how the two brothers sat for a while.

Cheyla was the first to speak. "It is what it is Pete, we can't change the past, so please don't be upset. I have to accept that fact. At least we have found each other, and I will always keep in contact. I will give Mary my address and phone numbers before I leave tonight. I can't do any more here because I know what the outcome will be! So, now as the eldest brother, I say we go to enjoy my party!" Then he stood up. "Are you coming?" he asked.

Pete could not believe the resilience Cheyla had, and tried to picture himself in his situation. Suddenly he rose, and grabbed Cheyls's arm. "You have to try once more! If you do? Then Mother is always at the cemetery at Shallow Downs every Sunday at 7.30am!" he urged with feeling.

"Umm!" pondered Cheyla as he thought on it.

Pete added as they walked. "Cheyla, Susan and I will definitely come to your wedding, just send my invite!"

By this time they had neared the door. "You had better attend my wedding Brother, or I shall hunt you down like a wild animal!" said Cheyla, then he started to chuckle.

For the first time that evening Pete Stringer laughed, and they both were laughing as they entered the room. 'God I love this boy's wit, what a dig at me!' he chuckled.

So they joined the party where the music was playing. Some people danced, others were just happy to talk, but Cheyla, and Tarryn sat very close together, their love for one another to be seen by all. Then it was all over, and they were saying their goodbyes outside in the carpark.

Cheyla folded her in his arms when they had all left. "Have I told you tonight how much I love you?" he asked.

"I am sure you just did! And I Cheyla, love you also! What a great Engagement party we had, so thank you!"

"You are most welcome! Now I have a couple of things to do. I have to go and thank The Manager, and pay his bill, and I will collect all our presents to put in the 4WD."

"Here are the keys, would you just have the boot open for me, and you can wait in the car. I won't be long!"

"Ok Cheyla, all good!" and he kissed her tenderly.

Back in Shallow Siding, Tarryn sat cross-legged on the big bed, and started unwrapping their presents.

"I just can't believe all the people at our party bought presents for us at such short notice, and will you look at these gifts, they are all beautiful Cheyla."

Cheyla walked over and stood beside her.

She held up large towels of high quality. There was a tea-pot, and dinner-set, and even a wall clock, but then she unwrapped some framed photos.

"Oh, you will love these Cheyla. Some framed pictures of Shallow Siding, and of Mary, and Drew. But look at these. These photographs are of your Mother, and Mary when they were young no doubt!" she said excitedly.

"That is the problem Tarryn. All the photos I have of my Mother even the painting, are when she was young!"

367

Tarryn looked up at him in puzzlement at first to see his disappointed face, until she realized why.

'Of course!' she thought to herself. 'Cheyla hasn't seen his Mother, so he doesn't know what she looks like now!'

'All the gifts are great Tarryn. I shall go in to see Geoff tomorrow. I am sure he will have some boxes to give me, so I will pack that all up ready for our trip. If you would like I can give you a hand tomorrow to pack your things, and move out of the quarters, and you can move in here with me until Sunday. I guess you will have to tell them at your work that you are leaving Shallow Siding."

"Yes, that is a good idea Cheyla, but maybe later in the day, as I will have to work tomorrow. I will give two days notice, so in the morning you can just drop me home, and I will go to work, and do my packing after my shift!"

"Ok then. I will visit Geoff when I get back!"

"There is something else Tarryn that I must tell you."

She looked at him with surprise. "What is it Cheyla?"

"It is about Pete Stringer. Do you know when we went outside? Well! It was then he told me we were Brothers! Near floored me that did! My Mother is his step-mother."

Tarryn was going to say she had guessed, but decided against it, so she just smiled, and said. "You know Cheyla, your family is getting bigger as we speak." she laughed.

Cheyla laughed too. "Plus, don't forget Melissa! She would be my little sister. How beautiful that child is. We had a conversation you know." he chuckled. "It was she, who led me to Mary, so I like it well enough to have all this new-found family, and of course, the love of my life!"

"Ah! Pleased you didn't forget about me my darling!"

"You would never let me do that Tarryn, would you? Maybe it's not the right time because I think I have spoilt you enough today but hell, it is our engagement, so I have more news. On Saturday, I have to get up early again."

"Whatever for Cheyla?" she asked.

"To visit the jeweller who made your ring. You see, I ordered a matching wedding ring for your engagement ring and it will be finished and ready to collect Saturday."

"You are too much Cheyla Stone, but I love you for it!" She rolled over and pulled him down to her.

"I love you also Tarryn Westley! But, I like you well enough too." They made love amongst all the presents.

For the rest of the week Cheyla, and Tarryn had a busy time planning out their trip, and packing. But still enjoyed their time together for the last few days in Shallow Siding.

All goodbyes had already been said, and the heat was setting in, so they lolled around the pool just relaxing for it was a long, long road to their destination in the N.T.

Before they knew it Saturday was upon them. Cheyla left early to go, and visit Joe, and to get his wedding ring, but he was surprised to find when he got there that Joe had made two matching rings. One for him, and one for Tarryn, and would not take any more money for them.

Cheyla was well pleased with himself, he had not even thought of a ring for himself, but now it was perfect.

When he got back to his room he found Tarryn sitting outside in a settee under the umbrellas by the pool, and the sun shone brilliantly over the pool to start their day.

"Oh! Show me quickly!" she screeched when she spied

Cheyla on the porch, but now he sauntered towards her, speaking to her as he walked. "I have had a surprise too, but I have come to decision!" he said, rather with finality.

"You know what Tarryn! I think you may have to wait for this surprise. After all, you will need some surprises on our wedding day. So no! I am not showing you! I will wrap it, and put it in a safe place so you can't find it!" then he laughed. "Just trust me. What I have here is beautiful, just like your ring, so be patient my love." he stated.

Tarryn looked at him in disbelief. "Oh Cheyla no! You can't be serious, just a little peek?" she pleaded.

"Oh, no you don't!" he replied. "You are not changing my mind, and you will thank me for that one day!" and with that declaration he turned on his heel, and walked off. "But I have ordered breakfast for you my darling!" he said over his shoulder. "We will eat out here! Love you!"

After breakfast Cheyla went to settle his bill, and then they sat around the pool, and swam a little, but he seemed reserved to Tarryn, but it wasn't until later after dinner that night that she realized something was worrying him.

They had gone back to the room, but instead of going inside he went to sit under the cabana where they enjoyed their first date. He sat brooding in the semi-darkness.

Tarryn went to sit beside him. "What is it Cheyla, what is troubling you? I know something is wrong just tell me!"

"Just to see her face is all I want!" he said softly.

"Whose face do you want to see Cheyla?" she asked.

"My Mothers! Pete said she goes to the cemetery 7.30am each Sunday. "Then you must go Cheyla, try once more!"

Chapter 27

It was still dark outside when Cheyla woke, but he was unsettled, and got up to put the kettle on. He made his coffee, and sat down as Tarryn rolled out of bed, and sat beside him at the table. He got up, and made her a coffee.

"Thank you darling!" she said as she sipped her coffee.

"Am I doing the right thing Tarryn?" he asked.

"Cheyla you have come a long way just to see her face, so if that is all you get, then so be it. You have tried, that is all you can do. I just know in my heart that if you don't go to see her today, you will regret it all of your life!"

"You do have a way of explaining things my love, and besides. I have already snatched the prize. Thank you for loving me. I will love you until the day I die!" he rasped.

Tarryn almost cried, as he was all choked up, and so was she, but she needed to be strong for him.

"Ok, so you buck up now. Finish your coffee, and get spruced up, and I will be packed up here, and ready to leave on our trip when you get back, and Cheyla! What will be, will be!" please remember that, and good luck!"

"I knew there was a reason I was marrying you Tarryn Westley. I must be the luckiest man alive!" he uttered.

371

Cheyla drove slowly through Shallow Siding. It was quiet, all the streets deserted in the early morning.

He took the familiar road out of town, and reached the turn-off to the property Shallow Downs just on 7.30am.

He drove on past the portals which stated the entrance to The Homestead, then he drove very slowly past Mary's turn-off, and on towards the mountain where he had seen the cemetery as he had passed it, only a few days before.

All was calm, not even a bird flitted through the trees, and for one fleeting moment something tightened in his chest. 'What if she doesn't come out today?' he stressed.

He drove on harboring that thought until he got much closer to where he thought he needed to turn in, when all of a sudden through the leaves of the tall gums, he noticed a vehicle. His heart tripped a little as he spied a brightly coloured Jeep with the roof down, parked in amongst the trees. So he drove ever so slowly into the turn-off, then parked on the side of the road in the cemetery grounds.

Calmly he got out to start walking the rest of the way.

He stood back under the gums trees and watched her. She seemed to be sobbing, her head bowed to a graveside, and his heart went out to her. He knew the graves would be of her parents, the parents that she had to leave behind, because of him, and that made him feel so bad.

She was beautiful beyond the telling of it, though he knew she would be in her mid-fifties now. Her hair was of gold and cropped short, but blew gently across her face in the early morning breeze. She was so petite, he felt he could hold her in one arm. 'If only?' he thought.

It wasn't until he moved that he saw her true beauty.

372

Her shoulders trembled he noted as he moved slowly forward. But suddenly, she turned quickly alerted as his boots rolled on gravel, in his approach behind her.

Tears streamed from her beautiful, deep green eyes.

'My exact same eyes!' he thought, as their eyes locked on one another, and immediately he detected something in the depths of them…'Recognition.'

Then she swayed, and fell towards him.

Cheyla raced forward but only just in time to break her fall, and he bundled her into his arms as if she was a child.

For that brief moment. All the longing, and yearning for her seemed simply to dissipate as her looked upon her beautiful face for the first time in his life. The face of his natural Mother. He wanted to remember every feature of hers, he wanted to treasure this time together forever.

Then her eyes fluttered so as he placed her back on her feet, she simply stared at him with confusion on her face.

"It is ok!" he said. "You only fainted, but I was there to catch you, so you shouldn't be hurt!" he said tenderly.

"My name is Cheyla, I am….

"I know quite well who you are!" she said abruptly, cutting his speech off in mid-stream.

"You have a face that was very dear to me, and to look upon it again is a shock, so you startled me Cheyla Stone!"

"I am sorry it was not intended." replied Cheyla softly.

"Don't you think for one moment young man that you can come into my life to turn it upside-down, just because you resemble my Father. No! That is just not happening!"

Her body seemed to tremble, and her lips quivered in her attempt to chastise him further by carrying on.

"I want you to go back where you came from Cheyla."

"You don't belong…."

Cheyla looked forlornly at her, and for the last time he looked into those beautiful eyes to try his hardest to remember them for the rest of his life. He interrupted her.

"Stop! Please stop Mother! I know quite well why you can't accept me. That saddens me, though I can say I can't blame you at all, instead I came only to look on your face for the first time in my life, and to thank you for my life!"

"Now after seeing you, and just to hold you for a short while, I may be able to be happy in life. I became engaged to Tarryn Westley this week and we will be married in the N.T where I have a Property. We are leaving this morning when I return to gt her. I guess this is hello, and good-bye Mother, but just know I understand, and will always love you!" then sadly Cheyla turned, and walked away.

Jacqueline stood rooted to the spot. Something in her heart wrenched, and her head began to spin. She looked at the huge figure, just like her Father's had been, walking away from her, and with him was the only physical thing that resembled her Father, his face. A beautiful face that she had thought of all the years of her messed-up life, and wondered if her child was male or female, what her child would look like? She looked at her Father's tombstone. It had a replica of him pictured next to the verse. Then she looked down the road at the figure getting into a 4WD, and she started to sob, heart-breaking sobs that shook her.

"Please god, please help me? Take back this pride that has always ruined my life, and is tearing me apart!"

She stood there, she knew not how long. It seemed like an eternity. Her body was shaking, her heart breaking until she sank to the ground sobbing, not knowing what to do, so she cried until her tears were spent.

Then she was up, and running, she knew not where to, but reached her Jeep, and climbed in to gun the engine.

She drove with a reckless abandonment of her inner self, and of her pride, as she pressed the pedal to the floor to go faster still, and to rid herself of the curse within her.

'Please don't let me be too late!' she prayed.

Cheyla drove his 4WD without really seeing where he was going. For the first time in his life he felt the hot tears scolding his eyes as he fought to repress them, but they rolled down his cheeks anyway. 'He knew what to expect, but the reality of it was just starting to hit home. Rejection was a bitter pill to swallow, but he would survive this. He had to, he had a new life now, so he could only hold onto the good things he had just experienced, and to move on.'

Tarryn was waiting for him on the porch. Just one look at his face was all she needed to know, so instead she said.

"Everything is packed Cheyla, would you like a coffee before we go?" she asked attentively.

"No thanks Tarryn, I'll pack the car up, and we will hit the road. Maybe we will stop later to have something."

"I thought you might say that so I took it upon myself to make some sandwiches, and coffee to take with us!"

"Good girl!" he replied with a wry smile.

They drove in complete silence until they made the main highway, and she watched as Cheyla's face set like stone.

Cheyla looked in the revision mirror, then looked back with a desolate face as he concentrated on the road ahead. He looked sideways at Tarryn, and thought it best to say something to her, he was being too abrupt.

"Tarryn, I just want to….

"Cheyla, just drive the car. You don't have to explain! When you feel up to it, we shall talk!" she interrupted.

He just shook his head, 'How lucky I am to have this woman by my side for the rest of my life.' he thought.

Though Cheyla had Tarryn Westley, the love of his life by his side, he looked forlornly back with regret of what could have been as he checked the mirror again. His heart beat faster. There was a tiny speck on the road behind him that wasn't there before, so he slowed down. He checked again, but this time he identified the unmistakable colour of the Jeep that was following him, and he hit the brakes.

"What is it Cheyla?" asked Tarryn with concern.

Cheyla smiled as he opened the door, then slipped out of the vehicle to stand on the Highway. "It is my Mother!"

Tarryn took a look at the vehicle quickly approaching. So she grabbed Cheyla's phone and hit the camera button. She got out of the 4WD discreetly. Just in time, as the Jeep stopped and the pictures she got were of Cheyla's Mother rushing into his arms, her eyes brimming with tears, and words of forgiveness on her lips, and Cheyla with a wide grin taking her into his embrace and spinning her around.

Tarryn got back in the 4WD, and smiled, as she knew. 'Now! Cheyla Stone had everything he always wanted!'

****